COLD HUNTER'S MOON

THOMAS DUNNE BOOKS   ST. MARTIN'S MINOTAUR      NEW YORK

COLD HUNTER'S MOON

K C GREENLIEF

THOMAS DUNNE BOOKS.
An imprint of St. Martin's Press.

www.minotaurbooks.com

Designed by Lorelle Graffeo

Library of Congress Cataloging-in-Publication Data

Greenlief, K. C.
    Cold hunter's moon / K. C. Greenlief.—1st ed.
        p.   cm.
    ISBN 0-312-27847-0
    1. Police—Wisconsin—Fiction.   2. Wisconsin—Fiction.   I. Title.

PS3607.R46 C65   2002
813'.6—dc21

                                                            2001041982

First Edition: January 2002

10   9   8   7   6   5   4   3   2   1

ACKNOWLEDGMENTS

I cannot possibly thank all the writers who have inspired me to finally write a book of my own. I can thank several bookstore owners who have nourished my interests in mysteries and overflowed my house with books. They include Mary Helen Becker, former owner of Booked for Murder in Madison, Wisconsin; Richard Katz of Murder One, Milwaukee, Wisconsin; Kate Mattes of Kate's Mystery Books, Cambridge, Massachusetts; Barbara Peters of The Poisoned Pen, Scottsdale, Arizona; and Tom and Enid Schantz of The Rue Morgue, Boulder, Colorado.

I am blessed with many friends who have encouraged me throughout this process, including: Debra, Alice Ann, Susan, Mary Kay, Connie, and Patsy. A million thanks.

Dan and Rick, you are the best brothers any girl could have. Thank you for supporting this project from the start. Zane, never quit writing.

A first-time writer needs help—at least this first-time writer did. Barbara Steiner, what a phenomenal teacher and manuscript editor you are. Carin Siegfried, you have been a delight to work with. Thank you for all the time you spent with me and for your superb editorial insights.

Last but not least, my husband, Roger. You are the best thing that ever happened to me. You can't help it if you read only nonfiction. Remember our bet!

COLD HUNTER'S MOON

What they say is true. When you're freezing to death you don't feel cold. She was lying in the snow watching her breath float up above her in frosty clouds and all she felt was very, very sleepy. She had done what she'd seen animals do in deep snow—burrow down into it. Snow is a good insulator but she knew it wouldn't work forever.

A bright, almost fluorescent, full moon lit up the dark cloudy sky off to her right. From the moon's position she figured it was either nine at night or three in the morning. Stars were everywhere, scattered amongst gray blots of clouds. The moon's reflection on the snow-covered ground created a ghostly light show all around her. Bare branches and huge tree trunks reached up towards the moonlight, casting strange shadows on the sparkling snow. When the wind blew, the trees and their shadows swayed back and forth ominously. The eerie whistling of the wind whipping through the trees should have already scared her to death, but she had always loved the sound of wind.

A helicopter flew over. She saw red and blue lights winking their way across the sky, and for a moment got excited that it was coming for her.

With tears freezing on her cheeks, she watched the lights fade into the distance.

She yelled for help again, but her voice was so hoarse that she wasn't sure anyone could hear her. She had never wanted to go to sleep as badly as she did right now but she knew if she did, she was dead. If she got up and walked maybe she could stay awake . . . stay alive.

She grabbed the dead tree limb she had used as a walking stick the last time she fell and jammed it down into the snow close to her left hip. She slid her left foot up underneath her and struggled up on her leg. The stick snapped and she stepped down on her right leg. She toppled to the ground, screaming as excruciating pain shot up her right leg. Her right arm hit the ground and the pain that shot through it put an end to her hopes that it was just sprained. She gave up and burrowed herself another hole in the snow drifted around a fallen tree. As she curled up in her makeshift igloo, she began to think about God.

When you lose hope, you lose everything, but she couldn't help feeling like there wasn't much hope for her. She wasn't one to pray for things. She had always believed that God helps those who help themselves. With all the poor, helpless people in the world, she had always felt like it wasn't right for her to beg God for help. She knew now that she wasn't going to get out of this without divine intervention. Sobbing with fear, she closed her eyes and began to pray.

She didn't know when she drifted off but she roused when something began tugging at the scarf around her neck. She heard a growl and thought about the wolves living in the area. The last thing she remembered was trying to bat the animals away from her face, and wondering if she was dreaming since she knew wolves didn't attack people.

Just as Ann drifted into a marvelous dream, the gunshot went off. She rolled over and dropped her feet to the floor just as two hundred pounds of dog slammed into her, knocking her back on the bed. Then she remembered she was in the middle of hell week, otherwise known as deer hunting season in northern Wisconsin.

"Get off me, you beasts," she yelled, struggling to see her alarm clock. She couldn't believe it was only 5:45 A.M. Surely it was a sin to be up this early, unless you hadn't gone to bed yet. In the midst of trying to kick the dogs off and gather enough covers to crawl back under, she heard footsteps on the stairs. She groaned and gave up any thought of getting back into her dream.

"Off," commanded a deep male voice, just as the ceiling light went on. All three dogs jumped off the bed and sat demurely at his feet.

"*What* is going on up here?" John asked, as he bent down to pick up Sheba, a black Schipperke, and pet the two golden retrievers. "Between the gunshots outside and the noise up here, it sounds like an invasion."

"I could swear that gun went off right in this room, so surely it must have been on our property." Ann yawned as she crawled out of bed and staggered to the sliding glass doors leading to the deck. She squinted, trying to see into the woods bordering their backyard. In a couple of weeks a full moon would reflect on the snow and make the woods come alive with light. Now it was moonless and pitch dark outside.

"It wasn't on our property but it was very close," John said, as he walked up behind Ann and wrapped his arms around her.

Meanwhile, the dogs took turns crowding each other to stand in front of the door and look out into the woods. Suddenly Duke, the oldest and biggest golden retriever, growled and lunged at the glass. Two more gunshots went off, seemingly in the next room.

Ann stumbled back to bed and crawled under the covers. "John, please go away and let me die in peace. And take these devil dogs with you," she said, trying to kick the dogs off the bed.

Ann swore she had just put her head on the pillow when her alarm went off at 9:30. She got up and went to look out the sliding glass door. The sun was shining on ten inches of new fallen snow. The thermometer hanging off the side of the house read five below zero. Weather reports had predicted nightly lows below zero for the rest of the week.

Ann grabbed her binoculars and scanned the woods and lake. She didn't see any blaze orange but she did hear gunshots every few minutes. Satisfied that they weren't being personally invaded, she headed for the bathroom just as the phone rang. No rest, even on vacation, she thought as she picked it up.

"Ann, I put the dogs in the garage. Don't forget and let them outside," John said.

"I knew it was too quiet in here."

"Can you do me a favor?" he asked, shouting to be heard over the construction noise.

"Sure."

"When I pulled out of the driveway this morning I saw something bright red lying up by the pond. I think it may be a deer part. Would you run up and get it before the dogs drag it all over the yard? God knows, they don't need to get any dirtier than they normally do."

"Sure. I need the exercise so I'll get out there in the next hour." They hung up after planning lunch for 12:30.

She hustled into the bathroom to get dressed, wondering what the dogs had dragged in. It wasn't unusual for them to drag in part of a deer carcass this time of year. Ann looked in the mirror and realized that while John was off on his construction site she was facing her own remodeling project. In the movies women always look like they have their makeup on and every hair in place when they get up. Her dark blonde hair was standing straight up on top of her head and smashed in on the sides. How could someone with absolutely no body in her straight, fine hair look like Don King first thing in the morning? She did her usual war paint, put a curling iron on the ends of her shoulder-length hair, and brushed it out. The mirror didn't crack, so she sprayed her hair and called it good.

On good days, after a week of sacrifice, Ann wore size 8 bottoms and size 12 tops. This was not a good week, so she headed to the size 12 section of the closet. Even so, she thought she should get a Congressional Medal of Honor for fighting the battle of the bulge every day of her life.

She pulled on jeans and sweatpants, two sweatshirts, and two pairs of socks and went downstairs. Northern Wisconsin winters are serious business. With at least sixteen inches of snow on the ground, below zero temperatures, and a brisk wind, it's possible to get incapacitated and freeze to death in just a few hours.

Ann put on boots and a red hooded parka. She wrapped a scarf around her face, leaving only her eyes uncovered. She stuffed a couple of trash bags into her coat pockets, pulled on thermal glove liners and a pair of heavy mittens, and headed outside.

As she hiked up the driveway towards the pond, she marveled at the beauty surrounding her. The snow John had bladed out of the driveway was heaped into three-foot piles lining the drive. The piles were the beginnings of the eight-foot snow tunnels they would be driving through by the end of March. It was one of those mornings when the snow seemed to stick to every tree branch, making the woods look like a winter wonderland. Except for the occasional gunshot in the distance and the wind in the trees, it was very quiet.

As Ann got closer to the pond, it was obvious that the dogs had been running all over this area. It didn't take her long to see something partially covered with snow near the pond. It was bright red, which made her wonder what it was. Blood didn't stay that red, even in cold weather. She pulled out a trash bag as she crunched through snowdrifts up to her knees to examine the thing.

Ann breathed a sigh of relief when she found nothing more than a shiny red rubber snow boot. As she stooped down to examine it, she wondered how someone lost a boot out in the middle of nowhere. She picked it up and noticed how heavy it was. Ann shook some rubbish out of the boot and bent down to inspect the clumps of brown soggy leaves and grayish white twigs that fell out. She yelled and startled back when a clump of leaves moved. A mouse, obviously scared to death, scrambled out from under the pile of leaf muck and scampered across the snow as she tried to maintain her balance.

Ann ended up on her butt in the snow with her hand buried in the muck from the boot. Silently admonishing herself for clumsiness, she got to her feet and shook the snow and leaf muck off her mittens. She bent down to brush away the twigs clinging to her sweatpants. Gasping, she stooped down to get a better look. The twigs looked just like the bones from a foot. She sifted frantically through the snow to find the rest of the twigs, or bones, or whatever they were, and pulled out what looked like a partially intact skeleton of a foot. In shock, she sat back on her heels and, for the second time, found herself on her ass in the snow.

Despite the cold, Ann felt warm and clammy. Sweat rivulets ran down her back and it felt like Krakatowa had migrated to her gut, prepared to explode. She scooped up the debris and the boot, wrapped them in the trash bag, and began walking home. If she had a boot and it had part of a foot in it, then it must be a human foot. If that were true, then where was the rest of the person? How did it get into her yard? She stopped and leaned up against a tree trunk, trying to focus and pull herself together.

A cacophony of barking greeted Ann as she entered her mudroom. She dumped the boot on the washer and got out of her wet outer clothes. The answering machine light was flashing, but she ignored it and ran upstairs to put on fresh jeans and a sweatshirt. She couldn't seem to get warm. Her mind was going a mile a minute trying to figure out what she should do about the boot.

She came back downstairs and listened to the calls on the answering machine. The director of nursing filled her in on yesterday's admissions and discharges and told her to enjoy her two weeks off. Ann was shocked to hear they had done five helicopter transfers in the last twenty-four hours. The second message was from John, asking her to have Gus Lowery's railroad lantern and pottery ready when he came home for lunch.

Shrugging off her concerns about the hospital, Ann called the sheriff's office. The dispatcher listened to her story and said she'd have someone get back to her as soon as possible. Resigned to the waiting game, Ann decided to have a cup of hot chocolate and get Gus's antiques ready.

She and John had gone to an antique show over the weekend. They were avid collectors and frequented farm auctions where things were sold in box lots. To get the one piece they wanted they usually had to buy a box of things they didn't collect. They had started selling antiques at the occasional show and many of their friends asked them to look for things they collected. The boxes piled in the family room attested to the fact that they'd found several items.

Ann unearthed Gus's box and lugged it to the table in the family room. Before she opened it, she decided to build a fire. Setting up the kindling, the paper, and the logs kept her hands busy but left her mind free to race forward. How long did it take for bones to be picked clean? How long would bones last when they were exposed? Where was the rest of the body? Once the fire was started she settled down to unpack the box.

The dogs, as usual, acted as an early warning system. Ann got to the front door just as a large, black-gloved hand reached past the sidelight to ring the doorbell. She opened the door smiling, expecting one of the deputies she knew. The guy standing on her porch was not someone she had met before.

"Hello Mrs. Ranson, I'm Sheriff Lark Swenson," he said in a deep voice as he pulled off his gloves and stuck out his hand. "I'm here to take a look at the boot you found."

In the mystery novels Ann read there didn't seem to be any middle ground for sheriffs. They were either dense and hard on the eyes or, if the lead character was a single woman, they were drop-dead gorgeous and unmarried. In real life the few police she'd met were average looking. Of course, she'd always met them bent towards the window of her car as they gave her a speeding ticket.

This guy was about six-foot-four with broad shoulders and a well-built frame. Dark wavy hair set off a tanned face and startling light blue eyes. He reminded her of a taller, darker, and, if possible, more handsome Mel Gibson. Even Ann, married to a man she adored, couldn't resist a sneak peak at his ring finger. She mentally thanked the goddess of curling irons and cosmetics that she'd bothered to pull herself together this morning.

"This is the Ranson place, isn't it?" His eyes glanced over Ann's face as she stood mute in the doorway.

"Ah . . . yes, it is," Ann stammered, ushering him inside. "I think I missed your name."

The sheriff stepped into the foyer and took off his topcoat. Ann hung it in the entry closet as he sat down on the bench to take off his boots.

"Most people don't catch it the first time. My name is Lark, like Mark, only with an 'L'. Lark Swenson."

Ann wondered who in their right mind would name their child Lark. She looked into his eyes and couldn't keep a straight face. Unfortunately, one of her least intelligent stress reactions was hysterical laughter. The remains of a human foot in her laundry room, coupled with the surprise of this guy's name, struck all at once. Ann bent over and started laughing and crying at the same time.

The sheriff stood up and took her arm. "Mrs. Ranson, are you all right? Why don't we sit down."

She raised up and wiped her eyes with the sleeve of her sweatshirt. "Please call me Ann and I'll call you"—more giggles—"I'll just call you Sheriff."

Ann walked the sheriff into the living room, and between laughing and wiping tears from her eyes, offered him something to drink. He accepted, and she escaped to the kitchen to get herself together.

When she returned with his coffee and her cocoa, he was standing in front of one of the corner cupboards looking at Ann's collection of carnival glass. "My grandmother had some of this glass. I've always thought it was very colorful," he said.

Ann laughed. "I love carnival glass but it isn't everyone's cup of tea." She smiled calmly at him. "Please accept my apologies for my earlier behavior; this hasn't been one of my better days. I just built a fire in the family room. Let's go back there and I'll tell you about the boot."

Lark took the tray and followed her. He stopped in front of the sofa table and set the tray down to pick up a blue pitcher she had just unpacked.

"Bleeding Heart," he murmured, staring at the pitcher.

Watching sadness play across his face, Ann asked him if he collected Roseville.

"My wife collected it," he said, gently setting the pitcher back down.

He walked over to the wall of windows and stood silently, looking out at Big Oak Lake. Ann sat on the sofa watching him. As she looked more closely, she saw a few threads of silver in his dark curly hair. She willed herself to stop staring when he sat down on the sofa and began his interview.

It didn't take Ann long to tell him the details of finding the boot. Lark then began asking questions about her and her husband. Ann told him the basics. She and John were married shortly after they met in West Virginia. After several job-related moves, they ended up in Madison, Wisconsin. Three years ago, one of John's clients left them land in Big Oak. Shortly after that, the hospital administrator position opened at Mason County Memorial Hospital. Ann got the job and John started his own residential design and construction company. They moved to Big Oak and built their house.

Once the sheriff was done questioning her, he asked to take a look at the boot. The dogs, still shut up in the garage, started barking when Ann and Lark got to the laundry room. Just as he unwrapped the boot, they heard a car pull up the driveway.

"That's probably John coming home for lunch," Ann said, glancing at her watch. "He'll think I've been speeding again when he sees a police car in the driveway."

"I'm driving my own car today," Lark said, studying the boot. "Everyone's working overtime and all the official cars were in use." He was putting on a pair of surgical gloves he'd pulled from his pants pocket when Ann left the room.

"Whose car is out front?" John yelled before she could get to the front door.

She rounded the corner as he hung his coat in the closet. "Who's here?" he asked, glancing at the boot tray.

She folded her arms and leaned against the wall. "You remember telling me about the red thing up by the pond?"

John nodded.

"It was a boot, and I think it had some bones in it. The car in the driveway belongs to the sheriff. He's in the laundry room looking at it."

"This is a joke, right?" John said, staring at Ann like she was crazy.

"No, I'm afraid it isn't," Lark said as he came around the corner. He shook hands with John and introduced himself. John didn't seem to notice his first name, which told Ann he was feeling the shock of this turn of events.

"Ann, I think you're right," Lark said. "I'm pretty sure it's the remains of a human foot. I'm going to send it to the state forensics lab in Wausau."

"Jesus Christ! A human foot? I don't believe it," John said as he walked into the kitchen and sat down at the table. "How long has it been out there?"

"I don't know, but I'd say quite a while," Lark said, sitting down across from him. "I'm wondering how it got into your yard and where it's been all this time."

"Uh, I'm pretty sure I know how it got here, but I don't have any idea where it came from," Ann said, sitting down. "The dogs probably found it and dragged it in." She fidgeted with the placemat on the table in front of her. "We didn't get home from Wausau until after eleven on Saturday night. It was so late, we figured it was safe to let the dogs out. Unfortunately, they took off towards the marsh, barking like hell. Remember," Ann said, looking over at John, "we thought we heard a snowmobile but didn't see any lights."

"I forgot about that," John replied. "You think that's when they found the boot?"

"They were out for three hours; they had to be into something."

"Well, if that's what happened, the rest of the body, if there's more, could be anywhere," John said, looking out the sliders. He glanced over at Lark. "I can't imagine trying to search all three hundred and sixty acres in this snow. In the spring you might have a chance, but I doubt it this time of year."

"How far do your dogs roam?" Lark asked.

"We don't watch them every minute but I doubt they leave the property. I've never seen them at the Lowerys', have you?" John asked Ann.

Frowning, she shook her head. "Nope, and I've never seen them at the Banskis' either. I think Duke and Buck routinely cover about twenty acres and range out around eighty to a hundred when they have time to fool around. They also wander out to the marsh when it's frozen."

Lark got up from the table and walked over to look out the sliding glass door at the lake. The sun was gone, hidden behind gunmetal gray clouds, and big, heavy snowflakes were rapidly falling. It was only one o'clock in the afternoon but it looked like it would soon be dark.

"I wonder if you'd even have a chance of finding the rest of the body right now. The dog tracks will be covered with the new snow and deer hunting season must be keeping all your people very busy," Ann said.

"I'll try to get some extra help from the state," Lark said, rubbing his forehead. He walked back over and sat down at the table.

"John, your crew can spare you for a day," Ann said. "If our dogs found that boot, why don't we see if they can lead us to the rest of the body."

"You've read one too many mysteries, sweetheart," John said.

She gave him a withering look.

"All right, all right. If the sheriff's interested, we'll give it a try."

"Give what a try?" Lark asked, not following their conversation.

"We'll see if the dogs can find the rest of the bones," John said. "Golden retrievers have a nose about three hundred times as sensitive as humans. I can pick up a rock from the gravel drive, roll it around in my hands, throw it a couple hundred feet, and they'll find the exact stone and bring it back. If there's more where that boot came from, they can find it."

Lark looked skeptical. John chuckled and shook his head "I wouldn't believe it either if I hadn't see it with my own eyes. It's the damnedest thing."

"While we're talking, I'm going to fix lunch," Ann said, heading for the pantry. "It's terrible to think about food at a time like this, but I'm famished." She heated up chicken noodle soup and made grilled ham-and-cheese sandwiches. They wolfed down the food and talked about hunting season accidents.

"I can't believe we've had the helicopter up here five times," Ann said.

"Believe it," Lark replied. "We've already had three tree stand falls, two of them with broken backs. We also had a woman shoot herself in the leg and hit her femoral artery. She damn near bled to death before her drunken hunting buddies got her to the ER. Pete Williams missed a deer he was shooting at from his kitchen window. His bullet ended up in Mrs. Hartley's sewing room wall after it went through her shoulder."

"Did Gus come down to take care of his father-in-law?" Ann asked John.

"He came down to check on the house. They want me to finish it in time for their big Christmas party," John replied. "He ended up bailing Pete out because Cathy was shopping. Cathy offered to come home, but he told her he'd deal with Pete. He said Pete is mad as hell. He has to go to Rhinelander for a psychiatric evaluation or stay in jail."

"The Lowerys go skiing at their cabin in Bessemer, Michigan, every Thanksgiving. Cathy spends most of the week shopping in Chicago because she hates to ski," Ann explained to Lark. "John's remodeling their house, so they're staying in Bessemer until it's done."

"Gus said Pete called Judge Holten every name in the book, right in the courtroom." John said, finishing his sandwich. "Pete told Holten that he got him elected and threatened to reverse that the next time he runs."

"Well, they're the richest family in Big Oak County, maybe even northern Wisconsin, so that's probably no exaggeration," Ann said. "Who knew you could make so much money with a string of sawmills and paper mills."

Lark changed the subject. He told the Ransons he would bring a team out first thing the following morning to search their property. He also told them that he was going to inquire about a police tracking dog from one of the neighboring counties or the state, although he didn't rule out trying to use their dogs if one wasn't available.

Before the sheriff left, he fingerprinted Ann and John, explaining that since Ann had handled the boot, he needed to eliminate her prints.

As Lark drove up the driveway, he thought about the Ransons and the trouble he expected was awaiting him somewhere on their property. His first impression of them didn't set off any alarm bells, but he knew to proceed with caution until he could dig further into their backgrounds. He made a mental note to get the details of their inheritance.

To his untrained eye, they had a lovely home. Lark thought about how much Maria would have enjoyed all the quilts and glass. He shook off the memories of his dead wife and turned his attention back to the bones. He stopped his car near the pond. As he tramped through the snow, he noticed several bird and deer feeders at the edge of the woods. Despite the snow and cold, birds and squirrels were everywhere.

He finally reached the area Ann had described. Faint, snow-filled animal tracks meandered from the woods to the edge of the pond. He saw the trampled snow where Ann had fallen. It didn't make sense that a person would retrieve the bones of someone she'd killed and turn them in to the police, but he'd seen stranger things in his career.

Lark studied the Ransons' house as he hiked back to his Jeep. If he didn't know it was new, he would have sworn the big, two-story, gray farmhouse had been there for decades. Mature trees and landscaping surrounded it. Smoke floated up out of the chimney and an evergreen wreath hung from the bright blue front door. The real show was Big Oak Lake. The twenty-four-hundred-acre lake, the largest in Mason County, spread out behind the house in a sea of white-capped gray.

Nothing had changed when he got back to the office; the place was crazy. He grabbed the messages from his spindle and headed for his office. Flo, the dispatcher, yelled that she needed to see him as soon as possible. He told her to stow it until later unless it was an emergency. She glared but waved him away. He noticed that she had changed the color on her claw-like fingernails. They were orange and decorated with decals of miniature turkeys. The new color scheme was an improvement over the green and yellow Green Bay Packer colors she'd been wearing for the last month.

Lark escaped into his office and called Joel Grenfurth. Joel and Lark met when Lark joined the Chicago police force. Shortly after they became friends, Joel got married and moved to Wausau. He had been a detective with the Wisconsin State Police for fifteen years. Lark told Joel about the boot and bones and asked him if anything about this situation rang a bell.

"What a piss-poor time for this to happen," Joel said. "Can you get the bones and the boot down to our lab? Everything has gone to hell this week. Wisconsin's full of FIB's getting drunk and trying to blow each other's brains out while they're shooting at the thirty-point buck." Joel paused. When Lark didn't say anything he continued, "You *have* heard that song about the thirty-point buck haven't you?"

"Yeah, yeah, I've heard the damn song so many times I could probably sing it in my sleep, especially the part about the Illinois lawman. Watch it with that FIB shit," Lark said, wondering who he could pull off to run to Wausau.

"You're exempt from Fucking Illinois Bastard status. The minute you made the move you became a Cheesehead." Joel chuckled, knowing how much Lark, a diehard Bears fan, hated the Packers.

"I think I'd rather be an FIB," Lark grumbled. "Hell will freeze over before I wear a piece of yellow plastic cheese on my head. I'll get the bones down to you in a few hours, but I need the boot back tomorrow morning. Do you have any tracking dogs we could use?"

"Tracking dogs? You think that skeleton left you a trail?" Joel asked. "You've been in boonie-land way too long."

"The people who found the boot think their dogs dragged it into their yard. They think the dogs can lead us back to where they found it," Lark said, wondering how stupid this sounded.

"What kind of dogs do they have?" Joel asked. "I've got a black Lab that could probably do the same thing."

"Golden retrievers."

"Smart dogs."

"So you think it's worth a try?" Lark asked, leaning back in his chair.

"Nothing to lose, is there? Otherwise you could be roaming the countryside until spring thaw. I don't think our dogs could help—they follow scent trails. Get the bones and the boot down here and we'll get to work on them ASAP. If your officer can wait, he can bring the boot back tonight. We could probably get you a couple of officers tomorrow, but there's no one available today. We're too busy dealing with live, law-breaking FIBs."

"Yeah, yeah, Grenfurth, always the joker. I'm not going out on this until tomorrow morning." Lark glanced out the window. "It's snowing like a bitch. It'll be dark in less than two hours and back down to fifteen below. We're covered over with deer hunters and problems after bar time. If there's something else out there, it can wait till tomorrow. It's been waiting this long." Lark yelled at an officer passing in the hall and waved him into the chair in front of his desk. "Joel, I'll get this stuff on the road in half an hour and call you tomorrow if we need help."

Jim Kryjack slouched into the chair, draping his arms over the arm-rests. He stretched out his long legs and poked his huge feet underneath the sheriff's desk. Despite all the food he packed into his six-foot-five frame, he was beanpole slim. Straight blond hair was combed to the side but occasionally flopped down into bright blue eyes set wide apart in his youthful face.

Jim could have gotten a law enforcement job just about anywhere but came home because he thought Mason County was the best place on earth. Unlike many of his friends who wanted to escape their roots, Jim just wanted to sink them deeper. His family had lived in northern Wisconsin for more than a century and he couldn't think of any-thing better than extending that tradition. He went to the University of

Wisconsin in Madison to get a degree in Police Science and came home as quickly as possible. Life in Madison had confirmed that he could not be happy in the city.

He had expected to work at the family resort until there was a job opening in the area, but Sheriff Dodge hired him right out of college. A couple of months later Dodge had his heart attack and Sheriff Swenson was hired. At first, Jim didn't think he would like working with a former Chicago cop. That feeling went away in a hurry when he figured out how much he could learn.

After finishing his conversation, the sheriff turned to Kryjack. Jim agreed to take the evidence to Wausau and bring back the boot. Lark gave him the bag and told him the details.

Jim looked stunned. "We've had the occasional arm or leg taken off in farm accidents, but nothing like this. That was a pretty isolated piece of property until the Ransons came. Old man Wazowski wasn't up here much. He allowed a few of us to deer hunt, but otherwise he was pretty strict about trespassers. Everybody was real surprised he let the snowmobile trail go through."

"What do you know about the Ransons?" Lark asked.

Jim thought for a minute. "Not much. My sister Janelle, she runs the restaurant part of Pine View for mom and dad." Jim continued when Lark nodded. "Well, the Ransons were at the Pine View the other night when I was there and I asked her about them. I'd just given Mrs. Ranson a speeding ticket."

"Speeding ticket," Lark said, and rubbed his hand across his eyes. "Tell me about it."

"She was doing seventy on Highway M. I could hear her radio clear back in the cruiser, but she'd turned it off by the time I got to her car. She seemed flustered but didn't try to lie her way out of the ticket," Jim said, grinning at Lark. "She said she had to stop listening to Motown when she's driving. I thought she seemed a little old to be listening to real loud rock."

"Jesus," Lark said, laughing and shaking his head.

"I thought that was pretty funny, too. Anyway, Janelle says the Ransons come out to eat a couple of times a month. They tip well and treat the waitress great. Mrs. Ranson used to be a waitress. Janelle thought they were middle-aged honeymooners until they celebrated their nineteenth wedding anniversary out there this fall. They're involved in this?"

"Yeah, the boot was found on their property." Lark hustled Jim out the door to Wausau. If the Ransons were middle-aged in Jim's eyes, then he probably was, as well. He sure felt like it at the moment.

He was astonished to find that it was almost four-thirty. Where does the time go, he wondered as he dialed the number for Dan Raeburn, the Madison attorney who had probated Wazowski's will. When he'd told the Ransons he wanted to talk with him about the details of the estate, they had supplied his name and number.

He was surprised to be put right through to the attorney. Raeburn described the Ransons' inheritance just as Ann had. They had befriended one of John's clients, an elderly man named Sam Wazowski, when John remodeled his house in Madison. Ann and Sam shared a fondness for mysteries, art glass, and Italian food. Both the Ransons were estranged from their parents and Sam was estranged from his children, so they became a surrogate family for each other. When he realized how much the Ransons loved to vacation in northern Wisconsin, Sam secretly decided to leave his Big Oak Lake property to them, with the stipulation that they never subdivide it. He also left them an ample trust fund to be used for taxes and property improvements, as well as a couple thousand first-edition mysteries. Raeburn admitted that he had convinced Sam to have the Ransons checked out prior to leaving the property to them, but they had found no financial, business, or social surprises.

It was after five by the time Lark completed his notes. He called Ann and told her they would be out to begin their search at 8 A.M. He leaned back in his chair and massaged the tight muscles in his neck. Sighing, he got up to go deal with the dispatcher's problems before she started a one-woman campaign to have him impeached.

Ann spent the afternoon unpacking the antiques they had purchased for their friends. John came home just before six, and they ate dinner and watched the news, thankful that there wasn't a story about the boot. There were, however, several deer hunting stories, including two shots of the medical helicopter landing at the hospital. They groaned when they saw the story about Pete Williams being transferred to Rhinelander. Everyone knew that the only reason someone went from Mason County Memorial to Rhinelander was for drug or alcohol rehab or a psychiatric evaluation. They were just clearing the table when the phone rang.

Ann got off the phone just as John put the last of the dishes in the dishwasher. "That was Myra. She's running over to pick up their books. She says Joe can't wait to dig into the Big Little Book. It's one he's never seen before."

Ann hurried into the family room. John followed her and picked up the tiny book, leafing through the pages. "*Tarzan and the Jewels of Opar*. I can't figure out what people see in these books."

Ann snatched it from him and slipped it into a small plastic bag. "You're messing with forty dollars' worth of book and that's a good buy. Joe should be tickled to death."

"Those two are as bad as you with their books," John chided as he picked up the Nancy Drew books Ann had found for Myra. Ann had just finished the invoices when the doorbell rang.

Myra breezed in, all four foot nine inches encased in an ankle-length mink coat and diminutive, black leather, high-heeled boots. Her short black pageboy peeked out from under a mink hat.

"How about something to drink?" Ann asked as Myra slipped out of her coat and boots.

"Thanks, but I can't stay. David's driving up from Madison with a friend and I want to get back as soon as possible." Myra and Joe were in their late fifties with three of their four children married and out of the house. David was the baby. Myra was collecting sets of Nancy Drew and Hardy Boys books for her future grandchildren, the first of which was due any time. Joe swore he was collecting Big Little Books for the same reason, but Myra was sure that the grandchildren were just an excuse for his collection.

"Well, at least come in and take a look at your books," Ann said as she and Myra sat down in the living room.

The Banskis were big city escapees just like John and Ann, only they were rich, early retirement escapees. They just couldn't seem to stay re-tired. Joe had inherited the family neighborhood bar and steak house right after he and Myra got married. Over the next thirty years, they turned it into a Chicago tradition, adding several branches throughout the city and suburbs. Their oldest son, Joe Jr., now ran the Chicago busi-ness. Ten years ago, Myra and Joe built their summer home on twenty acres of waterfront property adjacent to the Ransons' and moved up four years ago. Joe made it through one year of retirement before he gave in to the temptation to go back to work when one of the local sup-per clubs came up for sale. To keep Myra from killing him, he bought the restaurant with his daughter and son-in-law. Banskis' had become one of the most popular restaurants in the northwoods.

"Joe's gonna love this," Myra gushed as she leafed through the Tarzan book. "You've also found two Nancy Drews I don't have. I can't thank you enough," she said as she wrote out a check. "Hey, I heard the sheriff was over here today. What did you think of him?"

"How'd you know he was here?" Ann asked.

"Come on, Ann. A town this size with a single guy that gorgeous? Someone mentioned it when they made dinner reservations just a little while ago."

"I hear he's from Chicago. Do you know anything about him?"

"He's been in the restaurant a couple of times when I've been tending bar. He's always alone, and eats at the bar. He seems like a real nice guy. I asked Joe Junior about him. He said he was a detective on the Chicago police force and took early retirement after his wife died a few years ago. I don't think they had any children. I've tried to fix him up but he always has an excuse not to go. He's quite nice about it, he just doesn't seem interested. Well, gotta run, I want to be home when David gets in." Myra walked into the hall and sat down on the bench to pull on her boots. "Hey, you forgot to tell me why the sheriff was over here."

"It was nothing, just some trouble with hunters," Ann said. She hated lying, especially to friends, but if she told Myra the truth, all of Big Oak would know about it by tomorrow morning. Myra was a world champion gossip who couldn't keep a secret if her life depended on it.

"Well, honey, this is sure the week for that," she said, hugging Ann on her way out the door. "The helicopter has flown over so many times this week I feel like I'm back in Chicago, and that damn O'Hare's stuck in the mother of all holding patterns."

Tuesday morning came in a hurry. John kissed Ann good-bye at six, reminding her that he would be back to help with the search as soon as he got his construction crew started. Ann burrowed back down under the covers and the dogs cuddled around her. She was sleeping soundly when the doorbell rang.

"Shit, shit, shit," Ann yelled as she rolled over and looked at the clock. It was 8:15. She couldn't believe she'd overslept. She scrambled out of bed and lurched into the bathroom. She dragged a pick through her hair, grabbed her long blue robe, and ran downstairs. She realized the minute she hit the hallway floor that the tiles were freezing. She felt like she was walking on ice cubes. The dogs barked and crowded around her as she went to the door. She looked out the sidelight and saw the sheriff.

Pain shot through her left foot as Buck stepped on it. Meanwhile Sheba jumped up and down like her back legs were spring-loaded. Wobbling on one foot, Ann waved the dogs back and yelled, "Everybody sit!" They backed up, rumps hitting the floor. Glaring at them, she added,

"Stay." Buck slid down to lie on the floor. Nobody else moved. She took a deep breath and opened the door.

Lark smiled down at her. "I'm sorry if we woke you up. I have a couple of questions before we start the search."

"Please come in. I was just getting up when you rang the doorbell. Have you figured out where we'll start?" Ann asked, discreetly trying to stand on one foot and then the other to ward off the cold of the floor tiles.

The sheriff stepped into the hallway and introduced his two deputies, Paul Dolphson and Jim Kryjack. Ann smiled and shook hands with both of them, thinking that she must look old enough to be their mother.

Ann headed into the kitchen to find that there wasn't any coffee left, so she quickly made some. Fortunately, she had some leftover blueberry muffins. The officers and dogs followed her.

"Officer Kryjack, I wonder if you would do me a favor?" Ann asked, once everyone was seated in the kitchen with their coffee and muffins.

He looked at her nervously. "I'll try, ma'am."

"First of all," Ann said, brushing her hand across the table to get rid of a nonexistent crumb. "Please don't call me ma'am, my name is Ann. I'd also appreciate it if you wouldn't say anything to my husband about the ticket you gave me last week."

Lark was sipping his coffee and must have sucked some of it up his nose, because he was suddenly coughing, laughing, and choking at the same time. Ann gave him the evil eye.

His coughing subsided just as Ann was contemplating whether she should let him choke to death or offer to perform the Heimlich maneuver. He waved his hands and choked out, "I'm sorry, I'm so sorry. I didn't mean to laugh."

Officer Kryjack smiled. "Of course, ma'am—I mean Ann. I won't say a word, but you do know they put the names of all the people who get tickets in the paper."

"I've got that covered," Ann said as the sheriff started to laugh again. "Just what is so damn funny?" she snapped.

"Nothing, nothing," he said, trying to stop laughing. "Let's change the subject. I'd like to see if your dogs can help us track down the rest of the body."

Paul, who had been silent to this point, stood up. "If you have leashes we can take them out on, I'll be happy to get them ready. I grew up with golden retrievers."

"No need for that," Ann said. "I'll get the dogs ready as soon as I'm dressed."

"You don't have to go out in this cold, ma'am. We can handle it," Paul replied.

"Hold on a minute. You're not taking them without me," Ann said, looking back and forth between Paul and Lark.

Lark leaned forward in his chair and carefully put his coffee mug down on the table. "Ann, it's ten below and very windy. I don't think you should be out in this weather. I promise we'll take very good care of the dogs." Ann thought that women probably fell all over him. He seemed so sincere, looking right into her eyes as he talked.

"Look, Lark," Ann said, staring right back at him. "This is my property and those are my dogs. I'm going if they're going. I've spent a lot of time walking over this land and I know it better than the three of you. Besides, the dogs will work better with me there."

"I think this is a bad idea. I can't let you do it," Lark said, frowning. "I think your husband would agree with me."

Ann stood, slammed her palms down on the table, and looked directly into the sheriff's eyes. "Can't *let* me do it," she repeated, pointing a finger in his face. "I make my own decisions. You want to search this property without a warrant, dogs or no dogs, I'll be going with you."

"What the hell's going on here?" Ann turned around to see John standing in the kitchen doorway.

Lark stood up. "John, I was just explaining to Ann that it's very cold outside and I think it would be best if she didn't come with us to search. It's way too cold and windy for anyone to be out there let alone a—" He realized what he'd been about to say and had the good sense to shut up.

John looked from Lark to Ann. "Oh boy, you overslept, didn't you?'

Ann pulled herself up to her full five feet, two inches and crossed her arms over her chest. "The damn alarm clock didn't go off, the doorbell woke me up, the dogs have been nuts, you didn't leave any coffee, and they want to search our property without us."

"Ann, you always shut the alarm off and go back to sleep unless you're going to work. You know I never leave any coffee because you don't drink it, it just goes to waste," John said, patiently. "The dogs are always crazy when someone comes to the door."

Ann stared at him, her brown eyes snapping.

He came into the kitchen to get himself a cup of coffee. "I was planning on going with Sheriff Swenson. You can stay here and deal with those antiques you've got to get delivered," he said, not looking at her. He had developed an almost all-consuming interest in his coffee cup.

"No, dammit, that's not the way it's going to work," Ann said, settling her hands on her hips and staring daggers at him as he sat down at the table. "I'll be ready to go in ten minutes."

Ann took a couple of steps towards the stairs, turned around, and fired off her final salvo. "By the way, I got another speeding ticket last week. I'm up to nine points. This one's all your fault since you gave me that damn Motown CD," she snapped, and stormed out of the kitchen.

As Ann left she heard Paul say "Jeez, I'm sorry, boss, what did I do wrong?"

"Don't worry about it," Lark said. "You could have handled it better, but I have a feeling it wouldn't have made any difference this early in the morning."

"You're absolutely right," John said.

TUESDAY MORNING

NOVEMBER 21—THE SEARCH

Ann felt like a female relative of the Pillsbury Doughboy. She had on long thermal underwear underneath two pairs of sweats and two pairs of socks, one of them electric. John found her standing in front of their full-length mirror.

"I'll probably be yelling, 'I've fallen and I can't get up,' if I fall," Ann said.

He gave her a brief smile and sat down on the edge of the bed.

"Was I that bad?"

"You would have scared the shit out of me if I didn't know you," John said, pulling off his jeans. He went over to rummage in his dresser. "The sheriff's OK. The other guy, Paul, was just trying to be helpful. He thinks he insulted you. By the way, his sister's a nurse at the hospital."

"Do you think I should apologize?"

"That's your call," John said, pulling on his longjohns. "They don't want to search in this weather and neither do I, so they can't understand why you want to."

"Now I really feel like shit," she replied, sitting down awkwardly beside him.

"I didn't mean it that way," John sighed, tugging his jeans back on. "This isn't a case of the dreaded male chauvinist pigs at work. They're nice guys just like me." He gave her a sidelong grin. "Guys with great respect for a good-looking, barefoot woman."

"You asshole." He ducked as Ann threw a pillow at him. "Good-looking, my ass. I look like crap."

"Well, you do have a great ass, and a fabulous chest, I might add, but seriously—no, no, Ann." John crossed his arms over his face to avoid the pillow she swung at his head.

"I know what you're doing," she said, flopping back on the bed. "I'll let you get by with it because I feel a little better than I did a half hour ago but you can't butter me up and get me to stay home. I'll go make thermoses and apologize." She kissed him and heaved herself off the bed.

"Hold it," he yelled. "What's with you getting another speeding ticket?"

"I was hoping you'd forgotten that. I've been trying to watch it, but I just wasn't paying attention. I'll do better."

"Yeah, right," he said, heading into the bathroom. "One of these days you're going to end up in jail and I won't bail you out. If you keep it up, we won't be able to afford car insurance."

Ann left while the getting was good and went downstairs to apologize. Paul and Jim got the dogs on their leashes while she prepared the thermoses. The group set off down the driveway about nine. It wasn't snowing, but the dark clouds obliterating the sun foretold of inches to come. An arctic wind whipped through the trees and the men turned up the collars of their blaze orange coats. Even with her hood up and a scarf wrapped around her face, Ann was cold. Of course, she didn't say a word. She'd made her bed and now she was going to freeze her ass off in it.

The sheriff had brought two snowmobiles in the hope of speeding things up. John was concerned that the dogs would be distracted by the engine noise, so Jim took one of the radios and stayed behind with the snowmobiles. Lark kept the other radio in case they needed help. John took Duke and Ann took Buck and they followed the faint trail of animal tracks from the pond into the woods. Both dogs strained against their retractable leashes, but the occasional gunshot kept Ann and John from letting them out more than ten feet.

As they reached the edge of the woods, Lark pulled the boot out of a plastic bag. He bent down and let both dogs sniff it while John gave them the fetch command. Lark bagged the boot and put it in his backpack. Once the dogs realized they weren't getting their toy, they plunged into the woods, tails up and wagging. They meandered along a lightly snow-covered animal trail, stopping to investigate small tracks that skittered across the snow.

Squirrels and chickadees chattered down from the trees, periodically distracting the dogs. Buck veered off to follow a set of rabbit tracks, and further into the woods Duke sniffed fresh deer tracks and strained at his leash. John pulled him back. Duke snorted his discontent but trotted back onto the trail.

After meandering along for half an hour, they'd walked through a thousand yards of woods and come to the edge of the marsh that cut across the southern section of the Ransons' property. It was a quarter mile wide swath of sedge grass dotted with birch clumps, small thickets of sumac, and dead tree snags. In the summer it was impossible to cross without hip waders.

"Now what?" John asked as they took a break.

Paul took off his backpack and pulled out a thermos. "How about a cup of coffee?"

"Good idea," Ann said, brushing snow off a fallen tree. Unlike the manicured woods in parks, there were downed trees all over and no shortage of places to sit.

"Can you pour me some hot chocolate?" she asked, digging two rawhide treats out of her coat pocket. As she tossed them to the dogs, a barrage of gunshots went off on the other side of the marsh. Paul handed her a steaming cup and sat down beside her. The tree creaked but held their weight.

"I love this place," Paul said, looking across the marsh. "I was pissed when you posted it last year. Sam always let my family hunt here."

Ann sipped her cocoa. "I don't have anything against you hunting, I just can't feed all these animals and then kill them for sport. My father hunted just about everything and I ate a lot of game when I was a kid, so I can't be one of those 'ban all hunting radicals.' " She made quotation marks in the air with her free hand. "I just can't bear hunting on my property."

"Hey, Lark, get that boot out and let's get this show on the road," Paul yelled as soon as he finished his coffee. They refreshed the dogs' interest in the boot and restarted their search.

The marsh wasn't completely frozen. Between the matted sedge grass and snow, it was like walking on marshmallows. A hundred feet in, Duke wandered into a small grove of sumac trees and startled a flock of cardinals. The beauty of the bright red males distracted them. No one noticed Buck until he trotted up to them with something bright yellow in his mouth. Buck released his find, a yellow mitten, to John.

"Do you think it's anything important?" John asked as Lark put it in a plastic evidence bag.

"We won't know until we search this area," Lark said. "Why don't you walk the dogs on across the marsh. Yell if you find anything." He turned away to discuss the search with Paul.

Ann and John noticed a large number of fresh deer tracks as they crossed the marsh. They walked across the faint trail of a snowmobile and agreed that it must have been the one they'd heard on Saturday night. Neither of them could figure out who would be out without their running lights before the trails were open. Ann was sure they were up to no good, like poaching deer. They looked for signs of a kill but didn't find any.

When they reached the other side of the marsh, Ann sat down on a fallen tree. John joined her and lit a cigarette. They relaxed and watched Lark and Paul search the sumac grove. After fifteen minutes of waiting, they grew restless and wandered west along the edge of the marsh. The woods had a thick undergrowth of brambles and sumac that made it almost impossible to get through, summer or winter. Ann was content just walking along the edge. Suddenly, Duke swerved into the underbrush. John gave him some extra lead and the dog charged into the thicket. He started barking and Buck ran after him.

Ann heard twigs snapping. Four deer leaped out of the woods and ran past her into the marsh. The dogs crashed through the snow right behind them, dragging down the brush with their leashes. Buck galloped past Ann and pulled her off her feet. He dragged her fifteen feet before she came to a stop on her stomach. Buck's leash was still clenched in her outstretched hands and her arms felt like they might come out of their sockets. She rolled over on her back and lay in the trench her body had plowed through the snow, trying to catch her breath and sit up as Buck squirmed around her. She looked over at John. Duke was at the end of his leash, barking at the deer that had escaped back into the woods. Once again, she asked herself why they had such large dogs.

"My God, are you all right?" John yelled as he reeled Duke in and hurried over to her.

Ann couldn't answer because Buck was licking and nuzzling her. The more she protested, the more rambunctious he became. Even with John's help, she struggled to get up. In all the fracas, Buck pulled off one of her mittens. Swearing, Ann grabbed at it but Buck pranced out of her reach. She lunged towards him and slipped on the packed down snow, landing on her hands and knees and dropping the leash. He wasted no time dashing into the woods.

"Shit," John yelled as he rushed after Buck with Duke leading the way.

Ann turned around to see what the sheriff was up to, hoping he hadn't seen her Three Stooges act. He was only partially visible as he walked back and forth, searching the grove.

She was brushing the snow off her clothes when two men stepped out of the woods about a hundred yards from her. They wore orange jumpsuits and orange hats with the furry earflaps that make people look like they'd lost their last shred of intelligence. Ann jammed her naked hand down in her coat pocket and watched them approach. They both had at least two days' growth of beard and dark hair straggling out from under their hats. Looking across the marsh, Ann noted that the sheriff and Paul were also headed her way. John was not in sight, but she could hear the occasional unintelligible yell from the direction he'd taken into the woods.

Both hunters carried unsheathed rifles. As they got closer, she noted that the taller man's hair and mustache were a salt and pepper mix and his deep-set eyes were surrounded by heavy crows' feet and prominent bags. His face was ruddy. Ann figured it was windburn mixed with a healthy dose of alcohol.

When they got within five feet, Salt and Pepper pointed a black-gloved finger at her, "Hey, lady, what the hell are you doin' out here? We was trackin' some deer and your damn dog spooked 'em. I damn near shot him. Had him sighted in when I saw he was draggin' a leash."

"What are you doing on this property?" Ann asked. She crossed her arms, tucking her ungloved hand into the armpit of her coat.

The men looked at each other and laughed. Now that they were closer, it was obvious that the other one was a younger version of Salt and Pepper. His full mustache was reddish brown. His eyes were the same dark brown but the crows' feet and bags were only beginning to form. He unzipped his coat and pulled out a small flask, confirming Ann's suspicions. He took a swig before holding it out to her.

"No, thanks," Ann said, waving it away. "What are you doing on this property?"

"Ain't it obvious?" Salt and Pepper said. "We're huntin'. This ain't no time to be out for a walk. You could get yourself killed." They chuckled, their bodies weaving back and forth like trees in the wind.

John came out of the woods fifty yards from them. He doubled over and put his hands down on his knees. Ann saw his breath, rapid wisps of frosty air, and realized he was winded. The dogs stood docile by his side. She had a strong suspicion that corporal punishment, at a level frowned on by the ASPCA, had been administered while they were in the woods. When the dogs saw the two hunters, they started barking.

"That your old man?" The younger hunter nodded at John.

John lifted his head and looked at Ann. "I heard you talking to someone. I thought it was the sheriff." He walked over to them, restraining the dogs in the heel mode.

"These two men are a bit upset that the dogs spooked their deer."

"Oh, really," John said. "If you look to your left, you'll see two men who may be as upset about your deer being spooked as you are." The hunters swiveled around to see Paul and Lark, about forty yards away and approaching rapidly.

The younger man raised his hand. "We'll be on our way, we didn't mean any harm." He glanced at Ann. "Dad and I, we'd never shoot a dog."

"Why are you hunting on this property?"

"Well, shit, I've hunted here for years," Salt and Pepper bellowed.

"Poaching maybe, but you've never hunted here legally," Paul said. "Lonnie, you know Sam only let people hunt by invitation and you were never on the guest list. These are the Ransons and they own this land now. Didn't you notice the no trespassing signs posted all over?"

The younger hunter shook his head. "We didn't see any signs, but you know Sam always had signs and everybody ignored them 'cause he was gone."

"Good one, Ronnie," Paul said.

Lark stepped towards the two men. "Paul will take your guns. He'll return them once you're off this property."

"Who the fuck are you to tell me and Dad what to do?" slurred Ronnie.

Lark ignored him and turned to Paul. "Escort these guys back the way they came. If they aren't fit to drive, take them home or to jail, depending on how much trouble they give you." He radioed Jim to come to the marsh ASAP.

"Who the hell are you, asshole?" Ronnie shouted, handing his rifle to Paul.

"I'm the new sheriff and you're about this close to being arrested," Lark snapped, holding his finger and thumb an inch apart in front of Ronnie's face.

Salt and Pepper had been quiet, looking back and forth between people as they talked. He'd given his rifle to Paul without resistance. Suddenly, he turned towards Ann. "Did he say your name is Ranson?"

"Yes," she said as he walked over to her.

He poked his finger in her face, nearly hitting her cheek. He reeked of alcohol mingled with tobacco and sweat. His eyes were shot through with red streaks. "Are you that bitch that took over down to the hospital?" he asked, swaying back and forth. Both dogs growled and Duke lunged forward, snarling at him. John pulled them back and took a few steps away.

Lark walked over and stared into Lonnie's eyes. "Get your finger out of her face."

Lonnie dropped his hand. "Are you that fucking bitch from the hospital?" he yelled.

"I work at Mason Memorial," Ann said, standing her ground.

"If I'd known that, we woulda killed them fuckin' dogs," he shrieked, his face flushing. "You're making my wife's life a living hell. Making her work night shift and weekends. She hates you, you fuckin' bitch."

"That's enough," Lark said, stepping in front of him.

"Who is your wife?" Ann asked, her voice calm. She heard the faint sound of a snowmobile in the distance.

"Betty Chevsky," he screamed, his face reddening so dramatically that Ann thought he might have a stroke. "She hates your guts. They all hate you. It was a good place to work 'til you came."

"That's more than enough," Lark snapped. He grabbed Lonnie's upper arms and walked him over to Paul as Jim arrived with the snowmobile. "If these two give you any trouble, arrest them."

Ann watched Paul escort them away, Jim following on the snowmobile. John returned her mitten and she slipped it on, marveling that she hadn't noticed how cold her hand had become.

"Boy, I really need a break," she said. Even the dogs seemed tired, lying down in the snow rather than playing. Ann rubbed her mittened hands over her face. "I had no idea Betty Chevsky felt that way. She volunteered to work nights and weekends. I can't believe she's married to that bastard."

"Those guys are just one of the reasons I didn't want you out here today. They could have hurt you," John said, putting his arm around her waist. "Why did you challenge them?"

"Challenge them?" Ann muttered, stunned by his comment. She pulled away and turned to face him. "Jesus, John, after five years on night shift in the ER I think I can handle myself. What do you think I was doing? Having a tea party? I spent more than my fair share of time dealing with chauvinistic drunks, violent drunks, drunks with knives and guns, and women who had the shit beaten out of them by drunks. Believe me, these guys don't listen to shy, retiring women. Those are the ones who get beaten up or killed."

"She's right," Lark said. "How about we call it a day?" He dug his watch out from under his glove. "It's after eleven, we can head back for lunch."

"I agree. We can come back out this afternoon," John said.

"Lark, I almost forgot in all the excitement. Did you find anything in the sumac grove?" Ann asked.

"A couple of old beer cans and a lot of squirrel tracks, all covered with fresh snow."

Ann frowned and shook her head. "I don't think our dogs roam much further than this, so I'd rather continue to look and get it over with." She took Buck's leash from John.

They decided to search for a couple more hours. Once again Lark pulled the red boot out of his backpack. The dogs sniffed it and strained at their leashes.

As they moved through the snow at the edge of the woods, Ann found herself relaxing in the beauty of the marsh. The dogs flushed two enormous, shaggy rabbits. The size of their coats suggested that Big Oak was in for a long, harsh winter. Birds chattered at them from the brush and a hawk floated over, looking for dinner. Ann thought about how hard it must be for the animals to survive and made a vow to add more feeders before she went back to work.

They crossed the snowmobile trail again. Despite repeated attempts to keep the dogs together, Duke veered off into the brush on the south end of the marsh while Buck strained to go north along the trail. They decided that Ann would let Buck go where he wanted as long as she didn't leave the trail, and John and Lark would head into the woods.

Buck and Ann worked their way slowly along the trail. It was obvious that a snowmobile had recently been through the area. They had gone about three hundred yards when Buck swerved into the woods, following a set of animal tracks. Ann pulled him back but he whined and lunged forward, unwilling to return to the trail. Swearing, she reeled him in to ten feet of leash and followed, expecting another bunch of deer to fly by her. Thankfully, no deer appeared, but Buck did flush a rabbit that he chased halfheartedly before getting back on the trail.

Then Buck stopped about a hundred feet into a deep thicket of sumac. He began digging around the end of a snow-covered log, then ran to tug at something at the other end. Ann slogged forward and bent down to sweep the snow off it. It was a yellow mitten like the one Buck had found earlier. She stood up and scanned the log, suddenly realizing that she was looking at a snow-covered human body. She stooped down and attempted to turn it over. It was facedown and frozen stiff, the arms splayed out and bent at the elbows. It was impossible for her to move it by herself. The person was obviously dead. She dragged Buck a few feet, yelling at him to heel. He reluctantly fell in line beside her. They followed their own trail out of the woods.

Once Ann got out to the marsh, she looped her scarf around a tree branch. The trail was obvious to her but she wanted to be sure the sheriff could find it. She thought about the body. Obviously, it wasn't missing a foot because it had on a pair of black boots. She tried to absorb the ramifications of this as she walked back to where John and Lark had entered the woods. She was debating whether to go in after them when a snowmobile came roaring down the trail and stopped in front of her. Paul took off his helmet.

"Where's the body Lark radioed about?" he asked, getting off the snowmobile. Seeing the stunned look on Ann's face, he walked over and took her arm. "Ann, are you OK? You suddenly got very pale. Hey, you look like you're gonna be sick."

Ann didn't realize she'd covered her mouth with her hands. For once, Buck sat quietly at her side. "Lark doesn't know about the body I found," she blurted out.

"He must, because he radioed me just as we were dropping the Chevskys off at the station. He told me to get back here ASAP."

"I'll show you what Buck and I found. I know it isn't the body we were looking for because it has on two black boots." She pointed back up the trail.

Looking at Ann like she was crazy, Paul radioed Lark and asked for directions. Lark's voice crackled over the radio, telling him to stay put; they were on their way out.

While they waited, Paul explained that they gave out minimal information on the radio. Listening to scanners was a way of life in the northwoods. He stopped talking as Duke, John, and Lark emerged from the thicket.

"Did you find a body?" Ann asked.

"A skeleton and some clothing," Lark replied.

"I can't believe this. Buck and I found one, too."

"What the hell," John said. Both men started talking overtop of each other.

"Hold it," Lark yelled, waving his hands around.

"You found a body?" John asked Ann.

"Must be an animal," Lark muttered.

"No, it's a person," Ann snapped, beginning to realize the impact of what she had found. One body was beyond comprehension, let alone two. The possibility of a third and fourth crept into her mind. Things began to float around her. Lark grabbed her arms and lowered her onto a log. She saw his lips moving but his words didn't make sense. Through a haze, she saw John wrestling with both dogs, which meant that she'd let go of Buck's leash.

"I'm putting your head down between your knees," Lark said, pushing on her shoulders.

"Hey, I'm OK," Ann said, resisting his pressure. "I'm not going to faint. Let me sit up."

John dumped the dogs on Paul and sat down beside her, putting his arm around her shoulders. "Ann, you're very pale. Put your head between your knees."

"Jesus, you guys," Ann said, looking from one to the other. "I'm not going to faint. Besides, with all these clothes on, I don't think I can bend into that position."

"Are you sure you found another human body?" Lark asked, glaring at her.

"I'm positive. It's about three hundred yards up ahead." She pointed out her red scarf. "It has on a yellow mitten. Buck must have found the body earlier and stolen the other one. It has on two black boots and a red coat. There are animal tracks leading in to it. I tried to turn it over but it's frozen stiff."

"I can't believe this," Lark said. He closed his eyes and massaged his forehead. "We found skeletal remains and a mate to the red boot. Now I'm wondering how many bodies are out here." His face was grim as he surveyed the marsh. "John, why don't you and Ann take the dogs back to the house. Paul and I will meet you there later."

Lark gave several instructions over the radio and took the snowmobile to find the other body. John and Ann headed back to the house. It was only twelve-thirty, but it felt as if they'd been at it for three days instead of three hours.

As they walked back, John described what he and Lark had found. Duke had led them two hundred feet into a thicket and right to a snow-covered, partially dismembered skeleton. One of the hands was missing as well as the booted foot the dogs had found. Lark had searched the clothing for identification but none had been found.

"Probably a woman," Ann said as they trudged past the sumac thicket where they'd found the yellow mitten.

"Why do you say that?"

"Small shoe size, red boots, and no sign of ID," Ann said. "My ID is in my purse and I wouldn't take my purse on a walk in the woods. It all points to a woman."

"You're probably right. I thought it was a woman or a kid when I first saw the boot."

"How long do you think that body's been out here? The other one looks like it hasn't been here long. Until I realized it was frozen, I thought we might need the EMTs."

John stopped to light a cigarette. "Lark guessed at least a year but said it could be longer."

Tears spilled down Ann's checks. She brushed them away before they could freeze. "I wonder if there was something we could have done for either of them if we'd being paying more attention to what's going on out here." Hand in hand, they walked the rest of the way home in silence.

When Ann and John got home, they took a hot shower. As they came out of the bathroom, they heard Lark's voice on the answering machine saying he and Paul would be back in half an hour. John grabbed the phone and offered them lunch.

The front doorbell rang just as Ann was defrosting chili. "They got here early," she said, glancing at her watch as she hurried to the foyer. She opened the door to find Sara Waltner smiling at her.

"Hi, Ann. I thought I'd pick up my Venetian glass and Steve's Flow Blue. I just couldn't wait to see what you found." Ann stumbled back, shocked to see her, and Sara stepped into the foyer. For a minute, Ann couldn't figure out how Sara knew she had anything for them. Then she remembered the message she'd left on their answering machine over the weekend, back when life was normal.

"Let me run and get your glass. I don't have Steve's Flow Blue unpacked yet so I'll have to get it to you later. You can pay me then," Ann said, hurrying to the family room. "John and I are having company for lunch."

Sara yelled hello to John as she followed Ann into the family room. She picked up the heavy, white, heart-shaped bowl ribboned with burgundy glass and held it to the light. "How lovely. I can't thank you enough," she said, handing it to Ann to be wrapped. She pulled out a chair and sat down at the table.

"I hear the sheriff's been over here," she said, surveying the haul from the weekend. "What excuse did you use? I'd sure like to have that hunk stop by my house."

"Good grief, Sara," Ann said, sliding the tissue paper-wrapped glass into a paper bag. "What about Steve?"

Sara leered and raised her eyebrows. Ann thought Sara always acted like she'd hit the matrimonial motherload, even though rumors abounded in the community that Steve was having an affair with his assistant. Her interest in the sheriff surprised Ann. Steve Waltner, quite the handsome guy himself, owned several businesses in Mason County, all of them bearing his name and purported to be very profitable. If there was such a thing as high society in a county with more cows than people and more deer than cows, Sara and Steve were it. The Waltners appeared to be the personification of the American dream, complete with Michael, twenty-four, and Sandra, twenty-two, both attending the University of Wisconsin–Madison campus.

Ann studied Sara's peaches-and-cream complexion, mass of chestnut colored hair, and huge brown eyes. Sara was older than Ann but she looked thirty. Women joked that they'd never seen her in the same outfit twice. True to form, she wore a plum colored sweater and matching skirt that Ann had never seen. Ann felt positively frumpy in her forest green sweats and crew socks. She envisioned them together on *Glamour*'s Do's and Don't's page, Ann as the fashion Don't.

"Ann, we're married but we aren't dead. We can still look." Sara flashed Ann an amused smile and patted her arm, her well-manicured left hand showing off the biggest marquise diamond Ann had ever seen. "I'm sure John's just like Steve, he's not blind to a good-looking woman. Why should we be any different?"

Ann didn't have time to answer her. The oven timer went off just seconds before the doorbell rang.

"Can you get that?" John yelled. Sara followed Ann into the foyer and slipped on her coat, a gorgeous midcalf-length mink. She was sitting on the bench pulling on her boots when Ann opened the door. Sara's mouth dropped open when Lark leaned in.

"We don't want to mess up your floor. We'll come in through your mud room."

Lark turned to go but Sara was too quick for him. Smiling, she walked over to the door, and extended her hand. "You must be the new sheriff. How nice to meet you, I'm Sara Waltner."

Lark took off his glove and shook her hand. "Mrs. Waltner." He beamed her a hundred-watt smile. "I've worked with your husband on a couple of things. Please let me walk you to your car. We'd hate to have another casualty on top of all the deer hunting excitement." He stepped inside, slipped her package from her hands, and guided her out the door. Sara winked at Ann as she left.

"Well, Jesus Christ," Ann said, hurrying through the kitchen to unlock the mud room door. "That man's charm is wasted in law enforcement. He should be a politician."

Ann let Paul in. Exhausted, he flopped down on the bench. He looked at Ann's angry face and jumped up, "Jeez, Mrs. Ranson, is it OK that we came back here? If we're in the way . . ."

"No, no," she interrupted, raising her hand to silence him. "You're fine, there's nothing going on around here that a prostate exam or a giant dose of salt peter wouldn't cure."

Paul looked confused, but Lark, who had just come in, almost fell off the bench laughing. Paul glanced back and forth between them, trying to figure out what he'd missed. Ann shut the door and walked back to the kitchen before her mouth could once again betray her better judgment.

John had a pan of cornbread cooling on the island and was busy stirring a pot of chili. He glanced at Ann. "What did Sara want?"

"She came to pick up their glass and find out why the sheriff was here," she replied, scooping cornbread onto a serving plate. The cops walked in as Ann put out the soup bowls.

When they were done eating, Ann and Paul cleared the table while John and Lark built a fire in the family room. Fifteen minutes later, everyone sat down in front of the fireplace. It wasn't even three o'clock and Ann was ready for a nap. She pulled a quilt around her and picked up her knitting, trying to stay awake. Lark munched a cookie and sipped a cup of tea as he explained that the state police would help remove the bodies and search the marsh. Then he told the Ransons that he needed to interview them.

Ann grabbed John's hand. "Do you really suspect us?"

Lark sat his tea down on the end table and stretched his legs out towards the fire. "I don't think either of you are responsible for this, but we can't automatically eliminate you. Right now, you are the only people we have connected to these bodies. That will change as soon as we learn who they are and what happened to them." He sighed. "I'd like to interview you today."

The Ransons agreed. Paul set up a tape recorder in the study and John went to be questioned. Ann sat alone in the family room. She turned on the television but found the noise irritating and turned it off. She picked up the Janet Evanovich novel that she hadn't been able to put down prior to the weekend, but even it couldn't hold her attention. She pulled an unfinished quilt out of the trunk that doubled as a coffee table.

She willed herself to relax into the quilting and began thinking about how horrible it must have been to die like the two people they'd found in the marsh. She wondered if they were dead before they got into the woods. Did they know who killed them? Did they cry out for help? She wondered what caused their deaths. Did they suffer? Did someone betray them? Someone they loved? Someone they trusted? She worried about their loved ones not knowing where they were and racked her brain to remember if she'd heard about anyone missing from the area.

Most of all, Ann worried that if she'd taken the time to check out the snowmobile in the marsh on Saturday night, just maybe they'd only have one body. The thought that they might have saved a life was almost more than she could stand. She stopped quilting to wipe tears away with the sleeve of her sweatshirt.

All of a sudden, John's interview was over. Ann was so startled when she heard the study door open that she ran the quilting needle deep into her right thumb. In her effort to get it out, she ripped it across her thumb, creating a deep, half-inch cut. She jerked her hand away from the quilt and popped the cut into her mouth. She was in the kitchen running it under cold water when John came in.

Ann smiled with relief when she heard John and Lark talking about golf. They seemed very relaxed after the hour-and-fifteen-minute interview. John's smile vanished when he saw the blood in the sink. He rushed over and grabbed Ann's hand.

"What happened?" he asked, looking at the gash in her thumb.

Ann pulled her hand out of his grasp and stuck it back under the cold water. "I stuck myself with my quilting needle. I don't know how a needle that small can cause so much blood." She pulled it out of the water, saw that it was still bleeding, and plunged it back under. She didn't look up, concerned that she had mascara running down her face. After a few more seconds she turned off the water and wrapped her thumb in a paper towel.

"I'll get a Band-Aid and be right back," she said, heading for the bathroom. Ann glanced up to find Lark, Paul, and John staring at her, their faces creased with worry.

John took a hold of her wrist and turned her around before she could get away. "What have you been crying about?" he asked, putting his hand under her chin and gently raising her face so she had no choice but to look at him.

"It's just stress. I've been wondering if we could have saved the second girl if we'd checked on that snowmobile we heard Saturday night. Please let me go deal with this cut so I can get my interview over with," she said, not meeting his eyes, as she disengaged her wrist and went to the bathroom.

The view in the mirror was not good. She didn't have mascara running down her face; it was long gone. Her face was red and blotchy and her eyes were bloodshot and swollen. She felt a bit like a manic depressive who had hit both ends of the spectrum in twenty-four hours. Yesterday she'd been laughing hysterically and today she was in the crying phase.

Ann plopped down on the commode lid to think. Sometime during her hiatus, she heard the dogs bark and run through the house. Since the doorbell didn't ring, she figured the crime scene team had arrived. She finally got herself together by turning out the bathroom lights and putting a cool washcloth over her eyes. John knocked twice before she was ready to leave.

"Sorry it took me so long," she said to no one in particular when she came out and found the three men sitting at the kitchen table drinking coffee. "That stuff will keep you up all night," she said, getting a caffeine-free Diet Coke out of the refrigerator.

She walked over to the table. "Are you two ready?" she asked, glancing at Lark and Paul.

"Ann, we don't have to do this now. I can come back tomorrow morning," Lark said as he rolled his coffee mug back and forth between his hands and studied her face. "We're going to be out in the marsh most of the day so it won't be any trouble."

John wrapped his arm around Ann's shoulders. "That's a great idea. You can get a good night's sleep and do the interview first thing in the morning."

"I want to get this over with." She patted John's hand as she walked out of his embrace and headed to the study. She heard chairs scraping the tile floor and glanced back to see Paul and Lark getting up to follow her.

After Ann agreed to be taped and waived her right to an attorney, Lark asked her once more if she wanted to do this tonight. Despite, or maybe because of, his kindness, tears welled in her eyes. She retrieved a box of tissues from one of the bookcases as she assured him that she wanted to get it over with.

"I'm always fine when I'm in the middle of a crisis. It's later that I cry. Too many years as an ER and ICU nurse," she said, patting her eyes.

"I really think we ought to do this tomorrow," Paul said. "You look worn out."

"I look like hell but I'm fine," Ann said, glancing from one to the other. "You're both probably just like John. It drives him crazy to see a woman cry, especially if he thinks he had anything to do with it. My tear ducts may be in hyperdrive but my mind is fine. I don't have anything to hide. I'll tell you whatever you want to know if it'll help you figure out who killed those poor people. Let's get this over with."

The interview lasted until seven. Lark questioned Ann about their activities the last few days and the only thing out of the ordinary she could remember was the snowmobile on Saturday night. He probed about any significant events during the time they'd lived there, and she couldn't recall anything other than the construction of their house. She assured them that they'd never been to Big Oak until Sam left them the property. They had vacationed in northern Wisconsin, but they'd always been in the St. Germaine or Rice Lake areas.

Lark seemed uncomfortable but plowed ahead through the personal questions.

His eyes bored into Ann's and she broke eye contact. "Have you ever had an affair?"

"I haven't, and I'd have to see John in action to believe he has. We've been very happy."

"Do you and John have any family close by?"

She studied the colorful book jackets to the right of his head. "Our families live in Ohio and West Virginia. I'm the oldest of six. I have two brothers, a sister, and a stepsister. My other sister died five years ago in a car accident. My father died when I was fifteen. My stepfather died two years ago. My grandparents are dead. My mother and I aren't on the best of terms, but I'm very close to my brothers and sister."

Ann stared down at the table, deep in thought. All those things she thought she'd dealt with were coming back to the surface. The things she'd worked so hard to get beyond were creeping out of the dark recesses of her mind where she'd so carefully packed them away. The agony over not being able to have children; the painful deaths of close family members; her estrangement from her mother. She had a blinding realization that the experts she'd privately scoffed at were right. These excruciating things never truly went away, as she had been so cavalier to think. She could pack them up and send them back to their designated tombs in her subconscious. She could get them back into places where she could talk about them apathetically. But it was devastatingly obvious that any significant emotional event in her life could trigger their return. Lark interrupted Ann's reverie to tell her that he didn't have any more questions.

"When will you know how long the second person has been dead?" Ann asked. "I just can't get that snowmobile we heard on Saturday night out of my mind. What was it doing in the marsh without head-lights? Either someone was picking up a deer they poached or dropping off that body. If that person was still alive when she was dumped, it's going to be very hard for me to live with the fact we may have let someone die." A tear trickled down Ann's face.

"Is that what you're upset about?" Lark asked.

"Mostly." She reached for a tissue. "Let's not talk about this any-more," she said, wiping her eyes as she got up.

"Ann, wait a minute," Lark said, stepping in front of her. "I doubt there was anything you could have done and you might have gotten hurt if you'd gone out in the marsh after that snowmobile."

Ann listened, staring silently over his shoulder.

"I'll let you know what the autopsy says about the time of death." She nodded and he stepped out of her way.

John met them in the kitchen. He asked Lark and Paul to stick around and have a snack. Paul quickly accepted and Lark agreed to stay for a few minutes before going to check on the progress of the crime scene team.

Ann went upstairs to pull herself together. Twenty minutes later she was back downstairs after a modestly successful makeup repair. John had stoked up the fire and she was just settling down on the sofa with some cookies and a mug of hot chocolate when the doorbell rang.

"For chrissakes, what is this, Grand Central Station?" John asked as he went to answer the door. He returned to tell Ann that Betty Chevsky wanted to speak with her. Ann squared her shoulders and headed into the living room.

Betty was sitting in one of the navy blue wingback chairs in front of the living room windows. Ann was used to seeing her in a blue house-keeper's uniform. Tonight, she was wearing a neat, dark green skirt and matching sweater. Her black purse was perched on top of her knees and she clutched the top of it with both hands. Ann sat down on the sofa across from her, noting that the front-porch lights were on and big, fat snowflakes were coming down.

"Betty, what brings you out on a night like this? Can I get you some coffee or something to warm you up?"

"No, thank you," she said, staring up at the wall behind Ann. "That's a beautiful quilt." Sixteen angels in various shades of red were appliquéd on light blue plaid blocks. Betty's eyes shifted to the red, white, and navy Log Cabin quilt that hung over the other sofa.

"Log Cabin is my favorite pattern. I made me one just like it. I mean, not just like that one," she stammered, "not them same colors, but that same pattern."

"Thank you. These were my quilting projects for the last two years," Ann said, watching surprise cross Betty's face. People who only knew her from work never dreamed she quilted.

"I can't believe all your carnival glass. I have some of my mother's." Betty's eyes darted between the two corner cupboards. She continued to cling to her purse like it was a lifeline and she was drowning.

"My grandmother gave me my first piece and I've loved it ever since," Ann said, studying Betty's weary face, trying to figure out why she had come.

Betty leaned forward and stared down at the carpet. "Mrs. Ranson, I got to talk to you about my husband. Lonnie didn't mean no harm. I like working at the hospital and I don't mind the night shift 'cause I get more money."

"I'm glad you like your job."

"I told Lonnie you made me go to nights so he wouldn't make me go off 'em." She glanced up at Ann and rushed on. "I don't know why he said I don't like you. That ain't true. I never said it. I don't understand what you're doin' at the hospital, but none of us want it to close 'cause then we wouldn't have no jobs or insurance." She continued to study the carpet. "Lonnie was drunk today and he shouldn't have been hunting on your property. I'm begging you not to press charges against him." She looked up at Ann with tears in the corners of her eyes.

"There must be some mistake, we haven't pressed charges," Ann said, although she vaguely remembered someone telling her the Chevskys had been taken to jail. "Just a minute, the sheriff's here. I'll ask him what's going on." Ann got up.

Betty jumped up and reached out her hand to stop Ann. "Oh, no, Mrs. Ranson. I'd better be going if the sheriff's here. I don't want no trouble, I just come to ask for your help." She scurried over to the door and picked up one of her boots.

Ann put her hand on Betty's arm. "You're not going to have any trouble. This is obviously very important if you drove all the way out here. Let me get Sheriff Swenson so we can figure it out." Reluctantly, Betty went back in the living room and sat down. Ann went around the corner to get the sheriff.

"That's Lonnie Chevsky's wife. She's begging me not to press charges and I told her we haven't," Ann said, looking from John to Lark for clarification.

John squirmed around on the sofa. "I asked Lark to press charges after Lonnie made those threats against you. I'm worried about you being out here alone during hunting season with him loose."

Paul chimed in. "Betty's probably scared to death because Lonnie's beaten her up a couple of times. He's got one hell of a temper." He glanced over at Ann, gauging her reaction. "I think John's right. He needs to stay in jail and sober up."

"Do you have any reason to hold him if we don't press charges?" Ann asked Lark.

"Hunting on posted land and drunk and disorderly," Lark said, looking concerned. "Cutting him loose isn't going to help his wife. In fact, it may be the worst thing you can do for her. He's been drinking for days. He needs to dry out and jail may be his only chance."

"Betty has good insurance. Maybe we can get him admitted for treatment."

"Not a chance. This guy doesn't want to quit," Paul said.

"I don't want to be the reason Betty's husband is in jail," Ann said. "She's one of our best workers and doesn't deserve this. Besides, the guy didn't hurt me, he just insulted me. I don't want to press charges."

Lark stood up, scowling and shaking his head. He wagged his finger at John and Ann. "You're making a big mistake, one that Betty may pay for." Ann felt frustration emanating from him as he followed her into the living room.

Betty stood up, clutching her purse like a shield, when Lark and Ann came into the living room. She listened patiently while Ann introduced Lark and explained how they could get Lonnie admitted for detox.

"Detox is a good idea if Lonnie wants it," she said. "Otherwise it ain't gonna do him no good. If he don't agree, we'll just have to wait till he's ready." It was a pity, Ann thought, that Betty wasn't able to use that common sense to extricate herself from this mess before it was too late.

Betty listened politely but shrugged off Ann's concerns about her well-being and hurried to the foyer to put on her boots and coat. She thanked Ann profusely for not putting Lonnie in jail. As she went out the door, she asked if she could bring in some carnival glass for Ann to identify as soon as she came back from vacation.

Lark went to the kitchen to call and release Lonnie to his wife. Ann stood in front of the living room window to make sure Betty got safely out of the driveway. Snow swirled around the departing taillights of Betty's old, beat-up truck. Her brake lights flashed on and off like a Morse code message. Ann prayed silently that she wasn't seeing an early warning SOS and that she hadn't just made a huge mistake.

"Man oh man, Mrs. Ranson was really upset," Paul said as he and Lark trudged through the falling snow to Lark's Jeep. "I hate it when women cry. What do you think all that was about?"

Lark smiled at Paul's naïveté. "She wonders if they could have prevented the second death by checking out that snowmobile in the marsh on Saturday night. She told us she cries easily when she's stressed. I can understand that, my wife would have been balling her eyes out over something like this."

"Do you think either of them had anything to do with this?" Paul asked as they arrived at the Jeep. He brushed snow off the roof and windows with the arm of his coat.

"I don't think so, but we have to check them out anyway," Lark said, sliding into the car to start the engine and turn on the defrosters. "Before we head back to Big Oak, I want to stop and see how they're doing in the marsh." He grabbed an ice scraper and slipped back out of the car to clear the windshield.

"Do you normally get this much snow during hunting season?" Lark asked as they got in the Jeep to wait for it to warm up.

"We usually have snow but this is more than usual," Paul replied. "This winter is going to be a bitch. We'll have a bumper crop of snowmobile accidents, car wrecks, and drunk driving arrests."

Lark put the Jeep in gear and headed down the driveway. They found the state police vehicles about five hundred feet up the drive. He parked behind two Explorers, one from Mason County and one from the state police parked near a state-owned van. Both state vehicles had empty snowmobile trailers hitched to them. One snowmobile sat by the side of the road. Lark was deciding whether to take it out to the marsh when another snowmobile came roaring out of the woods. It plowed to a stop beside him.

Joel Grenfurth slipped off his helmet and yelled, "Damn, it's colder than a witch's tit in a brass bra." He climbed off the snowmobile, walked over to Lark, and kicked the tires of one of the Explorers. Dirty brown clumps of snow fell from his boots and the wheel well of the truck. Once his boots were clean he began brushing snow off his clothes and hat.

"For Christ's sake, Joel, you remind me of a dog shaking himself after he gets out of the water." Lark chuckled, stepping away to avoid his fallout.

"Hey, boss," Paul yelled, walking over to the still warm snowmobile. "OK if I go see if they need help?"

"Yeah, sure, I'll radio you when I'm ready to leave."

Joel waved his arm back in the general direction of the Ransons' house. "While you were up in the big house all cozy and warm, us peons were out here freezing our asses off."

"You're right, Grenfurth," Lark said, slapping Joel on the back and watching the snow fly like he'd beaten an old dusty rug. "I've got it made. Be sure and remind me to thank you for telling me about this job. It's days like today when I know, beyond a shadow of a doubt, that with friends like you I don't need enemies."

"Screw you, too, Swenson." Joel flicked his thumb back at the house. "They have anything to do with this?"

"I don't think so," Lark said, crossing his arms and leaning back against the Explorer. "So far their only connection is that they own the property and she found the boot."

"Both bodies are ready to come out," Joel said, rubbing his gloved hands up and down his coat sleeves. "We've done the scene photographs and a preliminary assessment of the areas around the bodies. I don't think we're going to be able to stay out here much longer. My guys are freezing."

Lark opened the rear car door and grabbed his thermos.

"Once we get the bodies out I say we call off the scene work for tonight. A snowball's got a better chance in hell than we have of getting this area searched in this snowstorm in the dark. Since you don't think there's anyone in danger, we should get a good night's sleep and come out first thing tomorrow." Joel stopped to take a sip of steaming coffee from Lark's thermos cup. "Sweet mother of God, this coffee is strong enough to strip the enamel off my teeth."

Lark raised his eyebrows. "Beggars can't be choosers."

"Did I complain? Shit, it's hot and it's available, what more could any man ask for?"

"Jesus, Grenfurth, that's terrible," Lark said, getting in the Jeep. "Get in here and warm up while I arrange guards for the night. What can you tell me about the bodies?"

"The most recent body is wearing gray University of Wisconsin–Madison sweatpants and a red UW–Madison sweatshirt. I'm sure you know how well that will narrow it down, since there are forty thousand students on the Madison campus alone and they sell that shit all over. The body looks like it's been out here a few days, but it'll be hard to be exact because of the cold. The coat has a Lands' End label in it and the boots are from L. L. Bean." Joel paused to sip his coffee.

"Any information about the skeleton?"

"I think it was a woman from the looks of the clothes and the boots, but I could be wrong. She had on gray UW–Madison sweatpants. The word Madison was printed in a different style than the sweats on the other body, in big capital letters down the pants leg. We found a dark blue UW-Madison sweatshirt and a dark green Eddie Bauer jacket. We've only found one of her hands. The mate to the boot you brought me was near the skeleton. It has a Lands' End logo."

"Did you find any ID?"

"Nope," Joel said, shaking his head. "But you never know. They both had on those yuppie coats with more pockets than a pro pickpocket could keep straight."

They looked up to see three snowmobiles, two pulling litters, coming towards them. "Thank God. Take me someplace with a bar, a bed, and cable TV and I can die a happy man. A shower would be nice, but it isn't required," Joel said.

After the bodies, evidence, and snowmobiles were loaded and headed south to Wausau, Jim and Paul stayed behind to take the first leg of guard duty. Joel and his partner, Lacey Smith, followed Lark through Big Oak and back out into the country. Fifteen minutes later, they pulled into the garage of a large, two-story log cabin surrounded by woods.

"Damn," Joel said as he got out of the Explorer. A tall dusk-to-dawn light had illuminated the cabin and the lake beyond it as they drove up. "Mason County must have some budget if you can afford these accommodations for your out-of-town help. I may be sorry I didn't take this job."

"I hate to burst your bubble but this is my home," Lark said, helping them with their gear. "There aren't any decent rentals available because of hunting season. Your choices were to stay in a dive, camp at the station, or bunk with me. I don't have cable TV but there is a satellite dish. I've got the alcohol basics and you'll each have your own bed and bathroom. Of course," Lark said, stopping halfway to the cabin, "if you'd rather sleep at the station I can run you back into town. Last time I checked we only had one person in a cell but it's several hours before last call. The place should be hopping about three A.M."

"Swenson, you're such an asshole," Joel said.

Lark unlocked the door from the garage and they stepped into a utility room. They stowed their coats and boots in the closet and Lark showed them to their rooms upstairs. They agreed to meet downstairs when they were unpacked.

Lark changed into fresh jeans and a sweater before going back downstairs. Even in this secluded area, he maintained his nightly house check routine left over from Chicago. He checked the living room and went across the hall to check the bathroom. A right jog off the entrance foyer took him to the hallway that led to his study, the utility room, and the garage. He walked through the hallway that led to the kitchen. The kitchen, dining area, and family room were one big, open, two-story space. The wall facing Logan Lake was mostly glass, and despite the dark, moonless night, it was pulling in a good bit of light from the floodlights on the back of the house.

He lit the fire he'd built in the family room fireplace before he'd left for work. He was standing in the middle of what passed for his dining room when he heard a door shut overhead. Lacey Smith, Joel's partner, leaned over the upstairs balcony and smiled down at him. She'd changed into jeans and a long, white, loose-fitting sweater. She was about five foot eight with a great figure and masses of long, dark auburn hair that she'd pulled back in a ponytail. She had the fair complexion of most redheads with a dusting of tiny freckles across her nose and sparkling green eyes. She looked very different from the person he'd been briefly introduced to at the scene. Of course, that woman had been wearing a hooded ski parka and a scarf around her face.

"You have a beautiful home," she said, and he realized he'd been staring at her. "Thanks for letting us stay here."

"You're welcome," Lark said, heading into the kitchen. "Did you already have dinner? I ate lunch about three but I'm starving."

"We had fast food for lunch on our way out of Wausau. Could we order a pizza?" Lacey asked as she came downstairs and wandered into the kitchen.

"Not likely," Lark said, amused at the thought of someone plowing through all the snow to deliver. "No one delivers way out here."

"Yeah, life's a bitch living out here in paradise," Joel said as he trotted downstairs and joined them at the dining table.

Joel looked much the same as he had for the past twenty years. He was balding with unruly, dark curly hair on the sides of his head. His dark brown eyes danced with merriment behind brown-framed glasses. At five foot ten, he had always been stocky. He now had a slight paunch hanging over his belt.

"I'm starving," Joel said as he sat down. "That damn Mexican take-out we ate for lunch was just like eating Chinese food. It only sticks to your ribs for a couple of hours."

"Joel, you're always starving," Lacey said.

Before Lark could respond, Joel pointed up at the balcony that served as the second floor hallway connecting the bedrooms. "You got yourself a great little love nest. If Molly and I bring the kids up, you'll have to do something about that balcony. Otherwise, the boys will do a circus highwire act off the second floor railing."

Lark burst out laughing, "That'll be the day, when you and Molly come up for a visit and bring the kids. If that ever happens I'll see what I can do. You and Molly could come up and use this 'love nest' to get away from the kids. Maybe make another one while you're at it." Lark patted Joel's shoulder as he headed into the kitchen.

Joel groaned and buried his head in his hands. "Don't wish that on us. With four boys under six, Molly says she'll need Prozac and a psychotherapist if she gets pregnant again." He looked up as he heard Lark open the freezer. "Ah, frozen pizza, the culinary basic of single men and poor people like Molly and me. Of course, Lacey, you could always rustle us up something."

"Yeah, right, Grenfurth," she said, following Lark into the kitchen. She pulled three beers out of the refrigerator as Lark put the pizza in the oven.

They drank beer and talked about crime in Wausau and the northwoods while they waited for the pizza to cook. After they ate, Lacey and Lark cleaned up the kitchen while Joel followed up with the crime lab staff and made a brief call to his wife. Joel got off the phone with a bit of good news. The lab had managed to work with Lands' End to identify the boot. Lands' End had agreed to have their purchase records together by morning. A request had also been made to University of Wisconsin–Madison police for information about missing students. They went to bed thinking they might just get a break in the case.

Wednesday dawned cold and snowy. Lark was up and ready to leave for the station when Lacey came downstairs. Her hair was pulled back in a ponytail, looking like it might escape any minute. She had on heavy white crew socks and a long dark green velour robe that accentuated her green eyes.

He watched her make herself at home, opening and closing cabinets until she found the cups. She grabbed a mug and filled it with coffee. Smiling, she leaned back against the counter, closed her eyes, and lifted the mug to her nose to inhale the aroma of the steaming coffee.

"I just can't get going without my coffee," she said as she took a sip and wandered into the dining room. She sat down at the table and pulled her right leg up underneath her. Lark noticed that she was wearing long, green, silky pajama pants.

"I slept like a log. It's so quiet and peaceful out here." She sipped her coffee and stared out at the falling snow.

Tongue-tied, he couldn't think of anything to say. She asked who would deal with Lands' End. He told her he wanted to handle that himself, and asked if she and Joel would take two Mason County officers and finish the search of the Ranson property. She agreed, saying she much preferred to work outside. She refilled her coffee mug and headed upstairs.

Lacey occupied Lark's thoughts as he drove into Big Oak. He found her very attractive and likable but she was probably no more than twenty-five. Much too young, he decided, putting her out of his mind. He barely noticed how dreary and snowy it was.

When he arrived, Flo asked if he could spare a minute. He grabbed a cup of coffee and pulled up a chair as she took a call. After dispatching for thirty-five years, she had forgotten more about Mason County than most people ever knew.

He studied her while she worked the call. Gold wire-rimmed glasses framed her brown eyes unless they had slid down her nose or been shoved on top of her head. A felt turkey decoration was pinned to her right shoulder and she had tiny ceramic turkey studs in her ears.

His reverie was broken when she radioed Jim Kryjack to check out an abandoned car. She then turned her full attention to Lark. Although there were only eleven years' difference in their ages, he somehow felt his mother was about to rip him a new one.

"You shoulda talked to me before you let Lonnie go last night," Flo said, jamming her glasses back up her nose. "He's just gonna beat the crap out of Betty and drink up her paycheck like he's been doin for weeks." Shaking her finger at him, she ranted on. "You had the perfect opportunity to keep him in jail and get him sobered up. You coulda had Mrs. Ranson press charges and saved Betty a ton of grief."

"Betty showed up at the Ransons and begged Ann not to press charges. Without the Ransons, we didn't have anything on him that would stand up in court." He paused to take a breath and held up his hand to keep Flo quiet. "Mrs. Ranson tried to get Betty to sign Lonnie in for detox, but she would only do it if Lonnie would go in voluntarily and he refused."

"It's a damn shame that asshole didn't get so drunk that he shot himself and put everyone out of their misery. He's such a snake that shooting him would be considered justifiable homicide by everyone but Betty." She glanced at Lark. "I'll bet you'd be real surprised at how fast the number of summer cabin robberies would drop if he wasn't around. He's also quite the poacher."

"Can you prove any of this?"

"Do you think he'd still be here if I could?" she grumbled. "I hear things. You fit them together and they point to Lonnie. How can he stay drunk and not work but still have a roof over his head? Betty takes all the overtime she can get but her paycheck only stretches so far. There's other money comin' into that house and Lonnie's not doin' any legit work for it."

"Thanks for the heads up, I'll keep my eyes peeled," Lark said as he got up.

"Hold it," she said, pointing her finger at him as she got another call. He sat back down and watched her take a message.

"I hear those two bodies from out at Wazowski's had on UW–Madison clothes."

"You heard right," he said, not bothering to ask how she got the information. Somehow she always knew everything.

"My Frank's on a long haul and won't be home 'til tomorrow afternoon, so I was free last night. I went over to the library and looked through the high school yearbooks. I made a list of the kids from here who went down to UW–Madison. I added the summer kids I know about." She held out three handwritten pages stapled together. "Both Jim and Paul are on the list."

Lark thanked her, took the list, and got up to leave. Before he could get away, she handed him the message slip she'd just written. "I told him you'd call him before eight."

The message was from Joel. Lark noted that it was seven-thirty and called him back. Joel answered on the second ring. "You becoming a donut-shop cop? Based on when the lovely Lacey told me you left here, you shoulda been there when I called."

"I was waylaid, but not by the donut shop," Lark grumbled, leaning back in his chair and stretching out his legs. "Our dispatcher did some detective work last night." He told Joel about the list she'd given him.

"Well, from what you've told me, the FBI probably doesn't have more accurate information." Joel chuckled. "Between her names and the list from Lands' End we'll be drowning in data. I'll see if we can spring someone in Wausau to help with the phone calls. Speaking of Wausau," Joel added, all business, "looks like our body was only out there two or three days."

"That jives with the snowmobile the Ransons heard."

"What's even more interesting is that both bodies have the same injury patterns. Depressed skull fractures of the right frontal and right parietal areas. For the medical terminology challenged, that's the right front and side of the head. They both have right humerus fractures, that's the upper arm, and right femur fractures, the big bone in the upper leg. The skeleton of Red Boot has a couple of old right radius and ulnar fractures, that's lower arm, that may help us with identification."

"Do they think the fractures were the cause of death?" Lark heard Joel shuffling papers.

"Jesus, I can hardly read the notes I just took," Joel grumbled. "The long bone fractures didn't do any healing at all and the skull fracture was very depressed. The lab concluded that Red Boot died right after they happened. The skull fracture is probably as close to the cause of death as we're going to get.

"The injuries on Yellow Mitten were all blunt. No penetrating wounds. She was hit with something very hard: crowbar, ball bat, a heavy piece of wood. According to the bruising around the wounds and the state of the fractures, she probably died a couple hours after she was hit. Looks like she was moved. She was on her back for a while and then dumped on her stomach. They can't say for sure how Red Boot was injured because there isn't any soft tissue to examine, but the fracture patterns look very much the same."

"Both have right-sided fractures and the head injuries are frontal and right side?"

"You got it, Kemosabe, probably a lefty."

Lark was trying to remember if either of the Ransons were left-handed. He wondered about Lonnie and closed his eyes, trying to remember how he handled his rifle.

"Are Yellow Mitten's fingerprints out yet?" Lark asked.

"Nationwide, but don't be surprised if that turns up a big fat nothing. How many college girls do you know who've been fingerprinted? I'll have the office fax you a summary of this as soon as it's transcribed. Gotta go, the lovely Lacey is done with her shower and raring to go," Joel said, laughing.

"Just behave yourself, Grenfurth, and remember your wife is a great friend of mine," Lark said with mock concern. As far as he knew, Joel hadn't seriously looked at another woman since he'd gotten married, but you'd never know it to hear him talk.

"The lovely Lacey would never look twice at me. She goes for the Gorgeous Georges of the world. You should see the Mr. Body Beautiful she just dumped. My nontraditional physical appearance and inner beauty are lost on her."

Lark hung up the phone and shook his head to get his mind back on business. He sorted through the papers on his desk for the Lands' End number. It was almost eight, and he wanted to get as much as possible done before things shut down for Thanksgiving. He unearthed the number and yelled at Flo to send Paul and Jim out to the Ransons'. After a pit stop at the coffeepot, he was on the phone to Lands' End.

He was put through to Janey Dawes, the director of merchandising. She told him the Madison television channels were carrying a brief news story about two bodies discovered in northern Wisconsin. Lark told her he couldn't comment. Janey confirmed that almost all of the five thousand size-seven red boots had been sold through the catalog four years ago. The remaining one hundred and two pairs had been sent to their outlet in Madison.

She was willing to fax him the list of catalog customers who had purchased the boot as long as none of the data was publicly released. Lark agreed. They ended their conversation with him reaffirming that he wanted the names faxed even though the list was one hundred and forty pages long.

Before he hung up, he asked if the state police had called about a red Lands' End coat. Janey said they hadn't. She told him she needed the request by noon to get him the data before Lands' End closed for the holiday.

Lark checked his watch, noting that it was eight-thirty, and called his house. He caught Joel just before they walked out the door. He agreed to light a fire under Wausau to get the information requests out to L. L. Bean, Eddie Bauer, and Lands' End.

Lark got off the phone and warned Flo that the fax from hell was coming. She rolled her eyes and told him he was just a little late, that it had already started. She also told him that if this was going to go on all day, someone had better run to the office supply store because they only had one ream of paper left. Swearing, he left to make the half-hour run to Park Falls.

When he got on the road, he realized he'd forgotten to tell Joel that the media had wind of the case. He leaned forward to look up through the windshield at the continuous cloud cover and the steadily falling snow and decided that no one in their right mind would come to Big Oak in this weather for a story. But Lark had never known any press people in their right minds.

He called Flo on his cellular to tell her he needed two additional officers to secure the Ransons' property. She got a good laugh out of that, saying all their officers for the day would be working this one case. She quit laughing when he told her that the Madison television stations were already broadcasting the story.

It was a good thing they were on the cellular or her "Oh, shit" would have gone out on the police band. Then some idiot with nothing better to do would bring up swearing on the radio at the next public works meeting. Flo assured him she'd get someone out there ASAP.

Lark decided he'd better stop at the Ransons'. It was only five minutes out of his way. There were three news vans with satellite dishes parked on the berm of Big Oak Road, and two more vans in the driveway. He met John Ranson's truck a hundred yards down the drive. John backed up to let him through just as Lark's cellular rang.

"Sheriff." Flo sounded very concerned. "I've got Mrs. Ranson on the phone."

"Tell her I'm out in her driveway with her husband. Get on the horn and see if anybody wants overtime. See if the other counties or Park Falls can give us some help. We're going to need two more people out here." He shut off the phone before she could respond with another expletive.

John climbed into Lark's Jeep, scanning the area like he was looking for terrorists. "I've got more officers coming," Lark said. "I'm really sorry about this."

"Don't worry about it," John said. "I grew up in a small town and my father was a deputy sheriff for years. If it gets too crazy, I'll pull some of my guys off the job and bring them over."

"Hopefully, that won't be necessary," Lark said as they pulled up in front of the house. Ann met them at the door.

"I told the reporters they were trespassing. I took down their license numbers and told them I'd have them arrested if they didn't get off our property. They left pretty quickly but I don't think they're clear on where the property lines are."

"We'll move them off," Lark said. He gave Ann his business card after writing on the back. "If they give you any more trouble, call the dispatcher or me at the number on the back of the card."

Lark and John drove up to the two press vans still parked in the Ransons' upper drive. John made it clear he'd bring charges against anyone trespassing on his land.

Once they realized there was nothing to see from Big Oak Road, the press left. Lark had his doubts that they'd find any motel rooms nearby and hoped that thoughts of a family Thanksgiving would draw them back to their homes. Nevertheless, he assigned an officer at each end of the Ransons' property and added two extra people to the search. It was almost ten before he got back on the road.

On the drive back from Park Falls, he called the University of Wisconsin–Madison campus police to see if they had the information on missing students ready to send. He caught the captain just before he went out of state for Thanksgiving. He informed Lark that there were four females and one male unaccounted for in the past four years. He agreed to fax information on each case to Lark. He had already faxed copies of their medical histories to Wausau. The chief gave him a cell phone number where he could be reached if anything looked promising. Lark thought back to the days before fax machines and cellular phones and wondered how anyone got anything done.

When he returned to the office, the fax machine was humming like it was about to take flight. He had calls from all of the area newspapers and most of the television stations in Wisconsin and Minnesota. He mentally began composing a press release.

He also had a message to call Janey Dawes. He picked up the Lands' End fax and leafed through it as he waited for the last two pages of the University police fax to come through. Finally, a place to start.

He got hold of Janey about eleven-fifteen. "I hope your day is better than mine," he said when she answered.

"It probably is. We're winding down for the holiday. I've got your coat information. That anorak is a standard in our line and it's been made for several years. The product number they gave us narrows it down to three production years, 1996 through 1998, and twenty thousand size-twelve coats. Eighteen-thousand-three-hundred-twelve of them were sold through the catalog and the rest sent to the outlets. That will be another five hundred and twenty fax pages once I get them off my printer."

Lark groaned.

"You sound like my printer. It's groaning, too."

"Five hundred pages?" Lark said, stunned. "I'm tempted to send someone down to Dodgeville rather than put my dispatcher through that. She's liable to take out a contract on me."

"I've got a better idea—that is, if it's not out of line."

"Let's hear it, I'll consider just about anything at this point."

"My husband and I are coming up to Rhinelander for Thanksgiving with his parents. We're leaving after work tonight and should get up there by ten. I'd be happy to bring the list with me if you could send someone over to get it. We're always up till at least midnight."

"Janey, you're a lifesaver," Lark said, wandering over to the map on his office wall to see how long it would take him to get there. "How about if I stop by around eleven tonight? That'll give you a little extra time in case the weather gets worse." He looked out his window and noticed that the snow had stopped, but the sky was still covered with a blanket of low-hanging, dark gray clouds. He got directions and gave her his cell phone number just in case their plans changed.

After John and the sheriff left, Ann went to the family room to get the antiques ready to deliver to the Martens. They had vacationed in the area for years, and when their last child went off to college two years ago, they sold their home in Milwaukee and built a house on Big Oak Lake. Abraham Lincoln Marten, otherwise known as Linc, and his wife Melissa were the only black family in the area. Linc, a family practice physician, worked at the clinic in Big Oak. Melissa worked part-time as a substitute schoolteacher.

Ann had found Linc two cobalt blue medicine bottles for his collection. Melissa collected cookbooks and Ann had found her two color-illustrated, advertising cookbooks from the early 1900s that she didn't have.

Ann had also found her a box full of old Valentines and holiday postcards. Melissa made decorative boxes in her spare time. She covered them with copies of old Valentines, postcards, and pictures from her collection of old magazines. They were selling like hotcakes in gift shops in the northwoods.

Ann dug out Steve Waltner's Flow Blue bowl and got the invoice ready, then packed up the two deliveries and drove to the Martens. Normally, their house was less than ten minutes away, but snow was pelting down and it took her more than fifteen minutes to get there. Their driveway was a white tunnel with hills of snow on either side. Two snowmobiles sat on a trailer in the parking area. The house, a modern cedar and stone two-story with a wraparound deck, was built near the shore of the lake on a ten-acre parcel of land. The back exterior wall jutted out like the prow of a ship. Ann could look across the lake at night and see the entire two-and-a-half story back of their house lit up.

Melissa met Ann at the door in jeans and a smudged sweatshirt. She had wrapped a towel around her paste-splattered hands to open the door. After shedding her winter gear, Ann followed her down to her workroom in the basement. Ann took one look at the Christmas boxes spread out all over the counters and began to salivate.

"I swear, I don't know why I come over here. It always costs me money. I'm going to have to have one of those," Ann said, pointing to a small heart-shaped box covered with Santas.

"I'll make you a hell of a deal," Melissa joked, working the picture of a fat, rosy-cheeked Santa over the curve of a box lid. When the picture was in place, she smiled at Ann. "The Artist's Gallery in Wausau is screaming at me to get these done." She began to apply another Santa to the lid. "Three of the kids decided at the last minute to bring friends up for the weekend. Jack and Bill and their friends will get in tonight; Shelley is driving up from Madison tomorrow with two of her girlfriends." She stood up, stretched, and walked over to the sink to wash her hands. Deciding it was time for a break, Melissa made hot chocolate. While they drank it, she oohed and ahhed over her new cookbooks and Linc's cobalt bottles.

Ann left about three o'clock and drove to Big Oak to drop Steve Waltner's bowl off at the marina. The office was open but both Steve and his assistant were gone. The guy manning the gas pumps declined to take the package, saying he was afraid it would get broken. He told Ann he would have Steve call her. Once again, Ann wondered if the rumors she'd heard about Steve and his assistant were really true.

Lark spent most of the afternoon cross-referencing lists. He compared the five names from the campus police against the list of boot purchasers faxed from Lands' End. No match. He compared the campus police list against the list of UW–Madison students from the area that Flo had provided. No match. No one from the Mason County list had purchased the red Lands' End boots.

He was interrupted several times. L. L. Bean had manufactured 7,500 pairs of the size-six black boot Yellow Mitten was wearing. Most of them were sold through their catalog. Eddie Bauer had made 15,000 of Yellow Mitten's medium-size coat, most of them also sold as catalog purchases. Eddie Bauer agreed to Express Mail the customer lists to him.

About three-thirty, Wausau called to tell Lark they might have a match between Red Boot and a medical record from the University police. Gemma Patterson, a student missing since 1997, had fractured her right radius and ulnar when she was fifteen. They were waiting for her X-rays and dental records to make a final determination. Lark culled through his other two lists but didn't find any link to her.

He realized he hadn't had any lunch and was headed to the Big Oak Diner when Joel and Lacey walked into his office about four-thirty. He forgot about being hungry and poured what must have been his tenth cup of coffee for the day. Joel was updating him on their search when Flo called Joel to the phone.

Joel didn't seem to be in his usual jovial mood when he got off the phone. "I'm going back to Wausau tonight. My oldest has chicken pox and Molly's mother is on her way up from Indiana for Thanksgiving. I'll stay home tomorrow, and if you need me I'll drive back on Friday. Lacey, can you stay and give Lark a hand with this?"

"Sure thing. Hope Robbie's OK," she said, glancing over at Lark. "Can your dispatcher find me a place to stay?"

"She'll try, but it may be a lost cause," Lark said, smiling at her. "You're more than welcome to stay at my place. I've got room, and I can assure you I'm harmless."

"Harmless, my ass," Joel said, smirking at Lark. "I remember when you were single."

"That was a long time ago," Lark said, turning away to replenish his coffee.

Joel took the hint and changed the subject. "As far as we can tell, the rest of the Ransons' marsh looks clean. We didn't go over every square inch, but I think we would have found another body unless it's been buried. If that's the case, we won't find it until spring, if ever."

"We didn't find the missing hand from Jane Doe Two, but there's a lot of wildlife in those woods. If it's been out there a couple of years, it could be anywhere," Lacey said. "We should search the woods on each side of the marsh tomorrow and call it good unless we find something."

Lark filled them in on his day, including the possible identification of Red Boot. He promised he'd call Joel at home as soon as he knew something and told him to watch the ten o'clock news. Joel left Big Oak a little after five.

Lark went over his progress on the list comparisons with Lacey and updated her on his trip to Rhinelander, planned for later that night. Flo wasn't able to find a motel room and they decided that Lacey would stay with him. He was just starting to write a press release on the two bodies when Jim and Paul staggered in. Between helping with the search and dealing with routine calls, they were exhausted.

Jim came into Lark's office to give an update on the abandoned car he'd investigated earlier that morning. "It's a 1998 gray Taurus registered to Lippert Motors from Wausau. Someone ditched it in the parking lot at Grezetski's Market." He flipped through his notebook. "I called Lippert's and, would you believe, they didn't have any idea they had a car missing."

"You're kidding," Lark said, leaning across his desk. "Was it hotwired?"

"Nope. We found the ignition and trunk keys under the front passenger seat. They were on one of those generic key chains with nothing else on it. There were lots of fingerprints on the car, but all the areas of high use. The door handles, steering wheel, instrument panel, and radio controls were smudged out, probably from someone wearing gloves. The woman who reported the car said it had been parked in the lot since Sunday morning. No one had any idea how it got there." Jim flipped his notebook shut and frowned at Lark. "I had the car towed to Tetzloff's garage until we decide what to do with it."

"Good work," Lark said, patting him on the back as they walked out of the office. "I'll drop by and take a look at it in the morning."

Jim and Paul clocked out, making plans to meet at the Pine View for dinner on Jim's family. Lark wished he was as carefree as they appeared to be. Flo clocked out and waved good-bye with a flash of her turkey decals. The decals reminded him that tomorrow was Thanksgiving and he had nothing to feed his houseguest; one more item on his endless to-do list.

By six-thirty the press release was ready for Mary Lou, the night dispatcher, to fax out. Lark gave her instructions on how to respond to any calls about the case. His stomach growled as he updated her on his trip to Rhinelander. He went in search of Lacey and found her asleep in the workroom. As he was debating whether to wake her up, she opened her eyes and yawned.

"Why don't we get the hell out of here and grab something to eat?"

Yawning again, Lacey dragged herself up out of the chair. "All that work outside seems to have worn me out."

Lark watched her shrug into her coat. The dark circles under her eyes stood out against her pale face. "On second thought, why don't we go home and I'll fix us something to eat. Then you can go to bed and I'll run over to Rhinelander."

"I've got a better idea," Lacey said, heading for the door. "Why don't

I take a quick nap while you eat something light to take the edge off your hunger. Then I'll ride to Rhinelander with you and we can have dinner in a great restaurant I know there. That way neither of us will be alone tonight."

"Deal," Lark said, glancing at his watch. "This doesn't give you much time for a nap. We've got to be on the road by eight."

"I can sleep in the car. God knows, I've slept in worse places."

Lacey dozed on the drive to Lark's house and went directly upstairs, asking him to wake her up thirty minutes before they were supposed to leave.

Lark rummaged around in the refrigerator, finally settling on a glass of milk and the last of a bunch of grapes to snack on. He settled into his favorite chair in the family room and fast-forwarded through the tape of the Wausau Channel Nine news, stopping to view all coverage of the murders. There was nothing new or particularly harmful, although he winced as he saw the amount of photo coverage on the Ransons' property. He trotted upstairs to get the tape he'd set for Channel Twelve out of Rhinelander. It was pretty much the same. He made a mental note to watch the coverage of Channel Thirteen out of Eau Claire as soon as he got back to the office. He popped both tapes back in the VCRs and set them to record the ten o'clock news.

Lark took a shower and threw on gray pants and a light gray cashmere sweater Maria had given him. He spent the time before they had to leave reading a few pages of the latest Dick Francis.

Miraculously, Lacey was ready to go in under thirty minutes. She looked spectacular in a long, forest green knit skirt and sweater. She had washed her auburn hair and left it hanging long. It was drying in curls around her face. She came flying down the stairs carrying a tall pair of black boots with her huge black purse slung over her shoulder. Lark noticed that the nap, or a good makeup job, had returned the color to her face. She dropped her boots and purse in the foyer and gratefully accepted the coffee mug he handed her. She repeated her routine of inhaling and sipping and Lark was once again fascinated. He shook off his thoughts as they got into their winter gear.

The phone rang as they were walking out the door. "Shit. This had better be important," Lark said, trotting into the kitchen.

He picked up the phone and Joel's voice boomed across the wires. "Glad I caught you. Our guys positively identified Red Boot as Gemma Patterson. The University police are faxing a copy of their investigation notes to you. I just got my copy."

"Give me the condensed version. Lacey and I'll read the report on our way to Rhinelander."

"Ah, so you're taking the lovely Lacey with you. Kind of like a date. Is she staying at Casa Swenson?"

"Get your mind out of the gutter and back on the report, Grenfurth."

"Put him on speakerphone, that'll shut him up," Lacey said.

Just as Lark turned to see her leaning up against the snack bar, she hit the speaker button.

"You're on speaker, Joel. Give us a quick overview so we can get the hell out of here," Lacey said, all business.

"Yes, ma'am. Gemma Patterson's old fractures positively match the old fractures on Red Boot. Her dental records are also a match. She was last seen leaving the UW–Madison campus on Tuesday, November twenty-fifth, in 'ninety-seven. She left her mother a phone message saying she was on her way home and was going to stay over Tuesday, and maybe Wednesday night, at a friend's house. She never made it home to Wayzata, Minnesota." They could hear Joel flipping through his papers.

"The kid's message said she would call later but her parents never heard from her. They didn't have any idea who the friend was. People from Big Oak as well as Marshfield, Wausau, and Eau Claire knew her and were questioned. She was born September twenty-seventh, nineteen-seventy-eight, so she had just turned nineteen. She was a sophomore majoring in business and talking about going to law school. One of our officers worked on the case with the Minnesota State Police and the Feds."

"At least we know who she was and how she died. Now all we have to do is figure out who killed her," Lacey said. "We've got to get going or we'll never get to Rhinelander, let alone get dinner. Who knows about this ID? Have you told the Pattersons?"

"Not yet," Joel said, papers rustling in the background. "Lacey, the University police are willing to transfer this case to us since the state police were already involved. I think we should take it. Lark, we'll work together on this as well as Yellow Mitten. I'll be back up Friday unless something happens before then." He stopped talking and a child cried in the background.

"Sounds like my idea of a good time." Lacey giggled.

"Someday you'll get yours," Joel said, the energy draining out of his voice. "When you're both up to your asses in dirty diapers, I'll be there to say I told you so. Take a hint from me and don't have kids. God knows, I love the ones I have, but if I knew then what I know now, I'd have stayed away from parenthood. Chicken pox, four kids, in-laws, and Thanksgiving all at one time is not a pretty sight."

"My heart bleeds for you, Joel," Lacey said, laughing.

"We'll call you if we find out anything new," Lark interjected, putting on his coat. "Will this identification be out in time for the ten o'clock news or can we wait until tomorrow?"

"We won't announce the name until we notify the Pattersons, but we'll probably have to say that we've identified one of the bodies," Joel said, his voice picking up energy now that his child was no longer crying.

Joel wished them a happy Thanksgiving and signed off with a reminder for them not to do anything he wouldn't do. When Lark and Lacey finally left they were behind, but decided to stop at the station to pick up the fax. Lark stayed outside and kept the motor running while Lacey ran in to get it.

So far, the weather was cutting them a break. Although the sky was starless, it wasn't snowing. According to the radio, it was seventeen below zero and falling, with more snow expected during the night. Lark marveled at the resilience of the people living in the northwoods. They seemed to take the weather in stride; many even seemed to like it. While he waited for Lacey, he cracked the car window. The air was redolent with wood smoke and the cool, crisp smell of winter. He was startled out of his reverie when the car door opened and Lacey climbed in the Jeep.

"Your dispatcher says the fax machine has been used more today than it has in the entire two years since they got it," Lacey said, slamming the passenger door shut. "Modern police work comes to Mason County. How about if I read the report out loud while you drive?"

"Good idea." He pulled onto south Highway 13 and turned on the dome light.

"No need for that." Lacey motioned up at the light and began digging through her shoulder bag. "I've got a flashlight in here somewhere."

"Christ, you could have half the state of Rhode Island in there," Lark said, glancing back and forth between the road and her search.

First came a set of car keys followed by: a hair pick; billfold; coin purse; checkbook; three tubes of lipstick; a couple of small, frayed notebooks; a jar of Carmex; a pair of black leather gloves; a bottle of aspirin; two Hershey bars; a compact; a handful of pens; two bottles of nail polish; a nail file; a couple of small pouches; and another key ring with a beat-up rabbit's foot on the end.

"Finally," Lacey said, pulling out a small flashlight. "I thought I was going to have to pour everything out to find the damn thing."

"That purse isn't empty?" Lark asked, watching her scoot the pile back in her bag.

"Almost. I didn't bother to pull out the kitchen sink I keep in here for emergencies," she said, smirking at him. "I also didn't pull out the really personal things that might embarrass you." She zipped her purse closed and dropped it on the floor.

As they sped south towards Highway 70, Lacey read large sections of the report out loud. Gemma had lived her entire life in Wayzata until she went to college in Madison. Her parents owned a marina on Lake Wayzata. She had planned to major in business and come back and help run the marina with her older brother, also a University of Wisconsin grad. Her grades were excellent and she was never in trouble with the police in Wayzata or Madison.

Gemma appeared to have adjusted well to college and seemed to have lots of friends. She had done a little dating but had not been serious about anyone. She'd last been heard from when she'd called her parents from her dorm room. The police tracked down a gasoline credit card charge in Marshfield on Tuesday afternoon, the same day she'd left, and another one in Eau Claire around 2 A.M. on Wednesday morning. Her car was found in a shopping mall parking lot in Eau Claire on Sunday, November 30, 1997. No one knew how long it had been there. One witness remembered seeing it on Saturday night.

Fingerprints from the car weren't any help, which wasn't surprising since most people wore gloves for driving that time of year. No traces of blood were found, although human hairs and clothing fibers had been found in the trunk. The hairs matched those found on Gemma's clothes in her dorm room. All the evidence was stored at the state police lab in Madison.

"Wonder how her body ended up here and her car ended up in Eau

Claire?" Lacey mused, taking a break from reading the report while they navigated through Park Falls.

"Car trouble? Hitchhiker? Maybe she brought someone with her from Madison."

"I can't believe a girl that smart would pick up a hitchhiker. The car was running fine and had a full tank of gas when they found it in Eau Claire."

"It doesn't sound right to me either, but stranger things have happened. Look at the women Ted Bundy was able to fool."

Their conversation drifted to a general discussion of crime and serial killers in particular. As they turned east on Highway 70, a light snow began to fall. Lacey leaned forward and glared out the windshield. "Will this stuff ever let up? I like snow but this is just plain ridiculous." She slouched down in her seat and stared out the window.

"I've been told that we're in for the winter of our lives," Lark said, glancing over at her. "Before we start on the file again, tell me where we're going to eat. I'm starving and it'll help my stomach to know that there really is food in its future."

"Depends on what you want. I'm in the mood for Italian. What's your pleasure?"

"Italian's good."

"Well, then there's only one place. The Sportsman's Inn. It's on Highway 8 as you get into Rhinelander."

"What if I wanted a steak?"

"I'd suggest we go to the Sportsman's."

"What if I said seafood?"

"We'd go to the Sportsman's," they said in unison, laughing.

"It took me forever to get used to the lack of variety up here," Lark said.

"What about theaters? I used to love to go to the movies. When I see a movie in Wausau, everyone knows the details of my social life the next day. There isn't any privacy."

"Tell me about it," Lark said. "I made the mistake of going to a movie in Park Falls by myself one night. It was right after I moved and I still haven't heard the end of it. For a couple weeks afterwards, everyone kept trying to fix me up. I haven't done that again."

"I do believe it's a mortal sin to go to the movies alone up here. The same thing happened to me. You can imagine how a bunch of macho cops reacted. I could have retired for life if I was into sexual harassment lawsuits." Lacey snapped her flashlight back on. "We'd better get back to this report if we're going to get through it before we get to the Sportsman's." She sorted through the papers, finding where she had left off.

"The remainder of the report summarizes the interviews of people who knew Gemma. The state and university police interviewed over a hundred people. Her roommates were all interviewed. They had solid alibis. They did interview a few people from Big Oak. Do you want me to go over their statements?" Lacey asked, flipping through the pages.

"Who'd they interviewed from Big Oak?"

"Let's see." More pages rattled. "They interviewed David Banski from Chicago, who summered in the area. Is his name familiar?"

"Yep. He must be the son, or maybe grandson, of the people who own Banski's, a restaurant over on Pine Lake. Nice people, this isn't going to be pleasant."

Lacey turned more pages. "It looks like they interviewed two kids named Lowery, Katey and Matt."

"The Lowerys are a prominent family in Mason County."

"There are also two Waltner kids listed here. Does that name ring a bell?"

"Yep," Lark said as his grip on the steering wheel tightened. "This only gets worse. Their parents own the Waltner Marina and Waltner Hardware and Sporting Goods in Big Oak. Their father is on the village board and their mother is on everything else. Although they publicly act like they couldn't be happier, Steve is rumored to be having an affair with his assistant. I think Sara's on the make for anything in pants, but that's beside the point."

"Shelley Marten, looks like she was from Cedarburg but summered up here. Does she ring a bell?"

"There's a new physician in town named Linc Marten. They live across the lake from the Ransons. Now that I think about it, the Lowerys live right next door to the Ransons and the Banskis live just down the road."

"What about the Waltners?"

"I can't recall where they live, just where their businesses are."

"My faith in male law enforcement officers is renewed just knowing that you don't know the address of Mason County's Miss Hot to Trot."

"I'm happy if you're happy," Lark replied, his tone scathing.

"Back to the suspects list," Lacey said. "Here's one you won't like—Jim Kryjack. He's one of the nicest people I've met up here, I can't believe he'd ever hurt anyone. In fact, he's too nice to be a police officer."

"Shit," Lark said, slamming his gloved hand against the steering wheel. "He's been involved in this investigation from the beginning. He took evidence to Wausau, he's guarded the Ransons' property, and he searched the marsh. Why the hell didn't he tell me about this?"

"Calm down. I'll bet he never associated the bodies with Gemma. She's been missing for three years and her car was found in Eau Claire. From the looks of this report, that's where most of the investigation took place. No one, except the killer, would have linked Gemma to the skeleton we found here. There's no reason to. Big Oak isn't exactly on the way to Eau Claire from Madison."

"You're right. I just don't want anything to go wrong with this investigation. I'd kind of like to be here for a while, and if this is botched that may not happen."

"It looks like we've got one more name from up here," she said, concentrating on the fax. "Ron Chevsky."

"You're shitting me. How the hell would he know Gemma Patterson?"

"Well, let's see what we've got here." Lacey read the interview details. "They took business classes together and dated a few times. He told the officer that it was casual and her friends agreed. She spent a few weekends up here with Katey Lowery and Sandi Waltner, and she met Ron when she was out with them at one of the supper clubs."

"I just met Ron Chevsky. He was hunting illegally with his father on the Ransons' property. He and his father were both drunk and obnoxious. I have a strong suspicion he's an alcoholic, probably a mean one, too." Lark's voice was full of concern. "He doesn't look like the type of guy who would run in this crowd."

"Want me to go over any others in detail?" she asked, gathering the pages together.

"Only Jim's."

"Says here that he went out with Gemma twice, once up here and once in Madison. He denies anything more than just a friendly relationship. Says there wasn't anything physical between them. He claims the only other time they met outside of class was to carpool home on the weekends. He doesn't remember seeing her at all the weekend she went missing, although he was up here deer hunting and working for his parents."

"Sounds innocent enough. Let's take a break. We've got another forty-five minutes before we get to Rhinelander. If you're still tired, that would make for a nice nap. There are blankets and a pillow in the back if you want them."

"I don't need a blanket. In fact, I'm kind of hot. I'd love to just relax and listen to some music if that won't disrupt your thinking," Lacey said, squirming out of her coat.

Lark tuned the radio to the Ojibwa reservation station. "This is it up here at night, a mix of rock and country oldies. If that doesn't sound good, there are some tapes in the glove box," he said.

The old Grass Roots song, "Two Divided by Love," was just finishing and was followed by Crystal Gayle singing "Don't It Make My Brown Eyes Blue." Lacey pulled off her boots and tucked her legs up underneath her. She settled back into the seat and pulled her coat over her like a blanket, snugging it up around her shoulders. "This is great. I love riding in a car in the dark listening to oldies. I always feel like nothing in the world can get to me here."

Lark listened to the music while his mind wandered. He suspected that he needed some food in his stomach to get himself back on track. He thought about how women behaved in cars. Maria used to take her shoes and coat off and snuggle up like she was home on the sofa, just like Lacey was doing. He didn't know a single man who would do that. He shook his head to rid it of painful memories and concentrated on the snow pelting the windshield.

He thought about how many kids from prominent families were mixed up in this investigation. For the first time in his career he had to be concerned about politics, and he didn't like it one damn bit. He thought about all the years he'd looked down on his superiors who had worried about the fallout from investigations. He knew, as with so many things in life, he was finally getting his comeuppance for some of the snide remarks he'd made about them.

Jim's involvement raised a red flag. Even without obvious links between the Gemma Patterson case and the skeleton in the swamp, he felt he should have known that Jim had been questioned in a criminal case. He wondered if Sheriff Dodge had known anything about it.

One of Maria's favorite songs, "Ain't No Mountain High Enough" by Marvin Gaye and Tammi Terrell, came on the radio. Lark was flooded with wonderful memories. He reached over and patted Lacey's arm. "Hey, wake up, sleepyhead, your song's on."

Horrified, he realized his mistake as soon as he'd made it. Lacey opened her eyes and straightened up in the seat. "Jeez, I must have fallen asleep. Is everything OK?"

"Everything's fine," he said, looking straight ahead out the windshield.

Lacey reached out and touched his arm. "Are you all right? Do you want me to drive for a while?"

"Heavens no. I'm wide awake. Get a little more rest before we get to Rhinelander," he said, staring out into the darkness.

"What did you wake me up for?" Lacey asked as she fumbled back under her coat. "I heard you say something."

"Nothing important. I was just thinking out loud."

"You shook my arm."

"Jesus Christ, it was nothing. There was a deer at the side of the road and I didn't want you to get hurt if it ran out in front of us," Lark said, exasperated at having to lie.

"All right, all right. You don't need to get so irritated." She glanced over at him. "You startled me and I thought something was wrong. I guess the lack of sleep is making both of us irritable." She rooted around in the seat trying to get comfortable. "Let's both shut up so I can listen to the end of this song. It's one of my favorites."

Lacey was so intent on getting herself situated that she didn't see the look of surprise Lark shot her way. He was relieved to see her settle down for a nap. He passed the last thirty minutes of the trip deep in thought. He tried to focus on the case, but he was flooded with thoughts about the woman sitting next to him intermixed with flashbacks to his life with Maria.

Although he had dated a couple of women in Chicago after Maria died, he hadn't been serious about either of them and they'd felt the same way about him. They had provided companionship, someone to go to dinner and a movie with, and occasionally sleep with. He reminded himself that Lacey was way too young for him and scolded himself for thinking about sex and not focusing on the case. He breathed a sigh of relief when the sign for Highway 8 to Rhinelander came into view.

He leaned over and patted Lacey on the arm again. "Time to wake up. I need you to tell me how to get to the Sportsman's before I pass out from hunger."

She smiled sleepily and sat up, stretching her arms towards the windshield. "Just keep going east. Believe me, you can't miss it. Wow, I slept like a log." She stifled a yawn with the back of her hand. "Now I'm raring to go. I'll be happy to drive back so you can get some sleep." She bent down to pull on her boots.

Before he could answer, a huge, neon red fish splashing up out of neon blue water came into view.

Noticing Lark's shock, Lacey poked him in the arm. "I told you you couldn't miss it."

"Hell, a blind man couldn't miss this. It's a wonder the neighbors don't complain," Lark said, alternating between watching the road and glancing up at the enormous sign.

They pulled into the Sportsman's parking lot at nine-forty-five. Despite the late hour, it was jam-packed with cars from Illinois, Minnesota, and Wisconsin.

"I think they serve dinner until eleven but we should probably get seated immediately if we're going to pick up the Lands' End data on time," Lacey said, climbing out of the Jeep. Grill smoke permeated the air and the restaurant sign proclaimed charbroiled steaks in bright red neon just below the fish. It was quite a sight with the snow swirling around it.

"I can just about guarantee that this will be one of the best meals I've ever eaten," Lark said, taking her elbow and steering her towards the entrance.

"The food's good, but I don't know if I'd go that far," Lacey said, trying not to slip on the snow-covered blacktop.

"Shoe leather would be a gourmet treat right now, I'm so hungry."

The entrance of the Sportsman's split off in two directions. To the right was the typical northwoods dark-paneled, smoke-filled bar, swarming with people who weren't feeling any pain. The walls were covered with mounted trophy Muskie and Pike mingled with large antlered deer and the occasional bear head. A few mounted raccoons and one stuffed owl rounded out the menagerie.

The dining room entrance was on the left. Lark was shocked by the difference in the decor. The walls were covered in a large floral cream-

and-rose-flocked wallpaper. Rose damask tablecloths fell to the rose carpeted floor and fan-folded, rose cloth napkins sat at each place setting. A fat rose-colored candle nestled in a clear crystal hurricane in the center of each table. They were immediately seated in a quiet corner booth. The hostess gave them their menus, lit their candle, and took off to get their Leinenkugels.

"This place must be owned by someone with multiple personalities," Lark said looking around the room in wonderment.

"Why do you think that?" Lacey asked, her eyes twinkling.

"I've never seen two parts of the same restaurant look more different than that bar and this dining room."

"You men are all alike. You wouldn't have thought a thing about it if I'd taken you to a restaurant decorated like that bar, but because this place looks so elegant," Lacey said, sweeping her arm around the room, "you're ready to say the owner must be crazy."

"Come on," Lark said, putting down his menu. "Don't you find this a little strange? Across the hall we have northwoods hunt camp decor and here we have"—he looked around the room, searching for the right words—"well, some sort of northwoods bordello motif?"

"Oh, for God's sake, I didn't take you for this kind of guy. Didn't you eat anywhere but sports bars in Chicago?"

"I've eaten in some of the best places in Chicago. That's not the point. You have to admit, these two restaurants, in a building topped by the largest red neon fish in North America, is pretty strange. And what did you mean by that remark?"

"Come again," Lacey said, her eyebrows raised in question.

"You know, that crack about what kind of guy I am."

"I just meant that when I first met you, you seemed like a pretty enlightened guy." She glanced at him over the top of her menu. "You don't seem at all like the typical male chauvinist cops I run into all the time."

"And now what do you think?"

She leaned back against the booth, tapping her lips in thought, her green eyes twinkling. "Let's see. You seem a little old-fashioned, kind of uptight and straight-arrow." She stared into his eyes. "The kind of guy Mom would have wanted me to bring home."

Lark was saved from the need to reply by the waitress bringing their beer. After giving their dinner orders, chicken parmigiana for Lark and lasagna for Lacey, they settled into an awkward silence. They had exhausted their discussion about the case on the drive and there was nothing left to talk about but themselves. They spoke at once and then stopped, laughing nervously. The tension was broken when the waitress brought their bread basket.

"How did you end up working for the Wisconsin State Police?" Lark asked, munching on a breadstick that he could have sworn was baked in heaven.

"I'm originally from Rochester, New York, but I got my bachelor's and master's in education at Penn State. When I was a student, I worked as a dispatcher for the Penn State University Police. I went back to Rochester and taught junior high math. Two years later both my parents were killed in a high-speed chase."

"The cops were after your parents?" Lark asked, as the waitress brought their salads.

"No, no," Lacey said, waving her salad fork. "My parents had gone to New York City to Christmas shop and see a couple of plays, one of their holiday traditions. The police were chasing some guys who had robbed a gas station. The thieves ran a red light and broadsided my parents' car. Dad was dead at the scene and Mom died a week later. She never regained consciousness." Lacey paused to eat a forkful of salad.

Lark tried to ward off thoughts of the loss of his wife.

"My parents were very much in love. They told me once that they wanted to die together and they wanted it to be quick. I remember them joking that when they got old and feeble, they would just drive off a cliff together like a modern-day Butch Cassidy and Sundance team. They almost got their wish. I don't think they ever knew what hit them."

"I'm so very sorry," Lark said, watching her fight to hold back tears. "It must have been terrible. I had a couple of high-speed chases on the interstate in Chicago, and as badly as I wanted to catch the bastards, I was always nervous that someone might get hurt."

They finished their salads just in time for their main courses.

"Your food looks delicious," Lacey said as she watched Lark dive into his meal. "I almost ordered the chicken parmigiana but it always reminds me of veal parmigiana, and I've seen one too many veal hutches up here to ever eat veal again."

"Gee, thanks ever so much for setting a great dinner mood," Lark said, popping a piece of chicken into his mouth. "How did you go from teaching to being a homicide detective for the state police?"

"Funny how many people ask me that question," Lacey said, dipping a breadstick in the sauce from her lasagna. "It's probably not the best dinner conversation topic."

"Go for it. Just about anything will beat a discussion about veal hutches."

"After my parents died I had to deal with their estate. I was an only child and they left me everything, including their home and a cabin in the Adirondacks. I was living in an apartment in Rochester and decided to move back home. They'd lived most of their married lives in a big old Victorian farmhouse on a two-hundred-acre farm. Both of them were pack rats and antique buffs so the house was jammed to the rafters. I discovered some letters packed away in my mom's things. I took them to my parent's attorney and got the shock of my life." Lacey paused to tackle another bite of lasagna. "I found out I was adopted."

"You didn't have any idea before that?" Lark asked, stunned.

"None. I couldn't believe my parents would keep something like that from me. It turned out to be like some gothic novel. They left a letter with their attorney. He was supposed to give it to me if I asked about being adopted or got engaged. I was adopted in Wausau, Wisconsin, when I was one week old. They assured me that my birth parents were intelligent, healthy people. My biological parents also left me a nest egg that my parents invested. It did very well."

"You came to Wisconsin to find your birth parents?" Lark asked, winding up a forkful of pasta.

"Clichéd but true. The more I thought about it, the more I just had to know. I moved to Madison and applied for a job on the city police force. The timing was right for women with degrees. I got a second master's in criminal justice at UW–Madison. In my spare time I tried to track down my biological parents."

"Have you had any luck?"

"There isn't any birth-documented-in-Wisconsin records with the exact date and time listed on my birth certificate. I've tracked all Wisconsin births for a week in either direction and can't find any discrepancies that point to me. I'm beginning to think I was born out of state."

"This must be really important to you."

Lacey took the last bite of her lasagna. "I loved my parents very much. We almost never had a disagreement, even when I was teenager.

They couldn't have loved me more or treated me better. No one can ever take their place; they'll always be my real parents. But I need to know who my biological parents were." Before she could go on, the waitress cleared their plates and offered dessert. They settled on coffee and a shared piece of chocolate silk pie.

Lacey smiled at Lark. "Let's change the subject. You know things that even Joel hasn't pried out of me. Tell me about yourself."

"Well, my life has been rather boring in comparison to yours. I'm the oldest of six kids. I have three brothers and two sisters. We were like stair steps, all one or two years apart."

"I always wanted a sister or a brother."

"Well, there were times when I was desperate to be an only child," Lark said, amused. "It just goes to show you that we're never happy with what we have. I was born in Chicago and always lived there until I took this job. My dad was a firefighter and my mom was a nurse. We were comfortably middle class with both my parents working a lot of overtime and each of us going to work when we were sixteen." Lark paused as the waitress brought their dessert and coffee.

"You go first," Lark said, shoving the decadent-looking pie towards her. "I've never known a woman who wouldn't all but kill for a good piece of chocolate."

"What a dangerous remark to make to a woman with a gun."

"Whoa," he said, raising his hands. "No offense meant. Feel free to slide it right back over here if I misspoke."

"Bullshit," Lacey said, pulling the pie towards her. "If you think you're getting first dibs on this, you've got another thing coming." She forked a large piece into her mouth and moaned with delight. "Just one more reason why all roads lead to the Sportsman's. They have heavenly desserts." She shoved the pie towards Lark.

He tried a piece. "This is good, but I'll never understand why women are so obsessed with chocolate."

Lacey snatched the plate back. "I guess that means you won't mind if that's the last bite you get." Her eyes twinkled. "I thought about getting my own piece but I didn't want to be a pig about it."

"By all means, enjoy it."

"You really don't know about the connection between women and chocolate?"

"Never understood it. My wife had to have chocolate every day."

"That speaks volumes," Lacey quipped, carving off another bite. "While I eat this, finish telling me about yourself."

Lark leaned back against the booth. "I always wanted to be a cop, but my parents wanted us to be professionals—lawyers, doctors, or engineers. Everyone met my parents' expectations but me. My parents are retired and living in Goshen, Indiana, on a hobby farm most of the year, and in Cabo San Lucas, in a place we kids bought them in the winter. I'm the oddball of the family."

"Why do you think you're odd?"

"As I said, my parents never wanted me to be a cop. They insisted that I get my degree, so I got it in criminal justice. When I joined the Chicago police force, my mother almost fell over. She was sure I'd be shot dead in days. Then they nearly drove me crazy insisting that I go to law school. They thought the reality of police work would hit me and I'd finally wake up. Much to their amazement, I got my master's in criminal justice."

"Parents are like that," Lacey said, polishing off the last bite of pie. "What brought you up here?"

He looked down at the table, lost in thought. Lacey was surprised by the sadness in his face. "My wife died two years ago. Nothing felt the same after that. I was a captain in Homicide and took early retirement when they offered me this job. Maria and I vacationed up here and talked about buying a cottage. We never did it because we were too busy, and I guess because we always thought we had all the time in the world. I had some of the best times of my life up here. This is one of the few places where I only have happy memories."

Lacey put her hands around his clenched fists in the center of the table. "I am so very sorry. She must have been a wonderful woman."

"She was the best thing that ever happened to me."

"It's ten-thirty," Lacey said, glancing at her watch. "We'd better go if we're going to find this house on time." She picked up the bill and scanned the numbers for her part of the total. Lark snatched it out of her hands.

"My treat," Lark said, pulling several bills out of his wallet.

"Wait a minute, this is business." Lacey reached for the bill. "Let me total up my half and we can each get a receipt."

Lark gave the bill and money to the waitress. "I'm just living up to my old-fashioned, straight-arrow image."

They walked out into a blowing, swirling mass of white. Lacey flipped up the hood on her coat and they hurried to the Jeep.

"God, this is awful," she said as they settled into their seats.

"If this doesn't quit, we may be stuck up here overnight," Lark said. He powered the side windows up and down and turned on the front and rear windshield wipers and defrosters.

"Big Oak, Rhinelander, who cares, as long as I have a warm place to sleep, and a bathroom," Lacey said as she dug out the directions to the Dawes' house.

"Are you familiar enough with Rhinelander to know where we're going?" Lark asked, studying the widening defroster pattern on the windshield.

"No, Captain, but I'm an excellent navigator."

"What did you say?" Lark asked, glaring over at her.

"I said I'm an excellent navigator," Lacey repeated, looking at him with concern. "Lark, are you all right?"

"I'm fine," he said, staring at the windshield. "Sorry I snapped at you. It was uncalled for. That's almost exactly what my wife used to say to me when we traveled. She was an airline pilot. The captain-navigator thing was a joke between us." He kneaded his forehead. "All this personal conversation seems to have brought back a lot of memories."

"You don't have to apologize," Lacey said, leaning over and squeezing his arm. "I've had such a sense of emptiness since my parents died. They were both only children and my grandparents died when I was very young, so I don't have any family. Sometimes the loneliness is overwhelming. I can't imagine what it must be like to lose a spouse. How long were you married?"

"Ten years," Lark mumbled. Lacey frowned down at the floor of the Jeep trying to think of something comforting to say.

Lark's voice interrupted her thoughts. "Let's get moving. Give me some directions, Navigator."

The Dawes' house turned out to be on the opposite side of town. Nearly every Christmas figure from Santa and his reindeer to Jesus in the manger were located somewhere on the house, the roof, or the lawn.

"I'd hate to pay this electric bill," Lacey said when they pulled into the driveway. "I wonder what the inside looks like."

"Let's go find out."

"I'll stay here. Maybe things will go faster if they know you've left someone in the car." She looked out the windshield at the big fat snowflakes coming down. "If you don't get going we're going to get stuck here."

Lark turned the ignition on and reached into the backseat. "Wrap yourself up in this if you get cold." He handed her a soft, plaid blanket.

Lacey watched Lark trudge up the driveway lit with red luminaries. It was time for her to be honest with herself. She had been attracted to him from the minute they met. She was used to guys coming on to her, but Lark was different; he didn't seem to notice her. She'd never had to compete with someone's dead wife and she didn't think she was up to it. She had just finished giving herself a lecture on getting her hormones under control when the car door opened and he climbed in the Jeep.

"Boy, did you miss out," he said, laying a thick manila envelope and a large Christmas-wrapped box between them in the seat. "The inside's worse than the outside. Every surface had Christmas stuff on it and the walls were covered with Christmas pictures and quilts." He backed the Jeep out of the driveway.

"That sounds just like my childhood. Every holiday was an excuse for my parents to go berserk. Halloween was beyond belief, all the other kids used to love to come over."

Lark swung the Jeep onto Highway 8, sliding on the snow-covered blacktop. "We never had time for that, but we had neighbors who decorated and I always loved their houses. I like a happy medium."

"Me, too," Lacey said, rummaging in the seat for her flashlight. "What's in the box?"

"Homemade cookies," he said, wagging his eyebrows. "At least we won't starve if we get stuck. There are several chocolate ones in there."

"Thank you, Jesus. As long as there's chocolate, nothing can go wrong."

She pulled a sheaf of pages out of the envelope. "Holy Toledo, look at all these names. I had no idea Lands' End did this much business."

"Let's not mess with this anymore tonight. I draw the line at eighteen-hour days and it's eleven-thirty now," Lark said as he pulled into the gas pumps at a brightly lit Stop and Go.

"Fine by me." Lacey stuffed the papers in the envelope. They were back on the road within five minutes, Lacey with a Diet Coke and Lark with a large coffee.

"You must be dog tired," Lacey said. "Why don't you let me drive?"

"Not on your life. I'm wide awake."

"I'm too tired to argue about it," she said, slipping off her boots and coat. "Wake me up when we get home."

Lark watched her rat around as he tuned in the radio. In a matter of seconds the snow went from large, slow flakes to near blizzard proportions.

"Jesus Christ," Lacey said. "I'm going to get an assignment with *Hawaii Five O* if this keeps up." A few minutes later, they burst into laughter when the radio announcer played Elvis Presley singing "Blue Hawaii" as a special request.

The trip back to Big Oak was uneventful. Lacey dozed and Lark listened to the radio. It was one of those nights when nearly every song brought back fond memories.

They pulled into Lark's garage just before 1 A.M. He realized how tired he was when it was almost too big an effort to get out of the Jeep. He called to Lacey but she didn't budge. She was sleeping soundly, her head resting against the door. When he shook her arm, she moaned and burrowed further into her coat and blanket.

"Lacey," he said, scooting over in the seat to shake her shoulder. "We're home. Let's go in the house."

"Um, let's just stay here where it's warm," she said drowsily, leaning into him. His arms went out to steady her and she snuggled against him, fitting her head against his shoulder. He was sitting there holding her, wondering what to do next, when she woke up.

"Jesus, I must have really been out." She pushed herself away from him.

Lark picked up the envelope and the box and got out of the Jeep.

Lacey opened her door and jumped down, letting out a howl. He rushed around the Jeep to see what was wrong.

"I forgot to put my boots back on," she said, rummaging around in the car. She grabbed her coat, boots, and purse and ran into the house muttering "Shit, shit, shit."

"That'll teach you to take your shoes off," Lark chuckled, watching her scuttle to get off the cold concrete.

"Hell, now I'm wide awake. I'll never get to sleep without some hot chocolate. Do you have cocoa and marshmallows around here somewhere?" she asked, rocking from foot to foot.

"Somewhere in the pantry," Lark replied, motioning towards the kitchen as he put his coat and boots in the closet.

Lacey dropped her boots and coat in the laundry room and went to search the pantry. "I don't believe this. You have Hershey's cocoa, sugar, and marshmallows. The marshmallows are old, but who cares. You've set a record," she said, looking for a pan.

"What kind of a record?" he asked, sitting down at the bar across from her.

"I've never known a single man to have all these ingredients." She glanced over at him on her way to the refrigerator for milk. "I'm impressed and I take back almost every chauvinistic word I said about you. Crap! You have regular milk instead of one percent."

"I hate low fat milk."

"Figures," she said, pouring the milk into the pan. "We need to have a little chat about men, dairy products, and heart disease."

"Maybe we should also have a little chat about the effects of sugar on a woman's body," he said as he watched her measure heaping spoonfuls of sugar and cocoa into the milk.

She rolled her eyes in disgust. "Where are your big mugs?"

"I only have beer mugs. Rather chauvinistic, don't you think?" He pointed above his head at the small cabinets over the bar.

"Why don't you go change clothes? Then you can stir while I change."

"I'm pretty comfortable the way I am, but I'll be glad to take over for you," he said, joining her at the stove.

By the time she was back downstairs in a pair of sweats, the cocoa was ready. She put some marshmallows in each mug, poured the cocoa over them, and popped in ice teaspoons she'd found in his silverware drawer.

Lark lit a fire and ran upstairs to get the tape from his bedroom VCR. They nestled into opposite ends of the sofa; Lacey curled up in the afghan Lark kept draped over the back. There wasn't anything new on the late news.

"Do you think the Ransons have something to do with these murders?" Lacey asked as the news ended.

"I don't think so," Lark said, propping his feet up on the coffee table. "They seem very honest."

"What's the husband like? Could this have anything to do with him screwing around?"

"We hit him pretty hard about extramarital affairs in our interview and he was adamant that he could never do that to his wife."

"There's a rarity."

"Contrary to the research done by *Cosmopolitan* magazine and Oprah Winfrey, not all men have affairs," Lark said, stifling a yawn.

"You're absolutely right. I believe the data says only about fifty percent of them do. What time is it?"

"One-forty-five and I need to be in the office by eight."

"On Thanksgiving?"

"Shit," Lark said, pounding his fist on the arm of the sofa.

Lacey jumped. "What's wrong?"

"I was going to stop and get a turkey but I forgot about it in all the excitement." Lark shook his head in disgust. "We'll just have to go out to eat."

"Don't give it a second thought," Lacey said, getting up and folding the afghan across the back of the sofa. She took their mugs to the kitchen. "We can grocery shop in the morning. Someone's bound to be open. I'll make a turkey dinner that will knock your socks off. We can go over the data and watch the games. Thanksgiving's my favorite holiday. Sports and good food, what more could you ask for?"

Lark followed her into the kitchen and leaned against the bar, watching her rinse the mugs and the cocoa pan. He said nothing until she opened the dishwasher. He rushed around the counter, grabbing a dish towel on his way.

"Maria didn't put those mugs or our pans in the dishwasher. I'll dry them."

"Sorry about that," she said, moving away from the sink and going into the foyer to put away her coat and boots, only to find that he'd already done it.

'What time do you want to wake up in the morning?" Lark shouted after her, not realizing she'd walked back into the kitchen.

"You pick, it's your house," she said, standing behind him, her arms folded across her chest.

"Jesus Christ." Lark jumped and almost dropped one of the mugs when he realized she was so close. "I thought you'd gone upstairs."

"What time do you want to go in? I'll set my alarm."

Lark felt as if he'd suddenly walked from bright sunshine into dark shadows. "How does nine sound?" he asked, trying to read her face.

"Fine by me. See you in the morning." She turned to go upstairs.

"Lacey, wait a minute, did I say something to upset you?" he asked, puzzled by the change in her behavior.

She turned around, the hint of a smile on her face. "Do you mind if I take a bath? Will that keep you up?"

"The H-bomb wouldn't keep me up. Please, make yourself at home," he said, sensing her reserve.

"Let me know what you want to do about Thanksgiving dinner and please don't feel like you need to entertain me. I didn't stop to think that you might have other plans. Jim told me the Pine View's open tomorrow."

"Lacey, wait a minute." He tossed the dish towel on the counter.

"Lark, we're both overtired and we've been thrown together without knowing each other at all. I apologize for intruding into your routines around here and making assumptions about how you do your dishes or spend your Thanksgiving. See you in the morning." She trotted up the stairs, not looking back.

He watched her go into her room. He felt as alone as he'd felt in years and couldn't quite figure it out. He sighed and finished straightening up the kitchen before going up to bed. Later, in his room, he listened to the sounds of the water running in Lacey's bathroom and wondered what he'd done to ruin the mood. He told himself he was being ridiculous, that she was way too young for him, and that he had to quit thinking with his dick.

Ann got up a little after six. John had gotten up earlier and gone to his office, hoping to get caught up on the work he'd missed during the last two days. Between John waking her to kiss her good-bye and the dogs jumping on and off the bed, she was restless and irritable.

She shuffled into the bathroom and then went over to the sliding glass doors to check out the view. It was dark with the slightest hint of pink on the horizon. The snow came down steadily. She slipped into her robe and opened the slider two or three inches so she could listen to the wind in the trees. Parts of the lake were covered with a patchy skin of ice, but most of the water was still free to flow into shore. She could hear the tiny ice chunks come tinkling in with each of the waves, kind of like a symphony of crystal bells. This phenomenon only came twice a year: in the fall, before the lake froze over, and in the spring, before the last of the ice left. Ann listened until she got too cold to keep the door open.

She walked over to the side window to check the deer feeders at the edge of the woods. She was disappointed to see that the feeders were empty except for one lone porcupine grubbing around. She wondered if the hunters had finally succeeded in killing every deer in the region.

The dogs were restless. She shooed them out, shut the door, and wandered back over to the window to see if any other critters had stopped by for breakfast. Her eye caught a glimpse of movement further back in the woods, but she couldn't make out what it was. She looked for the binoculars but they were nowhere to be found.

Disappointed, Ann headed into the bathroom to get dressed. She got about ten feet from the window and heard the deafening crack of a gunshot and the sound of glass breaking. She felt something slam into her shoulder. Everything went into slow motion. She looked down and saw blood streaming from her left upper arm. The nurse part of her said a silent prayer that the blood wasn't spurting, which meant her arteries were intact.

She stumbled over to the bed and grabbed the telephone to dial 911 before she remembered that they didn't have 911 in Mason County. She swore when she couldn't remember any of the emergency numbers. Jamming the receiver between her uninjured right shoulder and chin, she dialed zero and asked to be connected to the Mason County Sheriff's Office while she struggled to pull the belt from her robe. The dispatcher answered just as a second gunshot echoed through the bedroom. What was left of the window blew out and more glass shards scattered all over the bedroom. Ann felt spasms of pain in her back.

She heard the dispatcher yelling from the phone she'd dropped on the floor. During the second gunshot, she'd fallen off the bed, landing on her stomach. Ann didn't get up for fear she'd be shot at again. Instead, she slithered through the glass shards to the phone. She gave the dispatcher her name and address and asked her to call EMS for one victim of a gunshot wound. Never in her life had she been so scared.

The dispatcher tried to keep her on the line, but Ann hung up. She needed all her energy to take care of herself until the ambulance arrived. Her arm and back hurt like hell. She crawled into the master bathroom, dragging the cordless phone. Gingerly, she slipped her robe off her left shoulder and surveyed the damage. Her arm was covered with blood and the entire left side of her favorite nightgown was also soaked. She couldn't find a bullet hole but she did find a huge piece of glass sticking out of her upper arm. On closer inspection she found it had gone clear through her arm.

She sank down on the edge of the tub and leaned her uninjured right side against the wall. She heard the telephone ring but ignored it. Her options were to take the glass out herself or wait until she got to the hospital. Living in Mason County wasn't like living in the city in the middle of an episode of *911*. The county's volunteer emergency medical technicians were probably at home, sound asleep. Ann was hurting like hell and sure she had a greater chance of moving around and injuring herself with the glass left in. She decided the glass had to go.

She stood in front of the mirror over the bathroom sinks. The sight stopped her dead in her tracks. Her face was white as a sheet and there was blood everywhere, including smudges all over her face. She looked like an extra from *Friday the 13th*.

Shaking off her mounting fear, she grabbed the largest end of the glass shard, took a deep breath, and pulled it out. When she heard the sound of glass breaking, she looked down and realized she'd dropped the shard on the counter, where it had shattered into smaller pieces. A bloody five-inch wound gaped open in her arm. She mentally thanked her guardian angel, knowing she could have lost half her arm, or even worse, had she been in a different place when the gunshots went off.

The bleeding from her arm increased dramatically. She folded a towel over the wound and wrapped the tie from her bathrobe around it. The pressure she applied hurt like hell and she started crying. Dizzy and nauseated, she sat down on the bathroom floor.

Ann didn't know how long she waited for help, but she remembered soaking through several towels and being grateful that she'd had enough sense to sit down underneath the towel rack. She was rewrapping her arm when she heard the doorbell and the dogs barking. She dialed the operator, who put her through to the dispatcher, who told her the police had arrived.

Lark was sleeping soundly when the phone rang. He rolled over and grabbed the receiver as he swung his feet over the side of the bed. As he listened to the dispatcher, he pulled on jeans and maneuvered a sweater over his head. He hung up as he fished a pair of socks out of his drawer and yelled at Lacey to get up as he pulled them on. By the time he hit the hall, she was coming out of her room.

"I heard your phone," she said, following him downstairs. She had jumped into jeans and a sweater and pulled her hair up in a ponytail. Smudges of last night's mascara were still under her eyes. As they put on their winter gear, he filled her in. "Jim, Paul, and our ambulance crew are out on Highway 70, dealing with an accident. Our other unit is thirty-five miles away on a domestic dispute call. Ann Ranson called asking for an ambulance for one gunshot victim. She refused to stay on the phone."

"Jesus Christ," Lacey said as they raced out to the garage and hopped in the Jeep.

Lark backed out into a swirling mass of snow and gunned it down the drive. It was six-twenty and just beginning to lighten up. The road was drifted heavily in some spots and blown bare with an icy sheen in others. Lark slid the Jeep into four-wheel drive and worked the police radio. He asked Mary Lou to put the helicopter in Marshfield on standby and call out an EMS crew from Park Falls for mutual aid. She told him Park Falls was out on a call and she was already going through the township lists trying to find first responders who weren't busy.

Lark swore and pushed his speed up past sixty. It took them eight minutes to get to the Ransons'. The house was dark. It looked so peaceful that he hoped the call was a hoax. He rang the doorbell and heard barking and growling on the other side of the front door. The door was locked.

Lark shined his flashlight through the living-room window. Nothing seemed out of place, but the goldens were milling around, their tails up in alarm.

"How about if I check the other entrances," Lacey suggested, moving off the porch.

"Fine, radio me if you can get in."

He rang the doorbell again and debated on how long to wait before breaking in. He pulled up the porch mat, no key. He brushed his hand across the door lintel—no such luck. He did the same thing with the picture window. No key there either.

Just when he'd decided to break in, Mary Lou called. "Mrs. Ranson says there's a key in the left porch light globe. She's in the master bathroom. Someone shot out the bedroom window and there's glass all over the floor. She wants you to keep the dogs out."

"Who's hurt?" Lark asked, retrieving the key.

"Don't know, she hung up again."

"Shit." He unlocked the door just as Lacey came back.

"There's a huge hole in the upstairs west window. All the doors were locked."

"The window was shot out," Lark said, opening the door. The goldens greeted them, barking and wagging their tails. They galloped up the stairs, Sheba at their heels. Lacey and Lark pulled their guns, and after shouting police, followed them.

"These dogs have got to go," Lacey said. They dragged them into the bedroom at the end of the hall. The minute they shut the door, the dogs began barking.

Trying to ignore the cacophony, Lark eased open the master-bedroom door. "Ann, it's Sheriff Swenson," he yelled.

"I'm in the bathroom," she said in a shaky voice.

Lark raced through the bedroom, glass crunching under his feet. He entered the bathroom with Lacey on his heels. Ann was curled up on the floor by the tub. The countertop and the floor were smeared with blood and blood-soaked towels lay all around her. She had a bloody towel wrapped around her upper arm.

"Sweet mother of God," Lacey muttered, stooping down in front of her. Ann's eyes were enormous. Lacey gently pried Ann's hand from the death grip she held on her wound.

Ann glanced up at Lark. "I need another towel, it's really been bleeding, but not spurting, so I don't think there's arterial damage."

He gave Lacey a towel and took a look at Ann's wound.

"I thought I was shot but a big piece of glass went through my arm. I pulled it out."

"Judas Priest, you pulled it out yourself?" he said in disbelief.

"Somebody had to do it."

"You could have hurt yourself," he said angrily.

Ann ignored his outburst. "Either that hunter hasn't slept it off yet or he was firing at a deer the size of Godzilla." She glanced at Lacey, working away on her arm. "Since the ambulance isn't here yet, can I assume they're out on another call?"

"Auto accident on Highway 70," Lark said.

"Cancel them. I can move everything and I can breathe OK, so the glass didn't hit anything critical." She winced as Lacey tightened the new towel around her arm. "As soon as you pull the big pieces out of my back, you can drive me to the ER." She looked up at Lark. "Can you please call John and let him know what happened?"

"I'll call John and take you to the hospital, but we're not taking any glass out of your back," Lark said as Lacey gathered up the blood-soaked towels.

"Let's get you up off this cold floor," Lacey said, noting that Ann was shivering.

"I'd rather sit here and conserve my energy," Ann replied, leaning her head against the wall and closing her eyes. "Can you please get me a blanket?"

"I think we'd better get you to the hospital right now," Lark said. He took her wrist to check her pulse while Lacey rushed to get a blanket.

"What is it?" Ann asked.

"Ninety-six."

"I'll live. You don't have to worry until it hits about one-fifty, which won't happen unless some of this glass gets pushed into my back."

"We're going to the hospital right now. We're not going to piss around pulling out glass," Lark snapped.

Lacey brushed Lark out of the way and tucked a blanket around Ann's legs. Lacey pulled her forward, resting Ann's head on her shoulder to survey her back. Three shards of glass ranging from silver-dollar- to playing-card-size were imbedded in her upper shoulders.

"Lean against me and we'll get them out," Lacey murmured, holding Ann against her. She looked sternly at Lark. "Pull them out and be quick about it."

He frowned and stooped down. "I don't think this is a good idea."

"I'm the medical professional here and I say they need to come out," Ann said, her voice muffled against Lacey's shoulder.

Lark took a deep breath and pulled out the glass. Ann moaned and clung to Lacey as each piece was removed. Tears were running down Ann's face by the time they were done. Lacey pressed a towel against Ann's back and Lark stalked over to the other side of the bathroom. He placed the three glass shards on the counter and watched the women on the floor. Ann leaned back against the tub. Sweat had broken out on her forehead and upper lip, despite the room's plummeting temperature.

"Would one of you get me a Diet Coke?" she asked, wiping away tears.

Lark headed for the door but Lacey jumped up, saying she'd go. He started to protest but saw that she was crying. He let her go, realizing she needed time to compose herself.

"That hurt like hell, but it had to be done," Ann said.

Lark pulled a couple of towels out of the linen closet and knelt down in front of her. "I need to take a look at your back," he said, gently pulling her forward. The towel Lacey had just put there was soaked with blood. "I'm going to cut your robe and nightgown off your shoulders so we can see how bad this," he said, digging his knife out of his jeans pocket.

"Sure, go ahead and ruin John's favorite nightgown," Ann said, resting her head against his chest.

Lacey walked in as Lark finished cutting the back out of Ann's robe. "The ambulance will be here as soon as they drop their patient off at the ED." She opened a can of Diet Coke. "The helicopter is grounded because of weather."

Lark surveyed Ann's upper back. Three ugly gashes oozed blood. He put a towel against the wounds and leaned Ann back against the tub.

Lacey squatted down and gave her a drink of soda. Ann shuddered as she drank the cold liquid. She slumped back, holding the remains of her robe against her chest.

"Jesus, we've got to get her out of here. How long will that ambulance be?" Lark asked.

"Cancel the damn ambulance. How many times do I have to tell you, we don't need it," Ann yelled, her eyes settling on Lacey. "Sorry I'm so irritable. If you'll help me get dressed, I think we can get to the hospital on our own."

"We're not waiting for you to get dressed. You're going to the ER now," Lark snapped.

Lacey stepped in front of him. "Call off the ambulance and I'll help Ann get dressed."

When Lark protested, Lacey pointed her finger at him. "I wouldn't go to the hospital where I'm the boss in a sexy, blood-soaked nightgown unless I was half dead."

Lark protested again but Lacey cut him off. "We can stand here and fight or take that time and help Ann get dressed." Not waiting for an answer, she strode past him into the closet.

Lark walked out of the bathroom and sat down on the bed. He barely had time to call off the ambulance and direct Mary Lou to send Paul and Jim out to the Ransons' to start the scene work before Ann and Lacey came out of the bathroom.

The blood splatters had been washed off Ann's ghost-white face. She was dressed in a gray sweatsuit. Her blood-streaked hair was pulled back with a headband.

Lark and Lacey got on either side of her to make sure she didn't fall.

"I'm sorry I'm moving so slowly," Ann said, navigating the last step and flopping down on the bench in the foyer.

While she rested, Lark got her coat out of the closet. When she stood up, he draped it around her shoulders and noticed she was weaving on her feet.

"Lacey's going to pull the Jeep up and I'm going to carry you to the car," Lark said, tossing his keys to Lacey as he picked Ann up. She didn't protest, other than to groan in pain as his arm went across her shoulders. Lark called the hospital to notify them they were on their way, and the ER staff were waiting when they pulled into the ambulance garage ten minutes later.

Lark and Lacey drove to John's office. John's truck was parked on the street out front. The blinds were open and they could see him hunched over a drafting table. A small donut box from the Big Oak Diner lay open on his desk and a half full coffeepot sat on the credenza against the back wall of the office. John looked up at the sound of the door opening and his face broke into a smile. He glanced down at his watch, noting that it was only seven-fifteen.

"You're out early," he said. "Your invitation for Thanksgiving dinner is still open. Ann should already have the turkey in the oven."

"We just dropped Ann off at the emergency room," Lark said, studying the reaction on his face. "Someone shot out your bedroom window and she caught some glass in her arm and back."

John carefully put down his drawing pencil. "Is she all right?" he asked, scanning Lacey's blank face. He shrugged into his coat and snatched his truck keys off the desk.

"She's OK," Lark said. "I'll drive you over and Lacey can follow in your truck."

"That won't be necessary," John said, rushing for the door.

"I'll fill you in on the details on the way over," Lark said, right behind him.

"Fine," John snapped, lobbing his truck keys to Lacey. He slouched against the passenger door of the Jeep, his face a mask of despair, as Lark told him about the shooting.

"It must have happened right after I left. I stopped at the diner to get donuts and got to the office at six-fifteen. I was watching the time because I wanted to be home by nine to keep dinner on schedule. Ann makes the turkey and dressing, but the rest of the meal is mine."

Lark made a mental note to check the time of John's visit to the Big Oak Diner.

When they pulled into the ER, Lacey was already in the waiting room. "Ann's in X-ray. The doctor wants to admit her but she refused."

"Dammit," John muttered, rubbing his hand across his chin. "I don't know anyone as stubborn as Ann."

"We're going out to your house. Here's the number for my cellular." Lark handed John one of his cards. "Call me if you need anything. If I don't hear from you, I'll call you at home, or here, if she ends up staying."

"Yeah, right, like she's gonna stay here unless they tie her to the bed," he said, getting his keys from Lacey.

The ER staff assured him they would come and get him as soon as Ann was back from X-ray. John settled in to watch the fish in the waiting-room aquarium and figure out how to convince her to be admitted. She was back fifteen minutes later. John had never seen her so pale. She was sitting on a cart in a hospital gown, her left arm bandaged from shoulder to elbow. She had bandages on her back and an IV in her right arm.

"I hear they want to admit you."

"That's ridiculous. I can be here in less than fifteen minutes if I have a problem, and all I'd be staying for is IV antibiotics and fluids. I'm getting a fluid bolus and my first dose of antibiotic right now. They can cap this IV off," she said, lifting up her arm, "and reuse it when I come in for my antibiotic."

"Well, if the doctor's OK with your plan, then I guess I'm fine with it, too. If not, you're staying."

"Fine with me," Ann said. While they waited for the physician, she told him what had happened. She was convinced that she had seen something, or someone, by the deer feeder right before the gunshot went off. She couldn't remember if she told the police and asked him to call Lark.

When he got back, Dr. Kingsley was in Ann's cubicle. He discharged her and told her to come back at 9 P.M. He confirmed that her blood count was low, and warned her that she had a lot of muscle and soft-tissue damage that could give her trouble if she didn't take it easy. Ann nodded away like one of those dolls bobbing its head in the back window of a car. The nurse capped off her IV and gave her a bottle of pain pills.

They arrived home at nine. Two sheriff's department vehicles were in the driveway and the dogs were barking in the garage. The painkillers had kicked in and Ann could hardly keep her eyes open. She staggered into the house, leaning heavily on John, and curled up on the family-room sofa. He covered her with a quilt and went upstairs.

The master bedroom was freezing. He made a mental note to get plywood to cover the window. The rose-colored carpet had four platter-sized blood-soaked spots and was covered with glass shards. There were two holes in the wall above the bed. The bathroom was a bloody disaster. He left before he fainted.

He sat on the bed in the spare bedroom for several minutes, trying to calm down, and then went back to the master bathroom. Lacey walked in while he was surveying the damage.

"How about if I help you with this mess," she said, noting his terrified eyes. "We've already gone over this area, so it can be cleaned up." They had confirmed the time of his visit to the Big Oak Diner. He was in the clear for the shooting.

"We've been out behind the deer feeder and Ann was right. There are boot tracks, cigarette butts, and a snowmobile trail leading to the road. We lost the trail in a muddle of tire tracks out on the road. Paul and Jim are canvassing your neighbors to find out if they saw any-thing."

John stood mute as Lacey talked, his eyes scanning the room. Even in the movies, he'd never seen this much blood.

"Are you OK?" she asked, concerned by how pale his face had be-come.

"I gotta get out of here." He brushed past her and ran downstairs to check on Ann, Lacey right behind him. Ann slept peacefully on the sofa. He made coffee and sat down at the island.

"Do you think this shooting is related to the bodies we found?" John asked as he handed Lacey a mug.

"We're looking into that," Lacey replied, watching him stare at the sofa where Ann was sleeping. "I'll clean up that mess while you get Thanksgiving dinner ready. You're only a couple of hours behind. Lark and I will be here if your invitation is still open."

"Are you sure you want to tackle the upstairs?"

"Lead me to your cleaning supplies."

That finally coaxed a smile out of him. "You're a lifesaver. I just can't clean up Ann's blood right now. I'll get the turkey in the oven and then we'll get that window boarded up."

Ann awakened to the aroma of roasting turkey and couldn't figure out why John had put the bird in without her special stuffing. Pain shot through her left arm and shoulder when she tried to get up, and the memory of her early-morning activities came rushing back. She groaned but managed to sit up, flinching when she heard gunshots off in the distance. She stood up, pulling the quilt around her shoulders. She was still in the clothes she'd worn to the hospital and had an over-whelming urge to change them. She headed upstairs just as Lark came in the front door.

He broke into a grin. "Ann, I'm so glad you're OK. Can I do anything for you? Lacey got everything cleaned up, and she and John went to get some plywood to put over the windows. I was drafted to keep an eye on you while I make some phone calls."

"I don't need anybody to keep an eye on me," she snapped, hobbling up the stairs.

Lacey had done an excellent job. The glass was gone and the blood-stains were now only faint wet spots on the carpet. The bathroom was spotless. Ann wouldn't have known anything had happened if the window wasn't missing and there weren't two holes in the wall.

Even with the furnace running constantly, the bedroom was freezing, so Ann turned on the heat lamps in the bathroom. She decided to take a shower but needed to cover her sutures and IV. Sighing, she walked back out to the railing and yelled for Lark.

"Can you get the Saran Wrap from the top drawer left of the sink and toss it up to me?"

"Saran Wrap?" he asked, puzzled.

"I need to keep the moisture out of my IV and dressings while I shower."

He brought her the Saran Wrap without comment. Even with the heat lamps on and the door shut, the bathroom was freezing. Shivering, Ann convinced herself that the hot water would warm her up. Getting the Saran Wrap around her arm wasn't difficult, but covering the dressings on her back was impossible. She gave up and curled up under a quilt in the spare bedroom to wait for John. Lacey woke her up.

"What time is it?" Ann asked, struggling out from under the quilt.

"Twelve-thirty," Lacey said, sitting down on the chaise across from the bed.

"It's time for more pain pills," Ann said, grimacing as she sat up. "Where's John?"

"We couldn't find the boards he needed over at Lowery's so he called the guy who owns the lumberyard in Park Falls. Since he's such a good customer they're opening up for him. He dropped me off to see if you needed any help."

"You mean to keep an eye on me," Ann said.

"He's worried about you."

"Yeah, I'm sure he is, but I'm just like an old dog when I'm sick. I want to curl up in the corner and be left alone until I feel better." Ann slid her feet over the side of the bed and sat up. She groaned as pain shot through her arm and back.

"What can I do for you?" Lacey asked, reaching out to steady her.

She gave up and lay back down. "I'd be forever grateful if you'd get me some pain pills and a Diet Coke. The pills are in my purse downstairs. Please don't let Don Juan up here when I look like this."

"Don Juan?"

"You know," Ann said, motioning towards the stairs. "Mel Gibson's taller, better looking, twin . . . whatever."

Lacey burst out laughing. "Now that I think about it, he does look a little like Mel but he sure doesn't act like Don Juan." Still laughing, she went downstairs. Lark watched her dig around in Ann's purse as he talked on the phone.

"What the hell are you doing?" he asked when he hung up.

"Looking for Ann's pain pills."

Lark snatched a prescription bottle off the counter by the sink and tossed it to her. "John left them out so he could find them. Apparently, Ann's purse is just as bad as yours. No one in their right mind would leave them in that mess. They might never be found."

"Jesus, you're irritable," Lacey said, opening the refrigerator.

"You're right. Sorry I snapped at you. The only name on the Lands' End coat list that's connected to this case is Ann Ranson. She bought the same coat that Yellow Mitten had on."

"Didn't she wear a red coat to the hospital this morning?"

"I think you're right," Lark said, wondering why he hadn't remembered it.

They went to the foyer and pulled her coat out of the closet. The label read Lands' End.

"Well, I guess coincidences do happen," she said, breathing a sigh of relief.

"Did she do anything with the Saran Wrap?" Lark asked, following her into the kitchen.

"Saran Wrap?" Lacey asked, a bemused smile on her face. "I've read about alternative uses for Saran Wrap, but I don't think the timing is good for that right now."

"I don't have any idea what you're talking about, and from the look on your face, I'm not going to ask," Lark said. "About an hour ago, Ann asked me to bring her the Saran Wrap so she could take a shower. I went up to check on her and found her asleep in the other bedroom."

"First of all, Mel, you need to loosen up," Lacey said, patting him on the arm. "I'll check it out." She gathered up the pills and soda headed back upstairs.

"Hey," Lark yelled, looking confused. "Why did you call me Mel?"

"You're a detective," she quipped over her shoulder, "you figure it out."

Ann was dozing when she got back upstairs. She sat the soda and the pills on the table beside the bed and was just about out the door when Ann spoke.

"You don't have to leave, I'm awake. What took you so long?"

Lacey read the label, got out two pain pills, and opened the Diet Coke. "Did you get to shower?" she asked, noticing that Ann was in the same clothes she had worn to the hospital.

"No." Ann swallowed the pills. "Could you help me with the Saran Wrap?"

"Let's wait till your pain pills kick in," Lacey said, watching Ann wince as she got up.

"By then I'll be too sleepy. Let's get it over with. They say suffering is good for the soul. We'll do a little research and find out."

Ann had left the bathroom door shut and the heat lamps on, so it was a little warmer than the frigid master bedroom. With Ann giving directions, Lacey wound a piece of plastic wrap around Ann's arm dressing and smoothed a couple of large pieces over her shoulder dressing.

The shower was heaven. Ann's pain pills hadn't reached their peak and her arm was still sore, but it wasn't the excruciating pain she'd felt when she first woke up. She got out of the shower and wrapped herself in her old, ratty terry cloth robe. John walked in just as she was trying to figure out how to use the curling iron with her right hand. He helped her put on her makeup and get into slacks and a sweater.

They went downstairs. John and Lark carried the plywood upstairs as Ann shuffled into the family room and flopped down on the sofa. There was a roaring fire in the fireplace and the entire downstairs smelled like Thanksgiving dinner. She decided to fix herself a snack. Just as she got into the kitchen, the doorbell rang. Ann got to the door as John and Lark clattered down the stairs. She looked through the sidelight to see Myra and David Banski, their arms loaded down with bags.

"No need to bring out the guns," Ann said, noting Lark's hand resting on his shoulder holster. "It's only the neighbors."

Ann opened the door and Myra rushed in, bringing a sweep of cold air and snow with her. She handed two bags to John and then unloaded her son's two bags on Lark. "I brought you a ham and all the goodies," she said, studying Ann. "I heard you were shot and near death. I expected John to be here by himself. Thank God someone got their wires crossed." Lacey took their coats and they went into the family room to sit down.

"Where'd you hear that?" Ann asked, trying to keep irritation out of her voice. Myra's response was delayed while John took drink orders.

"David heard it from one of the IGA checkers. Her sister works at the hospital. You don't look like you were shot."

"Some crazy deer hunter shot out our bedroom window and I got some glass in my arm and back. They stitched me up in the ER."

"Ann, I'm so glad you're all right. I was so worried about you and John," Myra gushed.

"John's got a big turkey in the oven so we'll never eat all that food you brought. Should we send it over to the shelter in Park Falls?"

"Heavens, no," Myra said, waving her hand. "The restaurant sent a bunch of food over there this morning." She glanced at Lark. "The police went all around the lake asking if anyone saw anything funny this morning. Everyone knows something's up. You'll have lots of people checking up on you. That food will come in handy."

"Did either of you see anything unusual this morning?" Lark asked as John returned with a tray of drinks.

Myra shook her head and took a glass of white wine. "I didn't get up until eight-thirty. Did you see anything, dear?" she asked David.

"Nothing."

"Is this about the bodies found in the marsh?" Myra asked.

"Yes, it is. We're looking into several missing person cases from the past few years. David, do you remember a student from a few years ago who turned up missing? A Gemma Patterson?" Lark asked.

David scrunched up his forehead in thought and Ann wondered why she never ran into guys that cute when she was in college. He was clean cut with broad, football-player-type shoulders tapering to a narrow waist. His dark brown hair was cut fashionably short and his mouth was partially disguised with a newly grown goatee.

"You know, I do remember her. She came from Minneapolis. She and Sandi Waltner took a class together and hit it off."

"Did you ever date her?" Lark asked.

David smiled. "No, but I did go out to the Pine View with Sandi, Jim Kryjack, and Gemma once. Did they ever find out what happened to her?"

"No," Lark said, watching him.

Myra wasn't born yesterday. "Sheriff, was Gemma one of the bodies you found?"

"She's still missing. We'll be checking to see if one of the bodies is her."

"How about a little good news after this morbid conversation," Myra said, smiling at David. "Honey, why don't you tell them."

David shook his head and told her to break the news.

"David and Sandi Waltner are engaged. They're getting married next year after David graduates from law school. Isn't that wonderful?" Everyone congratulated David, which led to another round of drinks before the Banskis left for their own Thanksgiving dinner.

After basting the turkey, John, Lark, and Lacey went upstairs to hammer up the last piece of plywood. Against doctor's orders, Ann took two more pain pills on top of the two glasses of wine she drank and fell into the best sleep she'd had for several days.

Lark's cellular phone rang a little after three, just as they were putting the final nails into the plywood. Paul had arrested Ron Chevsky for drunk driving. Lark and Lacey drove through a blinding snowstorm to get to the station. Lacey rubbed her gloved hands over the passenger's side window and pressed her face up against the spot she'd cleared. She was able to get a look at the red swirling lights of Tetzloff's tow truck as it pulled a car out of the ditch.

They brushed off their coats and stamped snow off their boots as they trudged into the station. They met Paul at the coffeepot. He told them that Ron had failed his Breathalyzer test and was major league pissed that he'd been hauled in. They took a few minutes to warm up before interviewing him.

Ron looked worse than he had when Lark had last seen him. His long hair hung unkempt and matted around his face and his mustache was badly in need of a trim. His brown eyes were bloodshot. Blackheads pitted his nose and his face was an unhealthy ruddy color. He reeked of alcohol and body odor. A long underwear shirt, gray with dirt, stuck out of the top of his orange hunting jumpsuit. Lark suspected that he hadn't changed clothes since they had seen him in the marsh on Tuesday.

"What the fuck do you think you're doing dragging me in here like this? I tried to avoid that bitch but she was all over the fucking road," he yelled as they walked in.

"Watch your language," Lark said.

"Fuck you, asshole, and fuck that bitch cop you got with you, too," Ron yelled back.

Lark reached across the table and grabbed Ron's jumpsuit, pulling him up out of his chair. "I'm not going to tell you again, watch your language."

"Hurry the fuck up." Ron fiddled with a cigarette butt he'd crushed in the ashtray. "I got things to do."

"Yeah, we know," Lark said. "Do you remember a girl named Gemma Patterson?"

"Got a light?" Ron asked, putting a fresh cigarette between his cracked lips.

Lacey slipped out and came back with a book of matches. Lark lit his cigarette.

"Now tell me about Gemma Patterson."

"Fuck, I don't remember any bitch by that name," Ron said, taking a drag on his cigarette and blowing smoke in Lacey's face. She waved it away without comment.

"You were students at UW together and she went missing three years ago. Do you remember now?" Lacey asked, her voice full of contempt.

Ron began coughing and almost fell out off his chair.

"Do you remember being questioned about Gemma's disappearance?" Lark asked.

"Hell, you're still looking for that dyke bitch?" he asked, laughing.

"What do you mean by dyke bitch?" Lacey asked.

Ron's hands snaked out to touch her hair. Lark grabbed them and slammed them down on the table. "Keep your hands to yourself, Chevsky."

"I'll bet you don't. I hear you ain't had any in months, maybe years, since your wife kicked off. You fucking *her* now?" he asked, flipping his head in Lacey's direction as he coughed up a wad of yellow phlegm and spit it on the floor. "That why you're so touchy?"

Lacey left to get a box of tissues. When she got back, Ron was sitting quietly at the table and Lark looked like he was ready to explode. She wondered what had transpired between them.

"I'm going to ask you one more time. What do you remember about Gemma Patterson?" Lark asked, his voice barely controlled.

"She was a primo cockteaser, a fucking dyke," he yelled. "I took her out twice. She was all over me on the dance floor but later wouldn't have anything to do with me. Lesbo bitch."

"Did you see her up here or in Madison?" Lacey asked.

"One time up here, one time in Madison. Then the bitch wouldn't see me anymore. I guess I was too much man for her. You could probably handle me," he said, eyeing Lacey. He grabbed his crouch and leered at her, showing a mouth full of grungy teeth.

Lark yelled for Paul to take Ron to his cell.

"She must have rejected him, so in his eyes she was a lesbian," Lacey said, writing in a small notebook. "I think we should try to get him into detox. He's in bad shape."

"We'll see if we can get him admitted tonight. He's going to be tons of fun for some poor nurse."

"I'm sure they're used to drunks." Lacey stood up. "Let's find Kry-jack and get his interview over with so we can get back to the Ransons' for dinner. Do you want to do this with me in or out?"

"I'd rather talk to him alone. If I hear anything that concerns me, I'll pull you in."

"Fine by me. I'll go take a nap," Lacey said, ambling into the break-room.

Fifteen minutes later, Jim appeared in the doorway. "Happy Thanksgiving, Chief. What's up?" he asked as he sauntered into Lark's office.

"I need to ask you some questions."

"Shoot," Jim said, sitting down.

"Do you remember a woman you went to school with named Gemma Patterson?"

"Of course," he said, his face an open book. "She was from Minneapolis and getting a degree in business. She and Sandi Waltner and Katey Lowery were great friends, and she came up here several times to stay with one or the other of them for the weekend. She turned up missing, last seen in Eau Claire three or four years ago."

"Anything else you want to tell me?"

He lost his smile. "What's this about, Chief?"

"Just tell me everything you remember about Gemma Patterson."

Jim studied Lark's face. It revealed nothing. He shifted in his chair and stared down at his hands folded in his lap. When he looked up, he was as serious as Lark had ever seen him.

"I went out with her twice. She was the cutest thing I'd ever seen. She and I, Dave Banski, and Sandi Waltner went to the Pine View for dinner one Saturday. Later that night we went dancing over at the Town Line. She was a great dancer. When we got back to Waltner's, Sandi and David started necking. Gemma seemed uncomfortable, so we went for a walk on the Waltners' dock. We talked and held hands. I remember kissing her good night. But it was just a friendly kiss." He sat in silence staring at the wall behind Lark, remembering. "You know how it is when you like someone. I thought about her all the time, arranged ways to see her on campus and asked her out again." He glanced at Lark, blushing.

"I've been there," Lark said, smiling.

"We went to dinner and a movie, a chick flick." He gave Lark an embarrassed, lopsided grin. "I had a great time. The movie was a tear-jerker and she was leaning against me, crying. I had my arm around her, comforting her, you know the drill. I drove her back to the dorm. We sat in the car and held hands and talked. We kissed twice, little pecks. I asked her what was wrong and she said she just didn't know me well enough to get too friendly, and that she was very busy in school and didn't have time for a relationship. I asked her if she was giving me the brush-off. She acted surprised. She hugged me and told me that the timing just wasn't right. She said if we didn't meet anyone else that we might get together again later, but that she didn't want me to think she didn't like me because she did. She gave me a kiss, one with a little more soul, and told me she had to go. That was the last time I saw her other than to talk to for a few minutes on campus. It was about a month before she disappeared in Eau Claire."

"What makes you think she disappeared in Eau Claire?"

"Because that's where they found her car. I heard she gassed up there and was never seen again. Isn't that what happened?" Jim asked, glancing over at Lark.

"No, someone beat her to death and threw her body in the Ransons' marsh."

Jim sat forward, his eye big as saucers. "You mean that skeleton we found was Gemma?"

"Yes," Lark said, hating what he was doing to the kid.

"Oh my God, oh my God," he said, burying his head in his hands to hide his tears. "I remember that weekend. My parents were short at the restaurant so I helped out. I had no idea she was here." He stared at Lark, his face a mask of sadness, his eyes overflowing. "Do you think I had something to do with this? Is that why you brought me in here?"

"I need to know anything you can remember about Gemma's disappearance. You've been involved in this investigation from the start."

Jim wiped his eyes with a white handkerchief he pulled out of his pocket. Lark wondered how many men in their twenties carried handkerchiefs.

"I can't think of anything other than what I just told you. I only saw her a couple of times on campus before she disappeared. The campus police questioned all of us who knew Gemma, including me. The investigation was centered around Eau Claire because that's where her car was found. As I said, I was up here that weekend helping my parents." Jim stuffed his handkerchief in his back pocket. "I've got to get back to work, Chief. Check with Sandi Waltner and Katey Lowery. They knew her better than anyone else." He pulled himself up out of the chair and headed for the door.

"Jim," Lark said, raising his hand to stop him before he got away.

"Are you're going to tell me you don't want me to have anything to do with this case?"

"Let's sleep on that. We'll figure it out with Joel and Lacey tomorrow."

Lark jotted notes from his interview with Jim and called Joel to find out if they'd been able to locate the Pattersons. Joel told him the Wayzata police were still trying to track them down.

"How's Thanksgiving?" Lark asked, marveling at the racket he heard in the background.

"Thanksgiving sucks. Robbie has chicken pox and Joey has the flu and all its side effects. My mother-in-law is driving us berserk. Thank God she leaves tomorrow. It's so ugly here that Molly almost has me talked into getting my nuts cut."

Lark couldn't help himself, he started laughing. "Grenfurth, I know you're secretly loving every minute of your holiday."

"I don't think so. But you're so sappy about this that you must have your eye on someone to settle down with. The lovely Lacey must have gotten to you. Molly and I had been thinking of introducing you two to each other."

"She's way too young for me. Besides, she's not my type," Lark quipped, just as Lacey walked in the door.

"I'll be up tomorrow. I want to get my mother-in-law on the road before I leave. I'd hate to have to investigate my wife on a homicide charge even though every jury in the country would judge it a mercy killing. Then we can talk about fatherhood since you think it sounds like so much fun. Gotta go." Joel hung up.

Lacey stood in the doorway, hands on her hips. "Was that Joel?"

"Yep," Lark said, wondering what she'd overheard. "He'll be back up tomorrow. Two of the kids are sick, he's having murder fantasies about his mother-in-law, and Molly wants him to have a vasectomy."

Lacey sat down in the chair in front of his desk and crossed her legs, swinging one back and forth.

Lark focused on cleaning off his desk.

"So, how'd the interview with Jim go?" she asked, wrapping her hands around her knee, which she continued to swing.

"It was tough. He really liked Gemma but she let him down easy."

"Poor kid," she said, shaking her head. "He looked upset when he left. Jesus, aren't you starving?" she asked, grabbing her abdomen as they both listened to her stomach growl.

"Obviously, you are," he said, laughing. He looked at his watch. "Holy shit, it's five-thirty. Where does the time go?"

No one stopped them on the way out. The snow was on hiatus so they were able to get to the Ransons' by quarter till six. The dogs announced their arrival before they rang the doorbell.

Ann opened the door. Her face was puffy, but for the first time that day, she had color in her face and her eyes were bright. "John's in the kitchen wrestling with the last-minute details." She raised her voice. "He refused my help but he might accept yours."

"Bite me," John yelled. "Everything's under control. Go get dressed."

"He's just a little cranky," Ann said as she headed upstairs.

Lark and Lacey wandered into the dining room. John had turned on the deck lights as well as the lights along the walk down to the lake. The snow sparkled and glowed against the lights.

Lacey was pressed into service lighting the candles on the table and the buffet, with an admonishment not to light any of the turkey candles because "Ann will kill me if any of her precious turkey collection is damaged." Lark was put in charge of opening the wine.

Ann came down just as everything was ready. John and Lark got the turkey out of the oven and onto a platter. Ann and Lacey made gravy out of the drippings. Lacey stirred while Ann gave directions and asked about the latest on the two bodies. They got the mashed potatoes, John's stuffing, and vegetables onto the buffet. Then it was every man for himself.

The meal was a relaxing time after three stressful days. They tried not to talk about bodies or murder. To make the evening almost perfect, the nursing supervisor at the hospital sent a nurse out to give Ann's IV antibiotic.

By nine-thirty everyone had switched to beer. Ann had taken a couple more pain pills and settled in to try and figure out the football game, which had everyone else on the edge of their seats. She fell asleep against John's shoulder with Sheba curled up in her lap and Duke squeezed into the sofa beside her. She awakened briefly about eleven when Lacey and Lark left.

"What a great meal," Lacey said, staring up at a midnight-blue sky full of stars and deeply inhaling the cold crisp air.

Lark walked silently beside her.

"No snow. What a great evening," she said, glancing at him.

He smiled.

"Say something, dammit."

"It was very enjoyable," he replied, juggling the bags of leftovers John had given them. "I think you've had just a little too much to drink." The group had polished off two bottles of wine with dinner and dessert.

"You're right." She tried to control her smile. "I haven't had this much alcohol in years. It feels kind of good, kind of liberating, kind of like Christmas." She trotted ahead of him.

"Be careful," he called out.

Suddenly, she fell back in the snow. He ran to help her, trying to hold onto their leftovers, and found her laughing and making a snow angel. She stepped out of the angel and began brushing the snow from her coat.

"You scared the shit out of me when you fell down like that," he said, watching her shake the snow out of the hood of her coat.

"Obviously," she giggled, "you haven't had enough to drink, and I haven't made a snow angel in, um"—she thought for a moment, sucking in a corner of her lower lip—"twenty-five years. You oughta try it. It might loosen you up." She headed for the Jeep before he could speak.

Lacey hopped up in the seat and Lark gave her their packages. "This smells divine," she said, burying her nose in the bag. "I need to have some more dressing when we get home."

Lark groaned. "If I eat another thing my stomach will explode."

"Suit yourself. You probably can't handle the calories at this point in your life." She slammed her door shut.

He brushed snow off the windshield and tried to figure out what was going on. It hit him like a brick. She'd made two cracks about age. He realized she must have heard some of his conversation with Joel, probably the part about her being too young for him. If she'd heard that, she'd also heard the part about her not being his type. He groaned and decided to kill Grenfurth when he saw him. He took a deep breath, squared his shoulders, and got in the Jeep.

"Everything OK? I thought maybe something happened, as long as it took you out there."

"Everything's fine," he said, starting the car.

"You know, I just can't get over how beautiful it is tonight. Maybe it's just the reprieve from the snow or"—she giggled—"maybe it's the wine."

"Probably a little of both," he said, not wanting to rock the boat.

He turned on the radio, hoping it would preclude conversation. They listened to a medley of Motown songs and drove home in companionable silence.

Lacey plopped the food down on the bench in the laundry room while she hung up her coat and took off her boots. Then she ferried the packages into the kitchen.

"I'm going upstairs and change clothes, sixteen hours is enough in these jeans," she said, running upstairs as he walked in the kitchen.

Lark started to put the food away but the smell of the turkey changed his mind. He decided to change clothes, then have a snack. He threw on sweats and beat Lacey downstairs. He was dishing up plates of turkey and stuffing when she trotted onto the landing in emerald green sweats. Her red hair haloed out around her head as it caught the light from the chandelier. She came into the kitchen and hoisted herself up on the counter.

"I know it's not scientifically possible, but I'm starved." She flashed a radiant smile. "I think I'll have a beer if you've got any."

He stopped dead in his tracks, blown away by her beauty. She stared at him, waiting for an answer. He told her to help herself and turned away to get their plates ready.

She jumped down off the counter. "Would it be too much trouble to have a fire? It was great last night," she said, handing him a beer as she wandered past him into the family room.

"Sure, you finish the food and I'll get one started." He went out on the deck to get wood.

She watched him stand under the roof overhang, trying not to get his socks wet as he pulled wood from the covered storage bin. When he came back in the house, he brought a gust of bitter cold wind and snowflakes with him.

"Jesus, it's cold out there. Would you believe it's snowing again?"

"You're shitting me," she said, walking over to cup her face against the glass.

"This'll help," he said, turning on the deck lights. Lacey looked out beyond his deck just in time to see three deer, stopped in their tracks, mesmerized by the spotlights.

"Lark, get over here," she yelled, causing the deer to run like hell.

The tension in her voice caused him to drop the wood carrier.

"Shit," she yelled as she lost sight of the deer.

"What? What the hell is it?" he shouted, sliding up beside her on the hardwood floor.

"You missed them, they ran off," she said, staring out the door.

He flipped off the indoor and outdoor lights and wrapped his arms around her, pulling her away from the glass. "Who was out there?"

"Deer," she said, pushing out of his arms and going back to look out the glass. "You missed them. There were three of them, two doe and a buck with a huge rack. Oh, look at your floor," she said, seeing the firewood strewn all over. She knelt down and began picking up wood.

"This was all about deer?" he bellowed, staring down at her, his arms crossed. "You scared the shit out of me, I thought someone was out there." He stomped over and began tossing wood on top of the carrier lying open on the floor. She stooped down to help. "I'll get this," he snapped. He looked over at her, his eyes flashing, and motioned her back to the kitchen.

"Fine," she said, storming into the kitchen. "Asshole," she added under her breath, glad she'd overheard him tell Joel she wasn't her type. Funny, she was beginning to think he was just her type until she'd heard that. *Screw it*, she told herself. *Attractions come, attractions go.* Now she just wanted to get through this assignment and move on. She slammed their plates into the microwave.

She went to the doorway to ask him to let her know when the fire was set, but instead watched him kneeling down, intent on getting the fire going. He stood up and turned around, blowing out a long fireplace match. Behind him, she saw small wisps of fire licking up around the pile of logs. Lark saw her and started to say something, but she turned around and walked back into the kitchen, hitting the start button on the microwave with just a little more vigor than necessary. When she turned around he was leaning up against the bar, a sheepish grin on his face.

"I'm sorry I yelled at you like that," he said, trying to catch her eye.

"Forget it." She walked past him into the family room with their silverware. "No need to apologize. I overdid it when I saw the deer. They caught me off guard." She walked back into the kitchen. "Care if we eat on the coffee table?"

"Not at all," he said, unsure of her mood.

"Why don't you get the news tapes and we can watch them while we eat."

Lark came downstairs just as she carried two aromatic plates of turkey and dressing into the family room. They ate with minimal conversation as they fast-forwarded through the news. Lark got up once to get them each another beer and exchange news tapes. Both stations reported that one of the bodies had been identified but the name was being withheld pending family notification. Lark turned off the VCR and the beginning credits for *Holiday Inn* rolled onto the screen.

"Oh my God, I haven't seen *Holiday Inn* in ages," Lacey said. "It's one of my favorites."

"Mine, too," Lark said, smiling at her.

She snatched up her dishes. "I'll do these quick and go to bed and watch it."

Lark took her hand as she leaned forward to pick up his plate. "Why don't you stay down here? This isn't a movie to watch alone and I'd like your company."

She looked into his eyes, not saying a word.

"Look, I'm sorry I yelled at you. You scared the shit out of me. I thought someone was out there and I overreacted."

"I accept your apology. Let's get this stuff in the kitchen while there's a commercial on. I don't want to miss any of the movie."

They hurried into the kitchen. Lark rinsed and Lacey loaded the dishwasher. He grabbed a bottle of wine and a couple of glasses. She snagged the corkscrew and they hurried back into the family room just in time for the opening scene.

He sat down beside her. He poured their wine and stretched his arm over the back of the sofa behind her as they settled in to watch the movie. Thirty minutes later they were holding hands and leaning sleepily against each other.

Lark woke to that buzzing sound the television makes when all the programming is over. He needed a few seconds to grasp that it was his bladder, not the television, that had awakened him. It took him a while longer to realize that he and Lacey were twined around each other like pretzels. He tried to disengage himself but she hugged him closer. Freeing his left hand, he checked his watch, discovering that it was 3 A.M. Groaning, he told himself he was too old for this. He shook Lacey's shoulder, murmuring that it was time to go to bed.

"God, I'm beat," she mumbled, snuggling into him.

"Lacey, let's go upstairs," he said, shaking her a little harder.

She fluttered her eyes open and kissed him long and hard. "That was nice," she said dreamily, struggling up from the sofa.

He turned out the light on the end table and stood up. A little woozy himself, he put his arm out to steady her. Before he knew it, he'd pulled her into his arms for another passionate kiss.

"Wow," she said, leaning against him. "I can't imagine how much better you'd be at this if I was your type or the right age."

"What?" he squawked, not believing his ears.

"You heard me," Lacey said, pushing away from him.

"Shit, I had a feeling you overheard me," he said as she slipped out of his arms. "Listen, let me—"

Lacey held up her hand. "No explanation needed or for that matter, wanted." She stepped away. "I'll just take my thirty-six-year-old body upstairs for a little beauty rest. I've got to be prepared when someone more my age comes along."

Lark grabbed her upper arms. "Let me explain."

A thunderous blast went off, blowing out the French doors in the dining area. Glass fell like rain all around them. They dropped to the floor as a second gunshot went off, shattering the television.

"What the fuck," Lark bellowed, pulling Lacey against him.

"Where's your gun?" she whispered.

"Hall closet, same as yours." He crawled away from her as a third gun blast went off, ripping through another section of glass and showering the fireplace wall with pellets. A few seconds later, they heard the roar of a snowmobile.

Lark jumped to his feet and ran into the kitchen to look out the window. "He's going like a bat out of hell towards the road," he yelled as he dialed the station.

Lark fired off a barrage of instructions to the dispatcher. Jim and Paul, doing an overtime night shift, showed up twelve minutes after they received the call. They didn't run into a single vehicle or snowmobile on their way over. Lark was already outside inspecting the area behind the deck where he suspected the shooter had been.

Like the shooting at the Ransons', they found a snowmobile trail leading out of the woods. The area where the shooter had been standing was trampled down with boot prints. They found cigarette butts but no shell casings.

Jim and Paul followed the snowmobile trail and Lark went back inside. Lacey, dressed in her winter coat and boots, was taking pictures while the other night crew collected evidence.

"Did you find anything?" she asked, finishing the evidence photos.

"Same as the Ransons'," he said.

"I called your dispatcher and asked her to get someone to board up this glass," Lacey said as Lark picked a pottery shard out of the rubble. He told the officer sweeping up that he'd bag the debris. Mary Lou called, telling them that none of their usual glass repair contractors were available.

"Damn it," Lark yelled, grabbing the receiver from Lacey and banging his fist on the counter so hard the telephone jumped. "We sure as shit can't stay here with this mess."

"Maybe we can build a fire and dig in until morning," Lacey said.

"Yeah, right."

Before she could respond, Lark jabbed the speaker button. Mary Lou's voice stammered out into the room. "Sheriff Swenson, I don't know what else to do. I could try to find you a couple of motel rooms or you could always go over to my house—"

"Mary Lou," he interrupted, "give me the Ransons' number." He leaned against the counter, rigid with anger as he scribbled it on a notepad.

"Do you want me to call Mr. Ranson, sir?" Mary Lou asked.

"No, thank you, I'll do it myself." Lark hung up and dialed the Ransons'. He put the phone on speaker while it rang. John sleepily answered on the sixth ring.

"John, this is Sheriff Swenson, I need your help," Lark said, his tone professional.

"Damn, what time is it?" John asked. "What's wrong?"

"Almost three-thirty. Do you have any plywood left from boarding up your windows?

"Yeah, what happened?"

"Someone just shot the glass out of my family room. We can't seem to raise the people we usually use for this sort of thing."

"Jesus Christ, was anyone hurt? Did you get the guy?"

"Got away and no one was hurt."

"I'll be there as soon as I get dressed. Give me directions to your house."

It was 5 A.M. by the time the windows were boarded up.

"Do you think whoever did this also took a shot at Ann?" John asked as he packed up his tools.

"This is too much of a coincidence to be accidental," Lark replied.

"Then someone shot at Ann deliberately?"

"It looks that way." Lark watched anger flood John's face. "It wouldn't be a bad idea for you to stay around the house as much as possible until this is wrapped up."

"I'll take care of her," John said as he left.

The deputies left right after John. Lark called Mary Lou and let her know he'd be in by eleven, but to call him if they needed him sooner. He asked her to have one of the patrols check the Ransons' house at least every hour. The adrenaline surge he and Lacey had been running on was gone; they were both exhausted. The house was so cold you could see every breath despite the furnace running full blast.

"There's a fireplace in my bedroom. That room will hold the heat better than this cave," Lark said, lugging a load of firewood. "You're welcome to sleep there."

"Good idea," Lacey said, rubbing her hands up and down the arms of her coat. "I feel like I could sleep standing up. Besides, I take great comfort in knowing that I'm not your type."

"Fine," Lark said, plodding up the stairs. "All I want to do is sleep and keep warm. We can argue about types and age differences later."

He got the fire going and Lacey retrieved a couple of extra blankets out of the linen closet. They climbed into Lark's bed and were asleep as soon as their heads hit the pillow.

When the phone rang at 8 A.M. Lark was sleeping so soundly he didn't hear it. After four rings, Lacey crawled across him and grabbed it.

"Yeah," she said as she rolled back to her side of the bed.

"Uh, is this the Swenson residence?" asked a male voice.

"Yeah," she said, still half asleep.

"Lacey?"

"Yeah."

"What the hell is going on? You sound like you're nursing the worst hangover in history," boomed Grenfurth.

"Jesus, is that you, Joel?" she asked, gaining a bit more consciousness.

"No, Smith, it's the good fucking fairy. I repeat, what the hell is going on up there? The dispatcher said you and Lark had some kind of accident and wouldn't be in until eleven."

"Someone shot the glass out of the back of Lark's house last night. We didn't get to bed until after five." She stifled a yawn.

"Are you OK?"

"No problems a week of sleep wouldn't cure."

"Is that Grenfurth?" Lark mumbled. "If it is, tell him he'd better get off the damn phone unless he's called to tell us this fucking case is solved."

"Is that Swenson?" Joel asked.

"Here, talk to each other," she said, dropping the phone on Lark's chest as she got up.

"If you were here I'd put a stake through your heart," Lark said after he found the phone. He realized Lacey had left when he heard the door close just a bit louder than necessary.

"Wow, I can't hardly believe it. You two are already sleeping together. You're back to your old self. Molly and I knew you two would be perfect for each other."

"Shut up, Joel, it's not what you think. We slept in my bedroom in front of the fire so we could keep warm. We've both got on two layers of sweats. This was survival, not romance."

"Yeah, uh-huh, survival. That's gotta be the best line I've ever heard, even from you."

"What the hell did you call for? I've had less than three hours of sleep and my fuse is very short."

"I think we may have a line on Yellow Mitten."

"You're shitting me," Lark said, lurching up in bed.

"I'm serious as a heart attack. Get some coffee, and call me back at the office." Joel hung up.

Lark staggered out of bed just as the shower in the next room started running. He felt like he was ninety. He lumbered downstairs to make coffee only to find it already made.

He wandered through the first floor surveying the damage. His television looked like Elvis had taken a shot at it. Glass had been swept into three large piles on his floor. He went to salvage the pottery pieces from the rubble and found that someone had already placed them on a dish-towel on the dining-room table. Miraculously, the rest of the furniture was intact, with the exception of some gouges in the dining-room table. He was laying out the pottery pieces to see if it was worth having the bowl repaired when he heard the shower stop. He rushed upstairs to take his turn.

When he came downstairs Lacey was sitting at the bar drinking coffee. She had her coat on over top of her jeans and a sweatshirt.

"What did Joel want?" she asked, sipping her coffee.

"He has a line on Yellow Mitten. We're supposed to call him at the office."

Lacey hit the speaker button and dialed Joel.

"A Mrs. Foltz from Superior called the Madison campus police last night and asked them to check the dorm for her daughter, Terry. She was expected home on Monday but never made it. Campus police called us this morning. Terry Foltz fits the description of Yellow Mitten."

"Why did her mom wait so long to call and report her missing?" Lacey asked.

"Don't know. Mrs. Foltz is on her way down to take a look at Yellow Mitten. She's sure it isn't her daughter because she doesn't know why she would have come to Big Oak. She wants to see the body to put her fears to rest."

"Did Madison have a photo of Terry Foltz?" Lacey asked, jotting notes.

"Yep, they faxed it up just before you called. It's her, no question."

"Shit. How long ago did she leave?" Lark asked.

"Who?" Joel asked.

"Mrs. Foltz, dammit. How long ago did Mrs. Foltz leave for Wausau?"

"My, my, if you get any crankier we'll have to send you to charm school one-oh-one."

"Up yours, Grenfurth," Lark said, pausing to sip his coffee.

"They'll be here at noon. She had to stop and get her husband."

"We'll meet you there," Lark said. "Can you fax us what you got from Madison so we can read it on the way?"

"Sure thing."

After Joel hung up, Lacey went upstairs to change, and Lark called his insurance adjuster. He called Park Falls Furniture Mart and they agreed to deliver a new television if he came in by noon and picked it out.

Lark called the station and got George Knutson, who was working after having most of the week off for Thanksgiving. Lark asked him to have the notes and photos on the shootings at both his house and the Ransons' ready to pick up in half an hour. He also asked George to start files on David Banski, Michael Waltner, Sandi Waltner, Katey Lowery, Shelley Marten, Jim Kryjack, and Ron Chevsky. George had been with the sheriff's department for twenty-five years and, like Flo, knew everyone. He would have thorough information on each of the students when they got back from Wausau.

By the time he was done with his phone calls, Lacey was dressed. They left the house just after nine. Although they brought a thermos with them, Lacey insisted that they stop at the Big Oak Diner for pastries before they picked up the case file and the information on the shootings. After stopping in Park Falls to pick out a television, they headed for Wausau.

Usually, the trip from Big Oak to Wausau was a relaxing two-hour drive through some of Wisconsin's most beautiful countryside. Today the rolling hills were covered with snow. The radio informed them that parts of northern Wisconsin had received a record forty inches in the last ten days. They dodged huge snowplows, out in force to clear the snow and ice-covered roads. Despite the weather, the roads were littered with trucks and cars parked on the berm, and blaze orange suits dotted the fields.

They were fifteen miles out of Park Falls when five deer ran across the road. Ten miles later, Lark slammed on the brakes as four hunters ran across the road in front of them. One skidded and fell. In his effort to break his fall, he dropped his rifle, which came whirling down the highway towards their Jeep. Thankfully, the gun didn't discharge. The hunter sheepishly waved to them after he retrieved it.

"Jesus, there's living proof that God does take care of drunks and fools, or maybe that's drunken fools," Lacey said as they drove slowly by the group.

"Everyone's trying to get their deer before the end of the season."

"Up here it's always open season on deer. There were hundreds of poaching arrests last year in Wisconsin, and that's a mere fraction of what goes on. The only difference between deer hunting now and next week is that it's legal now."

"My, my, aren't we in a great mood," Lark commented, smiling over at her.

"Jeez, sorry about that. I normally do much better on three hours of sleep."

"Take a nap. We'll go over the case notes on the way back."

Lacey turned on the radio and settled in to doze with her head up again the car door.

When the alarm went off, Ann rolled over to hit the snooze button. She yelped in pain the minute her left shoulder hit the mattress. After getting herself into a more comfortable position, she glanced at the clock and groaned when she saw it was only 7:30. She felt as if she hadn't slept a wink. She rolled out of bed, pain shooting up her left arm and shoulder. Without bothering to put on a robe, she headed into the master bathroom only to remember that they were sleeping in a spare bedroom until the windows were replaced.

If she hadn't felt so bad she would have had a good cry. She didn't need a degree in rocket science to realize that she had to get her pain under control before she did anything else. She went downstairs to get her pain pills.

John had left a note on the island telling her to call him when she was ready to go in for her antibiotic. Knowing that he had gone from one construction job to three in less than twenty-four hours, Ann made a mental note to let him know she'd drive herself. She washed down one Tylenol with codeine with a glass of grape juice and fished a bagel out of the breadbox. She sat down at the kitchen table facing the sliding-glass door.

It wasn't snowing but it was dark and overcast. The thermometer said ten below. Water lapped up on the ice that had formed out to about ten feet from the lakeshore. The wind created small snow devils. Chickadees made perilous assaults on the bird feeders, snatching up sunflower seeds and speeding back into the bushes. Woodpeckers clung to the suet feeders as they swung in the wind, and half a dozen gray squirrels scampered around the bottom of the trees, picking up leftovers, fur puffed out to twice its normal size.

Ann had finished her breakfast and was thinking about getting dressed when the phone rang. It was Cathy Lowery calling to find out how she was.

"Are you guys home?" Ann asked.

"No, I flew up to Bessemer. I just wanted to check up on you."

"We're fine. Couldn't be safer with the cops everywhere."

"That's not what I hear."

"Tell me what's out there on the grapevine," Ann said, knowing that Cathy had the best network in Big Oak.

"I heard that you got shot and then refused to stay at the hospital."

Ann laughed. "I didn't get shot. A deer hunter shot through our bedroom window and I got some glass through my shoulder."

"I wish people would get it straight," Cathy said. "I also heard they've identified one of the bodies as Gemma Patterson. Katey's in shock. We can't imagine who would do such a thing to her. She was such a nice girl. Have they identified the other person yet?"

"Not that I know of, but then I didn't know they had officially identified the first body."

"Myra told me she heard about it when she came over to visit you yesterday. She said they questioned David about her."

"Cathy." Ann sighed. "They were questioning him because Gemma's missing, not because the body has been officially identified."

"Well, they must be pretty sure or they wouldn't have mentioned her."

"You couldn't prove it by me." Ann knew that every word she said would be all over Big Oak at the speed the rural long-distance lines would allow.

"How did Katey know her?" Ann asked.

"They were college friends."

"Well, if it's her, the sheriff will probably want to talk with all of you. If I see him, I'll tell him where he can find you."

They talked a few more minutes about the usual stuff: the weather, the holiday, the progress of her father's competency exam, the dastardly deer hunters, including Cathy's own husband and sons. By the time Ann got off the phone, her pain was starting to ease up.

She headed upstairs to get dressed and got to the top of the stairs just as the phone rang. She made it into the ice-cold master bedroom just as the answering machine picked up.

"Ann, pick up," John yelled overtop of the loud racket from a nail gun.

"I'll call you back from downstairs. I'm in our bedroom freezing my ass off."

"Just tell me what time you want to go to the ER."

"I can drive myself."

"Bullshit, you shouldn't be driving on these roads, full of codeine."

Ann pictured roads full of codeine and started laughing. She was fascinated by the little puffs of fog her breath made. At that point, she knew she wasn't in any shape to drive. They agreed that John would pick her up in an hour. She gathered up her clothes and headed for the bathroom.

She was doing her hair when the phone rang; Sara Waltner was leaving a message by the time she picked up.

"Sara, sorry about that. I just couldn't get to the phone in time."

"I'm surprised you can get to it at all. We just got back this morning and heard what's been going on. Is there anything I can do for you? I was going to bring over some food, but Myra tells me she has that covered."

"No, we're fine. How was your Thanksgiving?" Ann asked, trying to change the subject.

"We went to Wausau to see my family. A nice restful holiday until we saw the news. We came home this morning to hear that both you and the sheriff have been shot at."

"How'd you hear about that?"

"Steve called me. He heard about the sheriff needing new sliding-glass doors at the hardware store. He said the sheriff and the woman he's living with were nearly killed last night. He also said the sheriff has set up a command post at your house."

"They haven't set up a command post here, and Sheriff Swenson and Detective Smith aren't living together. She's a Wisconsin State police officer."

"Rumor has it that one of the bodies might be a girl named Gemma Patterson, a student that went to school with Katey and Sandi?" Sara asked.

"Where did you hear that?" Ann asked.

"Myra and Cathy called and told me. Did you hear that, too?"

"As far as I know the police haven't officially identified either of the bodies."

"Listen, I'm going to run some errands—grocery shop, dry cleaners, that sort of thing. Is there anything you need?"

"Not a thing."

"Call me if you do. We'll be home all weekend."

Sara hung up just as Ann realized she had forgotten to ask her when she wanted to pick up Steve's Flow Blue. She tried to call her back but the line was busy. Ann heard the front door open and close.

"Jeez, you're not ready yet?" John glanced up at her and then down at his watch. "Are you having trouble?"

"Just with the phone," Ann said, hugging him with her good arm before heading into the bathroom.

"Lark's windows and doors will be in this afternoon. They were able to get them on today's supply truck. I thought I'd try to get them in today," John said, following her into the bathroom. "If I don't get them in they're going to have to stay with us."

Once Ann was dressed, they headed for Mason County Memorial. It took about an hour for Ann to get her antibiotic and wound check. They were delayed from leaving when the Marshfield helicopter landed to pick up a man who had gotten drunk and fallen into his campfire. He had second- and third-degree burns over thirty percent of his body. Since his friends were also inebriated, it took them quite a while to fish him out of the fire.

They got home at eleven. Ann's shoulder was starting to ache, so she took two pain pills and lay down on the sofa. She slept soundly until the dogs awakened her. Although they stopped their tug of war when she yelled at them, Buck picked up what they'd been fighting over and brought it to her, his head down in submission. Visions of another body part flashed through Ann's head when she saw the fingers of a glove dangling from his mouth. Ignoring her pain, she ordered him to release and he dropped his prize into her hand.

It was part of an empty gray cashmere-and-fur glove. She picked up as many pieces as she could find but didn't see a label. It wasn't hers so she assumed it belonged to a visitor. She thought about their recent guests as she went into the kitchen to take a couple more pain pills. She washed them down with soda and noticed the pink-purple tones of sunset low in the west. The kitchen clock said it was 4:15. She was shocked to have slept the day away.

She got a piece of turkey from the refrigerator and sat down at the kitchen table to write down the names of everyone she could remember who had been in the house during the last week: Lark, Lacey, Paul Dolphson, Betty Chevsky, Jim Kryjack, Joel Grenfurth, Sara Waltner, and Myra and David Banski. She decided to ask Lacey if she'd lost a glove. She and Lark had been around the most.

The telephone stopped her musings. It was John letting her know he'd be working until at least eight that evening installing Lark's doors. Ann assured him she was fine and that nine would be a great time to take her to the ER.

As her pain wore off, she became fidgety. She tried knitting, needlepoint, and reading, but they didn't calm her restlessness so she decided to drive over to Lark's. She made enough turkey sandwiches for John and his crew, and slid wedges of pumpkin pie into some Tupperware. She threw a tub of Cool Whip into her care package along with a six-pack of Lienenkugels. The dogs were sound asleep, so she left them in the house.

It was dark as midnight even though it was only 5:45. When she backed out of the garage, she was shocked to see how hard it was snowing. She shut the garage door and put the Explorer in four-wheel drive.

Lacey roused once when Lark's cell phone rang but otherwise slept all the way to Wausau. The next thing she knew Lark was shaking her shoulder. They were in the parking lot of the Wausau state police office.

"Man, I really feel like I've been hit with a brick," she said, rubbing her eyes.

"A little caffeine will help," Lark said as he got out of the car. When she didn't follow, he walked around and opened her door. She sighed and slid out, her boots crunching on the ice-covered parking lot. Lacey led the way to the office she and Joel shared.

"Hell, I don't know who looks worse, the two of you or me," Joel boomed.

"Any word on the Pattersons yet?" Lark asked.

"No, they've gone out of town for Thanksgiving. Their marina is closed. The Wayzata police haven't been able to locate anyone who knows where they went."

"How are your kids?" Lacey asked, heading for the coffeepot.

"Scratching and puking, with a little diarrhea thrown in for good measure. Think twice before having your own."

"No worry there. The battery in my biological clock will have run down long before I find someone my type." She headed for the door without looking at either of them. "Call me when the Foltzes get here. I'll be going over the case notes in the work room."

"Holy shit. I guess she heard you yesterday," Joel said, once Lacey was gone.

"I always knew you were a rocket scientist," Lark said. "I told you she was too young for me. She's thirty-six and I'm forty-two."

"That's nothing. I'm five years older than Molly."

"Get off it Joel. It isn't going to happen. She's nice and she's very attractive, but I'm not interested in dating anyone right now."

"So, what happened at your place last night?" Joel asked, changing the subject.

Lark had just enough time to fill Joel in on the shooting before Mr. and Mrs. Foltz arrived.

Lark escorted them to an interview room while Joel went to get Lacey. Mrs. Foltz, a slim, attractive, gray blond of that indeterminate age between 45 and 60 had on a navy blue dress and matching jacket. A navy leather bag hung over her shoulder. The dark red coat slung over her arm was the only sign that she wasn't dressed for a funeral. The only hint that she was nervous was the death grip she had on a pair of navy leather gloves.

Mr. Foltz stood next to his wife, an intense look of concern on his face. He wore a navy plaid sweater and navy chinos. He towered over his wife by at least a foot. His light brown hair was peppered with gray and ruffled out of place as if he had been running his fingers through it. Even stressed, they made a handsome couple.

After introductions, Joel ushered everyone into chairs and left. Mrs. Foltz dropped her purse on the floor and carefully laid her gloves down on the table. She focused her attention on smoothing the wrinkles out of them. Mr. Foltz watched his wife but made no move to stop her.

When Joel returned with a manila envelope under his arm, Mrs. Foltz bolted up. "I don't understand why we're wasting our time in here. I want to see the body so we don't have to worry anymore."

"Before we do that, I'd like to get some information from you. It'll just take a few minutes." Joel pulled his chair between the Foltzes and sat down.

"No," Mrs. Foltz said, biting her lower lip and staring down at the floor.

"Please sit down for a few minutes," Joel said, glancing over at her husband, who looked away.

She sat back down, wiping the corner of her eyes with her fingertips. Lacey reached across the table, pulled a tissue out of the box, and quietly blew her nose. Mrs. Foltz watched her for second and then also reached for one. She proceeded to fold it into a fan shape.

"Mrs. Foltz, may I call you Marian?" Joel asked, trying to make eye contact.

"Of course," she said with a hint of defiance.

"Good. Can you tell me about the last time you heard from Terry?"

She sighed, her shoulders slumping, as she continued to focus her attention on folding and unfolding the tissue. "She called me last Saturday morning." She slammed her hand down on the table, crushing the tissue. "I just want to see the body. Once we know it isn't Terry, this conversation won't be necessary."

Mr. Foltz placed his hand on her arm. "Marian, let's hear the officers out." Silently, she began smoothing out the crushed tissue.

"What did you talk about?" Joel asked.

"The usual stuff college kids and parents talk about. When she'd be getting in, how her car was running, and how low on money she was."

"When was she supposed to get into Superior?"

"Monday or Tuesday evening," she said, resuming her origami exercise with the tissue.

"Did you discuss anything else, maybe have words?" Joel asked, trying to make eye contact with her.

"Yes," she said, almost inaudibly, shredding the tissue. Large tears began to leak out of the corners of her eyes. Mr. Foltz reached across the table to take her hand. She clutched his hand with both of hers, the tissue trapped between them.

"You had a disagreement?" Joel asked, prompting her.

"Not an argument," she blurted out, looking down at the table as tears spilled onto the Foltzes' clasped hands.

"Tell me a little more about it." Joel scooted his chair out from between them so Mr. Foltz could move closer to his wife. She fell into his arms.

"Could we have few minutes alone, please?" Mr. Foltz asked.

"No, Roger, I want to do this now. I might not be able to later." She swiped at the tears flowing down her cheeks. Roger settled his head on top of hers and held her.

"We argued over her wanting to take a few days out of her vacation to stop at a friend's house. I wanted her to come right home because we were having company."

"What friend?" Joel asked, mesmerized as tears streamed down Roger's face and seeped into Marian's hair.

"She didn't say. She was very angry and told me it was none of my business. I left to run errands right after her call. When I got home she had left a snippy message on the answering machine saying she'd call me later and might come home Monday evening."

"Our daughter had my temper, quick to flare, quick to forgive," Roger explained. "Marian and Terry were always having these kind of dust-ups. They never meant a thing." If anyone noticed his use of the past tense, they chose not to show it.

"Do you still have the tape?" Lark asked.

"No, I erased it," Marian said, her voice ragged from trying not to sob.

"Any idea where this friend lived?" Lacey asked, thinking how she would feel if she had erased her daughter's last words.

"No, I'm sure she would have told me when she called back, if I'd been home." Mrs. Foltz sobbed clinging to her husband.

"Can I please see the body now?" Mr. Foltz asked, glancing at Joel and then turning his full attention back to his wife as she eased out of his arms.

"We usually do this with photos. I've brought some for you to look at."

Both parents leaned forward, radiating tension, as Joel pulled the grainy faxed picture of their daughter and another 8 × 10 black and white photo out of the envelope. The photo showed a ghostly pale girl with her eyes closed from the neck up. It was gruesomely obvious that the person in the picture was dead. Joel placed them both on the table in front of the Foltzes. Both parents gasped as if they were having cardiac arrest.

"Oh no. No, no, no," Mrs. Foltz screamed. She picked up the morgue photo, crushing it against her chest as she rocked in her chair. Mr. Foltz pulled her to him, sobbing. She slipped her arms around him, the crumbled photo wadded into his back.

"We'll leave you alone for a few minutes," Joel said as the police left the room.

"Now I truly know the meaning of heartbroken," Lacey murmured as they stood outside the room, watching the parents cry and hold each other.

"I take back every ugly word I've ever said about my kids," Joel said as he ran his hand under his eyes.

"What's next?" Lacey asked.

"We let them calm down and then see if we can get any additional information from them before they leave," Lark said, not taking his eyes off the Foltzes. "Has someone gone through her dorm room?"

"Already done. The university police faxed me an inventory and closed it off until we can go down and look at it," Joel replied.

"Can you go down to Madison tomorrow and take care of the dorm room? We also need to interview her roommate."

"Fine by me."

Lark watched the Foltzes get up from their chairs.

"Before you leave, we'd like to ask you a few more questions," Joel said as they joined them.

"We really need to get home," Mr. Foltz said.

Marian reached for a tissue. "What would you like to know?"

"When did you first report your daughter missing?" Lark asked.

"I called her dorm Monday evening, Tuesday, and Wednesday," she replied. "Her roommate told me the same thing each time, that she'd left for Thanksgiving break. I called the University police Wednesday morning."

"We'll need the names of everyone you can think of in central Wisconsin, particularly the Big Oak area, that your daughter might know. We also need the names of her friends." Lacey fished a notebook out of her purse.

The Foltzes sat down and began to rattle off names. Like many married couples, they talked over each other, remembrances tumbling forth once they got started. As Roger talked, his tears dried up, but Marian continued to cry, piling up a small mountain of tissues. After an hour, the detectives had nearly fifty names to check out, including Katey Lowery, who had been interviewed when Gemma Patterson disappeared.

The Foltzes knew the Lowerys because they also owned sawmills. Roger explained that Gus Lowery had tried to buy their mills about ten years ago, but the Foltzes had decided not to sell. Instead, the two families had become friends, discovering that they had a lot in common, including children about the same age. Terry and Katey had known each other as teenagers and had gotten together frequently in Madison. The Foltzes thought their son Brian might know some of Terry's friends. Mr. Foltz agreed to have Brian contact them as soon as he came back from hunting.

The Foltzes accepted Joel's suggestion that they wait to see Terry at the funeral home. They left the station at 2:30 and the detectives left right behind them for lunch. They drove to the 2510 Club for lunch.

"That interview made it clear to me," Lacey said, after the waitress took their orders for burgers and fries. "The killer has to be local. There are too many things that tie both of those girls to Big Oak."

"Makes sense to me," Joel replied. "They both spent time with families in Big Oak. They were killed in the same way and dumped in the same place, three years apart."

"It could still be someone who vacationed or hunted in the area rather than a resident," Lark said, stopping as the waitress brought their food. "It could be a coincidence that the two were visiting here. Maybe they were selected at random by someone who was up here every year." He bit into his cheeseburger and listened to their protests.

Joel and Lacey agreed that it was possible but highly unlikely. After lunch they dropped Joel back at headquarters before stopping by Lacey's house for some extra clothes. Lacey guided. Lark to her house. The roads had been well cleared and snow was heaped along the curbs.

"Wow, I thought we had snow removal problems," Lark said, stopping suddenly as a car pulled out in front of them from a blind spot created by a massive snow pile.

They turned into the driveway of a small, white Cape God. Three empty bird feeders hung in the snow-covered yard.

"Damn things steal all the bird food even with squirrel-proof feeders," she said, watching two large red squirrels run to the tall evergreens along the side of her yard. Lark offered to fill the feeders while Lacey packed.

The first thing he heard when he walked in the mudroom was a man's voice. He shed his boots and walked into the kitchen to see who was there, only to find Lacey listening to her answering machine.

"Asshole," she murmured, stabbing a button on the machine to bring up another message.

"Lacey, I've been trying to get you all week," said yet another male voice. "I thought we'd have Thanksgiving dinner together but you never returned my call. If you want to go skiing, call me." The guy didn't feel the need to leave his name or number, so Lark figured Lacey knew him pretty well.

Lacey picked up the phone and punched in a number, leaving a message. "Phil, this is Lacey. Sorry I missed your call. I'm out of town on a case. I'll call you when I get back."

"You want some privacy?" he asked as she hit the play button on the machine again.

"Nope. This'll just take a second. There are only two messages left."

Lark wandered into the living room. Despite his discomfort, he listened intently as another male voice came across the machine. He was pleased to hear that it was a guy from a repair shop telling her she could pick up her VCR. The last message was a florist telling her she had a bouquet that they hadn't been able to deliver. Lark found himself wondering who had sent her flowers. He assumed it was Phil. He moved closer to the kitchen to listen as Lacey placed a call to the florist. She gave them Molly Grenfurth's name and address as the place to deliver the bouquet. Then she called Molly, telling her to expect a delivery. They commiserated over the kids, but Lark didn't hear any explanation of who the flowers were from. He didn't like how much he wanted to know. When Lacey came into the living room, he was studying her bookcases.

"Sorry that took so long. I'll get my clothes packed and we can go. Help yourself to the refrigerator." She trotted upstairs.

Lark focused his attention on her living room. The carpet was off-white. Two sofas in a dark green-and-blue paisley print flanked a painted brick fireplace and wall-to-wall bookcases. The bookcases were stuffed with books and pictures. In several of the pictures he recognized a younger Lacey with an older couple he assumed to be her parents. He found himself smiling at another display of pictures of Lacey with Joel and Molly's kids.

The books were arranged haphazardly. There were several rows of biographies, popular fiction, and mysteries. She had a small section on adoption along with several travel guides. A copy of *Women in Love* by D. H. Lawrence caught his eye, jammed between *Lady Chatterley's Lover* and a paperback copy of the *The Virgin and the Gypsy*. They were crammed onto the same shelf with several cookbooks and nature guides.

"Do you like to read?" Lacey asked.

"Jesus Christ, I didn't hear you come downstairs," Lark said, whirling around and bumping into her. He grabbed her arm to steady her.

"I flew in on my broom but you didn't seem to notice." She smiled up into his red face. "You were studying my meager book collection."

"Meager, my ass," he said. "You and Ann Ranson should pool your collections. Together you have more books than most libraries."

"See any titles you want to borrow? Topics you might want to brush up on?" she asked, her face innocent, her eyes twinkling.

"As a matter of fact I did." A smile played over his lips as he pulled a book off the shelf. "I don't have a copy of *Tracking Wildlife in Northern Wisconsin*. Mind if I borrow this?"

"Help yourself," she said, holding back laughter.

He grabbed her suitcase and they were out the door. They spent most of the ride with Lacey reading through the reports. "This is what we have so far," she said, once again curled up in the passenger seat. File papers were spread out between them and tucked under the edges of her coat. "Someone riding a snowmobile left several Marlboro cigarette butts and size-twelve boot tracks—we don't yet know the brand but the tracks look the same—outside your house as well as the Ransons'. I think it's a man, don't you?" she asked, looking at Lark for a comment.

"The shoe size seems to imply that, and these murders seem to be pretty vicious for a woman," he said, keeping his eyes on the road. It had started to snow just after they got out of Wausau and it was now coming down in blinding sheets that seemed to blow straight into the windshield.

"This weather is worse than what I expect to see in February, let alone November," Lacey said, trying to see out the window.

"You can say that again. I hope we get back to Big Oak tonight so we can get a good night's sleep."

"Why don't you let me drive?" Lacey asked, noticing how tired he looked. "I had a nap this morning, you didn't."

"No, you keep pouring the coffee and I'll be fine. I couldn't sleep right now—my brain is on overload trying to make sense of this case."

"I know what you mean," Lacey murmured. "Back to Shotgun Man. He must have a cloaking device or one hell of a snowmobile trailering system, because he's vanished both times. No one's seen a snowmobile trailer leaving either scene. They haven't been able to track any truck tires more than three hundred yards."

"Have they gotten anything back on what type of tires we're looking for? That might give us somewhere to start."

"Nothing yet. It's getting too dark to see. I'd better dig out my flashlight."

"I don't think we have enough room for you to empty that bag again."

"Very funny, Swenson. Ah, shit." A pile of papers she'd stuffed under the edge of her coat slid down on the floor when she reached for her bag. "Dammit, look at this mess." She raised up to show him the papers drifted all over the floor. "I can't believe this. Now we'll have to sort them back into the two files."

"I do believe this is the end of the world," Lark said, turning on the overhead light. "Stack them in the briefcase and we'll sort them out later."

Once she had the papers picked up, Lacey called Wausau only to find that Joel was on the road to Madison. There was nothing new on the tire tracks. They spent the rest of the ride listening to the radio, watching the snow, and talking about their observations from the Foltz interview. They made a quick stop to pick up the files that Knutson had prepared on the students and pulled into Lark's road a little after 6:30. About a quarter of a mile from his driveway, they came upon a snow-covered vehicle, lights on, nose down in the ditch. Their headlights showed a driver in the car.

"Shit, this doesn't look good." Lark said, stopping the Jeep.

"That looks like the Ransons' Explorer," Lacey said as she dialed the cell phone.

"I hope it's not John," Lark said, thinking that every third car in Big Oak was a Ford Explorer. He grabbed a large flashlight out of the backseat and got out of the Jeep.

"I'm not getting through on the phone or your radio. I'll keep trying and request an ambulance," Lacey said.

Lark walked up to the rear end of the vehicle and rubbed snow away to identify it. It was a dark-colored Explorer. He swore under his breath as he slid down through snow up to his thighs to get to the driver's side. The snow continued to pelt down and he pulled up the hood of his coat to protect his face from the sting of the flakes. The driver's side door was locked and the window was fogged, but he could see someone in the driver's seat. He banged on the door with the butt of his flashlight.

He breathed a sigh of relief when he saw the person's head move slightly. He was considering breaking out a window when Lacey yelled down from the road. She had to cup her hands and shout so he could hear her over the wind. "I'm going to drive up to your house and call."

He motioned her to go on and turned his attention back to the car. He rubbed out a spot on the side window. It didn't help much due to all the fog on the inside. He checked each door, including the hatch, to see if he could find one unlocked. By the time he'd gone full circle, his Jeep slid to a halt behind the Explorer.

Lacey jumped out of the driver's side and Lark trudged up to meet her. A big man in a hooded parka jumped down out of the passenger side and walked towards him. It was John Ranson.

"I found John and his crew putting in your new doors. The rest of his crew is coming down in his truck." She tried to position herself to keep the snow out of her face as they slipped and slid down to the Explorer. "The Big Oak ambulance is on the way to Wausau with another MVA. Your dispatcher is calling Park Falls to see if they can help and one of your patrols is coming."

They rounded the rear end of the Explorer and John let out a yell, stumbling through the snow to the driver's side. He rubbed newly fallen snow off the window and put his face up against it, trying to peer inside.

Lark grabbed him by the shoulders. "The doors are locked. Do you have a set of keys?"

"They're in my truck," he yelled as he broke away from Lark and half ran, half crawled up the drifted ditch bank. His crew pulled up in his truck just as he got to the road. He grabbed the keys out of the ignition, and slid back down to the Explorer. Lark grabbed him before he could put the keys in the door lock.

"Get the hell out of my way," John shouted, trying to get past Lark.

"John, wait a minute." Lark yelled, pulling the keys away from him and handing them to Lacey.

"Get out of my way, Ann's in there," John cried out, trying to get past Lark. Although John was a little shorter, it was a test of wills for Lark to keep him away from the door.

"Lacey will get the passenger door open so we can take care of her. We can't move her until we can get a cervical collar on her. Do you understand?" Lark asked, shaking his shoulders.

John looked at Lark, tears freezing on his cheeks. "You're right, I know you're right. I've had first-aid training."

Lark let him go. "There might be a cervical collar in my first-aid kit. I'll go get it if you promise me you won't do anything until I get back."

"I won't. I just lost my head for a minute."

Lacey had just climbed in the passenger side when John yelled at her to unlock the rest of the car. She found the electronic switch and popped the locks.

"Don't you lay a hand on her," she said, jabbing her finger at him.

"I know, I know," he said as he carefully opened the driver door.

Ann was still in her seat belt and shoulder harness. She was slouched over on her right side, away from the driver's door, leaning up against the headrest. She already had some redness and swelling on the left side of her head and there was a red line across her forehead. When Lacey called her name, she mumbled and batted the air with her left hand. The car reeked of beer and Lacey noticed that the floor on the passenger side was littered with broken beer bottles and Tupperware. Plastic-wrapped sandwiches spilled out of a torn paper bag.

Lark tapped John on the shoulder and motioned him out of the way, then leaned into the driver's seat and called Ann's name. She didn't respond. He asked Lacey to steady her head as he loosened the red scarf wrapped around her head and neck. When he wasn't able to get it off without manipulating her neck, he put the cervical collar over the scarf. He stepped out of the way so John could get back to his wife.

John gently picked up Ann's left hand. "She must have taken off her gloves like she usually does once the car warms up. She hates to drive in them." He rubbed her cold left hand between his two large warm ones. "Ann, can you hear me?" he yelled as he leaned in to stroke away the bangs that straggled down out of her scarf.

Her eyes fluttered open and she smiled at him. "I'm so cold, come over here and warm me up." She closed her eyes.

"Honey, open your eyes." he said, stroking her cheek.

"No, I'm cold," she whimpered as she tried to turn away from the bright light Lark was shining into the truck. "Turn out that light and come to bed."

"Ann," John said. "Do you know where you are?"

"Bed," she mumbled. "I'm in bed, turn out that damn light, it hurts my eyes." She pulled her hand away from John to shield her eyes.

Lark moved the light away from her face. "Ann, you're not home in bed. You've had a car accident. Do you hurt anywhere?"

"Car?" Her voice rose as she tried to right herself in the seat. "What am I doing in the car?" She fumbled with her seat belt.

"Just be still. Leave that on until the ambulance comes," John said, pulling her hands away from it.

Ann looked at Lark and Lacey, her eyes large and confused. "What are you doing here?" She looked around, as if seeing the inside of the car for the first time. "Please help me get out of here. I'm very cold. Oh my god, I have to get out of here right now."

"Ann, please be quiet until the ambulance comes," John pleaded, tension creeping into his voice as he tried to keep her from unfastening her seat belt.

"No," she yelled, swatting his hands and groping for the seat belt clasp. "I have to get out of here."

"Stop it," John shouted, "you're going to hurt yourself."

"John, take a break. I'll stay with her." Lark said, pulling him out of the way. John walked a few feet away and lit a cigarette. Lacey joined him.

"When is that damn ambulance supposed to get here?" he asked.

"As soon as it can. Do you know what she was doing out here?"

"Damn if I know, I was trying to finish up with Lark's windows," John said, pausing to take a drag on his Marlboro. "I called her earlier and told her that I wouldn't be home until late. I can't imagine why she'd drive over here in this weather."

"The car smells like beer and there's a sack of food spilled in the car. Could she have been bringing you dinner?"

"Shit," John said, rubbing his hand across his five o'clock shadow. "Yeah, she does that sometimes—brings us a surprise picnic supper when I'm working late." He flicked his cigarette butt into the snow and walked back to the car.

Lacey saw the flashing lights of the Park Falls ambulance. Thirty minutes later the ambulance crew was on its way to the hospital with Ann and John. Lacey and Lark walked the road attempting to trace Ann's skid marks and figure out what happened. It was next to impossible to find the Explorer tracks between the foot traffic and ambulance tracks. Within another thirty minutes, Ann's Explorer was loaded on Tetzloff's flatbed to be towed into Big Oak. Lark drove John's truck to the hospital on his way back to the station.

"Don't even think about it," John said as Lark and Lacey walked into Ann's room. She had been admitted to the ICU because of her loss of consciousness.

"I want to go home," Ann said. She was sitting up in bed, her back ramrod straight, obviously mad as hell. Her hair was frizzed out like she'd received a jolt of electricity and her hospital snap gown had slid off one shoulder. An IV dripped into her arm and she was hooked up to a heart monitor. John reached out to pull her gown back up on her shoulder and she smacked his hand away.

"I can tell you how to do a neuro check. I did the damn things for so long, I can do them in my sleep. They already said there's nothing on my head CT."

"That's what I've always thought. Now, at last we have proof," John said, humoring her.

"Asshole," she said, flopping down and turning away from them.

"Honey, I'm just teasing. I'm really afraid something will go wrong.

At least here they can help you if something happens." He walked to the other side of the bed and rubbed her shoulder.

"Fine," she shouted, pulling away from him.

John motioned for Lacey and Lark to leave. He kissed Ann's shoulder and followed them into the hall.

"Thank God she doesn't have a fractured skull, but she does have a concussion. They told me that people temporarily lose some of their inhibition control with frontal lobe concussions. That must be why she's reacting this way. She's never been a good patient, but I've never seen her like this."

"Does she remember anything about the accident?" Lacey asked.

"I don't know. All we've done is argue over going home. I think she might try and sign herself out," John said, stepping back to peek in the window.

"Would you mind if we talked with her for a few minutes?" Lark asked.

"OK, as long as you stop if she gets agitated," John said, heading back into her room.

When she heard the door open Ann turned over, tears streaming down her cheeks. "John, I'm so sorry, I don't know what's wrong with me," she sobbed.

"Ah, sweetheart," he said, pulling her into his arms.

"Ann, are you up to talking with us?" Lacey asked, pulling a chair up to her bed.

"Of course, anything to help." She wiped her tears with the corner of her sheet.

"Do you remember what caused your accident?"

Ann pulled her sheet up to her neck. "It was snowing hard. I slid a little bit and remember thinking how glad I was that John was just up the road in case something happened. I heard a loud noise and the car veered out of control. It was a blowout, wasn't it?" She looked back and forth between Lark and Lacey for confirmation.

"Blowouts can be very loud," Lark said, noticing that the left side of her lip was already swollen to twice its normal size. Her left temple was swollen and her forehead was abraded and reddened.

"The car was suddenly very hard to steer. It spun around and I hit my head and then nothing. How bad is the car?" she asked John.

"It's at Tetzloff's. Don't worry about it, we'll figure it out tomorrow."

"Ann, just one more question," Lacey said. "I hate to ask you this. There were broken beer bottles all over the floor of your car. Were you drinking?"

"Oh, no, I was bringing dinner to John and his crew and I threw in a six-pack of Leinies at the last minute. I'll sign a permit for a legal blood alcohol to be drawn. I don't want any question in the community or with the insurance company."

Lark and Lacey left to give John and Ann some privacy. John's crew was installing the last door when they got to Lark's. The house still felt like an icebox. After building fires in the family room and bedroom, they wolfed down cold turkey sandwiches while they watched the news tapes on Lark's new television. They were cleaning up the dishes when the phone rang.

It was Joel, calling from Madison to let them know that the Pattersons had been located at a relative's cabin in northern Minnesota. They had been notified about Gemma's body and had agreed to be interviewed in Eau Claire the next day at noon.

"How long does it take to get to Eau Claire?" Lacey asked, looking at her watch and yawning.

"Four hours in this weather. We've got to be on the road by seven-thirty," Lark said, dousing the family-room fire.

"I feel like I could sleep for a hundred years." Lacey yawned again and headed for the staircase. "Wonder how cold it is upstairs?"

"Too cold to sleep separately," Lark said, following her.

"I just want to get a good night's sleep and keep warm," she said, stifling yet another yawn. "At this rate I'll be asleep before my head hits the pillow." Lacey went into her room and changed into fresh sweats.

"My room's ice-cold, but with that fire and the door shut it isn't half bad in here," she said as she walked into Lark's room. "I can just barely see my breath."

He'd already changed into sweats and was stoking up the fire. She looked around the room, realizing that she'd been so tired the night before that she hadn't noticed much about it. His bed was a king-sized, dark cherry Shaker-style four poster covered with a navy-and-burgundy plaid comforter. A tall chest, two nightstands, and a long mirror-topped dresser, all matching the bed, were spread around the room. A burgundy leather recliner sat in the corner near the window. The bed was directly across from the massive floor-to-ceiling fieldstone fireplace—no small feat since the ceiling was vaulted. Old maps of northern Wisconsin were framed on the wall. A picture of a very pretty woman in an ornate gold frame sat on Lark's nightstand. Lacey's heart flew to her throat when she realized the woman was probably Lark's late wife.

She got into bed and crawled under the covers, snatching glances at the picture. The woman had a gorgeous smile and warm, friendly eyes. Lacey thought she looked like someone she would like to get to know. Rolling on her side away from the picture, she found herself staring out the window and discovered that Lark had left the perimeter lights on. They reflected on the falling snow, creating a fairyland effect. Lark snapped off the overhead lights and the room went dark except for the glow from the fire. She felt the mattress give as he got into bed beside her.

"In the right circumstances this could be heaven," she said drowsily.

"What? Sorry, I didn't hear you." He rolled over on his back.

"In the right circumstances, this could be heaven."

"Go to sleep," he said, turning on his side away from her. "It's after midnight."

She attempted to settle herself into a comfortable sleeping position. No matter what she did, the pillows were either too high or not high enough. The covers didn't seem to lay right and she couldn't get her body positioned to rest.

"What's wrong?" he mumbled. "You're whipping around like a cyclone."

"Can you believe it? Now that I'm in bed I'm not sleepy." She rolled over on her back and pulled the covers up under her chin.

He grunted.

"You've even got skylights in here," she said, looking up at the two glass domes in the ceiling.

Lark grunted again.

"Jeez, I can't believe this. Now that my eyes have adjusted, I can see a few stars."

"I'm going to 'jeez' you in a minute if you don't shut up and go to sleep."

"Crab ass."

"What did you—hey, what the hell are you doing now?" Lark asked, sitting up as she slid out of bed.

"I don't know." She walked to the window. "Maybe I should take the Ransons' up on staying at their place. Doesn't this setup make you a little nervous?" She turned around and looked into his eyes.

"I'm too damn tired to be nervous. How is this different than last night?"

"I was beyond exhausted last night. All that wine and the adrenaline rush with the shooting wore me out. I guess I'm not quite as tired tonight."

"Well, I am. What do you want to do?" he asked, his words coming out in white puffs.

"Do you care if I read?"

"Heavens, no. I could sleep if klieg lights were shining on me."

Lacey went to her room for her book. When she got back to Lark's room, he was sitting in the chair.

"I'll sleep downstairs on the sofa in front of the fire and you can sleep up here," he said, his blue eyes boring into hers. "Now that I think about this, it is a bit awkward."

"Don't be ridiculous," she said as she climbed into bed. "I don't know what got into me. This is fine. If I was in this circumstance with any other friend, I wouldn't hesitate to do this to keep warm. Why should it be any different with you?" She settled into bed, propping two pillows behind her back and pulling the covers up around her.

Lark continued to sit in the chair, his face impassive, watching her.

"Jesus Christ, Lark," she said, patting the comforter. "We're adults and we're law enforcement officers, for God's sake."

He climbed back into bed and they talked, avoiding any discussion about the case. An hour later, Lacey was talking about a case she'd worked on in Madison when she heard a faint snore. Lark was sound asleep. She slid down in the bed, suddenly very sleepy herself. The last thing she remembered was turning out the light.

SATURDAY MORNING

NOVEMBER 25 — ANN RANSON

Ann awakened with the mother of all headaches, confused about where she was. She knew immediately that she wasn't in her own bed because when she reached out to turn on the light, her hand hit something hard. As her fingers curled around it, she realized it was the side rail of her hospital bed. Flashbacks from the car accident flooded her mind. As her eyes adjusted to the dark she looked around the room for the clock she knew was somewhere on the wall. When she was unable to find it, she made a mental note to have all the clocks replaced with ones that glowed in the dark. Pain shot through her shoulders and back when she tried to sit up. Just as she got herself situated, a voice from the corner of the room startled her into agonizing pain.

"I'm so glad you're awake."

"Who is it?" Ann asked, peering into the darkness.

"It's me, Betty Chevsky." Betty came over to the bed and took Ann's hand.

"Betty, can you please turn a light on?"

The overhead light flashed on and sent shock waves of pain

through her head. Despite the pain in her back and shoulders, Ann pulled her arms up to cover her face. She cried out and Betty ran back to the bedside.

"Should I get the nurse?"

"No, just turn the light off," Ann said, gritting her teeth with pain. "Turn the bathroom light on."

The overhead light went off and the softer bathroom light came on. It dulled her headache to the point where it was tolerable.

"Is that better?" Betty asked, coming back to her bedside.

"Much," Ann said, attempting to smile. "How is your son?"

"He's in detox in Rhinelander. Things are really hard for him right now. I got to talk with him for the first time last night."

"Rhinelander will do a good job with him. They have a very good reputation," Ann said, closing her eyes in hopes of shutting out the pain. "What time is it?"

"Quarter after six. I get off at seven, but I wanted to check up on you before I left."

"Thank you for coming," Ann said, opening her eyes to see Betty staring down at her.

She took Ann's hand. "I'm sorry this is happening to you. I hope it stops soon."

"I had a blowout. My car went out of control and I hit my head. Good thing I had on my seat belt."

"Thank God it was just a blowout."

"It hurts like hell right now. Could you ask the nurse to bring me something for pain?"

"Yes, ma'am. I'll do that right now," Betty said, leaving the room.

Ann fell asleep dreaming that someone had her head in a vice. She roused enough to take a couple of pain pills and fell back into a troubled sleep. She woke up when John came in at 8:30 and was home in her own bed by early afternoon.

Lacey was having the most wonderful dream. She was toasty warm in a double sleeping bag in the northwoods. She was being kissed passionately, just like in the romance novels, and her breasts were being caressed. She was excited and way beyond ready to move on to better things when she heard a ringing in her ears. *This is it*, she thought as she rolled herself full length against her lover. Suddenly the kissing stopped and the wonderful hands and warm body withdrew. The ringing in her ears became the sound of an alarm clock.

"Turn it off. Let's stay here and make love all day," she said, reaching out to embrace her lover.

"Shit" was the response.

"Dammit." Lacey sat up so fast she was dizzy. "What happened?" she asked, pulling down her sweatshirt. She buried her face in her hands.

"The alarm went off," Lark grumbled.

"No, I mean what the hell just happened here?" she asked, her voice drifting out between her palms as she attempted to rub her face awake.

"I'm not sure," he said, reaching out to put his arm around her and then quickly pulling back. "I'm really sorry about this."

"Hell, it's not your fault." She pulled her left hand away from cradling her head just enough to look at him. "I must confess, I was enjoying myself until the stupid alarm went off."

"I thought I was dreaming," Lark said, his face beet red.

"Me, too."

They sat there for a few minutes in awkward silence.

"Well, at least the house is warmer." Lacey said, sketching her arms up in the air. "I feel like I need a cold shower, but considering it's still a bit chilly, I'll forgo it." She smiled at Lark's back and left.

"Jesus Christ," Lark mumbled, staring down at the floor. "What the hell is wrong with me?" He went to take his own shower.

Refreshed from standing under the hot shower spray, but no less embarrassed, Lark dressed and went downstairs to get the coffee started. Once again, Lacey had beaten him.

"How the hell do you get dressed so fast?" he asked, pouring himself a cup of coffee.

"My youthful beauty demands little primping," she said, not taking her eyes off the *Wausau Herald*. Her damp hair was fanned out around her face and curled down the back of her navy knit dress in an unruly mass. She looked as if she had on a hint of lipstick and mascara, but no other makeup was noticeable.

Lark sat down at the island across from her, saying nothing. He picked up the section of the paper she had left lying on the counter.

"Don't throw up when you read the headlines," she said from behind the paper.

He unfolded the front page. SECOND UW–MADISON COED FOUND DEAD IN MASON COUNTY screamed out at him.

"They have almost as much information as we do," she commented as she refilled her coffee mug and went into the family room to flip on the television.

"Assholes," Lark said, scanning the article.

Lacey flipped between the three network stations, looking for a local news update.

The *Herald* had an excellent biographical sketch of Terry Foltz but they did not have the link with the other UW–Madison students who lived in Big Oak.

All three news stations were carrying the same information. The Rhinelander station had sent a reporter to the Foltzes' house. Her live report consisted of telling the world that the Foltzes were in seclusion and not available for comment.

"Sharks," Lacey snapped. "Now everyone knows where these poor people live. No one gets a moment to grieve in peace anymore." She turned off the television and slammed the remote down on the sofa.

"We'd better get going," Lark said, filling a thermos with coffee. "This is going to be another long day. We've got to get back here and interview those kids before they go back to school tomorrow."

They pulled out of the garage into another overcast day. What had looked like a winter wonderland last night now looked like a scene from the movie *Fargo*; everything; everywhere, with the exception of the brown trees, was white. Big, fat snowflakes fell on a never-ending sea of snow. The road crew that plowed Lark's driveway had left a tunnel of snow almost as high as the roof of the Jeep.

"It's a wonder that everyone up here isn't on Prozac," Lacey commented as they drove to the station. The roads were surprisingly clear. There were still quite a few trucks parked up against the piles of snow left by the road grader. White fields were dotted with blaze orange specks that materialized into men with guns as they grew closer.

The station was abuzz with activity. After being reassured that everyone was working on routine stuff, Lark pulled George aside and asked him to set up appointments with all the UW–Madison students who lived in Big Oak. Ten minutes later he and Lacey were on the road to Eau Claire.

As they drove through town, Lacey was amazed at the number of vehicles with deer strapped to their tops. "This is disgusting," she said, craning her neck to watch an old station wagon drive by with a very small doe strapped to the roof, its head hanging down over the passenger side of the car as if it were looking into the window. "This feels like a sick *Far Side* cartoon."

"Be careful, Detective Smith, this is a multimillion–dollar industry in northern Wisconsin. It's sacrilege to criticize it," he said sarcastically.

"Yeah, uh-huh, I hear you. You must be running for election soon."

"Sooner or later, if I want to stay in this garden spot," he said with a sigh. "What I'm thinking about right now is that one of these guys who comes up here for deer hunting, a guy who will be leaving here today or tomorrow, may just be our killer."

"Don't even think that. It has to be someone local."

They agreed that so far they did not have a motive for the crime, let alone means and opportunity for anyone. Once their discussion of Patterson and Foltz flagged, they talked about the recent shootings. They both agreed that the connections between the cases was the snowmobile. After discussing the prevalence of snowmobiles in northern Wisconsin, they agreed that rather than checking out everyone who owned one, they would determine if the suspects had one.

They arrived at the Eau Claire state police headquarters only five minutes ahead of the Pattersons. Joel had called ahead and arranged for Captain Leonard Minor, the officer who had worked with the Pattersons when their daughter had first been reported missing, to sit in on the interview.

Despite the seriousness of the moment, the nursery rhyme "Jack Sprat could eat no fat and his wife could eat no lean" ran through Lacey's head as she shook hands with the Pattersons. Allan Patterson, was a long, tall study in brown. He was at least six-foot-six with a shock of straight brown hair that hung down on his forehead and huge, soft brown eyes set deep in a long, narrow face. His forehead was creased with worry lines which matched the long frown lines around his mouth. He shuffled into the center of the interview room, his shoulders hunched, his hands jammed in his pants pockets. Two camel wool coats hung through the crook of his right arm.

Yvonne Patterson followed close behind. At five foot four, she struggled to keep up with her husband's stride. Lacey was struck at how beautiful she was, complete with greenish brown eyes shimmering with tears and dark brown hair streaked with gray swirled artfully around her face. Her voluptuous frame was draped in a calf-length, dark brown cashmere skirt and sweater set. Although she now had the body of a Ruebens model, it was obvious from her style and grace that she had not always been built that way.

Everyone found a seat around the oblong table. After introductions, Lark started the interview by telling the Pattersons how sorry he was about their daughter.

"I think I knew she was dead but it helps to know that we can put her to rest," Mrs. Patterson said, her voice quavering. She pulled a tissue from the box on the table and dabbed at the tears that overflowed her eyes and dribbled down her cheeks.

"When will we be able to bring her home?" Allan Patterson asked in a deep but gentle voice. He leaned over and massaged his wife's shoulder.

"Maybe early next week," Lark said, observing the tenderness between them. "I've read the files, but I'd like you to tell me what you remember about your daughter's disappearance."

"It was a Tuesday afternoon and I was out grocery shopping for Thanksgiving." Yvonne smiled sadly at Lark. "It's Gemma and Allan's favorite holiday. We eat the same thing every year, no substitutions allowed." Her husband squeezed her shoulder. "When I got home, it was about three o'clock. Gemma had left a short message on our answering machine saying that she was headed home but was going to stop and visit a friend and maybe stay overnight." She stopped talking, overcome with tears.

Worried for his wife, Allan slid his chair closer to comfort her. "We didn't think too much about it when she didn't show up Tuesday night, but we got concerned when she didn't make it in on Wednesday evening. Minnesota and northern Wisconsin got a lot of snow that Wednesday and we were worried that she'd gotten stuck or had an accident."

Yvonne squared her shoulders and examined the black smudges on the water-logged tissue before reaching across the table for another. She smiled at Lacey. "I knew I shouldn't have worn makeup."

Lacey reached across the table and patted her hand.

"As I look back on this, I realize that I should have known something was wrong when she didn't call us on Tuesday."

"Why's that?" Lark asked.

"Because she said she'd call me back later and she didn't."

Allan nodded his head. "Yvonne's right. Gemma was very responsible. She would have called us if she had been able to."

"Do you remember any of her friends from the Big Oak area?" Lark asked.

Mrs. Patterson stuffed her tissue into the cuff of her sweater and reached down for her handbag. "I brought my notes."

"We went through Gemma's date book looking for names," Allan said, relaxing back into his chair now that his wife was less emotional.

Yvonne unfolded several pages of notebook paper with sections highlighted in yellow. "Let me see," she said, poring over the first page.

"Sandi Waltner," Allan said, glancing at Lacey's notes. "I know her father. He owns a marina in Big Oak. I can't imagine her being a part of this. Sandi has been to our house a couple of times."

"She was always a wonderful guest. She came with Katey Lowery, another friend of Gemma's from Big Oak," Yvonne said, flipping to another highlighted page.

"Did they both visit your home?" Lark asked.

"Yes, do you need to know when? I can go through Gemma's date book if it will help."

"I'd like to look over her date book myself. There are copies of pages from them in the police files but not a copy of the whole thing. You never can tell what might be helpful," Lark said.

"We'll get it over to you tomorrow," Allan said.

"David Banski is also in my notes. She gave him a ride to Big Oak once," Yvonne said.

"I can't imagine what kind of an animal could do this," Allan said, his hands gripping the arms of his chair.

"Honey, let's get going so we can spend some time with Mike," Yvonne said, one hand resting on his wrist, the other caressing his shoulder.

"In a minute," he said, staring at the calendar hanging on the wall across from him.

Not taking her eyes off her husband, Yvonne said, "Mike, our son, also went to UW. He's working with his dad at the marina. He and Gemma were very close, and finding Gemma's body has brought all the pain of her disappearance back for him. He's having a hard time right now."

Allan stood up and shook hands with Lark and Lacey. "Thank you for your time. Yvonne's right, we have to take care of the living. We'll get that date book to you tomorrow."

Allan reminded Lacey of an automaton, emotionless, going through the motions of being polite. Yvonne shook hands with Lark and gave Lacey a hug. "I don't know how you do this. I couldn't deal with all this sadness. I'll say a prayer for you both."

Lacey grabbed a tissue as she watched them reach for each other's hands as they passed the interrogation window. "Sometimes I don't know how we do it either," she mumbled.

Lark, his face grim, headed for the door. "I'm going to see if I can catch them before they leave and get a copy of her notes. There might be something in there that can help us."

By the time he came back with the copies and a refilled thermos compliments of the Eau Claire state police, Lacey had composed herself. They walked out into air laden with the smells of burning wood and snow. The moisture in the air was so thick that you could almost reach out and grab a handful of it.

After getting burgers and fries at a drive-through, they headed out of town. They listened to the Eau Claire radio newscast while they ate. It brought dire tidings of a residential roof collapse, presumably from the weight of the snow. There had also been two house fires, both started from space heaters, leaving two families with small children homeless. The Red Cross was asking for donations of clothing and household items, as one of the families didn't have insurance. Three hunters from Illinois had been arrested just north of Eau Claire for the 2 A.M. spotlighting and shooting of a deer from their snowmobiles while intoxicated. The six-day forecast called for two to six inches of snow each day. The county superintendent of roads was interviewed on how much their budget had been eaten into so early in the snow season. He got in his plug for emergency appropriations before the latest estimate on the Wisconsin deer kill. The broadcaster ended with a request for listeners to call in and comment on global warning.

They spent their drive back to Big Oak trying to ignore the overcast gray skies and the snow that continued to fall. While Lark drove, Lacey read Mrs. Patterson's twelve pages of notes out loud without finding anything they didn't already know. They planned their interviews for the evening, agreeing that the key to the case lay with the group of college students that kept surfacing around the two dead girls: Katey and Matt Lowery, David Banski, Sandi and Michael Waltner, Shelley Marten, Jim Kryjack, and Ron Chevsky.

They pulled into Big Oak at dusk. Lacey would have killed for a hot bath and Lark would have given a week's pay for a stiff drink and an hour under a hot shower, but it was not to be. Shelley Marten and her parents were waiting at the station for their 5 P.M. appointment.

The Martens had seated themselves together at one end of the table with Shelley in between her two very concerned parents. They stood up when Lark and Lacey entered the room. Lark studied Dr. Marten's craggy face and salt-and-pepper beard and wondered if his parents had had a premonition when they named him after Abraham Lincoln.

"Please have a seat," Lark said, waving them into their chairs. "Would you like some coffee or a soda?" he asked as he took a sip from his steaming cup of black coffee.

"Do you have any bottled water?" Shelley asked.

"Let me see what I can do," Lacey said after Shelley's parents declined refreshments.

"Can you tell me what this is all about?" Dr. Marten asked, his voice full of concern.

"I'm sorry to bring you in here on a Saturday night. We're interviewing several students from the area before they go back to Madison tomorrow. I'm sure you heard about the two bodies we found on the Ransons' property?"

The Martens nodded in unison.

"They've been identified as Gemma Patterson and Terry Foltz, both UW–Madison students."

The Martens nodded and Mrs. Marten reached over and squeezed her daughter's hand.

"Shelley, your name has come up as knowing both of these girls and we'd like to talk with you about them. You may be able to help us figure out what happened."

"I'll help in any way I can."

Lacey walked in with a bottle of water as Lark asked Dr. and Mrs. Marten to step out while they talked with their daughter.

"This should be relatively painless," Lacey said as she slid the water over to Shelley and flipped open her notebook.

"I didn't know Gemma or Terry well so this shouldn't take very long," she replied, her eyes flicking between Lark and Lacey as she opened the bottle.

As it turned out, Shelley was right. Other than riding up to Big Oak with Gemma twice during the summer before she died, Shelley and Gemma never crossed paths. She told them that Sandi Waltner and Katey Lowery had ridden up with them and that the three girls seemed to know each other well. Her knowledge of Terry Foltz was similar. She had hitched a ride to Big Oak with Terry, Sandi, and Katey on two weekends the previous spring and had seen the three of them with David

Banski out at the Mason County Country Club. Other than that, she didn't remember any other contact with the two victims.

Shelley could not remember exactly where she was on the Tuesday before Thanksgiving three years ago, but did know that she was in Madison in the middle of exams. She had driven up to Big Oak the Wednesday night before Thanksgiving with her brother. This Thanksgiving she had driven up on Thursday morning with two of her friends, and had been in Milwaukee with friends last weekend. Lacey wrote down the phone number of the family she had stayed with in Milwaukee, as well as the names of the instructors and classes Shelley had taken fall semester three years ago.

By 5:45 Shelley and her parents were gone and Lark and Lacey were organizing their notes before they did their next interview.

David Banski showed up with his mother precisely at six o'clock. Myra was decked out in her full-length fur coat and dangling diamond earrings. She hugged Lark and Lacey and talked about how concerned she was that two young girls had been murdered in Mason County.

"I feel almost like I'm back in Chicago," she said as she hustled into the interview room with David. She slipped off her coat and settled into a chair, refusing anything to drink.

"Myra, it would be best if we interviewed David alone," Lark said, smiling at her.

"Anything you have to ask David, you can ask in front of me."

"David isn't a minor and we really need to talk with him confidentially."

"I won't repeat anything I hear. You can trust me."

"Mom, go outside and wait. I'm twenty-two and more than able to take care of myself," David said as he got up and pulled out her chair.

"I know that, dear, but this is serious and you might need my help," Myra protested as David helped her back into her coat.

"Why don't you go on over to the country club and I'll meet you there. I'm sure someone here will give me a ride, and that way you won't be late for the party." David patted her shoulders, glancing at Lark for support.

Lark took his cue. "Myra, we'll get David out to the club. The last thing we want to do is make you late."

"You're all ganging up on me so I'll go," she said, wagging her finger at Lark, "but don't take advantage of my son. Treat him right."

"We'll do our best," he said, asking Lacey to escort her to her car.

"Mom's a bit over-protective," David said as he settled into his chair.

"You're lucky to have her." Lark sat down across from him. "You probably know why we want to talk with you."

"I've been watching the news and reading the paper, I can hardly believe it," he said, shaking his head.

"We need you to tell us what you know about Gemma Patterson and Terry Foltz."

"Well, let's see," he said, studying the imaginary graffiti he was drawing on the top of the table with his index finger. "I already told you about Gemma. She and Sandi became friends when they took a class together. Sandi introduced her to Katey Lowery and the three of them were inseparable. Gemma spent some weekends up here with them. Sandi and I went out to dinner with Gemma and Jim Kryjack one night at the Pine View. That's about it for Gemma."

"How well did you know Terry?"

"I met her a couple of times last spring when she was staying at Katey's. She drove up here a couple of weekends with Sandi and Katey, but that's about it."

"Do you recall where you were three years ago on Tuesday, November twenty-fifth?" Lark asked as Lacey walked back through the door with two more cups of coffee.

"Three years ago," he said, glancing at Lacey, "I was in Poughkeepsie, New York. I flew out of Madison on Wednesday afternoon and came back on Sunday evening."

"What were you doing in Poughkeepsie?" she asked, jotting down notes.

"This is not the best subject for me now that Sandi and I are engaged. I was serious about someone else and flew out there to spend Thanksgiving with her family. It didn't go well and we broke up before Christmas. Sandi and I rode up here together for Christmas break and spent a lot of time together. We've been dating ever since."

"I thought you and Sandi went out with Jim and Gemma prior to that," Lark said.

His face turned scarlet. "Sandi and I had been seeing each other off and on."

"So you were seeing Poughkeepsie and Sandi at the same time?" Lacey asked.

"Patricia, Patricia Spencer."

"You were seeing them at the same time?"

"Yes."

"Did they know about each other?"

"Sandi knew there was someone else, but Patricia didn't. What's that got to do with Gemma's murder?" he asked, irritated.

"Who knows?" Lacey said, smiling at him. "You can never tell what will lead us to a piece of the puzzle."

"Where were you this past weekend?" Lark asked.

"The UW law library. Several friends saw me there."

"Lacey will get some names from you before you leave," Lark said. "Thanks for coming in. Are you headed back to Madison tomorrow?"

"Yes, you can call me down there if you have any more questions," David volunteered. "I'll do anything I can to help. I've always wondered how Gemma could just disappear. It never entered my mind that Big Oak had anything to do with it."

He left by quarter to seven and Lark and Lacey wandered out to find out who was next. George had his coat on and informed them that the Waltners had changed their appointment to Sunday afternoon so they could go to the country club party. He told Lark that Ron Chevsky was coherent enough to talk with them and was scheduled for Monday.

Jim Kryjack was going off his twelve-hour shift and Lark decided to get his formal interview over with. Jim repeated the same story he had told Lark earlier in the week. Even after viewing a photograph of Terry Foltz, he wasn't able to remember her. Unfortunately, he had been in Big Oak during the time of both murders, working at his parents' restaurant the weekend that Gemma was murdered and on duty when Terry was murdered.

Lark and Lacey completed their notes and left the station a little after eight. The snow was on hiatus.

They decided to eat leftovers and made a pit stop at a combination video store and gas station to pick up a movie. Lark reluctantly agreed to Lacey's request not to rent a thriller or action flick. They agreed on a romantic comedy.

After two days of frigid temperatures, the house was finally warm and cozy. They changed clothes, heated up heaping plates of turkey and fixings and flopped down on the sofa to watch Julia Roberts find true love. They stopped the movie to watch the ten o'clock news. None of the networks had anything new to say about the murders despite the reporters they had dispatched to the victim's homes. They finished watching the movie just before midnight and went to bed, exhausted and barely able to stay awake.

As Lark undressed in his room, he heard water running in Lacey's bathroom and began to think about the last few days. His room felt cold and empty. It hit him like a rock that he would have preferred to have her in his bedroom rather than down the hall. He glanced at the picture of his late wife and mentally asked her for guidance. None came.

After thirty minutes of reading the same two pages over and over, he turned out the light and willed himself to go to sleep. He tossed and turned for fifteen minutes, then got up. He pulled on a pair of sweatpants and took his book downstairs, hoping that getting up and doing something would make him sleepy.

He wandered into the family room and decided to start a fire, thinking it would make him drowsy. Once he got it going, he went into the kitchen to get a beer and ended up rummaging around in the refrigerator for a snack.

"I see I'm not the only person around here who can't sleep."

"What the hell," Lark shouted, jerking up and slamming his head into the freezer handle. "Dammit, you scared the shit out of me." He rubbed a rapidly forming goose egg on top of his head.

A barefoot Lacey stood in front of him, grinning. She looked gorgeous in her dark green robe.

"Oh my God, I'm so sorry. Lean down here. Let me look at your head."

"Dammit, woman, you have a real bad habit of turning up without warning." He sat down on a bar stool to give her a better view of his bruise. "I'm beginning to think you really do have a broom."

"I was already down here."

"Already down here?" Lark echoed, raising his head to look at her. "Where the hell were you?"

"Hold still." She pulled his head back down. "You've got a bad gash in your head."

"Forget about that. Where were you?"

"The living room. You could use a few stitches. This gash is almost an inch long. Hold still," she ordered, grabbing a couple of paper towels to press against his wound.

"We're not going to the ER over a little cut like this," he snapped, pressing the paper towels to his head. "I'll put some ice on it and take a couple of aspirin. It'll be fine."

"Suit yourself. You'll have a lemon on top of your head in the morning." She filled a baggie with ice and wrapped it in a dishtowel.

"It'll be fine," he muttered, as his head began to throb.

"Do you have any peroxide?" she asked, handing him the ice pack.

"Peroxide will hurt like hell."

"Alcohol hurts but peroxide doesn't. Don't worry, I'll be gentle. We need to clean out that wound. If you don't have any in here, I'll get it out of your first-aid kit in the Jeep."

"There's some in the closet in the powder room," he said, resigned to his fate. "Grab me a Tylenol with codeine while you're in there. I've got a few pills left from when I sprained my shoulder last year."

"Having a little pain, are we?" she asked, on her way to the powder room.

"Just get the damn Tylenol."

She returned with the drugs, peroxide, and some towels. She draped a towel over his bare shoulders, cracked open the beer he'd managed to get out of the fridge before he hit his head, and handed it to him along with two Tylenol with codeine.

"I only need one of these and I shouldn't take them with alcohol." He put the beer and one of the pills over on the snack bar.

"For God's sake, who are you, Andy of Mayberry?" She handed him the second pill and the beer. "Take the damn pills."

"Yes, ma'am."

"Lean towards me so I can get this wound cleaned out." He rested his head against Lacey's chest as she parted his hair to expose the gash and pour a little peroxide into the wound.

"Damn, that hurts like a son of a bitch," he cried out, rearing away from her and whacking her chin with his head. Lacey stumbled against the counter, dropping the bottle and splattering peroxide over the tile.

"Oh, shit," Lark yelled, lunging forward to break her fall. He slipped in the peroxide and they both fell.

When the dust settled, they were both on the floor, Lacey on her back with Lark half on top of her. His ice pack had split open, sending ice cubes careening over the floor.

"We're not going to say a word about this to anyone," she said as she sat up. Ignoring the sharp pain in her right side, she wiped blood from the puncture wound her upper teeth had made in her lower lip.

"I'm so sorry," he said, scrambling to help her up. "Are you all right?"

"The Three Stooges couldn't have done any better." She got to her feet. "If Joel ever hears about this he'll make our lives miserable for years. How bad is my lip?"

"You've got a gash about an inch long," he said, gently assessing the damage. "It's pretty deep. You need to go to the ER for some stitches."

"Screw you." She brushed past him on her way to the powder room. "If you're not going, I'm not going."

"There's a little bit of peroxide left." He picked up the bottle and followed her. "If we need more, I'll get the first-aid kit from the car."

"Kiss my ass," she said, her eyes blazing at him from the mirror.

"You really do need to have that lip stitched. If you don't you'll probably have a scar."

"Didn't you hear me the first time?"

"You've said so many things."

"Screw you. Have I said that?"

"That and more," he said, trying to keep from laughing.

"Are there any butterflies in your first-aid kit?"

"Might be," he said, heading for the garage. He returned with a package of Steri-Strips.

"Those ought to do," Lacey said, pressing a towel against her lip.

"You sure you don't want to get a couple of stitches? It might heal without a scar if you get it sutured."

"We'll bandage it tonight and I'll decide tomorrow if it needs stitches," she snapped, studying her lip in the mirror. "Can you get me an ice cube?"

After ten minutes of pressure with an ice cube wrapped in a washcloth, the bleeding stopped. Lark cleaned out the cut with peroxide and carefully trimmed and placed the Steri-Strips on her lip. They went to the kitchen to clean up the mess before going to bed.

"I'm impressed that you didn't flinch with that peroxide," he said as he mopped the floor.

"Women handle pain better than men. I hesitate to think what the birth rate would be if men had the babies."

"That's original," he mumbled, mopping up the last of the mess.

"What time do we need to get up?" she asked, noting that it was after 1 A.M.

"We should be in the station by nine—our first interview's at ten."

"That sounds about right. I wouldn't know how to work this case with more than seven hours of sleep," she said, as Lark took the mop bucket to the laundry room.

He came back with the bottle of Tylenol with codeine, tossing it across the kitchen to her. "Your lip has to hurt. Take a couple of these."

She swallowed them without comment and they headed up to bed, each going to their own rooms. Exhausted, they slept until their alarms went off at 8 A.M.

Lark's alarm awakened him from a wonderful dream. He sat up on the side of the bed, ignoring a faint headache. He told himself he should be focused on the double murder case, not his middle-aged libido. He ran his hand through his hair and encountered two goose eggs. He groaned, remembering the fiasco in the kitchen last night and wondered how Lacey's lip was. He lurched into the shower, hoping that some hot water would soothe his headache and refocus his mind.

Lacey's alarm went off, waking her from the sleep of the dead. She was sure she hadn't moved a muscle since her head hit the pillow. Her lip throbbed and her right hip ached. The right side of her chest hurt like hell. She got up and tried to stretch out the soreness. She went into the bathroom, looked in the mirror, and got the shock of her life. The center of her lower lip was swollen to twice its normal size. She moaned and bent her face into her hands.

"Dammit to hell," she said. The cut in her lip was gaping open about an eighth of an inch. Reluctantly, she decided to stop at the ER on their way to the station and have her lip checked. She despised eating crow but, even worse, hated the thought of her lip healing poorly.

Hearing Lark's shower go off jolted her into action. She stumbled to the shower and stood under the spray, hoping it would wash away her muscle aches. When she washed her hair, she noticed that the pain in her right side got even worse. She tried to shrug it off, thinking it would go away once she limbered up.

Lark beat Lacey into the kitchen. He made coffee and thumbed through the paper. He was nursing his second mug when she came down. He did a double take when her saw her face.

"Does it hurt?" he asked, trying not to laugh at her pouting lower lip.

"Not as much as my pride." She got the Tylenol with codeine out of the powder room. "Want some?" she asked, holding the bottle out to him.

"Already had some." He watched her try to drink coffee and avoid the cut on her lip. "I'd offer you a straw but I don't have any."

"I'll manage," she said, attempting to sip with the side of her mouth. She swore as a few drops dribbled onto the front of her dress. "Shit, now I need a bib. I'm going to run up and change clothes. Do we have time to stop by the ER so I can see if this needs stitches?"

"We'll make time." He headed for the telephone as Lacey went upstairs. He let Flo know they'd be a few minutes late and asked her to have Jim Kryjack meet him at the ER in half and hour. She told him that Tetzloff was expecting a call from him about the Ransons' Explorer and the abandoned Taurus. Sighing, he realized the two cars had slipped his mind.

Lacey came down dressed in a red sweater and worn jeans, mumbling about how she needed to do laundry. They rode to the ER in silence. To distract herself from focusing on how bad her right side was hurting every time she took a breath, she read the Wausau paper.

The ER wasn't busy and Lacey got right in to see the physician. He took one look at her lip and told her that she should have come in the night before. He put in four small sutures. He noticed her wincing as she got down from the table and asked about her fall. An examination of her back revealed two bruises across her shoulders and a huge bruise on her right rib cage and hip. A chest X-ray discovered two fractured ribs. He told her she should be off her feet for the day and wrote her a prescription for Tylenol with codeine.

She got dressed and went to the waiting room to find Lark deep in conversation with her doctor and Jim Kryjack sitting in the corner of the ER.

"I've told your husband that you need to go home and rest," the doctor said.

"He's—"

"Come on, honey," Lark said, interrupting her as he took her arm.

"I'm not taking the day off," she snapped once the doctor left. "And what are you doing pretending to be my husband and soliciting private information about me?"

"I didn't solicit. He assumed and I listened," Lark said, letting go of her arm as he saw her grimace. "I'm going to run you back to the house and have Jim bring me back into town so you can have the Jeep in case you need it."

"No way."

"No choice. Doctor's orders."

"Asshole," she said under her breath as she stalked away.

"Should I call Joel and let him make the decision?" he asked, walking up behind her.

"No," she snapped. "Let's go."

"You can use my Tylenol with codeine and I'll get yours filled later."

"Fine," she said as they walked out the door. Jim followed, concerned over their fighting.

They rode in silence. Lacey got out as soon as the Jeep pulled into the garage and stomped into the laundry room. Lark followed her, dropping the keys on the kitchen counter.

"Need some help?" he asked, seeing her flinch as she bent over to take off her boots.

"No," she said, gritting her teeth.

"Take it easy and get some rest. We're going to Rhinelander tomorrow to interview Chevsky and I want you with me for that."

"Fine," she said, brushing past him on her way to the kitchen.

"I've cracked my ribs a couple of times, I know how it feels. There's a whirlpool tub in my bathroom. Take some pills and get in there and soak. If you take it easy, you'll feel better tomorrow."

"Yes, Doctor Swenson," she said pouring herself some coffee.

"Do what you want," Lark said, waving her off. "I'll see you tonight."

After he left, Lacey took a couple more Tylenol with codeine and wandered upstairs to check out Lark's bathroom. The tub was inviting, nestled underneath a window that looked out on snow-covered woods. While it filled, she laid out her nightgown and robe and tuned Lark's radio to the country station. When the tub was full, she slipped into the hot, soothing water. The whirlpool jets relieved some of the tightness in her back and side. The tub and the pain pills made her so drowsy she could hardly get out of the water. She wrapped herself in a towel and stumbled into Lark's bedroom. She turned off the radio and curled up under his quilt, comforted by the closeness of his smell.

Jim and Lark raced back to the station. Flo had delayed the Waltners until 10:30 and asked George Knutson to staff the interviews. Lark rushed through the back door of the station just before the Waltners came in the front.

Lark brought them into the interview room and explained the process. Sara requested to sit in on the interviews, but both children told her they would be fine. She threatened to bring in their lawyer, but Steve stepped in to say they would respect the children's wishes on the condition that Lark terminate the interviews if they wanted to stop. Lark agreed and Sara reluctantly left with her husband and Sandi, since Michael was to be interviewed first.

Michael was nearly as tall as Lark and very self-assured for a twenty-four-year-old. He had his father's good looks with dark brown eyes and curly black hair. He relaxed as if he didn't have a care in the world.

"How long did you know Gemma Patterson?" Lark asked.

"About a year," he said, his face impassive, his eyes flickering over Lark, sizing him up. "She and Sandi met in class and became friends."

"Did you ever go out with her?"

"No," Michael said, laughing. "She was too young for me."

"She was only two years younger."

"She seemed much younger than Sandi. Almost like a kid."

"Do you know who she dated?"

"I wouldn't know. Ask Sandi."

"Know anyone who was angry with her?"

"No," he said, shaking his head.

"When was the last time you saw her?"

He stared down at the table for a few seconds. "I figured you'd ask me that and I can't remember. It was either during one of her trips up here or in passing on campus."

"Did she and Sandi ever have words?"

"Not that I know of. Sandi only had nice things to say about her."

"Did she ever have a falling out with Katey Lowery?"

"Not that I know of."

"Anything else you can think of to tell me about Gemma?"

"No," he said, shrugging his shoulders.

"Where were you Tuesday, November twenty-fifth in 'ninety-seven?"

Michael adjusted himself in the chair. "Studying my ass off in the law library in Madison. I've got a couple of study group members who can vouch for me. We were preparing for a pretty nasty exam."

Lark waited while George took down his friends' names and phone numbers.

"How well did you know Terry Foltz?"

"Not very well. I only saw her a couple of times, once with Sandi on campus and once when we were up here together. I don't know anything else about her."

"Where were you last weekend?"

"Same place as before. The UW law library," he said with a lopsided grin. "Law school has not been easy for me. I've really had to hit the books. My study group will vouch for that. Nancy Schaub, my roommate, can verify that I was home every night until I came up here."

George took the names and numbers of the study group and Lark thanked Michael for his assistance.

"What did you think?" Lark asked as he and George went over their notes prior to bringing Sandi in.

"I've known that kid for years," George said as he sat back and stretched his legs. "He didn't seem any different. He's uncomfortable about spending so much time in the library. He was quite the jock in school. I don't think I ever saw him with a book."

Lark nodded, a bit of a smile on his face. "Happens to a lot of us sooner or later if we stay in school. Was he ever in any trouble?"

"Nope. He liked the girls and they were nuts for him. As far as I know, he never got anyone in trouble either, if you get my drift," George said.

Lark refilled their coffee cups and went in search of Sandi.

Sandi, dressed in black pants and a bright red sweater, brightened up the room just by her presence. Like her mother, she had masses of beautiful chestnut-colored hair and huge brown eyes surrounded by what seemed to be a double set of eyelashes. Lark had a feeling she was well aware of her effect on men, although nothing about her gave that impression. She accepted Lark's offer of a Diet Coke. They made small talk while they waited for George to return with it. Lark was amazed at how relaxed she seemed in the wake of the murders of two of her friends.

He started the interview by asking her to describe her relationship with Gemma.

"We met our freshman year at UW–Madison when we were taking history together. One of those cattle-call classes in an auditorium. A group of us got together to share notes when we couldn't be there. Gemma was in the group. We became friends."

"Can you tell me about some of Gemma's other friends?"

"Katey Lowery also became a good friend, as did a couple of other girls from the class." She beamed him a radiant smile.

"Any falling-outs that you know about?"

"None other than her freshman-year roommate," she said, her face turning serious. "I believe her name was Jasmine Milton. I don't know if she's still on campus, but you could probably find out at the registrar's office."

"What happened between them?"

"They were like oil and water. Gemma was neat and Jas was a slob. Gemma went to bed early and Jas stayed up till all hours." Sandi rolled her eyes as she described Jasmine's behavior.

"Did Jasmine know Terry Foltz?"

"I don't know, I lost track of her when she and Gemma split as roommates."

"Was she violent?"

"Not that I know of." She folded her hands together. "She sure had a temper, throwing things, cussing and swearing. Gemma moved out halfway through the fall semester."

"Anyone else who could have been violent towards Gemma?"

"I can't think of anyone." She frowned over at Lark. "I know Ron Chevsky got mad at her when she wouldn't go out with him. He's got quite a temper, but I've never known Ron to be violent until recently. I ran into him in the IGA parking lot before Thanksgiving. He screamed at me and called me a fucking bitch and pounded on the hood of my car so hard he put a couple of dents in it. He reeked of alcohol and looked like hell."

"You mean this Thanksgiving?" Lark asked, watching her face intently.

"Yes, just after the bodies were found. He scared the shit out of me. He's always been a drinker, but he's really gone downhill since he left school."

"Did Ron know Terry?"

"I don't know. Ask Katey."

"What about boyfriends?"

"Gemma dated occasionally, but she hadn't found anyone special," she said, staring down at her folded hands. "She was busy in school. You should ask Katey or Gemma's old roommate, Shannon Tallman, the one she moved in with after Jasmine. I heard she went skiing with her parents in Colorado over Thanksgiving but she should be back on campus tomorrow."

"Where were you on the Tuesday before Thanksgiving in 'ninety-seven?"

"I was in class in Madison. Michael and I talked about this," she said, grinning at him and waving her finger, as if to make a point. "We knew you'd ask us. We drove up together late Wednesday night. In fact, we got in after midnight on Thanksgiving morning."

"Now let's talk about Terry Foltz. Can you tell me about your relationship with her?"

"Sure." She grinned and crossed her legs as she took a big sip of Diet Coke. Lark had been flirted with by the best and marveled at how unaware she seemed to be of her effect on men. "I met Terry in Madison. She knew Katey and we had some of the same classes."

"When did you meet her?"

"Um, about two years ago, right after Gemma disappeared."

"Can you think of anyone who would have wanted to hurt her?"

"No one," she said, shaking her head. "She was a sweetie."

"Can you tell us about some of her other friends?"

"She was pretty close to her roommate. That's about it. Ask Katey, they were much closer than we were."

"Any idea about Terry's boyfriends?"

"I never saw her dating anyone other than a guy she knew from Wayzata. I've racked my brain," she said, tapping her lower lip with a red fingernail that matched her outfit, "but I can't remember his name. Ask Katey, she'll know."

"Where were you this past weekend?"

"Madison, studying. My roommate can verify that."

"Can you think of anything else to tell me about Terry?"

"Nothing, but I hope you catch whoever did this. It's kind of spooky that someone is killing UW students in my hometown."

More than spooky, Lark thought as he walked her out to her parents, thinking about her lack of emotion over the murders.

He quelled Sara's fears about needing to hire a bodyguard for Sandi and saw the Waltners out of the station. What Sandi lacked in emotion, Sara made up in dramatics. Steve seemed curiously detached from the whole situation, and Lark found it easy to believe the rumors he'd heard about his affair with his assistant.

Although they had started late with the Waltners, Lark still had thirty minutes before the Lowerys showed up at 1 P.M. He and George went to the Big Oak Diner for a quick lunch. On the way over, he found himself wondering how Lacey was doing. He restrained himself from calling, not wanting to wake her if she had managed to fall sleep.

They got back from lunch just as the Lowerys arrived. Katey was as blond as Sandi Waltner was dark, and as casual as Sandi was formal. She wore a dark blue ski parka and gray UW–Madison sweatpants. Black boots and blue ski gloves finished off her look. She didn't appear to be wearing any makeup. Her long blonde hair was pulled back with a dark blue hairband. Her cheeks were rosy from the cold and her deep blue eyes sparkled.

Her brother, Matt, was a tall, blond, Viking type. They agreed that Katey would be interviewed first. Matt made it clear that he didn't know much about either girl but he was willing to answer their questions.

"Tell me about your relationship with Gemma," Lark said, studying Katey. He came to the conclusion that she looked like the Nordic version of a California surfer girl.

Katey sighed and fiddled with the cuff of her UW sweatshirt. "Sandi introduced me to her freshman year and the three of us became friends. She came up here to visit several times, staying at my house or Sandi's, and I went to her place a couple of times."

"What did you two like to do together?"

"Hmm. We both liked to read, we went out to eat a lot and to the movies. We shopped and hung out together. That's about it." Katey slouched down in her chair, plopping a ski boot across her knee.

"Did you know Gemma's roommate Jasmine?"

"Yeah, nice but very temperamental," she quipped. An ironic smile crossed her face. "She and Gemma couldn't have been more different. They split up midway through fall semester."

"Did Jasmine also know Terry?"

"Not that I know of," she said without hesitation.

"Was Jasmine violent?"

"Um, I wouldn't say violent, more like very emotional."

"Can you think of anyone who would have wanted to hurt Gemma?"

"No, I've racked my brain and I can't think of a soul. She was one of the nicest people I've ever known." She looked over at him sadly. "I just can't believe this has happened."

"Do you recall who she dated?"

"She went out with a couple of guys from here, Jim Kryjack and Ron Chevsky, and she had a few dates with other guys on campus, nothing serious."

"How about you?"

"How about me what?" she asked, smiling at him.

"Dating. Do you have a steady boyfriend?"

"No. No steady boyfriend. I'm focused on school."

"Anything else you can think of that I need to know about Gemma?"

"Nothing. Everyone who knew her liked her."

"Where were you Tuesday, November twenty-fifth, that year?"

"That's easy," she said, slouching further down in the chair. "I was up in Bessemer, Michigan, skiing with my family. It's tradition. We always go up Thanksgiving week."

"What can you tell me about Terry Foltz?"

"I've known her since we were kids," she said, her eyes teary. "Our parents know each other through the mills. We became good friends when we both ended up going to school in Madison."

"What did you have in common?"

"Pretty much the same as Gemma: books, movies, music, hanging out," she said, wiping her eyes with the sleeve of her sweatshirt.

"Do you know anyone who had a reason to hurt Terry?"

"I can't think of a soul." She sat up in the chair, shaking her head.

"Did you know any of Terry's boyfriends?"

"No," she said, pulling her headband off and running her hands through her hair. "She dated a little, but I don't think there was anyone special."

"Where were you last weekend?"

"Skiing in Bessemer with my family." She replaced her headband. "I got up there late Friday evening."

"Anything else you can tell me about Terry?"

"Not a thing," she said, shaking her head and fiddling with her headband.

Katey left and Matt was ushered in. As he'd told them earlier, he knew next to nothing about Gemma and Terry. He'd met Terry several times at family gatherings, but he was three years older than Terry and Katey; just enough, he said, to make the girls giggling teenage pests when they were younger. He was far enough ahead of them in school that they rarely crossed paths on campus. On the downhill stretch for his Ph.D. in biology, he was totally focused on his goal of being hired to teach at one of the universities in the Midwest.

Matt recalled seeing Gemma only twice when she spent the weekend at his house. He, too, had been in Bessemer skiing when both girls were killed. He assured Lark that several family friends and ski resort employees would verify his presence as well as Katey's, and most of the Lowery clan for both time periods.

The Lowerys were on their way by 2:30. Lark and George sat down to organize their notes. They constructed a table on the marker board in the interview room to keep everyone's whereabouts straight. The only people in Big Oak for both murders were Jim Kryjack, the last person Lark suspected, and Ron Chevsky, the person most easy to suspect.

Lark made copies of his notes so he could review them with Lacey. He left the station at 3:30 and stopped at the store to pick up some groceries and two more movies. Both were videos that Lacey had mentioned she wanted to see. As he headed out of town, he passed Tetzloff's and remembered he was supposed to get back to Tom about the two cars that had been towed there.

As luck would have it, Tom was in the garage unloading a car with the front end smashed in. "Yet another drunken FIB providing business for us poor folk up here in the northwoods," he joked.

Lark ignored him and asked what was happening with the Taurus from Lippert Motors.

"They don't seem to be in any hurry to pick it up. If they don't show up soon, I may take it over, or I might ask Sara Waltner if she or one of her kids wants to run it over."

"Sara Waltner? Why would you ask her?" Lark asked.

"Sara was a Lippert before she married Steve. Everybody around here knows that," he said, wiping his hands on the legs of his grimy overalls.

"Well, I'll be dammed," Lark muttered under his breath.

"Had another stolen car from Lippert's turn up here a few years ago. If you ask me, it's one of them Waltner kids joy-riding."

"Do you remember when that was?" Lark asked

"Nope. I can have Edith check the books. Now, about the Ransons' Explorer." He walked to the other side of the garage where it was up on a rack. "There's something kind of peculiar here. I pulled the tire off and noticed that it had a big hole in each side. Doesn't look like a blowout, looks more like something went through it." He showed Lark the tire.

"What could have done that?" Lark asked, a feeling of dread forming in his gut.

"Look under here," Tom said, motioning him under the Explorer to look at a hole in the lower portion of the side panel.

"What caused that?" Lark asked, pretty sure he knew the answer.

"From the way the metal is punctured from the inside out, I think it was a bullet. It blew through the tire and the side of the truck, causing this hole. Must have been a drunken hunter. She was one lucky woman not to get herself killed."

"You really think it was a bullet?"

"Sure as sure can be," Tom said, running his blackened fingers back and forth through the hole. "Those hunters are a bunch of crazy fuckers. I give it up years ago. I got my trophy buck and quit. Never did much like the taste of venison. What the hell do you want me to do with this car? John and his insurance adjuster were in here today wanting to have it repaired. I told them I couldn't do nothing with it till you give permission."

Lark shook himself out of his reverie. "I'll send someone over to photograph the tire and the side panel and you can release the car to John tomorrow. Hang on to the Lippert vehicle."

Lark drove home deep in thought. He pulled the county Explorer into the garage and noted that his Jeep hadn't moved. The clock on the dashboard glowed 4:30 and he wondered where the day had gone.

He walked into a dark house. He was pleased, thinking that Lacey had taken his advice and gotten some rest. When he went upstairs to change clothes, he was startled to find her under his quilt, sound asleep. A nightgown and robe were draped over the chair.

Not knowing what to do, he wandered into the bathroom to think. He was saved from having to make a decision when he heard a muddled,

"Holy shit." Concerned that something was wrong, he went back into the bedroom and found her lurching like a drunk as she clutched the quilt around her and tried to sit up.

He eased her up into a sitting position.

"What time is it?" she asked, struggling to get her eyes focused.

"Almost five. Have you slept all day?"

"I think so. I made the mistake of getting in your whirlpool after taking two pain pills. It knocked me for a loop."

He sat down on the bed and put his arm around her just as she started to list back down. "Are you OK?"

"I feel like I could sleep for another hundred years." She extracted one of her arms from the quilt.

"Why don't you go back to bed?" He tightened his grip on her to keep her from falling over.

"Nature calls," she said, lurching out of his grasp and scooting to the side of the bed.

"Let me help you," he said, concerned when he saw how wobbly she was.

"Not on your life, buster, all I have on is this quilt."

"This could be very interesting," he said, doing a poor imitation of the Arte Johnson character from the old show *Laugh-In*.

"Good one, Lark. I'm black and blue, I've got cracked ribs and a busted lip. No question, I'm a real sex goddess." She bent over and picked up her nightgown and robe. Pain shot through her and she groaned, thinking her chest might explode.

Constrained by the quilt, she hobbled into the bathroom. She leaned up against the sink and watched in gratitude as Lark started the shower and laid out a towel and washcloth for her.

"A hot shower will help work out the cobwebs. If you're still tired when you get out of the shower, go back to bed. When you're hungry, let me know. I'll fix you my very best comfort food."

"What's that?" she asked, interest piqued.

"Grilled cheese and soup, as long as it's chicken noodle or tomato. But I could go out and get something else. It's not comfort food unless you have your favorite soup."

"Tomato's my favorite," she said, smiling even though it hurt her lip.

"Great. I'll be ready when you are." He started for the door. "Anything else you need before I leave?" He glanced over his shoulder at her.

"If you don't get out of here, all the hot water will be gone."

"I could help you wash your hair," he teased, coaxing another smile out of her, "or I could wash your back."

"In your dreams, pal." She used her free hand to wave him away. "Get out of here."

Laughing, he shut the door and headed downstairs. He marveled at how a little flirting had made his headache vanish.

Lacey steamed away her aches and pains, thinking about how she would have loved to have Lark wash her back, as well as more exciting things. "In my dreams," she murmured into the shower spray.

In her nightgown and robe, her hair turbaned in a towel, she wandered downstairs a half hour later to find Lark on the phone. She poured herself a glass of milk and pulled a straw out of a box that lay on the counter with cans of soup and a loaf of bread. Lacey listened to Lark request one of his teams to post itself on the road outside the Ransons' house. He demanded that the other team patrol the area whenever they weren't out on a call. He ended the phone call and dialed again before she could ask him what was going on.

Her concern grew as he called his colleagues in the four surrounding counties and asked for their assistance in covering calls for the next twenty-four hours. The sheriffs obliged, knowing the circumstances he was in.

When he hung up, Lacey attempted to ask him what was going on but he waved her off and dialed Joel. He found him at home just starting dinner, and for once there was no small talk.

"Joel, I need help up here for the next few days. Can you send a team to keep Ann Ranson under surveillance?" Lark punched the speaker button so Lacey could hear.

"Are you telling me you think she did this?" Joel asked, shocked.

"No, I think someone thinks she knows something and may be trying to kill her."

Lark glanced over at Lacey. "We thought she had a blowout on my road last night, but I just looked at the car. Her tire was shot out."

"No shit," Joel said. "Damn, are there snowmobile tracks at this scene as well?"

"Don't know. We haven't had time to look. I just found out about this an hour ago and I'm trying to put together protection for Ann. I'll look for tracks first thing in the morning."

"Your staff told me that you have most of the suspect interviews done," Joel said. "Anyone stand out?"

"No," Lark said, shaking his head as if Joel could see him. "Everyone has alibis. If they all check out, we've got no one left but Ron Chevsky and Jim Kryjack."

"Kryjack's your officer, isn't he?"

"Yep, and I'd stake a paycheck it isn't him," Lacey interrupted.

Joel hooted into the phone. "That's nice, honey, but we all know you've got that trust fund, so one paycheck isn't saying much."

"Eat shit, Joel. The kid didn't do it."

"You develop clairvoyance during your short stay in the northwoods?" Joel asked.

"I agree with her," Lark said. "I'd put my money on Ron Chevsky, but he isn't our snowmobiler. He's been in jail or in Rhinelander for two out of the three shootings."

"Maybe you've got yourself the mother of all rural crime sprees going on up there. One serial killer and one snowmobile sniper," Joel said, chuckling.

"Very funny Joel, very, very funny," Lark said, continuing to pace. "I also had an ugly thought that our murderer might be someone who comes up here for deer hunting season and could be from anywhere. But I don't think so."

"Why not?"

"Because both these girls have personal ties to Big Oak. They know a lot of the same people here. It's got to be someone with connections to this area."

Hearing the concern in Lark's voice, Joel assured him that he and four officers would be over by noon on Monday. After taking the names the UW students had identified as alibis and promising to get them interviewed ASAP, Joel hung up.

Lark called the station, asking the dispatcher to fax a copy of George's interview notes to Joel as soon as they were typed. Once again he stopped Lacey before she could ask a question and dialed the Ransons' number. When no one answered, he left a message for John to call him as soon as he got in.

"Now we can talk," he said, smiling at her.

"You really think someone's trying to kill Ann?"

"I believe someone deliberately shot out her bedroom window when she was standing in front of it. I also think her tires were deliberately shot out. All this started after we found the two bodies on their property. But I can't explain how that fits with my windows being shot out."

"Me either," she said, studying his face.

"Something isn't right and it's more than just drunken, accident-prone deer hunters. We've got the same type of boot prints, Marlboro cigarette butts, and snowmobile tracks leading to nowhere at two scenes. I bet we find the same thing out front," he said, gesturing towards the road in front of his house.

As promised, Lark fixed them a dinner of grilled cheese sandwiches and tomato soup. They ate watching the six o'clock news. John Ranson returned their call just as Lark finished the dishes. He was shocked when Lark told him about the car and grateful for the police guard. Lark and Lacey barely made it to the end of the second movie before stumbling to bed.

MONDAY MORNING

NOVEMBER 27—SWENSON

Lacey fell asleep as soon as her head hit the pillow and did not wake up until her alarm went off. She sat up and groaned in pain as her ribs rebelled. She willed herself out of bed and staggered into the bathroom. She glanced in the mirror and was gratified to see that most of the swelling was gone from her lip. She stood under the shower, and just as the hot water turned lukewarm, she felt her rib cage begin to loosen up.

Twenty minutes later she was sitting at the bar in the kitchen. Although she wasn't hungry, she forced herself to eat some toast and drink a glass of orange juice while she waited for the coffee to brew. She turned around when she heard Lark trotting down the stairs.

"Feeling better?" he asked, pouring them both a cup of coffee.

"Yep."

"Good thing," Lark said, popping a couple slices of bread in the toaster. "I'd hate to think I suffered though a cold shower for nothing."

"I'm sorry. That I didn't even think about you this morning shows how whacked out I must be."

"Didn't you sleep well?" he asked with concern as he slathered his toast with grape jam.

"So well I don't think I even moved."

"It's gonna be a long day. You sure you're up to it?" He studied her lip as he sipped his coffee.

"I wouldn't miss it," she said, guarding her side as she stood up. "Besides, if I sleep any more I'm in danger of turning into Rip Van Winkle."

When Lark realized it was quarter after seven, they hustled out to the Jeep. After a quick stop at the station, they were on the road to Rhinelander. The weather, while disappointing, was consistent. Snow was pelting down. From the look of the roads, it had been snowing for quite a while. They passed a salt truck and then slowed down to get around a road grader pushing brown-tinted drifts of snow to the berm. A few miles down the road they passed a convoy of dump trucks loaded with snow.

"At the rate we're going, it won't be melted by next winter," Lark said as they passed the huge truck.

"Such an optimist," she said as she answered the car phone.

It was Joel, who gave them an update from the University police. They had confirmed the alibis for Sandi and Michael Waltner and were faxing their reports to Big Oak and Wausau.

Lark and Lacey arrived at the clinic in Rhinelander on time and were ushered into a conference room. They warmed themselves with steaming mugs of sludgy coffee.

Ron arrived at 11:30, accompanied by a nurse who could double for Mrs. Claus. Santa's wife turned out to be a very jolly Mrs. Krejewski, who offered to stay for the interview. Ron politely declined. Before she left, she patted him on the back to get his attention.

"What?" Ron asked, a hint of irritation in his voice. Lark and Lacey were surprised to see that he was smiling.

"You remember what your mama told you and you remember what we talked about." Although she was smiling, her voice was as commanding as a four-star general.

"Yes, ma'am."

"You call me if you need anything." She gestured at a black rotary phone without any numbers on it.

"Yes, ma'am," Ron repeated.

"All you have to do is pick it up and I'll be right in here." She looked around the room, her cheerful glance taking each one of them in. She patted Ron on the shoulder again. "Now you behave and tell the truth."

Everyone took their seats. Ron pulled a pack of cigarettes out of his shirt pocket. "Do you mind?" he asked Lacey, gesturing with the crumpled pack.

"Not at all," she said, marveling at the change in him.

Now that his hair was clean and neatly combed, Lacey could tell that it was a rich brown color. It even looked like it had been trimmed. His straggly mustache was gone and his teeth looked like they had been professionally cleaned. The sickly yellow, bloodshot look she'd previously seen in his eyes was gone. He wore a red plaid flannel shirt tucked into worn but clean blue jeans that hung down over his tennis shoes.

"How have you been?" Lark asked, watching him try to steady his hands so he could light up.

"It's really tough," he said, in between drags on his cigarette. "I'd take a drink right now if you offered me one."

"At least you're honest," Lacey said, shocked at the hungry look in his eyes.

"I'm a third-generation drunk," he said, puffing on his Marlboro. "My grandfather died of cirrhosis of the liver in his fifties. I don't even remember him."

"I'm so sorry," Lacey murmured.

Ron flicked his eyes over her, trying to gauge her sincerity. "My dad's been a drunk for as long as I can remember."

"They say alcoholism can be genetic," Lark said, regretting it the minute he saw the despair cross Ron's face.

"No shit, man." Ron leaned over towards Lark, jabbing himself in the chest. "Look at me, take a good look at me," he yelled.

"Treatment can help," Lacey said.

"I've been treated before and so has my dad. It's never successful. We get sick of AA and crawl right back in the bottle." He stubbed out his cigarette butt.

"What are you going to do this time?" Lark asked, ignoring the emotional vibes emanating from Lacey and Ron.

"I'm doing thirty days here. I'll go back to daily AA and I'm going to take Antabuse," he said, staring down at the table.

"What's Antabuse?" Lacey asked.

"A drug that makes you sick as hell if you take it and drink. Mom says I'm a mean drunk. I guess I slapped her twice last week when she tried to get me to stop. I don't remember it." His trembling hand reached into his shirt pocket for another cigarette.

"Did you hurt her?" Lacey asked, her voice no longer sympathetic.

"She's got a black eye, says I gave it to her," he said, his voice hardening. "Scared the shit out of me that I could do that to her and not remember it."

"You ever get into fights when you're drinking?" Lark asked.

Ron took a deep drag on his cigarette and shot a plume of smoke upwards, watching it climb to the ceiling and dissipate.

"Did you . . ."

"I heard you the first time." He cocked his head to give Lark a sharp look. "I've been in fights with guys before but I've never hit a woman."

"You're sure about that?" Lark asked, staring into his face.

"Yep."

"How can you be sure when you don't remember hitting your mom?" Lacey asked.

"I've never been this bad before. This is a new goddamn low," he yelled.

The door swung open and Mrs. Krejewski leaned in. "Ron, I could swear someone called me. You need something?"

"No, sorry," he replied, slouching down in his chair.

"Don't you worry. The next time you holler I'll be right in." She pointed her finger at him as she closed the door.

"Old fucking battle-ax," he said over his shoulder, his voice raised.

"That's quite enough." A voice as cold as steel drifted through the door. "You're working yourself up to loss of privileges. Calm down."

"You said you've never been this bad before," Lark said, trying to get him back on track.

"I've passed out before, but never lost blocks of time like last week."

"Where were you the weekend before Thanksgiving?"

"Drunk," he said, his eyes flicking back and forth between Lark and Lacey.

"Drunk where?" Lark asked.

Ron stubbed out his cigarette. "Mom told me there was another body found at Wazowski's. A college girl, Terry somebody. I didn't know her."

"I didn't ask you that," Lark said with deliberate patience. "Where were you the weekend before Thanksgiving?"

"I'm not sure."

"What do you mean you're not sure?"

"Goddammit," Ron said, slamming his free hand down on the table. "Dad and I went hunting Saturday. We drank all day. I don't remember Saturday or much of Sunday."

"Where'd you hunt?" Lacey asked.

"We got up before dawn and drove to the Chequamegon State Forest around Clam Lake."

"When did you leave there?" Lacey asked, watching him light up again.

"I don't remember."

"Who was driving?" she asked.

"Dad."

"Did you stay overnight or sleep at home?"

"I got up at home on Sunday morning."

"What did you do Sunday?" Lark asked.

"We went hunting up around Grand View, in the Chequamegon."

"Do you remember when you got home Sunday?" Lacey asked.

"I couldn't tell you."

"What about Monday?" she asked, scribbling on her notepad.

"Pretty much the same as Sunday. We got up, ate, and went hunting. This time out by Big Oak Lake, but not at Wazowski's."

"Do you own any snowmobiles?" Lark asked, interrupting Lacey's line of questioning.

"Two of them. What's that got to do with this?" he asked, glancing at Lark.

"Someone shot out a couple of windows at the Ransons'. Ann Ranson also had her Explorer shot at. They also shot at my house." Lark didn't take his eyes off Ron's face.

"Sounds like hunting accidents."

"Somebody did all three on a snowmobile at night," Lark said.

"The trails aren't open yet."

"That doesn't seem to matter to this guy. Funny thing, he chain smokes Marlboros," Lark said, watching him for a reaction.

Ron lit a new cigarette with the butt from his spent one. "I got here Thursday night."

"First shooting happened early Thursday morning," Lark said.

"It wasn't me."

"Do you remember where you were Thursday morning?" Lark asked.

"At home. I was at home drinking."

"You sure about that?"

"Ask my mom. She'll vouch for that. So will my dad."

"We'll do that," Lark said, getting up. "Does your dad smoke Marlboros?"

"My dad didn't know those girls from Adam," Ron shouted as he shoved his chair back and stood up. "Leave him out of this, goddammit. He's got enough problems."

"I didn't say your dad did anything." Lark replied, watching Ron's frightened face. "I just asked if your dad smokes Marlboros."

"Yeah, right," Ron said, turning to watch Mrs. Krejewski walk in the room.

"Trouble in paradise?" she asked, surveying the two men standing opposite each other.

"We're fine. We'll be leaving as soon as Ron answers my question," Lark said, flashing her a smile.

"Yeah, he smokes Marlboros." Ron stomped out.

"I'll see you two out as soon as I get Ron back to his room," Mrs. Krejewski said, motioning for Lark and Lacey to sit down.

"He sure reacted when you asked him about his dad."

"I'd say he overreacted."

Before Lacey could respond, Mrs. Krejewski bustled back in the room.

"This is none of my business, but that's never stopped me before," she said, dropping into the chair Ron had vacated. "Ron was quite the high school football player. My son played against him in high school. During his senior year, the sports pages were full of stories about him and what a promising athlete he was. You know, he went to Madison on a football scholarship."

"How's he been since he got here?" Lacey asked, wondering why they hadn't heard any of this until now.

"Very depressed. Facing the fact that he's an alcoholic. There were always rumors that he had a problem with alcohol. I didn't know how bad it was until he was admitted." All traces of jocularity left her face. "Look, this is none of my business, in fact, I probably shouldn't be talking to you, but he's worried to death about his mom."

"He told us he gave her a black eye," Lacey said.

"He told me that, too, but I think his father has done far worse many times before. He's worried about her now that he's here and can't take care of her."

"Has he mentioned the two girls who were killed?" Lacey asked.

"Only the first one. He cried a couple of times when he talked about her."

"He hasn't mentioned Terry Foltz?" Lark asked.

"No, I asked him about her. He's been very concerned that someone else was killed. After more than twenty years here nothing surprises me, but I'd be shocked if he's your murderer. He's depressed, confused, and angry, but I don't get the feeling he's evil. Believe me, I've seen more than a few evil ones."

Just as Lark was going to ask her another question, her beeper went off.

"No rest for the weary," Mrs. Krejewski said, standing up to fish it out of her pocket. "Or was that the wicked?" She smiled at Lacey. "Gotta go. Never a dull moment."

"Just one more thing," Lark said as they headed for the door.

"Make it quick, dreamboat. I've got an admission."

"Has Ron's father been up to see him?"

"Been here twice," she said with distaste. "Both times reeking of alcohol. We wouldn't let him in. He took a couple of swings at the security staff. Thank heaven, he was so drunk he missed. We called the police but he left before they got here." Her beeper went off again and she set off down the hall at a surprisingly fast clip for a woman her size. She turned around and waggled her fingers at them just before she rounded the corner. "His father, now there's a slice of evil who could use a little time with us."

Lark and Lacey headed out the door, each lost in their own thoughts. They were pelted with a barrage of small stinging snowflakes. Lark forged ahead of Lacey to shield her from the blizzard. After cleaning three inches of snow off the Jeep, they crept out of town.

Joel had left a message on the car phone that all the Madison students' alibis had checked out. He also told them that Terry's car had been found in a strip mall parking lot in Wausau. They stopped at the Sportsman's Inn for lunch and devoured thick juicy burgers and fries in the nearly empty bar. They were back on the road by one-thirty.

MONDAY AFTERNOON

NOVEMBER 27—SWENSON

Once they were out of town, Lark called and asked Flo to have someone search the area across the road from his house where Ann Ranson had her accident. She informed him that there had been two car accidents so everyone was out, and that Joel had called to let her know he was not going to make it to Big Oak. When Lark cursed, she offered to call Joel back. He apologized, telling her he felt it was best that Joel not drive in this weather. She informed him that the state police were thinking about closing the roads and that the county road superintendent was debating pulling the plows off until the snow slowed down. In the background, Lark heard someone on the radio, squawking at her to respond, and quickly got off the phone.

Lacey was focused on the road. The snow was creating near whiteout conditions. Even with the defroster and the windshield wipers on full blast, it was difficult to see. One hour and twenty-five miles later, the Lake Tomahawk sign came into view.

"Do you think we should stop?"

"Let's go on to Minocqua," Lark said, his eyes riveted to the road.

It took them another half hour to drive the ten miles to Minocqua. The radio stations were predicting a record blizzard and the police were asking all motorists to get off the road.

Highway 51 looked like a bumper car rink with several vehicles in the ditch and half a dozen fender benders. On the outskirts of Minocqua, they encountered a police officer detouring traffic. He informed them that Highway 70 and Highway 51 were closed and gave them directions to the motels up the road.

The detour, although less than ten miles, seemed endless. They moved at two speeds, crawl and standstill. There seemed to be as many cars in the ditch as there were on the road. The relentless snow reduced vision to the end of their headlights when they kept it under ten miles an hour. Ninety tense minutes later, they pulled into the brightly lit Northwoods Inn, the only place that still had a vacancy sign blinking.

The exhausted woman at the desk told them they could have her last room. When they told her they needed two rooms, she called the other motels in town and informed them this was all that was left, take it or leave it. They burst out laughing and rented the room.

Lacey went to the room and Lark went to park the Jeep. When he didn't return, she went to the lobby to find him. He came back half an hour later, lugging three plastic bags and his briefcase.

"I thought you dropped off the face of the earth, but instead you bought out the store," she said, taking two of the bags from him as they plodded upstairs.

"A couple of stores were still open so I bought us some necessities," he said, handing her his briefcase so he could unlock the door. It was small but clean, complete with a refrigerator, coffeepot, table and chairs, TV, and a double bed.

"Home sweet home," she said, sitting down on the bed to investigate the shopping bags. She pulled out several travel-size toiletries, two cans of mixed nuts, a package of beef jerky, several candy bars, a bag of potato chips, and dip. He pulled a six-pack of beer and a six-pack of Diet Coke out of another bag. Two pairs of gray sweats emblazoned with the Green Bay Packers logo and two pairs of white socks embroidered with little footballs and Green Bay helmets were the last things out of the bag.

"At least we won't starve," he said, rationalizing his junk-food fit.

"Did you get us a cheesehead, too?" she asked, holding up an extra large sweatshirt to check it for fit.

"It just about killed me to buy these, but beggars can't be choosers. The shelves were almost bare and they were closing when I got there."

She glanced at her watch, surprised that it was only five-thirty. "Should we see if the restaurant is open or just depend on this feast?"

As she was talking, Lark called the dispatcher in Big Oak. Flo was getting ready to leave and informed him they had worried themselves sick over him driving in this mess. After a few minutes of reading him the riot act, she told him to call Ann Ranson at home and Brian Foltz in Duluth. He took down both phone numbers and dialed Ann first. She answered on the second ring, her voice irritable.

"You sound like you've about had it."

"This phone hasn't stopped ringing all day," she said. Lark could hear water running in the background. "And if it wasn't the phone, it was the damn doorbell. I don't know if people really care this much about me or they're just nosey."

"Both. Did I interrupt your dinner? If so, I can call back later."

"No, no, don't mind me. I think this attitude is from the concussion. I have a mother of a headache. The pain pills zone me out so I've quit taking them," she chuckled.

"Flo said you called earlier."

"I got an interesting phone call from a friend of mine in Madison. She's an instructor at the University. Barbara read about the bodies when she got home from Vermont last night. She knew Terry Foltz and Katey Lowery. What she had to say is news to me, but it probably won't be to you. First, you should know that Barbara is a lesbian. She's been out for quite a while and is very involved in some of the campus gay and lesbian groups. She called to find out how I was, and during our conversation she speculated that the murders might be hate crimes against lesbians. She was surprised when I asked her why. She was under the impression that Terry Foltz was a lesbian because she had seen her at several lesbian group meetings with Katey Lowery. Did you already know about this?"

"No, I didn't. Did you know that Katey Lowery was gay?"

Lacey, listening to Lark's side of the conversation while she put their purchases away, stopped dead in her tracks. "What the hell—"

He brought his index finger to his lips.

"I didn't have a clue, but now that I think about it, I've never seen her out on a date. A male date, that is. Maybe I've seen her on a date and didn't know it. I'm ashamed to say this, but I assumed since she was so gorgeous that she was straight. I told Barbara that and she gave me one hell of a lecture on stereotyping. I should know better."

"I do it, too," he said, his mind racing.

"Cathy Lowery just left here. She's here for a few days to check up on her father. I wanted to talk with her about this, but I just couldn't make myself bring it up. I don't know if she has any idea that her daughter might be gay."

"Ann, leave that to me," Lark said with concern.

After some discussion about the weather, Lark hung up and called Brian Foltz. While the phone was ringing, he told Lacey he'd fill her in on the details once they got downstairs. He left a message on Brian's answering machine and they went down to see if there was any food left.

The dining room was packed. Two smiling men raced back and forth behind the bar, serving drinks. A hostess was taking names for the dining room. She told them it would be a forty-five-minute wait, but gestured towards the seating area behind the bar as a spot where they could relax until their table was called.

Despite the crowd, Lark was able to get a beer for each of them while Lacey found a small table near the sliding-glass doors to the deck. They had a nice view of the massive stone fireplace that crackled with a warm, cozy fire.

"Isn't this incredible?" she said. The deck was infused with a glow from the perimeter floodlights. Silvery icicles hung off the gutters and the railing was heaped with at least a foot of snow. The woods beyond the deck, a mixture of white birch, pine, and bare hardwoods, sparkled with layers of snow. Fine flakes of snow continued to pelt down.

"It's great if you don't have to shovel it or deal with accidents as the result of it," Lark said, lounging down in his chair and watching the snow. "This is going to be a real bitch for us and the road crews. If it keeps up, we'll be lucky to get out of here tomorrow."

"Worse things could happen," she said, sipping her beer.

Lark studied her profile, wondering what was on her mind. He couldn't get the information Ann had just given him off his.

"Do you remember what it was like to get up after a huge snow and find out school was canceled?" she asked, grinning over at him.

A smile spread over Lark's face.

"Doesn't this feel just like that? Tons of work to do, but suddenly everything is brought to a standstill by Mother Nature." She raised her beer bottle in a salute towards the sliding-glass doors. "Not to change the subject, but what did Ann tell you?"

Lark pulled himself up, propped his elbows on the table, and filled her in.

"No shit," Lacey said, putting more pieces of the conversation together. She ate a few of the pretzels from the bowl the waitress had dropped off. "If this is true, I can't believe no one mentioned it."

"Someone did mention it. Ron Chevsky mentioned that he thought Gemma Patterson was gay during our first interview with him, but Ann's friend never mentioned Gemma," Lark said, waving his beer bottle at the waitress and motioning for her to bring them two more.

"Everyone says that Katey Lowery, Sandi Waltner, and Gemma were always together. And that Katey, Sandi, and Terry Foltz were inseparable."

"You're telling me you think Sandi Waltner's gay?" Lark asked, his eyes wide with disbelief. "She's a consummate flirt and engaged to Dave Banski."

"So what? She could be deep in the closet or maybe she goes both ways." Lacey waggled her hand back and forth.

"Ah, come on. Give me a break. No way."

"You're like every guy I know. You see a pretty face and a great body and you can't believe she'd waste it on another woman. It never enters your mind. Most of the lesbians I know are feminine and attractive."

"You're not one, are you?" Lark asked as he paid the waitress for their next round.

Lacey snorted as she sipped her beer and choked when it went up her nose. "Just call me grace," she said when she finally quit coughing. "No, I'm definitely straight, but there were women I knew in college who tried it both ways."

"Obviously, we're not done questioning Katey and Sandi. I can't imagine how the *Big Oak Bugle* will handle two gay hate crimes in their weekly summary of community news."

The waitress shouted their name for a table. All but the most expensive items on the menu were gone, so they feasted on Chateaubriand for two with the usual trimmings and split a bottle of red wine. When they got back to their room, Lacey took a shower while Lark made notes from his conversation with Ann. He called Joel to fill him in on the latest information. Molly answered, telling him Joel had been called out on an accident. She took their number and assured him Joel would call back.

While Lark showered, Lacey got into bed and checked out the TV channels. Lark came out just in time to catch the beginning of *McClintock*, an old John Wayne movie. They discovered that they both loved Big John and settled in to watch him fight it out with Maureen O'Hara.

The movie was over at eleven and they turned out the lights, agreeing they were exhausted. After sitting shoulder to shoulder and thigh to thigh while they watched the movie, they rolled over to go to sleep, backs to each other. Restless and wide awake fifteen minutes later, they turned over at the same time and rolled into each other's arms.

"I'm having a terrible time sleeping," he said, scooting himself back so he could focus on her face but keeping his arm around her. "Maybe it's because I'm hot. Would you mind if I took off my sweatshirt?"

"No problem," she said as he sat up on the side on the bed. "I'm hot, too, but I think there's more to it than that. I think we're attracted to each other."

"You're attracted to an old man like me?" he asked, looking over his shoulder as he pulled the sweatshirt off.

"Hell yes, I'm attracted to you. What woman wouldn't be?"

"A woman who likes women," he said, leaning back against the headboard, flattered by her admission.

"Men who like men would think you're a hunk, too." She broke into peals of laughter.

"Touché. What are we going to do about this?"

"Two options. Cold showers or maybe just some snuggling—you hold me or I hold you, and we drift off to sleep."

"Lacey, if I hold you right now, I don't think there's going to be much sleeping going on."

"Then take a cold shower." She stared down at the hillock her feet created under the covers.

"You're attracted to me but you don't want to sleep with me. Is that it?" He lifted her chin so he could look into her eyes.

"If we're going to start something, I don't want it to be while we're on a job together. If we decide to date later, that's one thing. This is something different." She looked at him steadily.

"You're right." He sighed. "I don't know what got into me."

"I do. How many women have you 'slept' with for three nights and not made love to?"

"None."

"Same for me. That's part of what makes this so awkward."

"You're right." He got up to get a Diet Coke. "Want one?" he asked, holding his up.

"Make mine a beer. Maybe it'll help me sleep."

"Great idea." He grabbed two beers and the bag of potato chips before he came back to bed.

They scooted away from each other and made small talk about the case, wondering why no one in Big Oak seemed to know Katey was gay, while they gobbled down chips and drank. After the beers were gone, they turned out the lights, rolled over on their sides away from each other, and attempted to go to sleep.

Five minutes later, Lacey started laughing. "You know what this is like?" she asked, rolling over on her back.

"What?" he mumbled, not turning over.

"A slumber party." She giggled.

"My sisters used to have them. They drove me crazy," he said, turning over on his back and staring up at the ceiling. "All these girls laughing and giggling whenever I came near them."

"This is a bit like having a slumber party with your big brother."

"Oh, so you see me as a brother?" Lark said, turning up on his side and looking down at her. "The sexy older brother. What would the psychiatrists make of this?"

"I didn't say you were sexy. I said you were handsome."

"So I'm not sexy?" he asked, rolling back over on his back.

"Oh, you're sexy, all right," she said, crossing her arms and glancing over at him. "And you damn well know it. This conversation is dangerous."

"Why's that?" He rolled his head over and looked straight into her eyes.

"You know why. You're not ready for anything other than a roll in the hay and I don't want to start anything that I have to get over later. I've been down that road."

"What road?"

She stared up at the ceiling. "The road where I fall into bed with someone I really like, have terrific sex, and begin seeing a future with him when all he sees is sex."

"That's happened to you? Some guy loved and left someone who looks as good as you?"

She snorted and looked over at him. "How long were you married?"

"Ten years." He thought of Maria and his mood deflated in more ways than one.

"You never went to bed with someone you liked and then distanced yourself because you didn't want a relationship?"

He blew out a big breath. "Yep, I've done it."

"As much as I'd love to jump your bones, we have to get up and have a working relationship tomorrow morning. I don't want any problems. I don't want one person to get up wanting something the other doesn't." She kissed him deeply, pulling away before he could wrap his arms around her.

"That stopped way too soon."

"That's exactly why it stopped." She turned over on her side away from him. "I'm a little vulnerable right now. For the first time in my life, I'm thinking about settling down. Neither of us needs this right now."

"Shh." He rolled over and put his arm around her. "We'll sleep better if we just snuggle up. In ten years of marriage I spent a lot of time snuggling. Let's curl up and go to sleep."

Wordlessly, she pulled his arm around her, relaxing against him. They were asleep within fifteen minutes. Although they slept soundly, they were dimly aware of turning over and refitting their bodies to each other throughout the night.

Lacey woke up at seven-thirty to find the other side of the bed empty. A note propped up on her nightstand read, "I'll be down in the bar reading the paper. Come down for breakfast when you get up." A large "L" and "0700" were scrawled at the bottom. She rolled out of bed, feeling more refreshed than she had in a week. Although her fractured ribs still ached, she decided against any pain pills and hoped that the shower would loosen them up. Lark had left half a pot of coffee and she poured herself a cup on the way to look out the window.

It was exciting to see how much snow had fallen the night before. The cars in the parking lot looked like snow-covered dinosaurs. She flipped on the television to hear that most of northern Wisconsin had gotten between eighteen and twenty-four inches and that many homes and businesses throughout the area were without power. Another three to six inches were expected by nightfall.

Shaking her head in wonderment, she headed for the shower. She had just gotten out of her clothes when the phone rang.

"What's up?" Joel asked.

"You sound like shit," she said, hearing his exhaustion through the phone.

"We've had a horrible, horrible night. I helped the county and state patrol with accidents. Wausau got at least two feet of snow and almost everything is at a dead stop." He took a breath and she could hear him sipping something. "I spent most of my night helping ambulance crews. I just got done ferrying a bunch of nurses to the hospital so they'd have enough staff to take care of patients. What can I do for you and what the hell are you doing in a hotel in Minocqua? Are you two having a little fun away from prying eyes?" he asked, the devil coming back into his voice.

"Good old Joel. Mind always in the gutter. For a minute there I thought you were too exhausted to make innuendoes this morning."

"What the hell are you two doing? I assume you're not there by yourself. Knowing you two, you're probably in the same room," he said laughing.

"We are, but you can rest easy. It was the last one left. Hold on." She dropped the phone on the bed when she heard Lark's key in the lock and dashed in the bathroom to put her sweats back on.

She came out to find a grinning Lark talking to Joel. "She just ran in the bathroom. No, nothing happened between us so there's no way you'll be a godfather anytime soon. I don't know if they're real, you'll have to ask her yourself."

"Give me that phone," Lacey said, grabbing the receiver from him. "We don't have time for this shit," she shouted. "Shut up and listen to Lark while I take my shower." She tossed the phone to Lark and stomped into the bathroom.

"One of these days you're going to go too far," Lark told Joel as he watched the bathroom door slam.

Lark finished his conversation just after she finished her shower. He hung up as she poured herself a cup of coffee.

"Wausau sounds like a nightmare," he said, surveying her face.

"You talk to anyone in Big Oak this morning?" she asked, working her fingers through her tangled hair.

"They did surprisingly well. No accidents after ten last night and no emergency calls. No one has reported any power outages, but with this amount of snow, who could get out to report it?" He poured himself the last of the coffee and sat down at the table. "The road crews have scraped most of the main roads. They're going to start on the side roads this afternoon."

"Did they get a chance to search that area across from your house?"

"They got out there yesterday afternoon and found the faint tracks of a snowmobile going up over the hill to a little dirt road that leads out to the highway."

She nodded and he went on, "They found boot tracks but couldn't identify them because too much snow had fallen into them. They also found half a dozen Marlboro butts."

"Maybe Joel can get someone up to help out. They have any breakfast down there? I'm famished."

"They've got a buffet. That's why I came up. I thought we could eat before the food runs out."

Ten minutes later, they were sitting in front of plates heaped with scrambled eggs, bacon, toast, and hash browns. Their table looked out on the deck. They ate quietly, watching the bird feeders that hung from the deck ceiling. Chickadees, woodpeckers, and nuthatches were the most common visitors. Doves and raucous bluejays scavenged up the leftovers from the snow-covered deck. Two standoffish pairs of cardinals waited their turn at the feeders. The radiance of the scarlet males against the snowy backdrop reminded Lacey of Christmas ornaments. The females in their dull brownish red feathers looked bedraggled in comparison.

After breakfast, Lark and Lacey wandered out to the motel entrance to see what condition the roads were in. They watched the road graders working away at snow removal while the police attempted to deal with the biggest obstacle to clearing the road: abandoned vehicles.

"We're not getting out of here any time soon," Lark said, surveying the mess. "Let's see if they have a conference room with a blackboard we can use."

Within thirty minutes they were settled into a small meeting room off the lobby. They reviewed their notes and compiled a list of questions for Ron Chevsky and Jim Kryjack.

"Did you tell Joel about last night's conversation with Ann?" Lacey asked, adding Katey Lowery and Sandi Waltner to the board with Ron and Jim.

"Yeah. He was quite surprised." Lark leaned back in his chair. "He hasn't picked up even a hint from anyone that Terry or Gemma were gay."

"Damn," Lacey said, sitting down. "You'd think someone would see that as an issue."

"If it's true." Lark rolled his pen between his hands. "What if there's nothing to it?"

"Did Joel pick up any names of boyfriends?"

"He didn't," Lark replied, making a note on his legal pad as Lacey got up to write "boyfriends" off to the side on the board. Radiating out from it she lined up the names of Katey Lowery, Sandi Waltner, Gemma Patterson, and Terry Foltz.

"Take Sandi off there, she's engaged," Lark said, waving at her new list.

Lacey stood back and surveyed the board. "Nope, she's staying."

"Suit yourself," he said, flipping through his notes.

"I'll never believe Jim did this." She sat down to copy the chart onto a legal pad. "We'll need to get details of every minute for Jim and Ron. There has to be something we're missing."

"The state police did a pretty thorough job of canvassing for any witnesses on Gemma's case. That's probably a dead end." Lark pulled Gemma's case file out of his briefcase and paged through it.

"If I remember right, the Foltzes said that Terry drove up on I-94 when she was coming home. We need to find out which way she would have driven to Big Oak." Lacey jotted another note on her legal pad. "Maybe Joel can get that route checked."

"Good idea," Lark said, distracted by Gemma's police report.

"You know who else we didn't question?"

"Who?"

"The Lowerys and the Waltners." When he looked at her blankly she went on. "She stayed with both families. Don't you think we should interview the parents as well as the kids?"

"Damn. How the hell could we have missed them? I must be slipping."

"We all missed it. Eliminate the obvious, and the kids are all obvious." She paused to scribble another note. "Plus all we've heard is Katey and Sandi, Sandi and Katey," she said in a sing-song voice.

"Shit, just when you think things have narrowed down, we get more people to screen."

Lacey fished the notes on Terry out of Lark's briefcase. They agreed that they would reread both files and see if they came up with anything new. Lacey quickly got through the scant notes from the Foltz case and wandered up to their room while Lark read the more voluminous Patterson file. At noon they sat down to review their notes while they took a break in the bar.

"What have you got?" Lark asked when he got back to the table with their soft drinks.

"Not much we didn't already have," she said. "Were there any boyfriends or any other intimate relationships? Gemma's car was found in Eau Claire and her body in Big Oak. Terry's car was found in Wausau and her body in Big Oak. Did someone move the cars and the bodies or both? How are these murders connected to the snowmobile shootings, or are they?" Lacey asked looking over at him. "That's all I found."

Lark nodded over at her. "The bodies were both moved. How far is the question."

"Do we go to Madison and interview Sandi and Katey again or do we have Joel send someone down?"

"We've got to talk to them. I also want to interview Ann's friend."

"Do we go straight to Madison or back over to Big Oak?"

"Back to Big Oak," Lark said, grinning over at her. "You don't want to spend the next two days in these Packer sweats do you?"

"I've been in less comfortable clothes," she said, fanning the waistline of the sweatshirt out. "It beats the hell out of pantyhose and heels, but it would be nice to have a change of underwear and some makeup."

"Surely you have an entire cosmetic counter in that purse of yours."

"I have things you'd never believe in this purse," she replied, with an evil grin.

He gulped down the last of his Coke. "Let's grab some lunch, and see if we can get back to Big Oak. Cathy Lowery's in town so we can interview her before she goes back to Michigan."

"We'll still have to interview Mr. Lowery," Lacey said as they trotted upstairs.

"We'll cross that bridge when we get to it."

When they got to their room, they had three phone messages. "Wonder why no one used the cell phone?" Lark grumbled as he played through the calls.

The first one was from Brian Foltz, who left a number for Lark to call after 7 P.M. The second was from Flo, asking him to call in and scolding him about not keeping his cell phone charged. The third was from Joel, telling them that he and two officers would be in Big Oak by noon tomorrow, if the weather held.

Lark called the Big Oak station only to find that Flo had gone to lunch. George was covering and told him that they had picked up Lonnie Chevsky drunk, his van in a ditch. He made Lark's day when he told him that Lonnie had his van rigged to haul a snowmobile in the back. He told Lark that Lonnie was charged with reckless driving and DUI and would be sleeping it off in jail.

Lark and Lacey ate lunch and were on the road by two o'clock. The police reported that the main roads, though slick, were open to traffic. The roads were much better than the day before, but there were several cars masquerading as snow-covered haystacks stuck along the side of the road. The forty-mile trip across Highway 70 was an hour and a half meander behind cars and trucks driving at minimum speeds. Although the roads had been graded, they were still snow-covered and there were only two narrow traffic lanes with no berm, which made it impossible to pass.

It was still snowing, but not in the threatening way it had come down the day before. The weather reports said it was five degrees and expected to drop down to fifteen below that night. Snow was predicted to continue over the next two to three days.

The hunting report brought dismal news no matter how you looked at it. According to the Department of Natural Resouces, the deer harvest was about 50,000 less than they felt was needed to keep the herd thinned down. DNR experts pontificated on how many deer would die of starvation if an organized feeding effort wasn't undertaken to save them. A list of the groups participating in feeding programs was provided. Many of the groups were gun clubs. The irony wasn't lost on Lark or Lacey.

Just past the intersection of Highways 13 and 70, they came upon an accident and stopped to call it in. No one was injured, just shaken up. As usual, all the Mason County patrols were out on other calls so they waited for the wrecker. Tom Tetzloff showed up an hour later with his tow truck. It took another hour to sort out the two vehicles. Before they left, Tom asked Lark what to do with the stolen Taurus he still had in his garage.

"I don't have time to deal with it right now, just get it back to Lipperts'."

"The wife looked up that other Lippert's car we found up here. It was from Eau Claire." Tom dug around in the pockets of his grimy overalls. "I got the dates here somewhere."

"Just call me when you find them," Lark said, brushing by him to get in the Jeep.

"Just hold your damn horses. I got it right here. It'll only take a couple seconds and then we can get on about our business." He pulled a black-smudged piece of paper out of one of his back pockets. "Found it," he said, triumphantly.

When he started rooting around for his glasses, Lark took the paper away from him. He opened the door and leaned in under the dome light to read *November 27, 1997*.

"Tom, are you sure about this date?"

"Sure as shootin'. My wife says we got to have our books gnat's ass accurate. She don't miss nothin'. You need more information on that car?"

"You've got more?"

"I'll find out and call ya," he said, heading for his truck. Just before he climbed in, he yelled at Lark. "You still want me to send that car back to Lippert's?"

"Hang on to it for a few more days," Lark said as he got back in his Jeep.

"That's what I figured," Tom said.

"What was that all about?" Lacey asked as Lark watched Tetzloff pull out.

"You remember that Taurus that was found at Grezetski's Market last week?" Lacey nodded. "Tom thought there was another car stolen from Lippert's that turned up here a few years ago. It was found two days after Gemma went missing. It was from Eau Claire."

"I'll be damned," Lacey said, sitting back in her seat, absorbing the facts. "Do you think this could be another connection between the two bodies?"

"Yep," Lark said, starting the Jeep, "and it's a connection right back to Big Oak. The cars came from different places, but they both ended up here."

"Holy shit," she said, her mind racing. "Someone up here has a connection to Lippert Motors. I can't remember who." She rummaged through her purse for her notebook.

"Sara Waltner was a Lippert before she got married. We haven't questioned anyone about the cars," Lark said, his voice clipped, "but we will shortly."

They pulled into the sheriff's office a little after 5 P.M. There was barely enough room to park in the back because of the mountain of snow taking up several parking places. The office was bustling and Flo motioned them over as she fielded a call. They pulled up chairs on either side of her.

"What's up?" Lark asked, noting the tiny white snowmen on her scarlet fingernails. Inch-long snowmen dangled from her ears and a three-inch felt snowman was pinned to her green-and-yellow Green Bay Packers sweatshirt.

"You all goin' for that matching look some couples get off on?" she asked, surveying their Packer sweats. Lark blushed a deep red.

Lacey leaped to his rescue. "This was all they had left in Minocqua last night. Beggars can't be choosers."

"Uh-huh," Flo said, looking them up and down before fielding another call. She dispatched George to deal with another accident and turned back to them. "Stupid bastard ran into a tree with his snowmobile," she said, shaking her head. "Nothing but idiots."

"Flo, what did you want?"

"Sorry about that, I was so bowled over by your matching Packer outfits that I forgot what I wanted to tell you. Betty Chevsky's waiting for you. She's got two black eyes and a bruise on her cheek. Says she fell down." She rolled her eyes. "Fell down, my ass. That drunken bastard beat her up again."

"We'll see if we can get her to press charges," Lark said, getting up.

"Wait a minute," Flo commanded, looking up at Lark and pointing down at the chair.

Much to Lacey's amusement, Lark sat down. "Sorry, Flo, I thought you were done."

"Did they tell you that bastard's got his van rigged so he can put a snowmobile in the back of it?"

"Yes, they did."

"She'll never press charges against him with Ron not here to protect her. She's too afraid of what he'll do to her. If you can find another way to arrest him, that would be best."

"I'll see what I can do," he said, standing up.

Flo fielded yet another call and glared up at Lark as she dispatched Jim to the Dew Drop Inn for a disturbance. Lark sat back down.

"Lonnie's got to be the one who shot out the windows," Flo said

"Why do you think that?"

"If it was someone going around town with a snowmobile trailer hitched to his truck, we would've found them by now. Lonnie's rig is perfect. That's why no one could find him when you and Mrs. Ranson was shot at."

"I'll check it out," Lark said, giving her a reassuring smile.

"Just don't let the bastard go until you know for sure. I've never seen Lonnie this bad off or Betty this beat up. He's liable to kill her the next time." She turned away to answer another call.

Lark and Lacey went to his office to lay out their plan. They decided to interview Betty and then take a stab at Lonnie. Lark asked Paul Dolphson to set up appointments to interview Cathy Lowery and Steve and Sara Waltner either that evening or the next day.

Lark was very alarmed when he saw Betty. The skin around her left eye was black and blue and her eye was bloodshot. The skin around her right eye was the purplish yellow rainbow color of a healing bruise. She had a fresh black-and-blue mark on her left cheek and her upper lip was cut and swollen. She stood up when she saw them and pain flashed across her face, indicating that Lonnie had not confined himself to her face.

"Betty," Lacey said, rushing to take her arm. "We need to get you to the hospital."

"No, I'll be fine. I fell out in the garage yesterday. All this snow makes it very slippery."

"You should at least go in and be checked," Lark said, watching her wince as she struggled to hold herself upright. "You've got good insurance, so it will be covered."

"I said I'm all right." She gave him an angry look as her hand flew involuntarily to her left flank. "I'm not here about myself. I'm here about Lonnie."

"Would you like something to drink?" Lacey asked as Lark led the way into the interrogation room.

"Coffee would be nice if you've got any fresh. Maybe it'll warm me up." She sat down and took off her gloves. Her hands were bruised and cut and her knuckles were swollen. Lark kept quiet, knowing better than to say anything.

Lacey had a bit more difficulty when she came back in the room. When Betty reached for the coffee cup, Lacey nearly dropped it in surprise over Betty's hands. She glanced at Lark, who gave her a nearly imperceptible shake of his head.

Betty took a sip of coffee. "How do I get Lonnie out of here? Can you release him to me like last time?"

"Not this time." Lark locked his eyes on hers. "He's been arrested for DUI and reckless driving. He'll be arraigned in Park Falls tomorrow morning. This time he'll probably go to jail and lose his license."

She sunk down in the chair, fixing her gaze on the table. "I'll get a lawyer and fight this."

"That's your right. You're looking at a couple grand in fines as well as lawyer fees."

"Why are you doing this to us?" she asked, her voice tremulous as she slumped lower in the chair. Her hands shook as she picked up her coffee cup.

"He could have killed someone driving drunk like this in the snow. You know we can't let him get away with that," Lacey said.

Betty looked away.

"Do you have a snowmobile?" Lark asked, changing the subject.

"Yes," she said, once again looking away, "just like everyone else up here."

"Your husband smokes Marlboros, doesn't he?" Lark asked the top of her head.

She said nothing.

"Your son also smokes Marlboros, doesn't he?"

Her head snapped up. "Don't you bring Ronnie into this. He has nothing to do with it."

"Your son and your husband both smoke Marlboros, don't they, Betty?"

"Why do you want to know?"

"Just answer the question."

"Yes! Who cares what they smoke?"

"Someone shot at Mrs. Ranson and shot out my windows. Whoever it was chain-smoked Marlboros and traveled on a snowmobile. That puts your husband and your son at the top of the list as suspects. Your son also dated Gemma Patterson, one of the dead girls."

"Ronnie's been in rehab. He couldn't have done this." A pleading tone crept into her voice.

"He was here in Big Oak when Mrs. Ranson was first shot at."

"I know he didn't do it," she whispered.

Lark watched two tears drip off her face and onto the tabletop. "I'm sorry, Mrs. Chevsky, I couldn't hear you."

"I know he didn't do it and you know it, too. Why are you doing this? Why do you want to hurt my son?" she asked, tears streaming down her face.

"Why would *you* want to hurt your son?" Lark asked.

"I would never hurt Ronnie," she snapped, wiping tears away with the back of her hand.

Before Lark could ask Betty another question, Lacey got up and left the room. The look she gave him would have frozen volcanic lava in its tracks. He sighed and went on with his questioning. "If you don't want to hurt your son, then why do you subject him to an alcoholic batterer as a father? What kind of an influence has he been for Ron?"

"Lonnie's his father. That's just the way it is," she said, her eyes overflowing with tears. Lacey walked back in, glaring daggers at Lark as she placed a tissue box in front of Mrs. Chevsky. Betty pulled out a handful of tissues, then wiped her eyes and blew her nose.

"That may be the way it is, but that isn't the way it has to be. Let's quit pussyfooting around here. Your son and your husband own a snowmobile and smoke Marlboros. They threatened Mrs. Ranson. One or both of them did these three shootings. I think Ron did the first one, and when he went into rehab, Lonnie did the other two."

"You're wrong. Ron would never hurt anyone."

"He gave you that black eye, didn't he?" Lark pointed to her right eye. "Don't try and lie about it, he already told us."

"He's a good boy, he's a good boy," she said over and over as she put her head into her hands and sobbed. Lacey reached out for her but Lark impatiently waved her back.

"He may be a good boy, but he admits that he's an alcoholic and he's terrified that he hit you. How is he going to get well and make something of himself living in the same house with your husband?"

"I can't . . . I can't do this," Betty cried into her hands. "I want to leave."

"Go ahead and leave," Lark said, standing up. "We didn't ask you to come here. You're free to go. We'll call you when we have the DNA done on your husband and your son, and see which one matches the cigarette butts we found at the scene. Whoever did it is going to jail for assault, maybe even attempted murder. We're also investigating Ron for the murders of the two girls."

Betty's words were unintelligible. All he heard were moans and sobs. Once again, he waved Lacey away from comforting her. After she'd cried herself out to the point of shaking, she began to talk.

"I can't tell you," she said in jagged, hiccoughing breaths. "He'll kill me."

"We'll try to keep him in jail this time," Lark said.

"He always gets out," she said, her voice rising as she swayed back and forth in her chair. "I can't tell you how many times he's been arrested, and he always gets out. The only reason he hasn't killed me is because I work. He needs my paycheck. I've even left him and he's found me and beaten me."

"We can keep him locked up for a long time if he did these shootings."

"Ron didn't do them," she said, wiping tears away. "He was passed out drunk when I got home from work on Thanksgiving morning. Lonnie had just come in and the snowmobile was in the back of the van. I couldn't figure out why he had it loaded up. He'd just started it up the day before. We live close to a trail, and he usually drives over to it when he rides. He only puts it in the van to haul it somewhere. He sold the trailer to get money for booze. Ron keeps telling him he's going to break the van down with that snowmobile in the back, but he's crazy." She paused to sip her coffee but her cup was empty.

"Would you like something else to drink?" Lark asked her. When she nodded, he waved Lacey out the door. "Should we go on?"

She nodded. "When I asked Lonnie why the snowmobile was in the van, he snickered and told me it was none of my damn business. He said I'd find out soon enough and if I told anyone he'd kill me. I started to worry right then that he'd done something awful." She paused when Lacey came back in.

"Take your time," Lark said when she choked on the first sip of hot coffee.

"I'm fine," she said, putting the cup down with a steady hand. "I just want to get this over with. I knew when I heard about Mrs. Ranson that he'd done it. He'd been ranting and raving about her since they were caught on her property. He's irrational when he drinks and lately he's been drinking all the time. I was working each time there was a shooting, but the snowmobile has been in the van all this time. He got angry with you once Ron went into rehab. The last time I saw him was last night. He was so drunk, he could hardly walk. I tried to take his keys away from him but he beat me up. I passed out on the floor and woke up this morning. He was nowhere in sight. When they called and told me he'd been arrested, I was overjoyed that no one else had gotten hurt." She slumped down in her chair.

"Anything else?" Lark asked.

"Ron had nothing to do with this. I know he didn't kill those girls. He could never, never do anything like that," she said, tears welling up in her eyes again.

"We're going to take you to the hospital," Lark said. When she started to protest, he raised his hand to quiet her. "If you want your battery charges to stick, you have to be examined. You've got to do this so we can keep him locked up as long as possible. You've also got to do this for your son. He won't be able to make it without you."

Lark and Lacey drove Betty to the hospital. The ER was quiet and she got in right away. Lark looked at his watch and was astounded to see that it was almost 7:30 P.M. He reached for his cell phone and swore when he remembered that the battery was dead. He sighed and went to the pay phone. George had left him a message that their three interviews would start at ten tomorrow morning. He also told him that Lonnie was sleeping fitfully in his cell and wasn't in any shape to be interviewed that night. A few minutes after Lark got off the phone, Dr. Kingsley came out to give them an update.

"We're going to keep her overnight. She's got fractured ribs, a bruise over her left kidney, maybe a fractured orbit, and a possible concussion." Lacey started to ask a question and he raised his hand to silence her. "She'll be X-rayed and photographed. Now what was your question?" he asked, turning to Lacey.

"What's a fractured orbit?"

"The orbit is the bone that surrounds the eye." He circled his right eye with his finger. "This woman has been badly beaten. Does she need protection?"

"Her husband's locked up," Lark replied.

"I hope you keep him there," Dr. Kingsley said, walking away. Lacey followed him. Lark watched them talk and then she followed him into the examination area. A few minutes later she came out, wiping her eyes with a wad of tissues.

Lark walked over to her, full of questions, but she ignored him and led the way out to the car.

"Can we just get a pizza and go home?" Lacey asked.

"Sounds good to me," he said. "I'll call it in." He got her request—anything except anchovies—before he went back into the hospital. When he returned, her head was back against the headrest, eyes closed, and the radio was tuned to the oldies station. He got in and started the car, not clear on whether he should ask her if she was OK or not. They drove to the Pizza Hut in silence, listening to the music.

Lacey appeared to be sleeping, so Lark went in for the pizza, then headed home. They drove in silence, the music washing over them. Lark wondered why she'd been so distant since leaving the ER and ran through the last few hours, trying to figure out what he'd done wrong. When they pulled into the garage, Lark turned off the engine and Lacey sat up, rubbing her eyes.

"Thank God this day is almost over," she said and stretched. "Sometimes I don't know how we get through it." She unbuckled her seat belt and opened the door. When she got out of the car and noticed that he hadn't budged, she asked him if he was all right.

"You haven't said a word in almost an hour. I've been very worried about you." He got out of the car, grabbing the pizza out of the back.

"I'm fine," she said, opening the laundry-room door for him. "I just needed some quiet time to recoup."

"Just tell me the next time I'm going to get the silent treatment, OK?" He brushed past her and dumped the pizza on the kitchen counter before coming back into the utility room to hang up his coat.

"You weren't getting the silent treatment," Lacey said, taking off her boots.

"Well, you could have fooled me. You weren't asleep when we stopped for the pizza. I know what you look like when you're sleeping. What was that all about?" Lark snapped, plopping down beside her. He pulled off his boots and slung them in the closet.

Lacey stood up and took of her coat. "No, I wasn't asleep, I just didn't want to talk. When I'm pissed at you, believe me, you'll know it." Her eyes drilled into him. "What happened earlier was about me, it had absolutely nothing to do with you." She stomped into the kitchen.

"Thanks for the news flash," Lark said, storming in behind her. "If you'd told me that earlier, I wouldn't have spent the last hour worried about you."

"I didn't ask you to worry about me. You took that on yourself," she said as she yanked a piece of pizza out of the box and took a big bite out of it. "I'm going to go upstairs, take a bath, and change. When I come back down here, I hope we're both in a better mood."

"Fine. I wasn't in a bad mood until you tuned me out back there in the car," he shouted after her as he snatched up a piece of pizza.

She remained silent until she got to the top of the stairs. She leaned over the banister and yelled down at him. "Well, I wasn't in a bad mood until you harassed poor Betty Chevsky and tuned me out in the interview at the police station, so I guess we're even." Seeing his jaw drop, she turned on her heel and went into her bedroom.

Shaking his head in disbelief, Lark plodded upstairs. He hesitated outside Lacey's door, thinking about asking her what she meant by her parting shot, but decided against it when he heard the water turn on. As he changed, he played Betty's interview over and over in his mind, trying to find Lacey's point of view. The only part he questioned was when he'd attempted to prevent her from comforting Betty.

With some trepidation, he went downstairs to find Lacey in her green robe, sorting slices of pizza onto two different plates. She turned around and smiled when she saw him. "Here's to surviving our first fight." She held up a plate in a salute.

"So we've survived it? It's over? Just like that?" he asked, surprised.

"Unless you want it to continue." Her smile faded as she gave him a sidelong glance. Before he could respond, she took their plates over to the microwave.

"No, no," he said, waving his hands at her. "I know when to quit." He saw a smile play across her lips as she slipped one of the plates into the microwave. He flopped down on a bar stool and waited for her to say something or for the food to get done, whatever came first.

Having also been trained in the art of waiting out the silence, Lacey busied herself exchanging the plates in the microwave and getting together napkins and silverware. When the pizza was reheated, she went over to the refrigerator and pulled out a beer. Innocently, she turned around and waved it at him, eyebrows raised in question. "Leinenkugel?"

He burst out laughing. "Yeah, thanks."

They ate pizza and watched the 6 P.M. news tapes. The latest storm front and the accidents and human interest stories that resulted from it were front and center. They cleaned up the kitchen and channel-surfed through the three ten o'clock newscasts. None of them carried anything about the murders, just more weather stories. They groaned when all three weather reports predicted two to four inches each day until the weekend, when another large storm would hit Mason County.

"Maybe they'll be wrong," he said, getting the tape out of the VCR to take back upstairs.

"Yeah, we'll probably get a foot each day and have the blizzard from hell over the weekend."

"Shut your mouth," Lark said as they approached the top of the stairs. He pointed his finger at her. "It's not nice to speak ill of Mother Nature. All the weather over the next few days is now on your head."

Laughing, Lacey flipped him the bird and went into her room. Just as he was opening his door, she popped back out and asked, "What time do you want to leave in the morning?"

"How about eight, and treating ourselves to breakfast at the diner? We can go over the transcript from Betty's interview before we meet with Lonnie."

"You're on."

He climbed into bed exhausted but couldn't get to sleep. His king-size bed suddenly felt as big as Alaska and every bit as cold and lonely. He tossed and turned for several minutes before hearing the faint sound of a radio coming through the wall from Lacey's room. He rolled over on his left side and turned on his own radio, thinking some music might help him sleep. Instead of the customary classical music he played at night, the radio blasted out a twangy female voice singing about love.

"Shit, country music," he said, rolling over to turn down the volume and change the station. Instead he shook his head and snapped the radio off. He rolled over and willed himself to fall asleep. His eyes fell on the picture of Maria. He looked into her smiling face, illuminated by the moonlight coming through his window. Usually, he could almost hear her voice when he looked at her picture. Not this time. After a few seconds, he rolled over on his other side and snapped the radio back on. He closed his eyes and listened to a woman sing about how she couldn't stop thinking about a man she was in love with.

Lark snapped off the radio, his mind flooded with thoughts about Lacey and Maria. Frustrated, he turned the radio back on and tuned it to the classical station. He rolled over on his back and willed himself to concentrate on the music. Within fifteen minutes, he was asleep, his cheeks wet with tears.

Lacey and Lark reviewed the notes from Betty's interview over Big Oak Diner skillet breakfasts with enough cholesterol to harden almost anyone's arteries. They were back at the station to interview Lonnie by 9:15. His six-foot frame was gaunt and his wind-burned face was sunken and covered with salt-and-pepper stubble. He looked like a concentration-camp victim. His hair looked like it hadn't been washed in weeks. His mustache was overgrown and unkempt, with flecks of God-knew-what in it. The crow's feet surrounding his dead-looking eyes were creased with dirt. Large purplish bags hung under his eyes.

He slumped in the chair and his hands began a jittery hunt through his clothes for cigarettes. When he couldn't find any, he glared at Lark. "I need a smoke."

"What's your brand?" Lark asked, getting up from the table.

"Marlboros," he said as his hands continued to skitter over his clothes. "I need a drink, too," he bellowed as Lark left the room.

Lark returned a few minutes later with a crumpled pack of Marlboros. "These are yours," he said, tossing them to Lonnie.

Lonnie tapped out a cigarette. He popped it in his mouth and held his head towards Lark for a light. "Where's my bottle?" he asked, after taking a drag.

"It's locked up. You won't be getting any of it while you're here."

"Fuck you," Lonnie said, blowing a long stream of smoke in Lark's face.

Lark stared at him, saying nothing.

"I won't make it without a couple belts," he whined.

"We'll take you to the hospital if you go into the DTs."

"How do I get out of here?"

"Answer our questions truthfully and we'll see what we can do."

"Shoot," Lonnie said, blowing a cloud of smoke up into the air.

"Let's get right to the point." Lark leaned across the table towards him. "Why did you kill those two girls and dump their bodies in the marsh?"

Lonnie jerked away, his mouth agape. "I didn't kill no girls," he stammered.

"I think you did," Lark said, getting up and walking around behind him. "Those girls were badly beaten. You know something about beating women, don't you?"

Lonnie said nothing. His fidgeting increased as he turned around to look at Lark.

"Those girls were put in the marsh by someone with a snowmobile."

"Everybody up here's got a damn snowmobile," Lonnie said, taking another drag.

Lark smacked his hands down on the table, making both Lonnie and Lacey jump in their chairs. He stared angrily into Lonnie's eyes. "Not everybody smokes Marlboros and leaves butts with their saliva on them at the scene."

Lonnie began to squirm in his chair. "I didn't kill them girls," he said as a long-neglected ash dropped off his cigarette onto his pants. Lonnie scrambled to brush it off his lap

"You robbed those summer cabins, you shot out Mrs. Ranson's windows, you shot out my windows, and you shot out Mrs. Ranson's tire and left cigarette butts at every scene. You killed both of those girls and did the same thing," Lark yelled, stabbing his finger at Lonnie with each accusation.

"No, no . . . I . . . shit, goddamn . . ." Lonnie said, flinging away the cigarette butt that had burnt down to his finger.

"What?" Lark yelled, leaning overtop of him.

"Shit, I damn near burnt my hand off." Lonnie popped a grimy finger into his mouth.

"Why did you do this?" Lark bellowed at him. "Why did you kill those girls?"

"I didn't kill nobody," Lonnie said, shrinking back in his chair, away from Lark's anger.

"The person who killed those girls is going to jail for life."

Lonnie was twitching in the chair. "Gimme a light," he demanded as he jerked another cigarette to his lips.

Lark lit him up again. After he took a deep pull, he faced Lark. "I swear I didn't kill them girls."

"Yeah, right."

"I really need a drink. I'm in bad shape."

Lark stared at him, his face like a thundercloud. "So were those two girls. If you go into the DTs, you'll go to a hospital. They died and Ann Ranson damn near died as well. I don't feel one bit sorry for you."

"I didn't kill them girls."

"If you didn't, your kid did. I'm tired of this." Lark nodded over at Lacey. "Let's go to Rhinelander and question Ron again. I'm tired of hearing the same old crap. Paul will be in to put you back in your cell," he said over his shoulder as he headed for the door

"My son didn't kill them either, leave him out of this," Lonnie yelled at Lark's back.

"Yeah right, just like you didn't do any of these other crimes either." Lark walked back over to the table.

"We didn't kill them girls," Lonnie said, sucking up the last of his cigarette.

Lark picked up one of Lonnie's cigarette butts. "You start talking or I'm headed for Rhinelander. We've got cigarette butts from the scenes of the shootings and the murders. All I have to do is match the DNA from the saliva on them to the DNA on this butt and the ones I got from your son." Lark leaned down into Lonnie's face, his jaw set in anger, his eyes as menacing as anything Lacey had ever seen.

"My son didn't do nothin'. I mighta done one or two of them other things, but I didn't kill nobody." Lonnie put a cigarette between his lips, leaning in for a light.

"No more lights until this is over with," Lark snapped, yanking away the cigarette.

"I don't have to tell you nothin'," Lonnie yelled, attempting to pull himself up in his chair. "Where's my wife? That bitch was supposed to bail me out."

"She was here but you were passed out. She almost passed out herself from pain, so we took her to the ER. She's in the hospital from the beating you gave her," Lark said, pacing.

"I didn't give her no beatin' but she deserves one for not getting me out."

"That's it," Lark yelled, throwing his hands up in the air. "Come on, Lacey, let's go. I've had enough of this. We're going to Rhinelander." Lark walked out of the room, slamming the door behind him while Lacey gathered up her notebook.

"No, no, no," Lonnie yelled. "Get him back in here."

"Why should I?" Lacey asked. "You'd rather see your son go to prison than admit what you did."

"Get that asshole back in here," Lonnie snarled.

"He's not coming back in here unless I can tell him something new."

"All right, all right," Lonnie said, fidgeting in his chair. "I robbed a few summer cabins. All them people got insurance, it's no skin off their ass."

"What else?" she asked, sitting down in the chair Lark had occupied.

"Jesus Christ, woman, ain't that enough?" He swayed back and forth in his chair.

"No, it isn't. George will put you back in your cell, we'll get details on the robberies later." She stood up. "How clever of you to admit to the crimes that carry the lightest prison sentence. Now your son will take the hit for the shootings and the murders. You're one sorry son of a bitch."

"Get back over here," he screamed as she walked out.

Lacey came back in and sat down, glancing at the window where she knew Lark was. As if on command, he came through the door. "What's taking so long? We've got to get going."

"Lonnie's got something he wants to tell us, he's already admitted to some robberies."

"I'm thrilled. We've got to get going if we want to get to Rhinelander today."

"Well, he's got another confession to make."

"This better be good." Lark sat down and frowned at Lonnie. "Let's hear it."

"I shot out Mrs. Ranson's window and your window," Lonnie mumbled.

"What about Mrs. Ranson's tire?"

"I did that, too."

"Why?"

"Because she's a bitch, makin' my wife work all them night shifts," he yelled.

"Why'd you shoot out my windows?"

"You took Ron away to that asylum against his will."

"Your wife signed him in and Ron has decided to stay."

"You're lyin'," he yelled.

"I'll see if I can get the DA over here from Park Falls so we can get this wrapped up." Lark tossed the matches to Lacey. "Have another cigarette to calm yourself down."

The remainder of the day's appointments were canceled while they worked to get the shooting cases wrapped up. By three o'clock, Lonnie was arraigned on six counts of burglary and three counts of assault and attempted murder. He was remanded into detox. Joel arrived with two other state troopers, who got the honor of driving Lonnie to Rhinelander.

Lark and Lacey took a break and ran over to the Big Oak Diner for a sandwich with Joel. Despite their large breakfast, they were both famished. Lark asked George to call and see if he could get Cathy Lowery or the Waltners in for early evening interviews. In the middle of their lunch, George let them know that Cathy Lowery would be in at four-thirty and Sara Waltner at six.

The weather was striving to fulfill the worst of the weather forecasts. Multitudes of huge, fluffy snowflakes rained down on them as they left the diner. Windshields on cars parked along the street, clear for most of the day, already had an inch of snow accumulation. Lark cussed and swore as they slipped and slid to the station.

Joel went off to set up interviews with Sandi Waltner and Katey Lowery for the next day while Lark took care of some local issues. The county already had both patrol cars out on fender-bender calls. Worried that he would need all the officers the county could muster, he called the Ransons, letting John know that he was pulling the guard off since they had a suspect in custody. When John asked for details, Lark told him about Lonnie's arrest.

Lacey and Cathy Lowery were settled in the interview room by the time Lark got there. Cathy greeted him cordially, volunteering that she would do anything to help solve the murders. Lark began by asking Cathy about her father. She informed him that after Pete's latest incident, they had decided to hire twenty-four-hour live-in help for him, their last-ditch effort before placing him somewhere since he refused to live with her and Gus.

Lark studied her while she talked about her father and realized that her daughter had gotten her blonde good looks from her mother. Cathy, in her midfifties, was a stunning woman. Her blond hair ended just above her jaw line and her sapphire blue eyes sparkled. She had a few crow's feet and smile lines but she didn't look like an average fifty-year-old.

Finally, they got down to business. Lark walked her through the times Gemma and Terry had stayed with them. Cathy had a very good memory, augmented by a set of date books she pulled out of her purse. She didn't have anything new to offer. When Lark asked her about Katey's friends, she named Sandi Waltner, stating they had been inseparable since kindergarten. When he asked her for the names of Katey's boyfriends, she grew reticent.

"Katey's never dated much," she said, glancing over at Lacey. "She's always run around with a group of girl and boy friends, but there hasn't been anyone serious that I know of."

"Are you concerned about that?" Lark asked her.

She hesitated for a few seconds. "No."

"Really?" Lark replied and let the silence do its job.

"Why are you so concerned about who my daughter dates?"

"We think she may have dated Gemma and Terry," Lark said, watching her face.

Cathy smiled wistfully. "I can't say I haven't wondered, but Katey and I have never talked about this. Gus also wonders why she doesn't date, but we've both left it alone."

"If your daughter is gay, will it cause problems for you?" he asked, noting her calmness.

"Being a lesbian is not the life I'd choose for my daughter, but then it's not my choice, is it?" she said, giving him a hard stare. "It won't cause problems for us. Does she know you're talking to me about this?"

"No, not yet."

"The only thing I'm concerned about is that someone has killed two of Katey's friends. I've been worried sick that she could be next." Cathy's voice shook and her eyes began to swim. "Gus and I begged her to stay in Bessemer until the killer is found, but she was adamant that she needed to get back to school to finish the semester. Should we hire private protection for her?" She glanced back and forth between Lark and Lacey as two big tears slid down her cheeks.

"I can't tell you what to do," Lark said, handing her the box of tissues. "Both girls were murdered up here, not in Madison, so she should be as OK as you can be on a campus that size."

Lark changed the subject to find out where Cathy was when the two murders occurred. She checked her calendar for 1997 and confirmed that she was in Chicago shopping during the time frame for both murders, volunteering the details of where she stayed in Chicago. As Cathy got up to leave, she said she would be in town for two more days before returning to Bessemer.

Lacey left the room to get a head start typing her notes. She was printing them when Sara Waltner walked in, stomping snow off her boots.

"Whew, it's a mess out there. I almost called to set up another time," she said, taking off her coat and shaking snow off her fur-lined hood.

Even in jeans and a University of Wisconsin sweatshirt, Sara was gorgeous. Lacey marveled at her smooth, flawless complexion. She knew that Sara had a twenty-four-year-old son, but she swore Sara looked thirty. While Lacey watched her fluff out her shoulder-length hair, she wondered who Sara's plastic surgeon was. Sara turned around and smiled, her huge brown eyes looking Lacey up and down. It was one of the few times in Lacey's life when she felt frumpy. As she stared back, looking critically at Sara's minimal number of smile lines and crow's feet, she didn't feel one bit guilty about thinking evil plastic-surgeon thoughts.

"Do you have any fresh coffee?" Sara asked, breaking eye contact to look around the station.

"There's coffee in the back," Lacey said, walking past her. "How do you take it?"

"Black," Sara called after her.

When Lacey got back she found Lark, Cathy, and Sara talking about everyone's favorite topic, the weather. Cathy already had her coat on and looked like she was anxious to leave. She took the opportunity to go when Lacey joined them. Lacey handed the cup to Sara as she watched her flirt with Lark. Even more irritating was watching Lark return the favor. After a few minutes of listening to them banter back and forth, Lacey had had enough and headed into the interrogation room. She had just settled into her chair when Lark and Sara came through the door, laughing. Sara seated herself in the chair furthest away from Lacey and kept all of her attention on Lark, who sat down in the chair across from her.

"I hate to do this to you, but we have to ask you some questions about the murders of Gemma Patterson and Terry Foltz," he said.

"I understand." She gave him a radiant smile. "This is so tragic. I can't believe those two young women are dead. Sandi and Katey were both very close to them. Such a waste."

"Can you tell us the names of any other people Katey and Sandi ran around with? Anyone they dated?"

"The girls were usually together when they were up here, kind of a girls' weekend," Sara said. "Sandi has been dating Dave Banski for a while, and before that she dated a few young men from Madison."

"Can you tell us their names?"

She glanced over at Lark, a bemused expression on her face. "I'm afraid I can't remember any of them. It really doesn't matter," she said with a wave of her hand. "There wasn't anybody serious until David."

Lacey's pen bore down so hard on the notebook, she thought she might rip the page as she watched Sara flirt. The word "bitch" echoed over and over in her head, startling her with its vehemence.

"Everyone tells us that Katey and Sandi are inseparable," Lark said.

"They've known each other since first grade or kindergarten. They were best friends from the moment they met."

"Do you recall any of the young men Katey dated?"

Sara glanced over at Lacey and then back at Lark with a quick smile. "No. Cathy would be a better source for that. I can barely keep up with my own kids, let alone someone else's."

"So, as close as the girls were, they never double-dated?" Lacey interrupted, bringing a curious glance from Lark.

"Oh, they went to proms with some of the local boys, but it was never anything serious," she replied to Lark, ignoring Lacey.

"Any local boys in particular that we should talk to?" Lark asked.

"None that I can recall."

"I'm sorry to keep pressing on this issue, but we've gotten some information that Katey may have been dating Gemma and Terry. Do you know anything about that?"

"Nothing at all," Sara muttered, breaking eye contact.

"Does that surprise you?" Lark asked.

"It's none of my business. Talk with Cathy and Gus about that," Sara said staring down at the table.

Lark leaned in towards her. "We've gotten some information that Sandi might have been dating Katey or one of the other girls."

"Dating a woman?" Sara said, her voice rising as she glared at Lark. "That's ridiculous."

"We've heard—"

"I don't give a shit what you've heard. My daughter is not gay!" she said, her voice rising in anger. "She's engaged to Dave Banski. Tell me, how could that happen if she's gay?"

"I didn't say your daughter was gay. We've gotten some information suggesting the possibility and we're trying to confirm or deny it."

"You've got your answer," Sara snapped. "My daughter is not gay. She's engaged. She would never be gay. She knows it's not the way we are meant to be. You'd better not bring this up when you talk with Steve. He'll go ballistic."

"When will he be back?" Lark asked taking his lead from Sara.

"He's in Atlanta on a buying trip. He'll be back on Saturday afternoon." Sara took a sip of her coffee and grimaced at the sour taste. She shot Lacey a look of distaste.

Lark asked Sara where she was during the time of the murders. Calming down, she told them that she was in Minneapolis, shopping. She gave them the name of the hotel she stayed in. Lark escorted her out of the room and helped her with her coat.

Sara had just turned towards the door when Lark called out to her. "Hang on a second. I almost forgot to ask you about this car we found."

Sara whirled around, a hint of irritation on her face. "What?"

"A few days after the second murder, we found a car at Grezetski's Market that was stolen from Lippert Motors in Wausau," Lark said, walking over to her. "Your maiden name was Lippert, right?"

"Yes."

"Any relation to the Lipperts who own Lippert Motors in Wausau and Eau Claire?" he asked, his eyes riveted on her face.

"My dad and my brothers."

"There was another stolen car left here a few years ago from Lippert Motors in Eau Claire. It was found the same week that Gemma was murdered. It seems like such a coincidence that you're a Lippert and two stolen cars from Lippert's were found where you and your family live. To top it off, we find two dead bodies the same week we find the two stolen cars."

"Lippert Motors is one of the largest dealerships in Wisconsin, and the weeks those girls were killed is one of the busiest in Mason County. Someone probably stole a car to get up here to hunt or to get home for Thanksgiving," she said, her face emotionless.

"Do you or your family have keys to the dealerships?" Lark asked.

"What a strange question. Are you accusing us of stealing those cars?" she asked.

"I'm just trying to unravel these coincidences," Lark said.

"Well, I can assure you that no one in my family needs to steal a car. If we needed a car when we were in Eau Claire or Wausau, we could just call up my family and ask. They'd be more than happy to loan us one." She slid the sleeve of her coat back to glance at her watch. "Anything else, Sheriff? I've got errands to run."

"No, that'll do it."

"Sweet mother of God," Lacey said once the door closed behind Sara. "That was almost like watching a split personality. One minute, she's trying to flirt your pants off and the next minute she's sounding like she could cut your balls off."

"I wonder if her alibi will hold up."

"You think she killed those girls?"

"She couldn't have gotten them out into the marsh alone. She doesn't look that strong."

"She keeps in shape," Lacey said. "She might surprise you."

"Let's check these alibis so we know what to do next." Lark glanced at his watch, shocked to find it was 7:30 P.M.

Since their appointments with Sandi and Katey were scheduled for the next day, Joel joined Lark and Lacey to check alibis. It took an hour to run down hotel managers and have them check their computerized records, but eventually both Cathy Lowery's and Sara's Waltner's stories checked out.

Cathy had driven to Chicago and stayed at the Ritz Carlton at Water Tower Place both times. Her bill showed daily parking-garage charges and room-service meals each day for both of her stays. From the looks of her bill, it was impossible that she could have driven back and forth between Chicago and Big Oak for the killings. Lark made a note to check airline lists on the date in question to assure that she hadn't flown back and forth. He asked Joel to check out the other airports to assure that she hadn't chartered a plane.

Sara had stayed at the Hotel Sofitel in Bloomington, Minnesota. She had driven to Minneapolis, but she didn't have any valet-parking charges. She did have sporadic room service and movie charges throughout her bill.

The three of them discussed their findings as they picked up a pizza and headed home. They settled down to eat around 9:30, and after planning the trip to Madison, they went to bed.

Lark stumbled out of bed at 6:30 to the sound of running water. He cranked his shower taps on and looked out the window. The sky to the east remained overcast. He stepped into a steaming hot shower, thankful at least one thing was going right.

He dressed quickly and headed downstairs. He found Lacey and Joel reading separate sections of the morning paper. Lark read the front page while he made a pot of coffee for their thermoses.

The trip to Madison was fast, despite the icy roads and the on-again, off-again snow. They hit the outskirts of Madison at 11:30 and threaded their way down East Washington towards the state capital. Lark's only exposure to Madison had been driving the interstate around it when he and Maria had vacationed in northern Wisconsin. He'd heard how big the campus was, but was surprised at how much of the city it usurped.

They pulled up at the side entrance of the student union just as Katey and Sandi walked out the door. The girls wore jeans, hooded ski parkas, and hiking boots. With mounds of snow on every street corner, it wasn't hard to see why they were dressed to climb Mount Everest.

They climbed into the Jeep and Lark drove to the University police headquarters. Joel went to talk with Ann's friend, Barbara Danner, and everyone else went to the interview room.

"I'm going to interview each of you separately and I'd like to talk with Katey first," Lark said, his smile gone, his voice all business. Sandi left the room.

"Why didn't you to tell us about your affairs with Terry and Gemma?" Lark asked.

"I didn't tell you because it isn't true," Katey replied, glancing at Lacey, looking for support. "Well, it's not exactly true," she said when Lacey scowled at her.

"What was your relationship with Gemma?" Lark asked.

"We were very good friends."

He snorted and glared at her.

"OK, OK, we were lovers."

"Why didn't you tell us this earlier?" Lacey asked.

"I didn't think it was important. We only slept together a few times. Gemma wasn't sure whether she was gay or straight. She was experimenting."

"Was Sandi also one of her lovers?" Lark asked.

Katey drew back from the table and looked away. "You'll have to ask her," she said, unable to meet his eyes.

"I'm asking you," Lark yelled. "Two women are dead and I'm trying to figure out why before someone else gets killed. I've had just about enough of your evasiveness." He slammed his fist down on the table. "Tell me what the hell's going on. Now!"

"If I knew, believe me, I'd tell you." Katey's voice was full of sadness. "I've been gay as long as I can remember. I've known Sandi since kindergarten and she's always been crazy about boys. Despite that, we're very close.

"Sandi was very promiscuous when she was in high school. She loves sex. I, on the other hand, didn't have sex until I came here. I think I was the only gay woman in Big Oak, maybe even in northern Wisconsin. No one ever guessed. They think I'm straight because I'm pretty. I went out with a few guys in high school, but it was always just a friendship thing.

"I went a little wild, when I got here. I joined a lesbian group and had a few short affairs, nothing serious. Gemma was one of those relationships. We spent most of our time talking about how unclear she was about her sexuality. I think she was bisexual but would have gotten married and had a very happy hetero life."

"What about Terry?"

"Terry was a lesbian and knew it just like I did. We were soul mates."

Lark nodded. "How does Sandi fit into this?"

"I told you, you'll have to ask her."

"I will, but right now I'm asking you."

"It's not my business to talk about Sandi. She can tell you what she sees fit."

"Have you heard of obstruction of justice?" Lark asked.

"Yes, but I'm not under arrest so that doesn't apply."

"You've got that wrong," Lacey said. "You can be arrested for obstructing justice."

"Ask your questions," Katey said, glaring at her.

"You said earlier that Sandi loves men and sex."

"That's correct."

"Have you had sex with her?"

Katey's face turned beet red. She looked past Lacey at the wall behind her.

"I repeat . . ."

"Yes, we've had sex, but that doesn't make her a lesbian," Katey snapped.

"What does that make her?" Lark asked

"Someone who loves sex." She gave Lark a withering glance. "She's in love with David and will probably never sleep with anyone else. She just wanted to try a few things."

"And you didn't have any problem with that?" Lacey asked.

"No, I was trying a few new things myself," she replied, not making eye contact with either of them.

"Did Sandi have sex with Gemma?" Lacey asked.

"Once or twice."

"Did Sandi have sex with Terry?"

"We both did."

"Meaning?" Lacey asked.

"We all three had sex together one time," Katey said, staring at the floor. "Sandi wanted to try it with two women."

"Does David know about this?" Lacey asked.

"You'll have to ask Sandi."

"Who else knows about it?" Lark asked

The color drained from Katey's face. "I don't know. I haven't told anyone. Terry may have told her brother Brian. He knew she was gay. I don't think anyone else knows."

"Anyone else you all were sleeping with who may have wanted to hurt Gemma or Terry?" Lark asked.

Katey studied him for a second before she spoke. "I'm sure this is all very shocking, but I can assure you, it was harmless sex. It was consensual and no one meant to hurt anyone. I've racked my brain and I can't imagine who would want to kill Gemma and Terry."

"Any jealous girlfriends in your past who might want to get at anyone you're close to?"

"No, my most serious relationship has been with Terry, and Sandi, of course, as a friend."

"And lover," Lark corrected

"Sandi and I aren't lovers. We just fooled around a little. It didn't mean anything to either of us."

"Do your parents know about any of this?" he asked.

"Are you kidding? My parents think I'm straight as an arrow."

"It's bound to come out that Terry was gay. Your relationship with her may also come out. I'd want to tell my parents before they heard it from someone else," Lacey said.

"It'll kill my dad."

"You may be surprised," Lark said. "I haven't talked with him, but I have talked with your mom and I think she can handle it."

They escorted Katey out and went to find Sandi. They started questioning her as soon as everyone was settled in the interview room.

"We don't think you've been honest with us about your relationship with Gemma and Terry," Lark said.

"Why do you think that?"

"Because you weren't honest about having sex with them."

"What does that have to do with them being killed?"

"We're not sure, but it would have been helpful to know," Lacey interjected.

"OK. I had sex a couple of times with Gemma and Katey, and once with Katey and Terry together. Do you want all the lurid details?"

"That isn't the point," Lacey said, maintaining eye contact with her. "We don't care who you sleep with. We're trying to piece together enough information to solve these murders."

"I'm not a lesbian," she said with defiance.

"But Katey is," Lark said.

"Yeah, so what's the big deal? God, you're as bad as my parents. My dad's always going on about how being gay is a sin."

"Who knew about your affairs with Gemma and Terry?" Lark asked, ignoring her outburst.

"I told David about Katey, but that's it."

"What did he think about it?"

"He was surprised but OK."

"Do your parents know about any of this?" Lacey asked.

"Hell, no," she shouted. "My father would go insane."

"Do you know anyone who might want to hurt Terry or Gemma because they were gay?"

"First of all, Gemma wasn't gay. She was just experimenting, sowing a few wild oats, like me. I can't think of anyone who'd want to hurt them, let alone kill them."

Their interviews finished, they offered to drive Katey and Sandi back to the student union but the girls declined. They found Joel sitting in the captain's office, his interview completed.

The sun came out as they left Madison. They spent the first part of their trip discussing the next steps, having exchanged information on their interviews over lunch. Joel's interview had not yielded anything new. He had blustered throughout lunch about how beautiful Barbara Danner was and how he was sure someone that gorgeous couldn't possibly be a lesbian. After a firm lecture from Lacey, he got back on track. There was no question that Barbara had seen Katey and Terry at campus lesbian group meetings. She identified their pictures to confirm it. She did not recall seeing Gemma or Sandi at any meetings, although she had seen Sandi and Katey together on campus.

They agreed that the students had alibis that would hold. With a growing sense of futility, they decided to reinterview Sara Waltner and Cathy Lowery and bring their husbands in for questioning. They agreed that they also needed to reinterview Jim Kryjack and the Chevskys. Lark called the station and asked Flo to make appointments for the following morning.

The remainder of the trip was spent rehashing the case. They discussed the two stolen Tauruses, coming to the conclusion that their appearance in Big Oak at the same time as the girls' deaths had to be more than coincidence. Lark called George and asked him to follow up with the employees at Grezetski's Market to find out if they had seen any of the suspects around the time the car was noticed in the lot. Joel suggested they interview employees of businesses around Lippert Motors in Wausau to see if they could get any leads. George was asked to assemble pictures of all the people they had interviewed so the state police could use them in their Wausau interviews.

It started snowing with a vengeance once they got to Marshfield. They spent the remainder of their time discussing the weather and watching for the deer and snowmobiles that seemed to be everywhere now that hunting season was over. Most of the bars and restaurants along Highway 13 had more snowmobiles than cars parked in their lots.

They were south of Park Falls when Lark got a radio call at 6:30 P.M. Flo told him that John Ranson had called, asking if anyone had reported his wife's car in an accident. He was concerned that she had not come home on time. She told Lark they were inundated with accidents due to the road conditions and George had authorized more overtime.

Lark called John. He answered on the first ring, sounding disappointed when it wasn't Ann. He told Lark that he had come home to find a note from Ann saying that she had to run a few errands. She was supposed to be home by 5:30 with pizza. Lark offered to stop by, but John told him it wasn't necessary. He asked Lark to be on the lookout for her. Lark called the station, requesting that an alert go out to all Mason County officers.

They made it into Big Oak just before 7:30 and had polished off a dinner of burritos and tacos when Lark's phone rang. The dispatcher asked him to call John Ranson ASAP. After finding out that none of the officers had seen Ann's car, he called John.

John was frantic. Lark cut him off when he began muttering about where Ann was and told him he was on his way. Lark and Lacey headed for the Ransons' while Joel got on the phone to round up staff to canvas Wausau the following morning.

John opened the front door before they even got out of the Jeep. While they took off their winter gear, he gave them an update on his attempts to find Ann. He walked them into the family room where there was a roaring fire.

John had already called friends as well as the various stores they frequented in Big Oak and Park Falls. Ann had stopped by the Martens' about 4:30 to pick up a box that Melissa had made for them. Melissa assumed that Ann was on her way home. The dogs began howling in the garage.

"They've been crazy since I got home," he said, as he went to let them in. "I don't know what's wrong with them." They snorted and wagged their tails and ran to the front door. After admonishing them to be good, John let them out.

"The deer must be moving," he said when he got back to the family room.

"Has anyone else seen Ann this afternoon?" Lacey asked.

"No one. It's not unusual for her to be thirty minutes, maybe even an hour late, when she's working, but this," he said, looking at his watch, "this isn't like her at all. She would have called me. Something's wrong."

"I put Ann's license plate number out right after our first conversation, but no one has reported her car," Lark said.

The dogs, barking and jumping at the front door, stopped their conversation nearly an hour later. John went to let them in. Lark slouched down in his chair and stared at the fire as he waited for John to return. He was startled back to reality when John yelled his name. Lark rounded the corner to the hallway with Lacey right behind him. They were met with a blast of ice-cold air. John was standing in the doorway, holding a red scarf caked with snow. Snow was blowing into the hallway, leaving traces of white on the tile. One of the dogs barked and pranced about in the snow. When John said nothing, Lark pushed past him and went out on the stoop to call the dog in. He darted away and ran towards the woods.

Lacey reached for the scarf but John held it tightly, staring down at it. "Ann must have dropped this in the driveway," he mumbled.

"Let me hang that up for you," she said. He gave it to her just as Lark walked in.

"That damn dog won't come in," Lark said, brushing snow off his sweater.

"I'll get them." John went back outside and called the dogs.

"There's only one out here," Lark said, following him.

"Buck's got to be close by, they're always together." John called the dogs' names over and over, oblivious to the snow and the cold. Duke ran up to him but pranced out of reach, barking and running towards the woods.

"Something's not right here," John said. "Duke acts like he wants me to follow him."

"That dog isn't that smart," Lark said as they walked back to the house.

"Yes, he is." John went to the utility room and began putting on his boots.

"What are you doing?" Lacey asked, sitting down beside him.

"I'm going to find Ann," he said, lacing up his boots. "Duke found her scarf and won't come in. He knows where she is."

"Like you said, she probably dropped her scarf in the driveway, that's how the dogs found it," Lark said

"No, now that I think about it, Ann couldn't have dropped her scarf out there. She gets in the car in the garage so there isn't any reason it would be outside. She has a car phone. She would have called and left a message if she was going to be this late. Something's wrong. Duke had her scarf and this is how he acts when he wants us to follow him. Buck's nowhere to be found. I think the dogs know where she is."

"We'll go with you," Lark said with a sense of foreboding. He and Lacey hurried to the foyer to put on their boots. Once they were dressed and armed with flashlights, they headed outside. Duke led them down the driveway, keeping about fifty feet ahead and trotting back to them when they got behind. While he waited for them to catch up, he ate snow and scanned the woods, his nose in the air. Once they got to the woods, he took off through the snow, leaping like a jack rabbit through drifts nearly up to his neck. John and Lacey took off after him but Lark called them back.

"This is the same trail we followed when we found the bodies," he said.

"I'm going to follow Duke," John insisted as the dog ran back to them. He reached down to pet him and Duke grabbed the arm of his jacket, pulling him forward. John shook him off. When Duke grabbed his arm again, John commanded him to sit. The dog sat down but continued to fidget, whining and craning his neck towards the woods.

"I agree with John," Lacey said, watching Duke. "Something's wrong. We need to find out where Buck is." She cocked her head, listening to what she thought was a faint bark. "Did you hear that?"

"Yep." John watched Duke squirm. "Go on," he said, flinging his arm out. Duke ran barking into the woods.

"I'm going back to the house and get the Jeep," Lark said, grabbing John by the sleeve. "I'll go with you as soon as I get back. We'll take the radio and the phone to make sure we maintain contact. Wait for me here. OK?"

When John said nothing, Lark shook him by the shoulders. "Did you hear me?"

"I heard you," John said, "but I can't guarantee I'll be here when you get back."

"Keep him here," Lark said to Lacey. He was back with the Jeep in less than ten minutes. He and John set out after Duke, leaving Lacey to wait for the additional officers and the county snowmobiles Lark had requested.

The snow was getting worse, making it slowgoing. It was above their knees in most places and drifted to the top of their thighs in others. Despite all the snow they'd had since finding the two bodies, their original trail was still visible. Lark also noticed fresh dog and deer tracks.

As they moved deeper into the woods, the wind cut down, but Lark was still amazed at the amount of noise it made as it blew through the leafless trees. Duke barked frequently, and as they got closer to the marsh, Lark could hear another dog.

By the time they got halfway across the marsh, John and Lark were winded. They stopped and bent over, hands propped on their thighs, as they sucked in air.

"Damn, I wish we had snowshoes," John said between breaths. He looked down at the snow that was just above their knees.

"I wish we had a snowmobile," Lark said, his chest heaving. "Slogging through this snow is harder than running a marathon." He radioed Lacey for an update. She told him the snowmobiles were due any minute.

As soon as they caught their breath, they trudged across the rest of the marsh. The snow continued to come down in small biting flakes. An owl hooted several times and Lark heard a faint response in the distance. Five minutes after they crossed the marsh, they walked into a grove of trees and Buck ran towards them, covered with snow. The dogs took off together back into the woods. The men picked up their pace, and within a few minutes found the dogs lying by a mound of snow. Buck whined and nuzzled the snow, revealing something red. John and Lark dug snow away to expose a coat. The dogs barked and leaped around them as they dug Ann out of the snowdrift.

She was breathing but her pulse was very slow. Her lips were blue and her skin was as white as the snow she was buried in. As they dug the snow away from her, Lark noticed that the hair on the right side of her head was matted with blood and her right arm and leg were bent at unnatural angles. His mind raced as his hands worked, taking in the fact that she had injuries like the two girls who had been murdered and dumped in the marsh.

Once they had Ann out of the snow, Lark radioed Lacey. Although it seemed like forever, it only took a few minutes for the snowmobiles to arrive.

Watching John rock his comatose wife back and forth, begging her to be all right, was more than Lark could stand. Memories of Maria flashed through his mind. He was unable to do anything more than step out of the way when help arrived. He watched as they put Ann on the portable litter. When they had her ready to go, John rode back with Paul. For once, the Mason County ambulance was free and waiting for them in the Ransons' driveway, but the medical helicopter was out on another flight. Lark and Lacey stayed behind to secure the scene until the state police got there.

They found a snowmobile trail that led away from the woods in the opposite direction from the Ransons' house. They followed it out to the road, where it was obliterated by fresh tire tracks. When they got back to where Ann was found, Joel and the state troopers were searching the area. They found footprints and a drag trail leading from the snowmobile trail to the area where Ann had collapsed. Someone had tried to cover them by dragging an evergreen branch over them. The few remaining footprints were good for little more than identification of shoe size.

They tracked Ann's attempts to get out of the woods, noting where she had fallen at least twice. Tears of anger froze on Lacey's cheeks as she imagined what the woman had gone through. Joel gave additional instructions to the two state troopers and they headed back to the Ransons'.

It took them forty-five minutes to wend their way back through the snow. Lark, worn out from his walk in, was quiet during their trek. Even

Joel said very little. Lacey was having trouble reconciling the horrors that had happened on this property with the incredible peace and beauty that surrounded her. The stillness was broken only by the crunch of their feet and the wind in the trees.

Paul radioed them to put the dogs in the garage, so they weren't surprised when Buck and Duke greeted them as they came out of the woods. The dogs rode to the house in the back of Lark's Jeep. Lacey and Joel cleaned them up in the mudroom while Lark called the hospital.

"She's still unconscious. The helicopter's grounded for weather. They're taking her to Marshfield by ground. Let's go," Lark said, brushing past them on his way out the door. They put the dogs in the garage and followed him to the Jeep.

They dropped Joel off at his Explorer and, for the second time that day, drove south on Highway 13. They caught up with the ambulance just south of Prentice. The EMTs radioed that Ann was still breathing but unconscious with a very low pulse and blood pressure. As Lark suspected, she had a broken arm and leg as well as a head injury.

Because Lark radioed ahead, wherever possible the police were out so they could get through the small communities without slowing down. Despite the snowstorm and icy roads, they made the ninety-mile trip in less than two hours. The ER staff were waiting for them along with an orthopedic surgeon and a neurosurgeon. A team of people swarmed over Ann, starting additional IVs and whisking her to X-ray. By one in the morning, it was confirmed that she had a broken arm, a very nasty broken leg, and a subdural hematoma in her brain. The neurosurgeon informed them that it looked like her shoulder had deflected the brunt of the hit to her head and probably saved her life.

Ann was admitted to the ICU and the staff made arrangements for them to stay at a nearby Super 8 Motel. They were told that the doctors would talk with them after their 7 A.M. rounds, or sooner if anything changed. When John insisted on staying, the staff informed him that he needed his rest so he could be there for Ann when she woke up. He reluctantly agreed to go to the motel, as long as they promised to call if her condition changed.

When they got to the Super 8, there were only two rooms available. Lark and Lacey agreed to room together. They realized they were once again stuck away from home with no toiletries or a change of clothes. The night manager directed them to a twenty-four-hour Kmart where they were able to buy the sundries they needed. Once they were back at the motel, Lacey showered and put on her newly purchased sweats while Lark called Joel. He looked desolate when she came out of the bathroom.

"No luck tracking the snowmobile. Apparently everyone in Big Oak has their snowmobiles out now."

"It's got to be someone around the lake or close by," she said, sitting down on the bed.

"Who, is the question. Everyone has alibis or no motive." He headed for the shower.

Ten minutes later, Lark came out of the bathroom, wearing his new sweatpants, to find Lacey propped up in bed reading a book.

"Once again, I'm not sleepy. Is the light going to bother you?"

"Not at all." He got into bed and rolled on his side away from her.

She spent the next half hour reading. Lark's rhythmic breathing told her he had fallen asleep. Her eyes began to get heavy, so she turned out the light and went right to sleep. She was awakened two hours later by Lark moaning and thrashing around.

She rolled over and put her arm around him, whispering, "Ssh, you're having a dream. Go back to sleep." He calmed down and she nodded off, curled around him.

The next thing she knew, the back of her neck was being kissed and her breasts were being caressed. She was in heaven. She roused up to roll away from Lark, remembering the last time this happened, but he pulled her close.

She rolled over and kissed him and he moaned, "Oh, Maria."

That brought her up short. She shoved her palms against his chest to get away from him. He opened his eyes and tried to pull her back.

"Wake up, Lark, you're having a dream. You called me Maria." She moved further away.

"Oh my God," he said as he sat up. "I'll sleep on the floor." He grabbed his pillows and got up.

"Don't be ridiculous. Get back in bed and go to sleep. Nothing happened." She turned away from him.

Embarrassed and not knowing what to say, he slid back into the bed, rolled on his side, and fell asleep.

Lacey vaguely heard the phone the next morning, but it stopped after only two rings and she fell back to sleep. When she woke up the next time, it was to Lark shutting the door.

"What time is it?" she asked, stifling a yawn.

"Eight-thirty," he replied, handing her a foam cup of steaming coffee.

"Holy shit, why didn't you wake me up?"

"John called for a ride to the hospital. You were sleeping so soundly I didn't want to wake you." He sat down at the table on the other side of the room and uncapped his coffee. "I got some bagels and donuts." He held up a crumpled bag.

"What's the latest on Ann?"

"They're taking her to surgery to remove the subdural hematoma. She may come back on a respirator for a while. If she can tolerate it, they're also going to fix her arm and leg."

Lacey hurried into the bathroom to get dressed.

"I'm going to get a paper," Lark yelled after her. "There's a coffee shop in the lobby. I'll meet you there when you're ready."

Lark slid into a booth in the restaurant and ordered a fresh cup of coffee from the grandmotherly waitress. He opened the paper to find that Ann's accident had not made it into print. He searched for news about the murders and, finding none, discovered that there was nothing else in the paper that could hold his attention. He folded it up and slid it across the table as the waitress brought his coffee. He took a sip and stared out the window at the icy, snow-covered parking lot. A large red pickup truck with a giant snow blade was clearing the snow the best it could around the cars in the lot. Although the snow had stopped, the sky remained overcast. The radio predicted more snow that afternoon.

His mind wandered off the weather and onto Lacey. He did not want to think about how much he wanted her. Vivid images floated through his mind. He leaned on the table and dropped his face in his hands, rubbing as if to erase the memory. Lacey found him in the same position a few minutes later. She got coffee to go and they headed for the hospital. Once Ann was off to surgery and they were sure that John had everything he needed, they drove to Wausau so Lacey could pick up more clothes.

Despite the snowy and icy roads, they made good time. Just west of Mosinee they slowed down to observe an unfamiliar site in Wisconsin: a herd of buffalo. The huge wooly beasts, their coats dusted with snow, wandered stoically in their snow-covered field.

"Wouldn't you hate to run into one of those on a dark highway?" Lacey asked, in awe of their size.

"Don't even think it," Lark said with a shudder as they drove on through town. Once they got off the interstate and headed into Wausau, Lark's eyes were drawn to the huge Lippert Motors sign. As they drove by the dealership, he looked at the number of cars in the lot and understood how the owners might not know if one was missing. Across the road from Lippert's was the strip mall where Terry Foltz's car had been found. The remainder of the area was built-up with fast-food restaurants and convenience stores. He turned around and went back to the strip mall, ignoring Lacey's questions about what he was doing. How the killer had pulled off part of the murder was suddenly clear to him.

"He dumped Terry's car here, went right across the road, and stole a car off the Lippert's lot," Lark said in wonderment. "Then he drove back to Big Oak and dumped the car in Grezetski's parking lot. We have to check every business in this area to see if anyone saw anything. Maybe the pictures will help jog someone's memory. We've also got to find out if the place where Gemma's car was dropped was near the Lippert dealership in Eau Claire. I can't remember, can you?" he asked Lacey.

She shook her head, trying to take it all in. "This makes so much sense. Why did it take us so long to figure it out?"

"It always makes sense when you have all the pieces," Lark said, pulling out of the lot. "No one linked Gemma to Big Oak until we found her body there, so no one could link her to the stolen car abandoned in Big Oak."

They discussed their next steps in the few minutes it took to get to Lacey's. While she packed, Lark checked in with Joel. They had checked the homes around the lake and found numerous snowmobile tracks leaving them, as most people were taking full advantage of the early snowfall. Ann's Explorer was still missing. All the students had been checked out and had alibis, in Madison. They were basically nowhere.

Lark told Joel about the discovery they'd made on the way up to Wausau and he agreed to speed up the canvassing of the businesses around Lippert's and the strip mall. Before they hung up, they decided that the state police would put a guard on Ann's door and admit no one but family. They hoped that when she regained consciousness, she could identify who had done this to her.

They got back to Marshfield just as Ann got out of surgery. The orthopedic surgeon was able to set her broken arm and leg at the same time the neurosurgeon drained the subdural hematoma. She was on a ventilator so she wasn't able to talk.

Joel drove to Marshfield, leaving his two troopers to scour the area for Ann's car and anyone who had seen her. He arrived in time to have lunch with Lark and Lacey. Afterwards they got a conference room at the hotel to review their information.

After four hours of rehashing, Lacey summarized what they agreed upon. "Whoever dumped Terry's and Gemma's cars stole cars from Lippert Motors and abandoned them in Big Oak. Whoever stole the cars was able to get in and out of the dealerships without leaving any signs of a break-in. All the UW students from Big Oak have strong alibis with the exception of Jim Kryjack and Ron Chevsky. Cathy Lowery and Sara

Waltner were out of town for both murders. Gus Lowery has an alibi for each murder; he was skiing in Michigan, as confirmed by multiple witnesses. Steve Waltner has yet to be interviewed and is purported to hate gays. He was supposed to be out of town for the murders, but that's not confirmed. Lonnie Chevsky doesn't have an alibi for either of the murders. Myra and Joe Banski have strong alibis—they were in full view of customers at their restaurant."

"This leaves us with Jim Kryjack, and Lonnie and Ron Chevsky for one of the murders," Joel said. "The Waltners have weaker alibis and connections to Lippert Motors. We need to check them out again."

"We probably ought to take Jim off duty," Lark said.

"These people will have to be interviewed for the attack on Ann," Lacey said, drumming her fingers on the table. "We know where Jim was this time, which should rule him out."

"Whoever did the girls probably also beat Ann," Joel said. "Her injuries are the same. Let's focus on who could have done all three."

"Ron and Lonnie Chevsky are both still up in Rhinelander, so they couldn't have done this to Ann," Lark said.

"Sara Waltner and Cathy Lowery were both in town and we don't know where Steve Waltner was," Lacey said, pacing around the room. "Why don't we bring those three in and question them? Look a little more into their alibis."

They agreed that Lark's staff would reschedule Sara and Cathy for interviews the following afternoon, and find out where Steve Waltner was since they had not been able to locate him in Atlanta. They decided that Joel and Lacey would do the interviews in Big Oak and Lark would stay in Marshfield to see if Ann regained consciousness.

Joel agreed to drive Lacey to Wausau so she could spend the night in her own bed. When he offered to have Molly get a babysitter so the four of them could go out to dinner, Lark and Lacey both refused, claiming they were exhausted and just wanted to get a good night's sleep.

"When did you two become party poopers?" Joel asked, studying them. "I've never known either of you to turn down a free meal."

"I'm really exhausted and tomorrow will be another long day," Lacey said. "I want to go home and have a nice soak in my own tub."

"Who the hell are you, Grandma Moses?" Joel asked, looking at her as if she'd grown a third eye.

"Joel," Lark interrupted, "I agree with her. I'm bushed and, besides, this is all I have to wear. My big plan for the night is to buy a change of clothes. We'll do it another time."

"Did you two have a fight?" Joel asked, glancing back and forth between them.

"We've been together constantly for almost two weeks. Lacey hasn't been home other than to pick up clothes. She deserves a night in her own bed."

Lacey grabbed Joel's arm and steered him to the door. "Let's get you home to Molly. We're going to swing through Taco Bell, I'm dying for Mexican."

"Guess we're leaving," Joel said, turning around to study Lark's face.

"I'll make those appointments and confirm the times later tonight," Lark said, staying behind to erase the board.

"Call Lacey," Joel said. "I'm taking my girl out to dinner."

Lark erased the board, thankful that he'd dodged a bullet. It was clear that Lacey felt as awkward as he did about last night. After taking the notes from the day back to his room and calling Big Oak to get them started on setting up interviews, he did as he had planned. Feeling a little more cheerful after doing a mundane errand like shopping, he went to the hospital to see if he could take John out to dinner.

He was heartened to find John at Ann's bedside. She was still on the ventilator and appeared to be sleeping. Her right arm was in a cast and a portion of her casted right leg showed below the sheet. A piece of gauze was taped to a shaved area on the right side of her head. She had three IV bags hanging around her and was hooked up to a machine that monitored her heart rate, blood pressure, and breathing. When Lark started talking with John, her eyes flew open and she started flailing her left arm about.

"What do you want, sweetheart?" John asked, leaning over her bed.

She pantomimed writing.

"We tried that before but no one could read it."

Ann's eyes got huge and she flapped her hand about, trying to mouth words around the breathing tube. The alarm on her ventilator went off. She rolled her eyes and pointed to the tube in her mouth, making a pulling motion with her hand.

"No," John said, taking her hand between his. He took a deep breath. "Remember, the doctor said not until morning. You've got a little pneumonia and he's afraid if we take it out you might not be able to maintain your oxygen level."

Ann rolled her eyes and pulled her hand away from him, slamming it down on the bed. Her ventilator beeped after she made what sounded like a very long sigh. Her eyes glaring, she again pantomimed writing a note.

"All right, all right, we'll try it again." John handed her the clipboard from her nightstand. She snatched the pencil out of his hand and began printing.

"With the anesthetic, pain medication, and brain surgery . . ." His voice trailed off as Ann looked up, her eyes snapping.

After what seemed like an eternity, she handed John the clipboard. He and Lark studied the scribbles. They looked like chicken scratches.

"Honey, I can't read this," John said.

She slammed her hand down on the bed and tears dripped out of the corners of her eyes. One of the alarms on her monitor went off and she strained around to look at it. She then settled herself down and closed her eyes.

"Her blood-pressure alarm went off and she's trying to relax herself and get it back down," John said, watching the numbers fall as a nurse walked into the room.

"What's going on with you, Ann?" the nurse asked, smiling at her as she reset the alarm. "Are you having any pain?"

Ann shook her head and pantomimed that she wanted her breathing tube out. The nurse explained why it needed to wait until morning.

Ann pantomimed writing a note and the nurse looked around for the clipboard. John showed her the scribbles and asked if there was any other way for Ann to communicate.

"We've got letter boards around here somewhere. She can point at the letters and spell out words."

They turned around at the sound of a side rail rattling and found Ann nodding. The nurse returned with a board with some common words like 'time,' 'pain,' 'yes,' and 'no' printed on it in big letters, along with the alphabet and the numbers 0 through 10. She gave Ann a pointer and set up the board on the easel that came with it. Ann began spelling out words. First came: *Where am I?*

John told her that she was in Marshfield.

She'd spelled out *What hap* when John interrupted to explain how they had found her.

She frowned and spelled out *Very cold.*

"I'll get you another blanket," Lark said, heading for the door.

Ann tapped the word *No* over and over, causing John to grab Lark and pull him back in the room. Ann then spelled out, *In the snow, very cold, frostbite.* She looked at her white fingertips.

"The doctors think you'll be all right. You broke your right arm and leg." John stopped when he saw her looking back and forth between her casts as if she'd just seen them for the first time.

Wolves? Ann tapped out, looking at them.

"We didn't see any wolves," John said, "but Duke and Buck led us to you. Buck stayed with you while Duke came back to the house with your scarf." She dropped the pointer and settled back down in the bed, her face very pale.

"Are you all right?" John asked, concerned over her sudden change in demeanor. He stroked the hair off her forehead.

She picked up the pointer and taped out *Tir.*

"Tired?" John asked.

She nodded and closed her eyes.

John kissed her forehead. "I'll see you in the morning."

They left the room a few minutes after she fell asleep. They ate a quick dinner and were back at the hotel by 10:30 P.M. When Lark got back to his room, he found a message from Big Oak telling him that the interviews were set up. Lark called Lacey's house and left a message about the interview times on her machine when she didn't answer. He told himself she had decided to go out with Joel and Molly after all.

He settled himself into bed and began reading the new Robert Parker he'd picked up at the mall. After reading the same page three times, he turned out the light in disgust. Unfortunately, he wasn't able to turn off his mind, which was busy imagining where Lacey was since she wasn't home to answer her phone.

The next morning came quickly for both John and Lark. They were delighted to see Ann sitting up in bed without her breathing tube. She was receiving oxygen from tubing under her nose and looked much better.

"The tube came out early this morning," she said. Her voice was raspy but her grin was radiant. The gauze bandage was gone from her head and in its place was a small incision.

"She talks again. My worst nightmare come true," John said, leaning over to kiss her.

Dr. Pine, the anesthesiologist, came in on rounds. "What's this I hear about you pulling your tube out last night?" He pulled his stethoscope out of his lab coat pocket and helped Ann sit up.

"I didn't pull it out, it fell out."

"You sound pretty good, so I'll forgive you," he said after listening to her chest and back. "If you keep your oxygen level up, we'll pull some of your IVs and let you leave the ICU."

John followed him out of the room, a worried look on his face. The doctor assured him that Ann wasn't suffering any ill effects from the tube coming out. When John got back in the room, Ann was ready for him.

"I swear," she said, her hands held up in defense. "I didn't intentionally pull it out. I woke up in the middle of the night with alarms going off and a bunch of nurses around me. The tube was out." She shrugged and stared down at the bed. "Sometimes it just happens that way."

"I'm not mad," he said, giving her a big hug. "I'm just glad you're OK."

"Have you figured out what happened to me yet?" she asked Lark.

"We're hoping you can tell us." He watched for any hint of recollection.

Her eyes bored into his. "I remember being in the woods and not being able to walk very well. I kept falling down. I didn't know where I was or how I got there. I burrowed down in the snow, trying to keep warm until someone found me. I remember yelling for help and feeling very cold. Then I remember thinking I was being attacked by a wolf. That must have been the dogs." She shuddered and pulled the covers up over her shoulders. "I remember thinking that I was going to die and praying." She reached out from under the covers to grab John's hand.

"Do you remember anything before the woods?" Lark asked, watching her eyes dart around the room.

"No." She frowned. "I don't remember anything about the rest of the day."

"Honey, you left me a note saying you were running errands and would pick something up for dinner," John said. "Does that ring a bell?"

"No. Dr. Lane, the neurosurgeon, said something could trigger my memory now, or months from now, or it might never come back." She signed and leaned back against her pillow.

"We're going to grab some breakfast and let you rest," John said, kissing her forehead. "The auction notices are piling up and I want you home so we can do some big-time antiquing over the holidays." They headed for the door.

Lark grinned back at her. "I hear you shop for special requests. I need to replace a piece of Roseville that got broken when Lonnie shot out my windows. Can you do that for me?"

Ann stared at him, her eyes big as saucers, a look of terror on her face.

"Ann, are you all right?" John asked, scurrying back to the bed.

Oblivious to them, Ann let out a wail and buried her head in her hands. She began rocking back and forth as if she were in excruciating pain. The alarms on her machines went off as she screamed, "No! No! Please don't . . ."

"Jesus Christ," John yelled, trying to calm her down. "Ann, what's wrong?" She slid down in the bed and curled up in a ball, trying to cover her head. She continued to moan and cry out and began to hyperventilate.

"I'll get someone," Lark shouted as he ran out to the nurse's station.

"Don't hit me," Ann gasped. "Please don't hit me."

"Who hit you?" John asked.

She leaned back against her pillow, gasping for air, her lips pale, her face white as the sheet she lay on. Tears ran down her cheeks. "Don't hit me, don't hit me," she repeated over and over as Lark, Dr. Lane, and the nurse ran through the door.

"Everybody out," the doctor ordered, waving his arms. "Now," he yelled when John and Lark continued to stand by the bed.

Thirty minutes later, Dr. Lane came out to talk with them. "She's calmed down. Sorry I yelled at you, but we needed to get her blood pressure down ASAP."

"How is she?" John asked.

"Her blood pressure's back to normal and her oxygen level's under control. We didn't have to intubate her, but we did have to give her some medication to calm her down. She's having flashbacks of being beaten. This isn't unusual in these situations. I'm glad this happened while she's here so we can keep the complications to a minimum. The psychologist will see her as soon as she wakes up. We'll let you know when you can go back in and talk with her. You," he said, nodding at Lark, "are going to have to wait until she's ready to talk." His beeper went off and he headed down the hall. "Have the nurses page me if you have any more questions. I'm around all day."

Lark went to the phone and called Joel, only to find that he had just left to pick up Lacey. He called Lacey and caught her still at home. He told her about Ann's flashback. They spent the next ten minutes planning their afternoon interviews with Sara Waltner and Cathy Lowery. They all headed for Big Oak when they hung up. Lark got to the station at twelve-thirty, right behind Joel and Lacey. Joel had great news. They had finally hit pay dirt in Wausau. They settled into the interview room to discuss the new evidence.

Joel was so excited he could hardly contain himself "One of the clerks at the service station across the road from Lippert's recognized a picture of Sara Waltner. He confirmed that she purchased gas late on Saturday the eighteenth."

"Sara was supposed to be in Minneapolis shopping that weekend. She was checked into the Sofitel that night. Is he sure about the date?" Lark asked.

"The kid goes to college and works weekend-evening shifts. The night guy called in sick and he worked a double." Joel checked his notes. "Sara tried to pay for gas with a credit card at the pump, but it wasn't working so she came in and paid cash. He thought she was the most beautiful woman he'd ever seen. She wasn't very friendly. She bought a Diet Coke and was mad because they didn't have caffeine-free."

"You sure he can put her there on that date?" Lark repeated.

"Sounds that way. The night is very vivid to him—a double shift, quiet night, beautiful woman, a new gray Taurus," Joel said, grinning at Lark.

"You're shitting me."

"He told us she was driving a new gray Taurus and wearing a black coat with a fur-lined hood. Sound familiar?"

"Will he give us a written statement?" Lark asked, unable to believe their luck.

"It'll be faxed over as soon as it's signed. We've got another team checking out this kid to make sure he's on the level. The store has a videotape security system. We're checking to see if there's any tape on her."

"Does Waltner Marina rent snowmobiles?" Lacey asked, pacing around the room.

"How the hell should I know?" Lark asked, not following this change of thought.

"Damn, I'll bet they do," Joel said.

"What's that got to do with this?" Lark asked.

"The Taurus was left at Grezetski's Market, across the road from Waltner Marina. The Taurus from a few years ago was left at the Big Oak Diner, down the block from the Marina."

"Everything's just down the block from everything else in this town," Lark grumbled, his mind racing.

"If you'd stolen a car and didn't want it near your house but needed to get home in the snow, what better way to do it than to borrow one of your own snowmobiles. Also use the rental snowmobile to take the body out to the marsh, so if anyone found out, it couldn't be pinned on you. After all, anyone who used that snowmobile could have done it," Lacey said, sitting down.

"Brilliant, and very hard to prove if that's how it went down," Joel said.

"I'll find out if the marina rents snowmobiles." Lark said, heading for the door.

"They either rent them or sell them," Lacey commented, "because they have a bunch of them in their parking lot."

Lark went out and asked Flo to call Waltner's to see if they rented snowmobiles, noting that Sara would be in for her interview in ten minutes.

" 'Course they do," she said. "I don't need to call unless you want to know the price."

"No shit," Lark said. "Get the DA on the phone. Tell him to get over here right now. Sara's coming in at one-thirty."

"We've got enough circumstantial evidence to read Sara her rights," Lark said as he walked back in the door. "Flo's calling Tom Jenkins, our DA. I want to make sure we do this right."

"Did you find her husband yet?" Lacey asked.

"Not that I know of," he replied, heading back out to ask if they'd tracked Steve down. Flo told him that Steve and his assistant weren't back from their meeting in Atlanta. Deep in thought, Lark headed back to the interview room. His reverie was interrupted when he heard someone call his name.

He looked up to find Sara standing in the doorway with Tom Jenkins. Lark asked her to take a seat, telling her they'd be with her in a few minutes, and motioned Tom into the interview room. They outlined the case for him. He reluctantly agreed that they needed to read Sara her rights and offered to call her attorney since the evidence was so circumstantial.

Sara came into the interview room, looking drop-dead gorgeous in a red cashmere twin set, a short black skirt, and black boots. She carried her black coat with the fur-lined hood slung over her arm. She greeted Lacey warmly and flirted shamelessly with Joel, then asked Lark how Ann was, her face full of concern. Watching her, Lacey felt a twinge that they might have the wrong person. She had to remind herself of the photo identification they had from the convenience store in Wausau.

Lark sat down across from Sara and everyone got quiet. She surveyed their faces. "What's wrong?"

"Do you know why you're here?" Lark asked.

"I was told it was to answer some more questions about Gemma and Terry." She looked back and forth between them.

"Would you like anything to drink before we get started?" Lacey asked, breaking some of the tension.

"Diet caffeine-free Coke would be great," she said, settling her eyes on Lark.

"We need to ask you some more questions about Terry and Gemma's murders, but this time we need to read you your rights and let you know that anything you say can be used against you in a court of law—"

"What the hell," she yelled, standing up so fast she knocked her chair over. "What the hell do you think you're doing?"

"I'm reading you your rights," Lark said.

"I want my attorney," she snarled, stalking towards the door, her eyes blazing. "Where the hell is Tom Jenkins?"

Jenkins met her at the door. He cajoled her back into the interview room by explaining that she could be arrested if she tried to leave. He told her he'd already called Brad Clapton, her attorney in Park Falls. She reluctantly agreed to stay. Jenkins told her that he'd called the hardware store to round up Steve and had been told that his plane was due in the next hour. He guided her over to the table, giving her the Diet Coke Lacey had handed him on his way in.

She looked contemptuously at the can and threw it across the room into the trash can. "Goddammit, I said caffeine-free," she yelled.

They left her stewing in the interview room until her lawyer appeared an hour later. Jenkins and Clapton listened as Lark laid out the evidence against Sara.

"This is all circumstantial," Clapton said.

"It may be circumstantial, but it all fits," Jenkins replied.

"I'm going to advise her not to talk to you. If you arrest her, we'll have her bailed out this afternoon. I've got Judge Holten standing by. Old man Williams has given him so much trouble that I'm sure he isn't going to want to hold Sara on circumstantial evidence. He'd be voted out of office for sure."

"Don't forget about Ann Ranson," Lark said.

"I heard she had brain surgery yesterday. She's not in any shape to give a statement."

"She's awake and starting to get her memory back."

"You're going to use a witness who's lost her memory and had brain surgery?" Clapton asked.

"We'll have a statement naming your client as the person who assaulted her and left her for dead in the same place as the other two victims."

"When you get it, let me know," Clapton said, standing up. "Let's get this show on the road so we can get over to Park Falls and Judge Holten before dark."

Clapton met briefly with Sara and then they all sat down in the interview room. They questioned her for an hour, but she stuck to her story that she was out of town at the time of both shootings and was home alone when Ann was beaten and dumped in the marsh. When she was asked about being identified by the kid at the convenience store, she denied that it could have happened, since she was in Minneapolis. When she was asked about her daughter's affairs with Katey, Gemma, and Terry, she became belligerent, denying that her daughter was a lesbian. Clapton calmed her down.

After the interview, they conferred with Jenkins on whether to turn her loose or arrest her. Joel left the room to call and check on how they were doing in Wausau, and Lark called Marshfield to find out if they could get a statement from Ann. John told him that Ann was sedated and back on the ventilator. She had been having quite a bit of trouble with flashbacks and elevated blood pressure.

Joel faired a little bit better. They had gotten a signed statement from the convenience-store clerk who had checked out as a good kid without so much as a speeding ticket. The store had surveillance tape, but they had not yet found Sara on it.

After hearing their information, Jenkins decided not to arrest Sara until they had positive identification on the surveillance tape or a statement from Ann. When Lark and Joel protested, he informed them that the county could not afford the lawsuit they would get if they were wrong and that one more day wouldn't hurt anything.

A disheveled Steve Waltner came flying through the door as they headed back to the interview room. After reassurance from Clapton, he went to see Sara. She glanced at him but did not acknowledge his presence. Jenkins informed Sara that she would not be arrested but was expected back at the station at three o'clock the next day for more questioning. Clapton agreed that she would be back and he and the Waltners left.

The police spent another half hour with Jenkins, planning their next steps. It was decided that Lark would drive back to Marshfield to be available to take Ann's statement. Joel and Lacey would go to Wausau to complete the review of the surveillance tapes. They had a quick dinner at the Big Oak Diner and got on the road in the middle of yet another snowstorm.

Sunday morning dawned as usual in Marshfield, gray and cloudy with a new layer of snow. Lark and John met in the restaurant at the Super 8. While they ate, Lark updated John on the case.

"Why would Sara do such a thing?" John asked, shocked at what Lark told him. "She must have really hated those kids to do that to them and leave Ann out in the snow to die." He stopped when he heard his voice quavering, and sipped his coffee.

"Jenkins doesn't want to arrest her until we have better evidence. Joel and Lacey are in Wausau trying to identify Sara on the surveillance tapes, but the strongest evidence will be what Ann can tell us."

"I don't want her to talk about this if it will harm her in any way."

"I don't either," Lark reassured him, "but if she's ready to talk, I'd like to take her statement."

Breakfast finished, they went to the hospital. They were surprised to find Ann sitting up in bed with her breathing tube out.

"Did you pull it out again?" John asked, kissing her forehead.

"They took it out about five." She nudged the oxygen prongs back up to her nose. She still had two IVs and the heart and blood pressure monitors on.

"You look like you're feeling better," Lark said, not knowing what else to say.

Her brown eyes bored into him. "I remember."

"Ann, you don't have to talk about this right now," John said, taking her hand.

"I've got to get it out. I want this past me so I can put all my energy into getting well." Lark pulled a tape recorder and notebook out of his coat pocket and they began.

"I felt so much better on Thursday, I decided I had to get out of the house," she said, playing nervously with the end of her top sheet. "Melissa Marten called and said she'd finished a box for me and wanted to know what time she could bring it over. I told her I'd come and get it. I still had Steve Waltner's Flow Blue and I decided I'd drop it off, pick up Melissa's box, and then get us a pizza. I left you a note," she said to John.

When he nodded she went on. "I got to the Waltner's at five. Sara seemed surprised to see me and I apologized for not calling. We went into her kitchen and she got us Diet Cokes. I noticed that a glove on her counter matched the gray cashmere-and-fur glove the dogs tore up. I asked her if she'd lost the mate and she looked at me kind of nervously. She said she couldn't find it and I told her I thought our dogs had destroyed it." Ann reached for the foam cup on her bedside table and found that it was empty. She held it out to John. "Could you fill this up with ice?"

"Can't we ring the bell and have them do it? I don't want to leave you."

"This will be much faster. You have no idea how dry my mouth is after having that tube in." John left to get the ice.

"I hate having him in here when I'm telling this. It will upset him. Anyway, back to Thursday. Sara was chopping some vegetables at the island. I was sitting at the bar. She told me that she didn't think she'd left the glove at our house." She glanced over at Lark and shook her head. "Oh, how I wish I'd left right then. Hindsight is a wonderful thing. I asked her how Sandi was dealing with the murders. She said Sandi was fine, but she was thinking about hiring a bodyguard for her. We talked about violence a few more minutes and then I asked her if she knew Katey Lowery was gay. She whirled around from the island with that big knife in her hand and asked me why I'd say a thing like that. Funny, she didn't scare me," Ann said, looking up as John walked in with her ice and a spoon.

She spooned some of the crushed ice into her mouth and went on. "I told her that a good friend of mine had seen Katey at lesbian-group meetings on campus and I was beginning to think that these might be gay hate crimes. She seemed angry and I asked her what was bothering her. She walked over to her pantry. It was off to my right and a little behind me. She said she didn't understand why I was saying these things to her. I turned around to see what she was doing just as she walloped me with the baseball bat. The next thing I knew, I was on the floor." Ann spooned more ice into her mouth.

"I had a few seconds before the pain took over. I remember looking up at her and asking why she was doing this to me just before she hit me again. She called me a meddling bitch and told me that no one was going to hurt her daughter. She hit me twice in the leg and once in the arm. I remember curling up in a ball. I must have passed out. The next thing I remember was her dragging me out to the garage. I must have moaned or something because she got down in my face and yelled that Sandi had been raped by those dykes. I remember her shaking me and thinking that I was going to die from the pain. I don't remember anything else until I woke up out in the snow. I couldn't remember how I'd gotten there or what had happened. I remember trying to walk and falling down because of the pain in my leg." She didn't seem to notice the tears streaming down her face.

"I gave up on trying to walk out and burrowed down in the snow, like animals do to keep warm." She bit her lip and reached for a tissue to wipe the tears away. "I prayed to God that I'd be rescued and I tried hard not to fall asleep. I yelled for help and sang, anything to let someone know I was out there. Then I didn't feel cold anymore, just warm and drowsy and I finally just let go. The last thing I remember was the dogs. I thought they were wolves."

She looked over at Lark, her eyes swimming in tears. "What will they do to Sara?"

"Life in prison's too good for her," he said, turning off the tape. "We'll transcribe this and have someone run it back down for you to sign."

He and John went out in the hall and conferred. It was decided that the guard would stay until Sara was in permanent custody.

Lark's pager went off just as he headed out of town. He tried his cellular phone and realized he still hadn't charged it. Swearing, he called Flo on the radio.

"Don't you answer your phone anymore?"

"It's not charged," he snapped, letting her know he wasn't in the mood for any attitude.

"Call Joel at the office in Wausau. He called twenty minutes ago and said it was urgent."

"Guess you'll have to patch me through since I can't call." She snorted her disdain as she made the transfer.

"Where have you been?" Joel asked. "I've been trying to get you for half an hour."

Lark informed him he had gotten what he needed in Marshfield.

Joel whooped into the radio, unable to contain himself, and told Lark that they had gotten the same. They signed off, agreeing to meet in Big Oak. Lark got into town at noon and Joel pulled in fifteen minutes later.

"Where's Lacey?" Lark asked, surprised that Joel was alone.

"This case is almost wrapped up and we needed her in Door County. We got our statement plus a damn fine picture of Sara on tape," he said, watching Lark's face.

"I didn't get a chance to thank her for all her hard work."

"Call her. Even better, drive over and take her out to dinner."

"Right," Lark replied. "Let's call Tom."

Tom Jenkins was there within fifteen minutes. He agreed that they had more than enough to arrest Sara and called Brad Clapton. After hearing what they had, Clapton agreed to pick Sara up rather than have them go out to the house and arrest her. Joel and Lark slipped over to the Big Oak Diner for lunch, knowing it would be way into the night before they got their next meal.

At two o'clock, Lark's beeper went off. He used Joel's cellular to call the station.

"You'd better get over here right now," Flo said.

"What the hell's going on?"

"Not on the phone," she said, and hung up.

"Damn that woman." Lark and Joel wrapped their cheeseburgers in paper napkins so they could eat them on the way.

Jenkins met them at the door, his face ashen. "This is awful, she took an overdose."

"Who overdosed?" Lark asked, a sinking feeling in the pit of his stomach.

"Sara Waltner," Jenkins said, guiding them into the interview room.

Lark tossed his half-eaten burger in the trash. "What happened?"

"Brad called me right before I called you." Jenkins slumped into the chair. "He went out to the house and found Sara and Steve nearly dead. She overdosed them on something. We'll know after they do the blood work. They just got to them in time. They were barely breathing when the ambulance got there."

"How the hell did this happen?" Lark asked.

"Clapton stayed at the Waltners' until midnight, trying to impress upon Sara how important it was that he knew the truth so he could help her make the best decisions. He said he made it clear that if Ann could identify her, she was in big trouble."

"Did she confess?" Joel asked.

"He says no. He spent most of the time refereeing a fight between them over Steve's affair with his assistant."

"Jesus Christ," Lark said, disgusted.

"Clapton left when Sara went upstairs to bed," Tom continued. "When he went out there this afternoon, no one answered the door. He went around back and saw Steve lying on the floor, so he broke in. He called the ambulance for Steve and found Sara upstairs in bed, nearly dead. He called me as soon as he found her."

CLOSURE

A week later, Ann was home, learning how to walk with crutches. No small feat since she also had an arm cast.

Steve and Sara Waltner lived. Sara had given them both a large dose of Seconal, a sleeping pill for which she had a prescription. She was not at all happy to be alive and had been transferred to Rhinelander for a psychiatric evaluation. Her physician finally gave Joel and Lark permission to interview her two weeks after her overdose. Lark was delighted to find out that Mrs. Krejewski, forever Mrs. Claus in his mind, was Sara's nurse.

"Who would have thought the beautiful Sara Lippert would come to this?" she said, her face full of sadness as she led Lark and Joel to Sara's room. "She's still very fragile, so I'm going to stay in here with you. If she has any problems, I'm going to ask you to leave. You agree?" she asked, looking at them as if she were setting ground rules for a couple of teenagers.

"We agree," Lark said. They followed her into the room.

It was difficult for Lark to hide his shock at his first sight of Sara. He knew they were about the same age, but she now looked like she was in her late fifties. Her eyes were focused but dull. Her face was devoid of makeup and her forehead and cheeks were lined with wrinkles. Someone had made a crude attempt at styling her hair by brushing it back from her face. Her once beautifully manicured nails were free of polish and chipped and bitten to the quick. She didn't seem to be aware that her hospital gown had slipped down over one shoulder.

"Sara, I'm going to fix your gown," Mrs. Krejewski said as she reached her hand out towards Sara's shoulder.

"Get away from me, you fat bitch," Sara yelled, swatting at Mrs. Krejewski's hand.

"Sara, we discussed this. Another outburst like that and the police will have to leave."

"Fine, just keep away from me," Sara snapped, yanking her gown back up on her shoulder.

Lark was so stunned by the change in Sara that he didn't notice Brad Clapton in the room until he spoke. "Sheriff, now that you've got your tape recorder set up, I want to go on record that I object to this interview. Steve and I have advised Sara against this, but she has chosen to ignore me."

"Didn't they determine that I was competent at that hearing we went through?" Sara asked, glaring at Clapton.

"Yes, Sara, you were judged to be competent but that doesn't mean that you should incriminate yourself."

"I want this over with. I want my children to get on with their lives and Steve to rot in hell with his harlot." Her voice was eerily calm.

Lark read Sara her rights and asked her if she understood them. When she stated that she did, he began questioning her.

"Sara did you kill Gemma Patterson and Terry Foltz?"

"Yes."

"Why did you kill them?"

"They raped Sandi. She would never have had sex with them if they hadn't forced her. She knows that sex between two women is an abomination," Sara snapped, her hands twisting into fists on top of the sheets. Lark noticed the wrist restraints that dangled from either side of the bed. He wondered if they would get through the interview without restraining Sara again.

"How did you know Sandi had sex with Terry and Gemma?" Lark asked, trying to make eye contact with her.

"I found Sandi's diary when I was cleaning her room. She forgot to take it back to Madison with her. She wrote about having sex with Gemma. I knew from her diary that she had been raped. She would never have written about it the way she did if Gemma hadn't forced her."

"I don't understand," Lark said.

"Sandi was traumatized by the rape. She wrote that she wanted to have more sex with that little bitch. I knew I had to do something to save my baby." Sara's eyes were full of hatred. "I called Gemma and asked her to help me plan a party for Sandi's birthday in December. She agreed to stop by on her way home for Thanksgiving. I asked her not to tell anyone about it so we could keep the party a surprise." Sara stopped to take a drink from a glass of water on her bedside stand. She gripped the glass so hard, Lark was afraid she might break it.

"When she got to the house, I invited her into the kitchen and gave her something to drink. She asked if she could use the phone to call her mother and tell her where she was, because she hadn't been able to get her earlier. I keep Michael's old baseball bat in the pantry for protection. It was so easy. I got the bat and hit her a couple of times. She was unconscious when I loaded her in our two-man snowmobile and took her out to the marsh."

"How did you get her in the snowmobile?" Lark asked.

"You men are all alike," she said malevolently. "You see a pretty woman and you think she's weak. I dragged her out to the garage and lifted her into the snowmobile. I carry forty-pound bags of water-softener salt down to the basement. I can drag a body a few feet."

"What did you do with her car?"

"I drove it to Eau Claire and used Gemma's credit card to fill it up with gas. Then I left it at a shopping center across from Lippert's. I took a Taurus off the lot and drove it back to Big Oak. I left it in the parking lot at the diner. I got a snowmobile at the marina and rode it home. Steve and the kids use the store snowmobiles all the time. I put it in the back of the garage until Steve found it later in the winter. Then I drove back over to the Sofitel." She looked at them defiantly, daring them to challenge her.

"What did you do with Gemma's purse?"

"I tossed it in a trash Dumpster in back of a restaurant in Ladysmith on the way home."

"Why did you kill Terry?" Lark asked.

"Things were so much better after Gemma went away." She stared at the wall as if she were daydreaming. A smile flickered across her face and Lark caught a glimpse of the woman he had known before this tragedy. "Sandi started dating David and they were in love. I knew everything was going to be all right. To make sure, I read her diary whenever she came home. Things were good until she let that dyke Terry get too close to her. Terry raped her just like Gemma and brainwashed her into thinking she might be gay. They were doing sinful things. I did the same thing to her I did to Gemma. Exactly the same," she said. Her eyes blazed into Lark's.

"Why did you try to kill Ann?"

"The bitch wouldn't leave things alone. When she asked me if Katey was gay, I knew she had figured it out. It would have ruined my baby's life if Ann told anyone. I just snapped."

"What did you do with her car?" Lark asked, since they still hadn't found it.

"It's under a tarp in one of Steve's boat storage buildings out on Highway T, the furthest one in the back. I didn't have time to dispose of it. You wouldn't have found it until spring. No one goes out there until people start taking their boats out of storage."

"Why didn't you kill Katey since Sandi and Katey slept together?" Lark asked, bracing himself for the worst as he watched Sara become enraged.

"Katey's a victim. Those bitches raped her, too," she yelled, flinging herself up in bed towards Lark.

"That's enough," Mrs. Krejewski said as she pushed the screaming and crying Sara down on the bed. Lark didn't think he'd ever get the sound of Sara's crying out of his head.

"The world gets stranger everyday," Lark said as they walked out of the hospital into the first sunshine they'd seen in over a month. "This is a vicious hate crime where the murderer claims she killed two innocent girls out of love for her daughter."

"She's sure going to have problems in prison," Joel said as they headed for their car.

"If she makes it there. She may be legally competent, but she's the sickest woman I've ever met. I doubt she'll ever get to the pen," Lark said as they drove away.

EPILOG—DECEMBER 31

When Lark, Joel, and Molly walked into the Park Falls Country Club, they were greeted by Ann and John. John was smiling from ear to ear. Ann wore a big grin along with a small cast on her arm, a floor-length, dark burgundy velvet skirt and a matching sweater studded with pearls. When she saw Lark, she stepped away from John and embraced him in her best imitation of a one-armed bear hug.

"It's so good to see you," she said, stepping back to look him over. "How have you been? I haven't seen you for the last two weeks."

Before he could get a word in edgewise, John came over to shake his hand. "Where the hell have you been? I haven't seen your Jeep around town lately."

"I went home to see my family over Christmas," he said, blushing at the attention.

Joel introduced Molly to the Ransons and the five of them were standing around talking and joking about the antics of the Grenfurth children when another group of people came around the corner. Molly and Joel moved into the ballroom after receiving instructions from John on how to find their table. Before Lark could follow, John pulled him into conversation. They were interrupted when Ann called to them.

Lark looked over to see what she wanted and his heart fell to his knees. As she walked over to them, he found himself making a detailed study of the paisley pattern in the carpet.

"Look what blew in from Wausau."

"Hello, Lark, how are you," Lacey said, smiling up into his face and reaching out to shake his hand.

"Great, and you?" Lark asked, with just the hint of a smile despite his rapidly beating heart. Lacey was a vision in a long, dark green cut velvet skirt and matching jacket with a black, low-cut lace camisole underneath. Her hair was in masses of curls around her face and hanging down her back.

"Wow, you look fantastic," John said, giving her a hug and then stepping back to look her over. "In fact, you look almost as good as my wife."

"He's living proof that love is blind," Ann said, taking John's arm. She glanced down at her watch and scanned the entrance of the club. "It's past time to start dinner and it looks like no one else is coming. Let's go eat. By the way," she said over her shoulder to Lark and Lacey, "don't even think about slipping away after dinner. We've got music and dancing planned, although that'll be hobbling for me." As she walked into the dining room, Lark noticed that John's hand under her elbow provided support; she was still walking with a slight limp.

John led the way to a table for six consisting of the Ransons, Joel and Molly, and Lark and Lacey. Dinner passed in a fog for Lark, seated between Ann and Lacey. Although he made polite conversation with Lacey about the Patterson/Foltz case, the continued bad weather, and the Green Bay Packers, he couldn't bring himself to get into more personal issues. Lacey was also seated next to Joel, who kept up his usual banter with frequent gooses from Molly to watch his mouth. During conversation lulls, Ann kept Lark busy talking about his family.

The lights went down after dinner and the DJ started playing a mix of holiday carols, oldies, rock, and country. In no time, everyone was dancing. Ann only danced about once an hour, claiming that her leg cast made it difficult. While everyone else danced, she had a delightful time talking to the people who stopped by their table. Lark, a very good dancer, found himself having fun, dancing with several women he knew from Big Oak. Much to his relief, he and Lacey were rarely at the table at the same time.

Shortly before eleven, Ann and Lark were talking when Lacey and John came back to the table. When Ann refused to dance to a fast song, Lacey stepped in to dance with John again.

Ann leaned over to Lark so she could be heard over the music. "What's going on with you and Lacey?"

Lark was thankful that the room was dark so Ann couldn't see him blush. "Nothing's going on. Why do you ask?"

"Yeah, right." Ann snorted. "Nothing's going on. Here's a news flash. You can cut the tension between you two with a knife."

"Ann, I think you're imagining things," he said, staring at the dance floor to avoid her eyes. "We worked together on your case. There isn't anything more between us."

"Excuse me, but that's nothing but pure bullshit." Ann craned her neck around to look at him, forcing him to look in her eyes.

"You're right, this *is* bullshit," he said, exasperated. He picked up his empty beer bottle and attempted to drink out of it. "Shit," he said, getting up. "Would you like something else to drink?"

"No, and you don't need anything else either." She grabbed his hand and pulled him back down in his seat. "We're going to finish this conversation."

"You're way out of line here," he said, his voice stern. "Despite your good intentions, this isn't any of your business."

She hesitated, breaking eye contact to watch John and Lacey on the dance floor. She took his hand in both of hers and looked into his eyes. "You're probably right, but I care very much about you and Lacey so I'm making it my business. Since you've seen me nearly naked and almost broken emotionally—I'll take the risk and wade into this. If I'm wrong, I'm sure you'll forgive me."

Lark groaned but didn't move away from her.

"At the risk of sounding sappy, we both know how short life can be. Love and happiness are rare commodities, truly to be cherished when you're lucky enough to find them."

When Lark said nothing, she plunged on. "I'm so sorry that I never had the chance to know your wife. Joel tells me she was remarkable and that the two of you were very much in love."

"I don't want to talk about this," he said, staring out at the dance floor.

"Someone that remarkable would not want you to be alone. She would want you to find someone to love and have children with."

"So you say," Lark mumbled, looking down at the table.

"I know it," she said, her hands tensing around his.

When she said nothing more, Lark looked into her eyes and found them sparkling with tears.

"Just hear me out," she said. "When I was out in the marsh, I nearly gave up on being rescued. I got to the point where I thought I was going to die. I remember looking up at the stars and marveling at how bright they were despite all the snow we were getting." Tears flowed down her cheeks. "I remember wishing that I could see a falling star so I could make a wish. I know it sounds trite, but you had to be there to understand."

"I was there," he said, staring down at her.

She ignored him. "When I didn't see one, I decided to wish anyway."

Lark, unable to stand her tears, picked up a napkin with his free hand and brushed them away. "Ann, don't put yourself through this."

She went on as if she didn't notice him. "I wished that if I couldn't live, John would find someone wonderful. Someone he loved madly, who would love him and give him beautiful children. When you love someone as much as I love John, and your wife must have loved you, you want them to be happy. Maria would want you to be happy. Don't let her down."

She let go of his hand and shoved herself to her feet.

"Are you all right?" he asked, getting up to help her.

"Of course I'm all right. I'm alive and here with people I love. I'm going to the ladies' room to fix my face. Think about what I said. You'll never hear it again. You saved my life a couple of times. Let me return the favor and help you get yours back." She limped off to the ladies' room just before John and Lacey got back to the table.

"Where's Ann going?" John asked as he set drinks down on the table.

"Powder room," Lark said, staring at her retreating back.

"Lacey," John yelled over the music as he headed away from the table. "Make her sit down and relax when she gets back, and for God's sake, don't let her get snapped up to dance with someone else. I want to pull off this surprise."

"What's he doing?" Lark asked.

"He's crazy, simply crazy."

"I don't understand."

"I know," she said, staring into the dancing crowd, her face sad. "What's he up to?"

Lacey sighed and looked over at him. "He's requested a couple of love songs he knows she likes to dance to."

They watched John intercept Ann on her way back to the table. Their conversation was very animated, with Ann pulling him towards her and cupping her ear so she could hear him. She pulled away, laughing, and shook her head coquettishly. John shoved his hands down in his pockets and smiled as he rocked on the balls of his feet and said something to her. She laughed, smacked him playfully on the arm, and then threaded her arm through his as they headed towards the dance floor.

"Would you like to dance?" Lark asked.

"No." Lacey dug her purse out from under the table and stood up.

"What would you like to do?" he asked, a sinking feeling in his chest.

"I think I'm going to cut out early." She smiled down at him. "It's been so nice seeing you again."

"It's much too early to go home," he said, standing up.

She put her hand on his arm and leaned up on her tiptoes to kiss him on the cheek. "Take care of yourself," she said, smiling into his eyes. "I hope we get to work together again."

He stood there stunned, watching her walk away.

"Buddy, you're a fool," Joel said into his ear as they watched Lacey walk out of the room.

"I know," Lark said, jamming his hands down in his pockets.

"You know, *you know*," Joel yelled, jerking him around by the shoulders. "Then what the hell are you doing standing here? This isn't a damn rehearsal—this is your life. Wake up." He let go of Lark's jacket and gave him an old-buddy punch in the arm.

"Joel," Molly cried out, hurrying over from the bar with their drinks. "What the hell are you doing? That's it. I'm giving this drink to someone else. You've had enough."

"Life support, I'm giving life support," he said as he watched Lark walk towards the hallway. "And just maybe we've had a successful resuscitation."

Lark walked around the corner and into an empty hallway. He went into the coatroom, ripped his overcoat from the hanger, and headed for the door, stuffing his arms into it as he went. He got outside and realized he had no idea what kind of car she drove. He charged out into the parking lot, slipping and sliding on the patchy ice. He looked for car lights but didn't see any. After scanning the parking lot for what seemed like hours, he walked back in the coatroom. He took his coat off, but just before hanging it up, put it back on. He realized that his best plan was to find Joel and ask him what kind of car Lacey drove. Deep in thought, he walked into the back of a woman, almost knocking her over.

A muffled expletive drifted up from the hood of the woman's coat. He grabbed her by the shoulders, trying to keep from falling himself as he righted them both.

"I'm sorry. I wasn't watching where I was going. Are you all right?" he asked as the person turned around.

"You're leaving, too?" Lacey asked, a look of astonishment on her face.

"Yes. I mean, no, I mean . . ." Lark stammered, so shocked at finding her after he thought she'd left that he was nearly tongue-tied.

"I don't think I've ever seen you speechless," she said, grinning at him, her face surrounded by the hood from her black coat. "It's not an unpleasant picture." When he continued to stare at her, saying nothing, she grabbed his arm. "Lark, are you OK? Have you had too much to drink? Do you need a ride home?"

"No, it's not that." His eyes bored into hers.

"Thank goodness you can still speak. I was wondering if you were having a stroke in your old age. I'd better get on the road." She headed for the door. "I've got a long drive ahead of me. I was going to stay over with John and Ann but I've decided to go home."

He followed her outside. "Lacey, why don't you stay over and we can have brunch tomorrow. I'll cook or we can go out."

Her eyes bored into him. She pulled her hand out of her pocket and laid her palm against his cheek. "I can't. It wouldn't be right."

"Why not?" he asked, taking her hand and kissing the tips of her fingers.

"Because I want something you don't want."

"What do you want?" he asked.

"I want what they have," she said, flipping her head back towards the ballroom. "What John and Ann have. I won't settle for less."

"I want the same thing," he said.

She rushed on as if she hadn't heard him, staring down at the hole she was toeing into the snow. "I've been dating an attorney in Wausau. He's out of town visiting his family for the holidays, but he'll be back tomorrow. We've made tentative plans for brunch. I just left a message on his machine that I'll meet him at noon, so I need to get back. Call me if you get to Wausau and we'll have dinner." She patted his arm and stepped off the curb, her coat swirling around her as she walked out into the parking lot.

Speechless, Lark watched her walk away. It had never entered his mind that she might be serious about someone else. Dejected, he walked back into the club, hung up his coat, and wandered back to the table. Molly and Joel were the only ones sitting there.

"How'd it go?" Joel asked. "From the look on your face, not well."

"She's serious about someone else."

"Bullshit," Joel said, dumbfounded. "She's been our baby-sitter for two Saturday nights this month and I haven't heard a thing about another man."

"Some attorney in Wausau who went home to see his family for the holidays."

"She's dated that asshole off and on since she's been up here. He doesn't mean jack shit to her."

"He must, she went home to be with him," Lark said, listening to music.

"She left because you were ignoring her and she told you this guy is important to her because she was embarrassed."

"What kind of car does she drive?" Lark asked, watching the Ransons walk back to the table.

"Dark green Grand Cherokee," Joel said, smiling. Lark grinned and raced towards the parking lot after Lacey.

3 2005 0135811 4   12

Greenlief, K. C.   1-23-02
   Cold hunter's moon

	DATE DUE		
MAR 1 2002			
FEB 02 2009			